RETRIBUTION

ALSO BY VANESSA KIER

<u>The Surgical Strike Unit (SSU) Series</u>

Vengeance

Betrayal

Retribution

Payback

Aftermath

Undercover (Prequel Novella)

<u>The WAR Series</u>

WAR: Disruption

WAR: Intrusion

WAR: Opposition

RETRIBUTION

THE SURGICAL STRIKE UNIT
BOOK THREE

VANESSA KIER

CHAPTER ONE

Dusk
Adirondack Mountains

"Well, lookee here, boss. Your lady sure does get around."

Surgical Strike Unit team leader Rafe Andros took the binoculars from Muldovsky and focused on the rock face below the laboratory they'd been observing for the past two days. Part of the rock had slid open, revealing the narrow door caught on photos taken by the SSU's satellite. Just outside that door, under one of the exterior lights, two women stood at awkward angles to each other.

Rafe felt a tingle of excitement across the back of his neck. The SSU had been watching the compound via satellite for a week prior to his team's deployment. Thanks to the satellite photos, Rafe knew several troop transport trucks had driven through another door further down the rock formation, indicating a probable garage or loading dock. The women's stark white lab coats suggested there were also labs on that lower level.

He didn't recognize the dark-haired woman on the right,

smoking jerkily on a cigarette. She wasn't part of the group of scientists and other staff members that was bused to and from the housing village every day. Since the mystery woman had to be sleeping somewhere, it was likely the underground portion of the facility also held living quarters.

Which meant more places for Rafe and his team to search for Nate Ngoro, their missing teammate.

Rafe shifted his binoculars to the woman on the left. Dr. Gabrielle Montague. One of the scientists the SSU's satellite had recorded entering and leaving the upper lab.

His men liked to tease, but damn, she made him hot. He'd always loved smart women, and intelligence was stamped on every line of her face. A clip held her honey blonde hair behind her ears, revealing a long, stubborn shot of jaw that ended in a slightly square chin. Rafe found perfectly symmetrical beauty boring and Dr. Montague's slightly too-wide nose pushed her past beautiful straight into fascinating.

The photos in her background file showed a woman with the sensual, curvy body of a flamenco dancer, but looking through the binoculars at the baggy fit of her institutional gray pencil skirt and bulky lab coat, he'd have to say she'd lost weight. Still, even with her being too thin he had a hard time keeping his eyes off her.

Too bad her presence made her a suspect in Nate's disappearance.

"Yo, Addison," Muldovsky called through the com link. "Guess who's outside? It's boss man's lady. And he's staring at her legs again."

"Hey, can you blame him? She's looking mighty fine for a dead woman."

There was no disputing that comment. Four months ago Dr. Montague had been listed among the fatalities in a bus crash on her way home from vacation. In fact, all of the staff here, except for today's mystery woman, were similarly not-dead-as-reported.

Of those staff they'd managed to identify from the photos, all had worked in the medical field. Dr. Montague's expertise was treating veterans who'd been exposed to chemical or biological agents. The other doctors specialized in such diverse topics as drug rehabilitation, hypnosis to cure obsessive-compulsive disorder, and the use of growth hormones. There were three psychiatrists, ten medical doctors, sixteen lab assistants, and six administrative staff. All working at a facility that didn't show up on any public or private records.

A snort came through the com link. "Hell, you boys got it wrong," O'Ryan pitched in. "Andros thinks the doctor has Ngoro stashed up her skirt. Never mind that Ngoro's like, six-four and a gazillion pounds, and Montague's lucky if she's five-seven and a hundred thirty."

Rafe ignored the gibes of his men. They'd caught him doing a double take over Dr. Montague the first time he'd seen her on the other end of his binoculars, and suddenly she'd become "his" lady. Like none of them had admired the feminine shape of her legs or the curve of her ass. Out of the handful of female staff, her combination of mature intelligence and sexy grace caught his attention over the perky young lab assistants or the dour senior female scientist.

The corner of Rafe's mouth lifted as he was hit by a memory.

"Why do you get to go after the girl?" Rafe had groused to Kai Paterson when he'd been given this assignment two months ago, "while I'm off trekking in the woods with a bunch of smelly, foul-mouthed men?" But he hadn't been able to stop the smile from teasing the corners of his mouth.

Kai, Rafe's brother-in-law and fellow SSU agent, had laughed and lightly punched him on the shoulder. "Because you're the ex-Ranger, my friend. You're the one trained in covert rescue and assault. I'm just a scientist turned spy."

If Kai could only hear the teasing Rafe was getting from his men, he'd bust a gut laughing.

Rafe saw the women's mouths move even though they stood at right angles to each other, heads turned down and away from the rock face. "Christ," he breathed. "Even a two-year-old could tell they're not gossiping." The smoker jerked her cigarette to and from her mouth like a sideshow robot and Dr. Montague had her arms wrapped around her torso so tightly she was in danger of breaking her own ribs.

"They might as well wave a sign saying 'We're up to something,'" he muttered in disgust, handing the binoculars back to Muldovsky.

Muldovsky focused the glasses, then nodded. "Yeah. Amateurs."

Even without the binoculars, Rafe continued to stare in the direction of the women. Unpredictable events always added spice to a mission. Maybe the women were just griping about their boss, or maybe they were planning trouble. Either way, he'd make sure nothing stopped his team from finding Nate.

"Bus is here," Willits announced from his spot closer to the upper level entrance.

As if she'd heard him, Dr. Montague glanced at her watch then bolted back into the building. The other woman stayed to finish her smoke, then she, too, retreated into the rock face.

Rafe touched Muldovsky on the shoulder and nodded toward the upper entrance to indicate he was switching locations. Moments later, Rafe slid into position beside Willits in time to watch the last of the scientists exit the building.

Where was—?

Dr. Montague dashed out the door and joined the end of the line.

Ah. There she was.

As the staff members shuffled toward the waiting bus Dr. Montague swayed, then stumbled against the man in front of her. He turned and grabbed her arm, helping her regain her balance.

The man's sharp expression of concern had Rafe zooming his binoculars onto her face.

He frowned. She had the tightly drawn expression of someone barely hanging onto her strength. Was she sick? Reacting to some chemical in the lab? Or was her stumble faked?

Rafe shook his head. Not his problem. She was involved in whatever was going on here, which made her weakness his advantage.

Two months ago, the privately run SSU had been hired by the Department of Defense and the FBI to look into the reappearance of military and federal law enforcement personnel who'd supposedly been killed in action. In each case, the circumstances surrounding the deaths had made body retrieval impossible. At least two of the "dead" later turned up in remote towns not far from this compound, pumped up on a new blend of steroids and homicidally insane.

Rafe's teammate, Nate Ngoro, had been reported as being killed during a joint special operations training exercise three months ago. Only, Nate's subdermal tracking device—which ran off his body's electrical impulses—had continued to transmit to the SSU for a week after his "death" until the signal finally vanished at these coordinates.

"I count Dr. Montague as the last one out," Rafe said over the com link as she leaned heavily on the handrail in order to pull herself onto the first stair of the bus.

"Ditto," O'Ryan answered.

The door closed behind Dr. Montague and the bus pulled out of the small parking lot. As it disappeared into the trees, Rafe announced, "Bluebird is on the move."

"Roger that, Team One." Six of Rafe's men had stayed behind to search the staff village, and would take up positions along the perimeter to watch the scientists during the night.

"Don't worry, we'll keep your lady nice and safe," Rick

Depaoli, the head of Team Two drawled. "Got to admit, though, her underwear drawer was a disappointment. Boring white cotton. I was hoping for at least a little lace to counteract that mind-numbing gray uniform."

"Asshole," Rafe said with a laugh. He shifted his binoculars back to the building that housed the labs and waited. Exactly ten minutes from the moment the bus pulled out, the interior of the building went dark, leaving only the exterior security lights to provide illumination.

"Is the security night shift here yet?" Rafe asked.

"Heading your way," Addison replied from his spot further down the road.

Rafe signaled for his men to return to camp. They'd grab a quick bite to eat, then sneak into the building once the guards had a few hours to grow complacent.

By now, the bus would have reached the gate in the chain link fence that enclosed the three wooded acres with walking paths immediately surrounding the lab. Two acres beyond that first fence, though, was a second fence, well hidden by bushes. The type of fence usually only seen at high-security prisons. Electrified. Slanted in at the top and capped with enough razor wire to make Edward Scissorhands jealous. The gate to that fence always slid into an opening in a fall of rock just before the bus came into view.

Why did the facility need a fence built to keep people inside? And why didn't they want the scientists to know about the second fence?

Tonight, Rafe intended to find out.

Fingers shaking, Gabby Montague flinched as she pulled out the clips that kept her chin-length hair from swinging into her eyes. Dammit, she couldn't go on like this. After just seven days of working in the clandestine part of the lab, there were hollows under her cheeks. Dark pools of fatigue lurked under the thin skin around her eyes.

Thank heavens, it would all end tonight. Her nerves were so taut, even with sedatives she couldn't sleep more than an hour or two at a time, jerking out of a sound sleep with her heart racing and her body poised for flight. Tension had stolen her appetite so completely, she barely managed to eat enough to keep her strength up.

God, what Kaufmann did to his subjects sickened her.

And she'd been helping him.

Gabby shivered. Four months ago, after the veterans' home she'd been working at had burned down while she was on vacation, a slightly distant, unfailingly polite and supportive man calling himself Dr. Pierce had offered her a job continuing her work. He'd had references from a researcher she'd trusted, so Gabby had agreed to join Dr. Pierce at this remote location.

She'd thought she'd been working on a legitimate project aimed at lessening rages in veterans exposed to biochemical agents. Until last week, when she'd returned from her lunchtime walk and found the front door locked due to another glitch in the spotty security system. While searching for another way inside, she'd stumbled across a door set in what she'd thought was a wall of rock and discovered the secret lab.

The red power lights of the security cameras had been dark when Gabby entered, indicating they weren't working. Hoping to find a way back upstairs, she'd started exploring, and come across a scene that starred in her nightmares. Her patient, Michael du Braise, knelt over a man in a sandy arena. Du Braise lowered his mouth to the man's throat and tore into it with his teeth while scientists looked on, writing furiously in their notebooks.

Horrified, and determined to figure out what the hell was going on, Gabby had snuck into some of the labs and stolen notes and test tubes.

She pressed the heels of her hands against her eye sockets.

All illusions about her mission had shattered that day. As soon as she'd managed to get back to her lab and look at the samples under the microscope, she'd known she was onto something deadly.

There had been traces of Agent Styx in one of the samples. The same Vietnam era biochemical agent that had driven her father into uncontrollable rages. The U.S. government insisted they had stopped producing Agent Styx in 1971 and that they'd destroyed all existing samples.

Except Gabby possessed two vials of Agent Styx that her father had left her upon his death. Proof of the government's horrible experiments. She'd studied Agent Styx. Seen traces of it in the blood of several of her patients who'd served in Vietnam. But she'd never found the chemical in anyone under the age of thirty. Until those samples she'd stolen.

When she'd seen the familiar marker glowing under her microscope, she'd thought wildly of running. Of taking the evidence to the authorities.

How naïve she'd been.

Gabby turned on the faucet and shoved her wrists under the cold water, adding soap and scrubbing until her skin was red. But no amount of soap could cleanse her of what she'd done.

She hadn't realized that the security cameras had come back online in time to catch her leaving the secret lab. The next day, Dr. Pierce had confronted her in his office with proof of her trespassing. He'd threatened to throw her to his subjects as a target for their rage.

He'd bound Gabby's hands behind her and marched her through the corridors into the secret lab. To what Gabby had believed would be her death. Dr. Kaufmann had explained that he'd been using her research to help mitigate chemically triggered, berserker rages that made his subjects impossible to command. And since the goal of his program was to create mind controlled superhuman soldiers, obedience was mandatory.

Kaufmann had offered Gabby one chance to save herself. She could work with him to overcome the men's rages. Or she could die at the hands of his subjects.

Gabby splashed water on her face, wishing she could go back in time and tell Kaufmann no. He'd agreed so quickly, she wondered if she'd been manipulated into helping him. Still, she hadn't seen any other way to stay alive. At least by easing the men's rages, she'd thought she'd lessen their suffering.

Now, after a week of watching man after man put through mental and physical experiments that left them screaming in agony, she was ready to break. She wanted to tell Kaufmann she'd changed her mind.

Let him kill her.

Because she now believed that curing the rages would do more harm than good. Anger gave the subjects a degree of power. A chance to strike back at their tormentors. And a mental break from the constant orders of the scientists.

Gabby's help only made their situation worse.

She scrubbed the towel over her face, but still didn't feel clean.

Few of the men remained sane. Yet, if she could remove all the subjects from the program within a couple of days and get them into treatment, she thought most of them could regain some degree of mental clarity.

Which is why she and her co-conspirator had originally come up with a plan to free them tomorrow. Instead, Gabby had told Laurel this afternoon that they had to move the timetable up to tonight. Gabby feared that with her own shaky mental and physical condition, she'd give them away if they waited much longer. Already she'd made some mistakes in the lab—dropping a beaker, mixing the wrong chemicals—that had Kaufmann's head of staff eyeing her with suspicion.

Knowing she was being watched and judged only made the sea of acid in her stomach burn that much hotter.

If she had to work at the lab for even another two days, Gabby thought it was very likely she would be the one who ended up insane.

Or dead.

CHAPTER TWO

THE LAST OF his team had just slipped through the breach in the electrified fence when Rafe's radio vibrated.

"We got activity at the rock face, boss," Muldovsky said from his perch watching the back of the lab. "Part of it's raising up, like a garage door."

Rafe signaled his men to hold positions. "O'Ryan, you see any headlights coming our way?" The former Marine was stationed up a tall pine, with a clear view of the single road.

"Negative, boss."

Rafe studied the lab. It appeared as deserted as the last two nights. The security guards were out patrolling the perimeter. If they held to schedule, this sector would remain clear for another ten minutes.

"We're staying on plan," Rafe announced. The wind had picked up, stirring the scent of pine and earth into a potent musk. Rafe knew the sounds of moving branches would help mask any sounds his men made, but a quieter night would have let him hear any approaching danger.

Rafe found himself smiling. Without a blueprint of the building and a security diagram, tonight's maneuver was strictly improv from here on out. He loved missions like these, when success depended more on his team's ingenuity than planning and technology.

"Well, well, lookee what we've got here," Muldovsky murmured. "One of those transports from the satellite photos is leaving the building."

"I'm on it." In its earlier flyovers their satellite hadn't even picked up a heat signal from the drivers of the trucks, which meant someone was going to a lot of trouble to hide what was going into, or coming out of, the hidden section of the lab. Rafe needed to know what was on those trucks.

He motioned for two of his men to head back to the road. Because the team had walked in, they didn't have their own vehicle to follow the truck. But the road wound through the compound, so his men would have plenty of time to get in position and hit the truck with a tracking device. Then the satellite would be able to locate it and send back photos.

"Hold up, boss. It's not going down the road. It's heading into the trees... Okay, good, the truck's moving slow enough that Willits is gonna sneak onboard."

"Roger." Rafe shifted his attention from his radio to the men around him as they approached the compound. At the signal from his point man, Rafe dashed across the lawn and onto the building's tiny front step. He pulled the dummy passkey out of his pocket and was just raising it to the electronic reader, when Muldovsky's voice crackled through the radio at his ear.

"Fuck!"

Rafe froze, then gave one quiet click of his mic to let his teammate know he'd been heard.

"Boss, Willits reports dead bodies in the back of the truck."

Rafe squeezed his eyes shut. He knew they were all wondering the same thing. Was Nate's body among them?

Rafe shook his head. He couldn't think about that now. He gave another click of the mic to acknowledge Muldovsky.

Then he proceeded with breaking into the lab. If Nate was indeed one of the dead, Rafe was damn well going to find out how and why he'd died.

GOD BLESS JANEY REESE, Rafe thought ten minutes later as the light on the lab's electronic lock turned green. The SSU's self-styled Gadget Goddess was the female equivalent to James Bond's "Q." Sixty if she was a day, she ran rings around her younger counterparts when it came to practical innovations. This dummy passkey was a perfect example. It had gotten them into the building and now allowed Rafe and his men to access each individual lab.

Unfortunately, the labels on the neat rows of chemicals and test tubes in this small room meant little to Rafe. His brother-in-law was a biochemical expert, but Kai was currently recovering from a severe malaria attack caused by a mutated parasite that didn't respond well to current drugs. Sparing a quick prayer for Kai's health, Rafe asked, "Anything look out of the ordinary to you, Addison?"

"Besides the fact that there's no power in the lab, not even a live battery backup for the computer, and there isn't so much as a Post-it in sight?" Addison whispered dryly. "Not a thing."

Yeah, the sterility of the room also bugged Rafe. He had no way of knowing if the lab was about to be closed down for good, or if removing all notes and disconnecting all power to the labs was standard post-hours procedure.

"Chemicals all seem pretty standard," Addison added. He was the only one on the team who'd taken chemistry in college, so he was the de facto expert. He waved a handheld sensor over the bottles and test tubes, across the counter, around the sink and underneath to the empty trash can. "No traces of any known biochemical or radioactive weapon-grade material," he announced.

Rafe nodded. The sensors were designed to detect the slightest residue that even a thorough cleaning might miss. He signaled Addison to follow him and stepped out into the hallway. "Anyone else have better luck?" he breathed into his lip mic.

"No smoking guns, or smoldering cauldrons, boss," Teng replied. "But I do have a locked door that our guru's passkey isn't opening. They've got a second layer of security here."

"I'll be—"

"Boss," Muldovsky's voice cut in. "You boys done something to draw attention to yourselves? I've got a team of six guards leaving the lower level and heading your way."

Fuck. Rafe met Addison's eyes, seeing the same suspicion reflected there.

"We must have triggered a silent alarm," Rafe murmured. "Time to head out. Muldovsky, any word from Willits?" Rafe jogged down the corridor toward the front door.

"Negative boss. He's still with the truck."

"Keep me posted. Going radio silent."

With the coordination of long practice, Rafe and his men slipped out the door, across the lawn, and back into the trees with mere seconds to spare before the compound's security team moved stealthily into view.

As they headed back to the rendezvous point, Rafe started plotting how to get access to that hidden room.

WILLITS STALKED into camp a good hour after Rafe and his team. The other men stepped out of his way, aware from the muscles working at his jaw that their teammate was furious and looking for a fight.

Rafe stood slowly from his crouched position by the food pack. Willits stopped a foot from Rafe. "Nate wasn't on the truck, sir."

Rafe nodded and felt the fist around his chest loosen. He'd

been prepared to deal with the news of Nate's death, but all of them would sleep better tonight knowing their missing teammate could still be alive and inside the lab.

"Tell me what you saw," Rafe commanded quietly.

Willits's blue eyes lost their angry glitter and turned bleak. "Seven dead men. Cause of death—" His lips twisted and he looked away. One shuddering inhale later, he swung his eyes back to Rafe's, his anger back. "One had his throat torn out. The teeth marks looked human."

"Shit."

"Three more had dried blood at their eyes, nose, ears and mouth. It looked like Ebola, but my sensor didn't pick up any known virus. The others appeared to have died from having the living hell beat out of them." Willits shook his head. "They were just fucking dumped in the truck, then driven out to a huge underground crematorium and tossed inside like fucking garbage."

Rafe watched Willits's fists open and close, and knew that wasn't the end of the story.

"And?" Rafe prompted.

Willits notched his chin up. "I recognized one of the guys with the bloody eyes. Bert Landers. Lying, troublemaking sack of shit from the last basic training class I ran for the army before I joined the SSU. Three months ago, I heard he'd been killed in a training accident. But his body tonight in the truck...dead no more than a few days at most. And two more of the bodies were men on our list of missing personnel."

"Fuck." The soft expletive came from O'Ryan. He and the rest of the men weren't even pretending not to listen.

"Here." Willits thrust his smartphone at Rafe. "I took photos."

Aware that the eyes of every one of his men were on him as he scrolled through the photos, Rafe kept his breathing even and his jaw relaxed even though he wanted to hurl the phone across the campsite. *They'll face justice,* Rafe promised himself. *One way or another we'll make certain they pay.*

"Teng," he snapped to his communications expert when he could trust himself to speak without snarling. "Get Ryker on the line. Willits, you have anything to add?"

There wasn't much more. Willits had stayed in the back of the truck until it stopped, then slipped into the woods and watched as the driver and another man carried the bodies to the crematorium, tossed them in, then pushed the button to set the fire.

"Yo boss. Ryker on line one." Rafe dismissed Willits with a clap on the shoulder, then grabbed the satellite phone Teng held out to him.

Rafe walked out of camp as he greeted the director and founder of the SSU, then launched into an account of tonight's developments.

After Rafe had finished, Ryker cursed softly. "Those symptoms sound like the ones reported with some of Nevsky's subjects." Rafe could just make out the faint sound of his boss spinning the antique globe he kept in his office, a sure sign Ryker was deep in thought. "We found Nevsky's body, but not Kaufmann's. It's possible Kaufmann survived and started his own program."

Rafe barely held back his own curses. Their surveillance hadn't shown anyone matching Kaufmann's description exiting or entering the facility, but if the man lived inside the compound he wouldn't need to leave. A select team of personnel drove into town once a month to pick up supplies. Aside from the staff that was bused to and from the housing complex, the SSU had been unable to get an accurate count of how many people stayed inside the compound around the clock. The buildings had been built in such a way that infrared couldn't penetrate.

"Any luck tracing the money?" Rafe asked.

"No. Whoever set up the bank account to cover the compound's expenses in town buried the details well. It will take time to unravel all the connections and I suspect in the end we'll run into a dead end. I'll tell our researchers to add Kaufmann's name to the search, but since he's presumed dead, any money he's getting for running the program will likely be under a false name."

"Yeah. That could also explain why there wasn't a single piece of branded paper in the labs or even a pencil with a customized logo on it. In case of infiltration, no one would know where to start looking for records tying the program back to its funder."

Rafe hoped to hell the leader of the program wasn't Kaufmann. Dr. Leonard Kaufmann had been the right hand man of Dr. Mikhail Nevsky, a scientist who had worked for the United States government to develop a program for creating super-human spies and soldiers. Using a combination of drugs, hypnosis and gene manipulation, Nevsky had made advances in physical strength, speed and immunity. There was just one problem. None of Nevsky's human subjects had survived past three or four months. They either went insane and committed suicide, or they died from massive organ failure.

Rafe paced along the bank of a small stream, wishing he had his boxing gloves. The thought of Nate going through such a program made him want to hit something. The fact that Rafe felt attracted to one of the scientists involved in such horrific experiments made him sick.

Between the reports of men from this facility going on murderous rampages and Willits's description of the state of the dead men in the back of the truck, Rafe suspected Ryker's conclusion about Kaufmann was correct, and this lab was based on Nevsky's research.

"Could Kaufmann have found Nevsky's microchip?" Rafe asked.

Kai had been undercover at the lab when Dr. Nevsky killed himself by triggering the self-destruct feature. All of Nevsky's work had been destroyed, except for the notes he'd encoded on a microchip and hidden away in an undisclosed location.

"No," Ryker said. "Kai said Nevsky was too paranoid. He didn't even trust Kaufmann with the chip. Kaufmann must have smuggled out his own copy of the notes."

"Shit." Kai had been searching for Nevsky's microchip for over two years now, racing to make sure it wasn't found by a terrorist or criminal organization. Once Kai recovered from the malaria, he was heading out to follow a strong lead regarding the chip's location.

But if the news got out that another superhuman program was up and running, the key players would shift their attention from the chip to the live data. The SSU needed to shut down this facility before word got out about its existence. "Whether this is really Kaufmann or not, they're using the missing service personnel in their experiments," Rafe informed his boss. "I believe they're holding Nate in the underground section of the lab."

Rafe paused. "I'm not leaving without him."

There was a long moment of silence. Rafe knew the situation had escalated far beyond just a simple locate and rescue, but he didn't care. He wasn't risking Nate becoming another cremated body.

"I assume you have a plan on how to get inside," Ryker said.

Rafe glanced at his watch, then ran through his options. He still had several hours of darkness left. "Yeah. Here's what we're going to do..."

CHAPTER THREE

"WAKE UP."

The command in the unfamiliar male voice jerked Gabby out of a sound sleep. Her eyes flew open and her lips parted, but cotton cloth clogged her mouth, blocking her scream. The faint light from the clock radio outlined the shape of a man's head and gave the whites of his eyes a greenish cast.

Terror shot through her. Oh, God. Her heart thundered in her chest until she thought it must be loud enough to wake the entire state. She attempted to sit up, to strike out, but her hands were tied in front of her. She tried to yank them apart, but the tight rope didn't give.

Why had she even allowed herself to sleep? The plan was for her to sneak out at one thirty in the morning and hide in the woods. At that time the chemicals she'd mixed earlier would reach their peak potency and explode in her lab. Laurel and her guard buddy would free the subjects in the lower lab, load them into the back of one of the cargo trucks, then swing by to pick Gabby up.

After turning out the light at her usual bedtime, Gabby had

stretched out on her bed to wait until it was time to meet Laurel. But sleep had snuck up on her.

Had Dr. Kaufmann discovered their plan? Was this man one of the guards come to take her back to the lab, where Kaufmann would fulfill his threat to turn Gabby over to his subjects?

A fresh burst of terror broke through her paralysis. She bent her knees and pushed with her feet, trying to make like an inchworm and move closer to the opposite end of the bed.

The man put his hand on her shoulder and held her in place.

"We're not going to hurt you," he said, his voice little more than a hoarse whisper.

We're? Oh, God, there was more than one man in the room with her?

She twisted away from the man. With one more shove of her feet, she toppled off the other side of the bed. She'd no sooner landed on the floor, though, than large hands reached down and picked her up, setting her back on the bed.

"Like the boss said," whispered a new voice. "We aren't gonna hurt you, lady. Just calm down and listen."

Calm down? She didn't—

The first man put his hand on her throat, using just enough pressure to let her know he could crush her windpipe if he chose. She couldn't stop herself from swallowing nervously, wincing as the muscles of her throat tried to move beneath the constriction of his hand.

The bed coverings moved as the man shifted closer. Her breath hitched.

"Easy," he whispered. "Just relax." His thumb and index finger began a slow, soothing massage under her jaw and to her utter shock and disgust, she felt her muscles ease.

"That's it," he murmured. "As long as you cooperate, I'm not going to hurt you."

Meaning he'd hurt her if she didn't cooperate? Her heart rate spiked again.

But he kept up the slow kneading of his fingers and her body responded to his warm, calloused touch. Not just relaxing, but stirring slightly with arousal.

What the *hell* was wrong with her?

"We're going to remove your gag. If you scream..." He tightened his fingers until she gasped for breath. "Do you understand?"

She nodded.

"Good." He relaxed his grip and it took every ounce of control for her not to gulp in air. But she'd be damned if she'd give him that satisfaction.

The other man's fingers swiftly found the knot on her gag and loosened it. She spat out the cotton and inhaled deeply.

"We cool?" the man asked, tightening his grip on her throat in warning.

Her mouth was too dry to talk, so Gabby merely nodded again.

"I want you to tell me where in the lab this man is being held." A penlight turned on. She winced, turning her head away until her eyes adjusted to the brightness. Then she glanced at the photo in front of her.

It showed a tall, muscular man with ebony skin, wearing military fatigues and a troublemaker's grin. She worked some moisture into her mouth. "I've never seen him before."

The fingers pressed down on her throat. "Wrong answer."

"I swear! I've never seen him before."

"Don't lie to me." There was a hint of violence in the voice now, along with greater pressure on her throat. "We tracked him here. We know he's inside the compound. He's not in the upper level, so he must be downstairs, where you work."

"I don't know what you're talking about." But even to her own ears, her protest sounded false.

Dr. Montague was hiding something. Rafe pressed a little harder on the fragile throat beneath his hand. He hadn't missed the way her pulse had kicked just now. Or the extra layer of wariness in her eyes.

Damn, but he wished they had full light. He wanted to see the color of her eyes. He thought they were hazel, but he couldn't be sure. What he could say for certain was that she was much more fragile in person than she'd appeared tonight when she'd stumbled leaving the compound. Her body shook continuously with tiny shudders he didn't think she was even aware of, and her wrists when he'd bound them had been little more than taut skin over bone. Part of him wanted to gather her in his arms and comfort her. To take away her fear.

Thinking back to the photos of the dead men in the truck, Rafe reminded himself that she didn't deserve his compassion. Her weakness just meant she'd be easy to break. And if his conscience cringed at the thought, he ignored it. He'd do whatever necessary to find Nate.

"Inside where?" Dr. Montague asked. "The compound houses our labs and a few other rooms, none of which are occupied." She nodded at the picture of Nate. "I've certainly never seen him around the property. Is he one of the guards? Are you?"

Her pulse leapt again under his hands. Interesting. So, she didn't like the idea of him being part of the security team? He leaned in closer, so close he could smell her warm, womanly scent underneath the institutional soap and shampoo. "What are you hiding that you don't want the guards to know?" he demanded. "That had you lying on top of the covers, fully dressed, with your shoes on?"

Her pulse went wild, and he knew he had her.

She didn't give in, though. Either she was unaware that his hand on her throat gave him a guideline to the pulse of her emotions, or she had more courage than he'd given her credit for.

She kept her mouth shut, her eyes watching him like a mouse waiting for the snake to strike.

"What are you hiding?" he repeated, tightening his grip on her throat.

She shook her head. "Nothing." But her pulse gave her away.

"Depaoli," Rafe called softly. "Do a more thorough search of these rooms." The cabin was more sparse than a military barracks. The living room held a couch, a coffee table and a small television on a stand. No bookcases. No extra chairs. Bare walls.

The bedroom was just large enough to hold the twin bed and dresser. Not many hiding places, but his gut still insisted she had something here she didn't want found. "You must have missed something the last time," Rafe told Depaoli.

Her breath hitched and her eyelids slammed shut. Her upper teeth captured her lower lip and started gnawing on it.

"Oh, no you don't, sweetheart. Keep those eyes open. I want you to look at this photo again." He put enough pressure on her throat to have her gaze flying to meet his. He saw resentment vying equally with fear and had to admire her backbone.

She flicked a glance at the photo. "I've still never seen him."

Oh yeah, there was no mistaking the aggravation behind that almost snarl. He had to clamp his teeth together to stop himself from grinning at her spunk.

Unfortunately, he believed her. She hadn't seen Nate. "Okay. If you don't know where he is, then tell me how to get access to the lower level of the lab. The place where the trucks come and go."

He felt her stiffen.

"Wha-what do you mean? Our labs take up only one level."

"Wrong answer and you know it. We saw you with your friend on her cigarette break. You definitely came out of a door underneath the upper labs." Rafe motioned to Willits. "Show her the photos you took."

The slight hesitation before Willits pulled out his phone was a sure sign he disapproved of Rafe's order. Tough. They were running out of night. He needed Dr. Montague's cooperation so they had enough time to break into the other part of the lab before daylight.

The first photo came up on the phone's screen. The back of the truck had been dark, so the only illumination came from Willits's phone, but the image of the dead man's face clearly showed dried blood at the eyes, nose, and mouth.

"Maybe you recognize this man instead?"

GABBY GASPED. Du Braise. Dead, with dried blood at his nose, mouth, and ears. She'd seen him alive this afternoon being escorted back to his cell. Du Braise had been maddened to the point of insanity, but otherwise healthy. What had happened in the few hours since she'd seen him?

"Where did you get this?" Her voice trembled and she hoped they thought it was anger, not fear. She hated the idea of showing fear.

"You know this man." The voice was hard. Uncompromising.

Damn it. Maybe she should have hidden her reaction. Too late now. "Who are you? What's going on? You're not part of the lab's security team, are you?"

The man let the silence stretch on. Gabby was acutely aware of the heavy pressure of his hand against her throat. She wondered if he was aware that his fingers were stroking her throat again, sending tiny little currents of arousal through her. Dammit. This was wrong. He could kill her in an instant, yet she found his touch erotic?

If she didn't know better, she'd think she'd been drugged.

"No," the man finally admitted. "We're not security." He cocked his head toward the other man. "Show her the rest of the photos."

By the last photo, Gabby couldn't hold back a whimper. Seven dead men. Two others besides du Braise had been part of the subject pool Dr. Kaufmann had provided to her and the other scientists in the upper labs. Of the seven, she'd only seen du Braise in the lower level, but she had no doubt that's where they'd all died.

Bile climbed up the back of her throat. She'd… She'd… Had her work contributed to their deaths? She swallowed heavily then shook her head. This wasn't the time for guilt or recriminations. She had to focus on getting away from these men.

"Where did these photos come from?" she demanded.

The man holding her studied her for several agonizing heart-beats. In the faint light he appeared cut from stone. Cruel. Totally without mercy.

Yet the tips of his fingers caressed her throat so tenderly. The contrast made her dizzy.

"He," the man nodded to his colleague holding the phone, "took these in the back of a truck that left the underground portion of your lab tonight."

"Tonight?" Her voice cracked. She needed to know what time it was. God, please don't let her have slept through the rescue. Gabby craned her neck, but the man's head blocked the clock's display.

Or had something gone terribly wrong with their escape plan and this was the result? She looked at the man with the phone. "Explain."

Phone Man cocked an eyebrow at her command, but obeyed. When he was finished, she lay in stunned silence. She'd known Kaufmann's program had nasty side effects. But this was far worse. And these men…

"You think I had something to do with that?" Outraged, she tried to sit up. But the man's hand didn't release her throat. With a grunt of annoyance, she glared at her captor. "Let me up, damn you. I refuse to let you accuse me while I'm flat on my back."

The man's mouth twitched and for an instant his fingers tightened, but to her surprise he released her. He even helped her sit up, then cut the ropes binding her.

Narrowing her eyes at her captor as she rubbed feeling back into her wrists, she tried to ignore the chill at her throat now that his warm hand wasn't touching her.

"You're afraid the man in that picture is going to end up like the men in the truck. And you think I know what's going on," she said. Her hands moved of their own will, shoving the man in the chest hard enough to make him grunt in annoyance.

"I had nothing to do with whatever happened to those men." Please let it be so. She'd been trying to help. To give the men some ease while she tried to find a way to free them. She'd never be able to live with herself if Kaufmann had once again used her data in unforeseen ways.

"Oh really?" It was the voice of the man who'd been searching her cabin. She'd totally forgotten about him. But now he stepped into view, holding her smuggled test tubes and notes.

"Then how do you explain these?"

CHAPTER FOUR

GABBY STARED in horror at the man holding the test tubes and the wrinkled notes. She thought she'd been so clever, inserting the test tubes into tampon wrappers, so at first glance they'd look like the other tampons in the box. And the notes were folded into several squares and stuck in between the folds of unused sanitary pads.

How on earth had he known to look inside? Weren't all men allergic to feminine hygiene products?

"Found these in a packed duffel bag just inside the front door," the man continued. "Looks like the doctor was ready to run."

Gabby sucked in a breath, nearly choking on the tension coming off the men as they waited for her to explain. But there was nothing to tell them. They said they weren't part of security. Maybe so. They still might be reporting back to Dr. Kaufmann.

She couldn't trust them with the truth.

The man who'd been holding her throat had his head turned toward the other man. Gabby took advantage of his distraction by pushing off the bed and leaping across the short expanse of floor to the wall with the window.

She had her fingers on the clasp, struggling to open it, when an arm snaked around her waist and a large hand covered her mouth. She clawed at the man, taking some small satisfaction in feeling skin shred beneath her nails, but her struggles didn't stop the man from lifting her off the ground and tossing her facedown on the bed.

"That was a mistake," his voice murmured against her ear. Even though he kept his words quiet, she felt the anger pulsing underneath.

His hand pressed on the back of her head, smushing her face into the pillow, while his knee rested on her lower back, pinning her to the mattress.

She kicked, but that didn't stop them from tying her feet together. Then retying her hands behind her.

"Boss, you'd better take a look at this," the harsh whisper whipped across Gabby's flesh. She'd hoped they wouldn't look at the notes, because there was no simple way to explain why she had them. Or why her name repeatedly came up.

"This here is some serious shit."

Gabby's breath stilled in her lungs. This was it. If they were part of Kaufmann's project, or even some outside force looking to destroy all evidence connecting Kaufmann's work to Agent Styx, then she was dead.

The man holding her down moved off her, then flipped her onto her back. He yanked the gag back into place over her mouth, tightened it, then moved away.

Gabby heard him cross the room, then the rustle of papers followed by a sharp inhale.

"Jesus H. Christ." Rafe held the creased paper closer to Depaoli's muted penlight so he could read the notes Dr. Montague had stashed away. No wonder she was nervous. The pages were part of the lab's treatment plan. The poor bastard who was the subject had been given drugs, been put under hypnosis, and been infected with a virus to deliver altered genes. All with the intent of making a mind-controlled killer.

Dr. Montague's name was mentioned frequently in the notes. Apparently she was working on a formula to counteract the uncontrollable rages experienced by some of the subjects.

Rafe shot a look of pure fury toward the woman on the bed. She looked so innocent. He'd started to believe her. But this...

He turned away. With a sharp jerk of his head, he indicated that the others should join him in the tiny bathroom. Once they were all crammed inside with the door closed, he flipped on the overhead light. The room had no windows, so they were safe from detection.

"Where'd you find these?" he asked Depaoli.

"She's quite ingenious, actually. The test tubes were disguised as tampons, the notes folded among the sanitary napkins."

Rafe skimmed the notes again. The tests described went beyond cruel into inhumane. And the list of known side effects would have made an ethical scientist stop work immediately.

Not here, though. These notes were cold. Showing no regard for the physical comfort or mental health of the subjects.

"What now, boss?" Willits asked.

Rafe shook his head, barely able to think past the hard punch of fury coalescing into the need to break the woman in the other room. The woman who'd willingly participated in this program.

But this was no time to lose control. His men were looking to him for guidance. Even though his first impulse was to throw the woman over his shoulder and take her back to camp for interrogation, he couldn't afford to reveal his team's presence. A missing scientist would do just that.

So Rafe reined in his temper. A quick check of his watch showed that their time was running out. Dawn would hit in a couple of hours and they needed to finish their assault on the lab and be gone by then.

He studied the men with him. Depaoli, Willits and O'Ryan. Of the three, Willits was currently the most dangerous. He practically vibrated with menace. His shock and disgust over the dead bodies in the truck were an asset.

"Willits, go get Dr. Montague. Leave her bound and gagged, and hold your knife to her throat. Get her nice and scared. Then bring her in here." Rafe walked over to the tiny bathtub with shower. He drew back the curtain, but saw that the tub was too narrow for what he had in mind. He considered the possibilities, then with a nod, pulled the curtain back into place. "When you bring her in, I want her on her knees, here." He indicated a spot in front of the shower.

"Sit on the edge of the tub like this," Rafe demonstrated. "Bracket her with your legs. Make sure she feels trapped. I'll let you know if I want you to cut her, but feel free to play with the pressure of the blade against her throat. O'Ryan, you sit on the toilet. Invade her space. Let your knees touch her. I want her to feel threatened. Play with your knife or your gun if you want. Depaoli, you'll be next to me. This isn't going to be a good cop, bad cop scenario. Her name is mentioned in these papers. She's directly involved. I want her terrified. I want her to know her life is in our hands."

Under normal circumstances, none of the men would lift a finger to harm a female. But Rafe didn't see even a flicker of unease on their faces now. Just grim determination. Right now she wasn't a female. She was an obstacle. An enemy.

"We're going to do whatever's necessary to find out where Nate is and get him out."

Satisfied that they were all on the same page, Rafe nodded at Willits, then flipped off the light before the man opened the door. Interrogating the doctor with only their flashlights as illumination would add to her stress. The shadows would make them seem monstrous, and with the shower curtain closed, she wouldn't know if someone else was behind her, waiting to attack.

Gabby tugged against her bonds the instant the bathroom door shut behind the men. Her fear had dissipated under a cloud of surreal calm and the firm determination to get away. But not only were the ropes bound so tight she felt no give at her wrists or ankles, a short length of rope connected her hands to her feet, severely limiting her range of motion.

Meaning her chances of escape were low, dammit. She couldn't even manage to sit up, despite muscles toned from years of practicing ballet. If she rolled over and let herself tumble to the floor, the thump might alert the men, but there wasn't enough play in the ropes to allow her to slide just her feet off the bed and stand up.

Her calm wavered and fear started to return. No! She had to stay focused. There had to be some way she could get free. Because the longer the men stayed in the bathroom, the greater the chances they'd be furious with her when they emerged. She knew those notes were damning. Unless she could make them understand she was a victim, innocent of the atrocities committed against the men in the truck, then her chances of being killed tonight were high.

Unable to just lie there waiting for death, Gabby took a chance and rolled off the mattress. For an instant she wondered if she could fool them by scooting under the dust ruffle and hiding under the bed.

But she would feel too much like a rabbit in its hole, praying that the hawk passed by. Instead, she rolled awkwardly into the living room.

She made it as far as the couch before she was yanked to her feet, then thrown over a hard male shoulder. Shock at the man's silent approach kept her still for precious moments. How had he snuck up on her like that?

But then her fear kicked back in. The gag muffled her cries as she tried to wriggle free. She might as well have saved her breath.

Her captor held her far too securely. Her struggling didn't even loosen his grip.

He wasn't the same man who'd held her throat. This man's scent was sharper, heavy with sweat and dirt. He didn't speak as he moved. His silence, combined with the darkness, increased her terror. Made her certain she was about to be killed. Tears leaked out of her eyes, running into her hairline as her upside down head bobbed with each step he took.

The bathroom door opened, then shut behind her. There was enough light from a flashlight for her to see the boots of the other men.

Her captor dumped her on the floor, then jerked her hair and used it to position her on her knees. He moved behind her, sitting on the edge of the tub so his thick legs bracketed her torso. He twisted his fingers in her hair and tugged, moving her head so her chin was slightly lifted.

Then he pressed a knife against her throat.

Gabby froze, not even daring to take a breath. She could feel the low vibration of his hatred and knew he wanted an excuse to kill her.

Another man lowered himself onto the closed toilet lid. He was close enough that she felt the heat of his anger as he leaned toward her, but what scared her most was the way he shifted his knife from hand to hand, as if eager to take his turn with her.

Lungs screaming for air, Gabby sucked in a breath. The knife at her throat dug further into her skin. She couldn't think past the fear. Couldn't see any way out of here but death.

Tears slid off her cheeks onto the man's hand. God, she'd been so close to freeing the men in the lab and escaping.

"We're going to try this again." The icy voice belonged to the man who'd held her throat. Who'd caressed her so gently. Surely she'd find some speck of mercy in his eyes?

But when the flashlight moved, illuminating his face, all she saw was cold fury.

Then the light hit her eyes and she couldn't see anything at all. She flinched and turned away, but the man behind her used her hair to yank her head forward again. She closed her eyes against the painful glare. Visions of interrogation scenes in old black-and-white movies raced through her head. Now she understood how isolating it was to be unable to see the man who held all the power.

"Cut the gag away," the voice said.

The knife moved from her throat up to a spot in front of her ear, burrowing under the cotton gag. The blade turned, so one edge lay against her skin and the other sawed at the cloth.

Gabby held very still, but even so, she felt the sting of the blade nicking her skin. An ache in her fingers made her realize that she had her fists tightly clenched in response to the pain. But she was afraid that if she loosened the tension in her hands, the rest of her body would follow, letting go until she was nothing more than a terrified puddle on the floor.

The cotton broke, and she spit out the gag. She desperately wanted some water for her parched mouth, but when the knife returned to its original position under her chin she didn't dare to even work the stiffness out of her sore jaw muscles for fear of being cut more.

"Here's the deal," the voice said. "I'm going to ask questions. You have one chance to give me a satisfactory answer. If I think you're lying, you'll be cut. Do you understand?"

"Y-yes." Her voice was a parched, frightened rasp.

"This is our missing teammate, Nate Ngoro. Where are they holding him?" The light lowered away from her eyes and she blinked them open. The man held up the same photo as before.

"I told you. I've never seen him before."

There was a long pause. The light returned to her eyes and she closed them. But even with her eyelids down, the light was bright enough to make her wince through the pink filter of her closed lids. Then the light shifted away, leaving her in blessed darkness.

"Have you ever seen any of the men in these photos?" he demanded.

Gabby reluctantly opened her eyes and peered at the sheet of paper displaying five color photographs. She leaned forward a little, trying to clear the dots of color dancing across her vision so she could make out the detail of their faces. "I—" She squinted and tilted her head, wincing as the knife pricked her throat. She pulled back before the blade cut her. "Maybe the last one. The one with the beret. I think I might have seen him waiting in one of the upper level examination rooms. But that would have been a couple of weeks ago."

The silence that followed her statement sparked with anticipation and she knew this was why these men were here. They were looking for the men in the photos. They weren't Kaufmann's men after all.

"Take another look at these men. Tell me which ones you recognize. Their names. How you know them." He held out the camera phone with the pictures of the dead men and Gabby flinched.

She didn't want to see the battered bodies of those men again. But the knife tip prodded her chin, reminding her of the consequences if she didn't obey.

"Michael du Braise," she identified the first photo. "One of the veterans I've been treating. He was alive as of four o'clock this afternoon."

The silence in the room was suffocating. She expected a barrage of questions. Instead, the man scrolled through the rest of the photos.

"No... No...Yes. I don't know his name, one of the other doctors was treating him, but I remember seeing him in the hallway being led to one of the treatment rooms. I thought he looked like Bruce Willis with a goatee… No…Yes. Again, the man wasn't one of my patients, but I recognize the scar behind his ear." Which was about the only identifiable aspect, the face in the photo had been beaten nearly unrecognizable

"No." Thank God that was the last photo. Her stomach had lodged somewhere in the vicinity of her throat. She fought to take shallow breaths so she wouldn't gag at the horror of the violence done to those men.

"You still claim you don't know anything about how these men ended up dead in the back of the truck?"

"That's right." God, she knew helping Kaufmann to save her own life had been a questionable move, but she'd never have agreed if she'd suspected men were dying.

The light flipped back up to spear into her eyes.

"Then how do you explain these notes?"

He didn't lower the light, but he didn't need to. Her stomach took a nosedive. She knew what he was holding up.

"I stole those notes and the vials from the lower level lab," she answered. "A lab I knew nothing about until last week. See the crease marks on the notes? You saw how small a square they were folded into. That's because I smuggled them out in my clothing, hiding them from the evening body check."

"Why did you need to steal the notes when you're working on the lower level?"

"I wasn't working on the lower level. Not then." She closed her eyes, thinking what a fool she'd been. "I was hired to work in the upper lab, for what I thought was a legitimate project." Her lips twisted in self-disgust. "Then last week I stumbled across the lower lab and discovered another program. A program that turned men into monsters." Her cheeks heated with outrage.

"I smuggled out the notes with some idea of escaping and letting the authorities know what was going on." Panic sent adrenaline through her veins exactly as it had when Kaufmann confronted her in his office. "But the security cameras I thought were off had come back online and caught me exploring the restricted area. The director threatened my life unless I joined the team in the lower lab."

She opened her eyes and tried to see the man behind the light. "I had no choice!"

CHAPTER FIVE

"Very touching." Rafe clapped. She was good. He'd give her that. She sounded truly outraged. "But somehow I'm not convinced that you were forced to work in this monstrous program."

She shifted, trying to see past the flashlight to his face. He kept it aimed at her eyes, and ignored his awareness of how attractive she looked even with her lips swollen from the gag and her hair tangled around her face. The long line of her jaw was tight with anger and defiance, in contrast to the sheen of frightened tears that reflected light off her cheeks.

Still, something about her pulled at him. He wanted to soothe her. To run his mouth over her neck and lick away the few drops of blood from where Willits's knife had nicked her. To dry her tears with his tongue.

But he wasn't some dumb hormone-crazed teenager. He knew evil could hide in beautiful packages. Dr. Montague was an enemy. Not an innocent.

"The director threatened to throw me to his subjects," she snapped. "When I discovered the lab, I saw du Braise in a berserker rage. He took a *bite* out of a man's *throat*. I'd never seen rage like that. I thought my work could give the men some degree of sanity back until I found a way to free them.

"That woman on the cigarette break? Laurel?" Her voice took on an earnest, cajoling tone. "We have a rescue planned for tonight." She glanced around, as if searching for something. "What time is it? The rescue is scheduled to start at one thirty. We left chemicals mixed in our labs that will set off a series of explosions. One of the guards is going to help us."

"Ri-ight. How convenient." He flicked a disdainful glance over her. "You seriously expect me to believe that two scientists and a guard thought you could take out a well-trained security team and help these monstrous subjects escape?" Gutsy, but hopeless. *If* she was telling the truth.

"We had to do *something*. The men are in extreme physical and mental agony. Forced to commit hideous acts of violence. Dr. Kaufmann has to be stopped."

Fuck. "What was that name?" Rafe asked with soft menace.

"Dr. Kaufmann. He called himself Dr. Pierce when he offered me the job, but his real name is Dr. Kaufmann."

Holy. Crap. They'd guessed right. Kaufmann had survived and started his own program.

Rafe studied Dr. Montague. He still wasn't sure if he believed her, though her outrage seemed real enough. There was more than a hint of evangelical fervor in her tone. If she was telling the truth, this could be exactly the situation they needed to get to Nate. He signaled subtly with his chin and Depaoli slipped out the door to tell the other team to keep a sharp eye on the lab. It was almost one thirty, so they'd see soon enough if she'd lied about the rescue. If she had, he'd make her give him access to the lab if he had to drag her there himself.

"Start at the beginning," he told her. "From the moment you faked your death."

She blinked once and her mouth fell open. "What are you talking about? I never pretended to be dead."

"Then why are you listed as a fatality in a bus accident on your way home from Aruba?"

"But...Dr. Kaufmann picked me up in a private plane. I was never on any bus."

Her pouty, puzzled frown seemed real enough. But he didn't trust his instincts tonight. Because despite the evidence of her guilt, he wanted to believe in her innocence. Not because of deduction, but because he wanted her in every way a man wanted a woman.

He saw the instant she made the jump in logic. Her back stiffened and her eyes narrowed. "You're saying Dr. Kaufmann faked my death? Why? What did it gain him?"

"Once you were declared dead, you fell off the radar," Rafe explained. "You didn't have any family to raise questions about what happened to you and your friends had no reason to suspect they'd been lied to. They believed you had died." The documentation surrounding her death had been expertly done. Another sign that Kaufmann had a powerful backer.

"No one searches for a dead woman," he continued. "Which means no one accidentally stumbles upon the work that's being done here. Kaufmann did the same for all the other staff." The others also had no immediate family.

"Everyone? No, that's impossible," she protested. "We have almost three dozen people on staff. Surely someone would notice such a high number of deaths."

Rafe shook his head, then remembered she couldn't see him past the light shining at her, although at some point his aim had shifted unconsciously to her chin rather than her eyes. "Do you have any idea how many accidental deaths occur every day? Besides, back in your former lives, none of you worked or lived in the same area, so no one would see a pattern. He was safe." But the staff weren't. Rafe wondered if Dr. Montague would reach the same conclusion he had.

She pursed her lips as she thought. When the edges of her

top teeth peeked out to worry her bottom lip, Rafe was hit with an unwelcome surge of lust.

Dammit. Not now!

"If we're already dead, then there's no way Dr. Kaufmann would want us to draw attention to ourselves and his project by suddenly returning to our lives." She squinted into the light as if trying to read his expression. "He never planned to keep us alive, did he?"

Rafe was impressed. So much for her naïveté. "No. Probably not."

He'd expected to see fear on her face. But instead, she looked pissed. And damn if he wasn't starting to believe she really was telling the truth.

Depaoli slipped back into the room. "Boss, Team Two reports a disturbance at the lower level of the lab. And there's a team of two security guards on their way to this cabin."

GABBY FROZE at the man's words. The one holding the knife jerked her hair, forcing her head back so she was almost staring at the ceiling, then dug the point of his knife into her throat until it broke the skin. A warm rivulet of blood slipped down her neck.

But it was the man behind the flashlight who snarled, "What the hell have you done? Sent out a silent alarm?"

"No!" Tears stung her eyes again. It wasn't fair. He'd been softening toward her, she'd heard it in his voice. Now he thought she'd betrayed him, when the only explanation was that something had gone wrong with the rescue and she'd been found out. "I—"

"Can it." The man switched off the flashlight. In the dark, she was acutely aware of every little sound. Her own panicked breathing. The scratch of her shirt sliding against the jacket of the man with the knife as his arms caged her in. The faint creak of the door opening. Soft rustling that was probably her bedcovers.

She sensed more than heard the man reenter the bathroom. Her night vision was coming online. He'd left the door cracked just enough for her to see the glow of the clock radio.

As the silence lengthened, it felt like the men around her were growing in size and weight, until they took up all the room and stole all the air. Her rapid, shallow breaths sounded as loud as a rocket engine.

She knew it was her panicked imagination, she really did, but that didn't calm her down. A scream built up in her throat, demanding to be let loose. She clamped her back teeth together, swallowed the scream and fiercely told herself that if she lost it she'd give away their position and get them all killed.

As if to punctuate her thoughts, the main bedroom door squeaked open. Gabby heard two faint pffts, like air being discharged from a pressurized canister, then heavy footsteps crossed her bedroom. A man swore softly.

Faster than she could track, the men around her rushed out of the bathroom.

Except for the one behind her. He released the knife from her throat, picked her up around the waist and tossed her into the bathtub.

"Don't move," he breathed. He pulled the shower curtain closed.

And left her alone.

WHAT THE FUCK was going on? Rafe stared at the pillows he'd shoved underneath Dr. Montague's covers when Depaoli had reported the security men heading toward the cabin.

He'd figured Dr. Montague had betrayed them and had braced for an assault aimed at his team. He hadn't expected an assassination attempt against her. But before he'd died, the older of the two security guards had admitted their orders were to kill Dr. Montague, then dump her body in the woods outside the compound's lower level, where a truck would pick up her corpse. Just another body for disposal at the crematorium.

Fuck. She'd been telling the truth. The thought of her dead, of her body burning, made Rafe want to hit something. Instead, he scrubbed his hand over his hair.

"Boss, we've got smoke pouring out of the lower level labs," Muldovsky's voice came over the com link. "The garage door is opening. People are streaming out. There's fighting...Fuck."

"Report," Rafe snapped.

"It's Nate. Christ, he's like the Tasmanian Devil on steroids. Fighting like a wild thing. Tearing at the security guards with his bare hands."

Screw this. Rafe gave orders to his team to move out. "We're heading your way," he told Muldovsky.

O'Ryan nodded toward the dead men on the bedroom floor.

Rafe muted his mic. "Bring 'em," he said. "We'll dump them at the compound."

"Yee-haw!" Muldovsky crowed over the com link. "One of the transport trucks just came racing out of the garage like Indiana Jones escaping the Nazis. And Nate just jumped on board."

"Get control of the truck," Rafe told him. "Then load up your team. Watch for us along the road. We're driving to the rendezvous tonight." They had Nate. Mission accomplished. It was time to get the hell out of Dodge.

"What about the lady doctor?" O'Ryan asked.

Rafe thought about large, frightened eyes and the courage it had taken to plan an escape. He'd find some way to make up for scaring her.

Shoving open the bathroom door, he said, "She's coming with us."

CHAPTER SIX

GABBY LAY HUDDLED in the bathtub, fighting to hear something, anything over the frantic beating of her heart. She needed to know what was happening in the other room. Was there a fight? Had her mysterious visitors left? Were Kaufmann's men waiting for her in the cabin?

Or was she alone?

Whatever was going on, she refused to just lie here, waiting helplessly for someone to come fetch her. Using her shoulder to brace her body against the side of the tub, she tucked her bound feet underneath her and shoved upright into an awkward kneeling position.

Unable to see which way was up through the impenetrable darkness, she felt for a moment like she was falling. She pressed her bound hands against the wall and flexed her toes against the bottom of the tub to force her brain to recognize where she was in space.

When her inner ear had adjusted to the new position, and her breathing was calm enough to allow her to hear, she strained to pick up any sound from the bedroom. But the men had shut the door behind them and she couldn't judge whether she was alone or not.

Still, maybe it was better to stay safely here in the tub, hidden by the shower curtain. That way, if Kaufmann's men were out there, she'd have a few precious moments to prepare for attack once the bathroom door opened. After sorting through her options, she decided to lie on her back in the tub despite the pain that caused her bound arms. Bending her knees and raising her feet, she prepared to kick out at any attacker. The position seemed rather silly, but at least this way she didn't feel so helpless.

To give her tired legs a break, she lowered her heels until they rested on the rim of the bathtub. And waited in suffocating silence for something to happen.

An interminable amount of time later, the sharp snick of the bathroom door handle engaging caused her whole body to jerk. She bent her legs, prepared to strike.

"Dr. Montague," a familiar voice said as the light from a flashlight glowed beyond the shower curtain. It was ridiculous the way her heart leapt to hear the voice of the man who'd pinned her to the bed. But there it was. His husky whisper, despite having threatened her life minutes ago, now gave her a sense of security.

"You need to come with us." He pulled back the shower curtain. His brows lowered as he spotted her and his eyes traced the short distance from her bare feet, poised to strike, to his vulnerable crotch. Then the corner of his mouth lifted in amusement. The hand that wasn't holding the flashlight came up in a gesture of reassurance. "Whoa. It's okay. You're safe."

She narrowed her eyes. "Am I?" she responded in a fierce whisper. "Aren't you the man who had his colleague hold a knife to my throat?"

"Yes." His tone was completely unapologetic. He nodded over his shoulder. "But two security men just shot up your bed, thinking you were in it. Whatever's got them thinking you're such a threat can only be good for us."

He held out his hand. "Come on. I'll untie you. Then you have five minutes to grab what essentials you need. You won't be coming back."

Gabby lowered her legs, then stared up at him in shock. This was the first time she'd seen his face. Even though the flashlight left more of it in shadow than she'd like, she only had one word for him. Stunning.

His face was an intriguing mix of planes and hollows. Pure male strength with a hint of sensuality that made her blood quicken. Dark eyes. Dark hair. A slightly Roman nose. And a mouth made to give a woman pleasure.

Gabby shook her head, wondering if she had a mild concussion. What else could explain this reaction?

"I promise not to bite," the man said. His eyes laughed down at her, then sparked with wicked intent. "At least, not unless you ask."

Huffing out a thoroughly confused breath, Gabby nodded agreement and tried to pretend that his change from tormenter to flirt was perfectly normal. A second later she squeaked as he reached down, grabbed her by the upper arms and lifted her out of the tub.

He set her on her feet and they stood facing one another. His fingers drew tiny circles on the bare skin of her upper arm beneath the sleeve of her t-shirt. She was trapped. Engulfed as much by the intensity of his gaze, as by his grip on her arm.

It was the strangest thing, staring at him in the dark, knowing he would have authorized his man to do serious harm to her in order to get the location of his teammate. Yet sensing that now, inexplicably, she was one of the ones he would protect. And she swore she felt something shift inside her. Something that made her blood warm, her nipples tighten, and caused her body to sway toward him.

She thought she saw an answering flare of heat in his eyes before he gave a muttered curse and turned her to face away from him. A second later the bindings at her wrists, then her ankles, fell off.

"Boss?" The quiet question from the doorway snapped the spell.

"Coming," the man replied. With a tug on her arm he led her into the bedroom.

She stopped cold, staring in horror at the two dead bodies on the floor. Her eyes rose to the leader's face, but he was deep in discussion with one of his men. Swallowing heavily against the sick fear of violent death, Gabby grabbed her overnight bag containing the rest of her notes, the other vials, a change of clothes, and her wallet.

Hoping she wasn't making the biggest mistake of her life, she let the men lead her into the night.

RAFE KEPT an eye on Dr. Montague as he led his team toward the rendezvous point. He was thankful there hadn't been any backup waiting outside for the two dead security men. It meant his team had been able to slip undetected into the woods. But as they drew closer to the point where they were supposed to meet Muldovsky and the others, he heard gunfire. Both single action and automatic fire. "Muldovsky, we're in position," he breathed into the com link. "We've got Dr. Montague with us."

"The more the merrier, boss, the more the merrier. We should be seeing you any...there you are."

The stolen transport truck slowed as it came into view. Rafe grabbed Dr. Montague's wrist and pulled her into a jog. She barely kept up with him as the rest of the team raced past. "Come on," he urged. "Just a bit further." But when it was their turn to climb into the truck, her arms didn't have the strength to pull herself aboard. Not surprising after all she'd been through. So

Rafe boosted her up, then slipped over the tailgate after her. "Go," he commanded Muldovsky through the link.

The truck leapt forward.

A dark blue sedan hurtled around the bend behind them, its headlights illuminating the interior of the truck. Jurgenson, their medic, was patching up a bullet graze on the side of Thompson's neck. Dr. Montague and the rest of Rafe's men crouched or sat along the truck's walls. Eight unconscious men, including Nate, lay on the floor in the center of the truck. "Shit," Rafe swore quietly.

"Sorry, boss," Brown murmured as he and Daniels secured the unconscious men's hands. "But they went berserk. We had to knock them out for our own safety."

Dr. Montague made a soft sound of sympathy deep in her throat and Rafe glanced over at her. He was still reeling from how close he'd come to kissing her back in her bathroom. How easily he'd put aside his anger and his doubts regarding her innocence and moved her from the category of enemy to potential lover.

"Wha—what happened to my friend?" Dr. Montague stammered. "To Laurel? She was supposed to leave with the men. And..." She nodded her head, mouthing numbers as she counted the unconscious men. "There should be sixteen more men who escaped the lab. Where are the others?"

Daniels raised his head and met Rafe's eyes briefly before looking at Dr. Montague. "This Laurel, did she have long, dark hair? Not very tall?"

Dr. Montague nodded.

"The guards shot her. She's dead."

Dr. Montague winced and caught her lower lip between her teeth, clamping down hard. "And the other men?"

"Five dead." Daniels shrugged. "We didn't see any others."

Dr. Montague's shoulders sagged. "Then they're still inside. Is...the lab still operational?"

Daniels nodded.

Dr. Montague's breath hissed out. Her gaze lifted to Rafe's. "The lab was supposed to be destroyed. We set chemical reactions to catch fire tonight and explode. We wanted the buildings destroyed and all the notes, too. The project was supposed to end tonight. We—"

Bullets pinged against the raised tailgate. "Down!" Rafe ordered.

The truck veered to the left, then slid around a curve, throwing Rafe and the others hard against the side of the truck. Dr. Montague gasped as Rafe's shoulder collided with her chest. Once the truck's balance returned to center, Rafe pushed away from her. "Sorry," he said, although he'd enjoyed the brief contact with the softness of her breasts.

Willits grabbed an automatic rifle, took aim over the tailgate and shot out the windshield of the sedan. The car swerved into a tree. Willits stayed in position, waiting for additional pursuit.

"We can't go back tonight for the other men," Rafe told Dr. Montague. "It's too dangerous."

She nodded, her eyes on Daniels and Brown as they finished securing the hands of the unconscious men. She rubbed her arms as if cold, even though with this many bodies in the truck the temperature was comfortable.

"Where are we going?" she asked.

"Headquarters is sending a plane to extract us."

"Headquarters? Who *are* you guys?"

Rafe shot her a grin. "We're the good guys, of course."

Dr. Montague rolled her eyes. "I want to check their vitals," she said, kneeling before the first unconscious man. She took his wrist in her hand, then shook back her sleeve on the other arm so she could see her watch.

Jurgenson started doing the same to the escapee closest to him.

The truck made another sharp turn and Rafe darted forward just in time to save Dr. Montague from crashing to the floor.

"Here, brace against me as you work." He wrapped one arm around her waist and grabbed hold of the side of the truck with his other hand. She glanced at him in surprise and shifted her body to give her arms more access, but he was pleased she didn't fight him.

With her pressed against his side, he could feel how delicate she was, and feel the small tremors of exhaustion still shaking her body. He was just about to take off his jacket and offer it to her when one of the unconscious men started to gasp for air.

Dr. Montague broke free of Rafe's arm and slid across the truck bed to the man. "Flashlight," she ordered, all signs of her fatigue disappearing.

Daniels swung his light over, revealing frothy, dark liquid bubbling from the man's mouth and nose.

"Christ." Rafe grabbed Dr. Montague's arm, holding her back from touching the man. "Are you nuts? You can't touch them without gloves."

She ignored him, twisting to get free. "Let me go. I need to help him."

"How?" Jurgenson demanded. He moved his own flashlight toward the sound of choking coming from his left. "Here's another one. Fucking bleeding from every hole he's got." He quickly spotlighted every unconscious man, but only those two were bleeding.

Jurgenson glared at Dr. Montague as if it were all her fault. "You got some miracle cure, sister? 'Cause otherwise, these men are dead."

"There is no cure," Dr. Montague snapped. She jerked free of Rafe's grip and turned the choking man onto his side, tipping his face slightly down so that the bloody froth spilled onto the truck floor. When the man stopped choking, she slid one of her thighs forward, then set his head on her leg.

She returned Jurgenson's glare. "I just want to make him more comfortable before he dies." Her voice thrummed with frustrated anger that contrasted with the gentleness of her actions. Pulling a tissue from her pants pocket, she wiped the man's face.

On the opposite side of the truck, Jurgenson scowled and mirrored her actions.

Rafe raised his brow. Jurgenson was former Force Recon with a bedside personality like a pit viper. All the men were wary of him. The worse they were hurt, the surlier his mood and the more forceful his treatment. They'd all learned to keep their mouths shut and play submissive.

Watching Dr. Montague put the surly medic in his place totally turned Rafe on. He loved confident, intelligent women. Add compassionate and brave and he was in trouble.

Rafe wet his handkerchief from his canteen and handed it to her. She flicked him a grateful smile then stroked the damp cloth over her patient's face. Watching her tend the man so gently, Rafe had to admire her strength. Her body was still shivering slightly, but all her focus was on the dying man.

The man coughed, then gave a wheezing death sigh. Dr. Montague gently closed his lids and murmured some benediction Rafe couldn't make out, before sliding her legs out from under his head.

She ran her hands up and down her arms. "They didn't have to die like this," she said almost too quietly for Rafe to hear. "He could have changed the formula."

Rafe removed his jacket and draped it over her shoulders. "Here," he said. "Come sit down." He led her over to the side of the truck as nearby, the man in Jurgenson's arms gasped out his last breath.

Dr. Montague slid down to the floor, pulled her knees to her chest, and wrapped his coat tighter around her torso as she tilted her head back against the wall. "Why," she breathed, rolling her head back and forth. "Why didn't Kaufmann care that his formula killed?"

A single tear slid down her cheek, breaking Rafe's heart.

She'd cried way too much tonight. He wished he could have spared her tears.

"If Kaufmann is the same man we think he is, all that matters to him is the end result."

"To create the ultimate soldier," she supplied wearily. "A man deprived of all traces of humanity in order to protect our country." She shook her head. "I wouldn't wish that on our worst enemy."

Rafe couldn't argue with her. He looked over to where Nate lay unconscious. Nate had chosen to serve his country. To place his life on the line. But he'd never volunteered to give up his humanity. And because that choice had been forced on him, Nate was going to die a horrible death.

Dr. Montague lifted her head and stared at Jurgenson as he eased the dead man onto the floor of the truck. Another tear slipped free, then she closed her eyes and leaned her head against the truck wall.

She was silent for so long, Rafe thought she'd fallen asleep.

"You've heard of Kaufmann," she said, not opening her eyes. "How? Are you military?"

Rafe almost gave her his standard reply, a light, teasing remark that only hinted at what he did. But after what she'd been through tonight, much of it his fault, he figured she deserved the truth.

"We're a private special operations force that does mostly contract work for the government."

She opened her eyes and studied him. Her hazel eyes probed deep, stripping him bare as she searched for an answer to a question he couldn't even guess at.

He had the strongest urge to squirm under her scrutiny, wanting to give her whatever she sought.

Finally, without any change in expression, she asked, "Do you have a name, or do you go by a number?"

Normally, Rafe would wink and give her his best James Bond

impression. But something about the way she looked at him, the focus in her eyes despite the lines of exhaustion on her face and the dried tears on her cheeks, killed his instinctive flirtation.

A part of him knew if he treated her question lightly he'd lose any respect he'd earned since leaving her cabin. And having her respect was suddenly as vital as breathing.

"Rafe Andros." He offered his hand for a shake. "I apologize for scaring you earlier."

Shit. Where the hell had that come from? Since when did he apologize for carrying out his mission? He'd needed information on Nate's location. Given the same situation, he'd do it again.

So why did it matter that she forgive him?

She eyed his hand with the same solemn regard. Damn, he wished he knew what was going on in that amazing brain of hers. Finally, the corners of her lips lifted in a small smile and she took his hand.

"Gabby Montague." Her handshake was firm, but her slender fingers were cold. He wanted to warm them. To pull all of her against him and give her his heat and strength. Her hand was so light and fragile inside his, filling him with the need to protect.

But before he could act, she withdrew, crossing her arms over her chest. "Apology accepted," she said quietly, her eyes drifting over the unconscious men. "I suppose I might do violence, too, if one of my friends suffered in such a program."

Her eyes sought his. Beneath the sorrow and the remnants of fear, he saw the slow burn of anger. Oh yeah. She might seem the cold scientist, but she had fire within her just waiting to be released.

Another of the men began coughing. Gabby threw off his jacket and beat Jurgenson to the man's side.

Rafe met O'Ryan's worried eyes and they both shifted closer to Nate. None of the dead men had shown any external symptoms before dying. Had they come all this way only to watch Nate die?

CHAPTER SEVEN

SSU Compound
Oregon

GABBY PULLED crisp mountain air deep into her lungs as she followed the last stretcher off the plane. They'd lost a total of four men during their escape from Kaufmann's lab. Three died in the back of the truck. One more died after they'd taken off in the small plane sent to meet them at a nearby airport. At some point after the fourth death, Gabby's energy had deserted her and she'd dozed just long enough to leave her groggy and emotionally vulnerable.

Uneasy over the strange events of the night, Gabby remained tense and wary, keeping an alert eye on the pine forest ringing the landing strip. Ahead of her, silhouetted by the early morning sun, men in civilian clothes pushed stretchers holding the survivors toward a transport truck. The airfield remained quiet except for the squeak of the stretchers' wheels over the tarmac and the distant call of what she thought was a hawk.

When she reached the truck Gabby averted her eyes, unable to bear watching the body bags being loaded. She didn't understand why the men's bodies had failed, and so dramatically. Throughout the trip she'd asked herself what she could have done to save them. Each time the answer had been the same. Nothing.

She couldn't fight what she didn't understand. Unfortunately, she also couldn't shake the suspicion that her research had contributed to the men's deaths.

She shook her head. No time to worry about that now. Or to wallow in guilt. She had to make certain the same fate didn't await the survivors.

Particularly not to Rafe's friend, Nate.

"These men aren't sane," she warned the short, muscular man with a stethoscope around his neck who was examining one of the survivors. The doctor looked up at her with compassionate eyes refreshingly different from the brusque medic onboard the truck. "And their physical strength is above normal. Ordinary restraints won't hold them. Sedate them like you would an elephant. They need—"

"You can finish giving Dr. Smith instructions later," Rafe interrupted, grabbing her arm. "The director wants to talk to you."

"But—"

"Now, doctor." Rafe pulled her away from the truck.

Gabby scowled at him, then turned her head back toward the medical team.

"It's okay," Dr. Smith assured her. "We'll be careful with the men."

Gabby searched his face and saw nothing but genuine concern. Maybe these really were good people who'd treat the men with the decency they deserved instead of like disposable lab rats.

She nodded and let Rafe guide her across the tarmac.

"What's the hurry?" she snapped.

"You've got information the director needs," Rafe replied. Then he grinned at her. "And I want a hot shower."

"Oh, well then," she answered drily. "Maybe we should run?"

"Nah, we're almost there." The glint of laughter in his eye emphasized the difference between Rafe the deadly soldier who'd terrorized her during his mission to rescue Nate, and Rafe the man who flirted as easily as other men breathed. Still reeling from the night's events, Gabby let Rafe's good humor surround her, further soothing her overloaded nerves.

Minutes later, Rafe led her through the stained glass door of a stately Victorian mansion. "This is the administration building."

Gabby gaped. The exterior might be pure 1800s, but although the interior retained the charming molding and scrollwork on the ceiling, it had been modernized into a high-tech office complex complete with palm readers at the doors and security cameras in the corners.

A sharp-eyed young man with auburn hair stepped out from a room to the right of the foyer.

"McDermott, this is Dr. Montague. Director Ryker is waiting for her."

"Yes, sir."

Rafe turned to Gabby. Before she knew what he was about, he took her hand and raised it to his mouth, placing a kiss on the back.

"I'll catch up with you later, doctor."

Gabby shivered at the warm press of his lips. She sincerely hoped she *didn't* meet this sexy, deadly man again. Her equilibrium was unsettled enough as it was. "Good-*bye*, Mr. Andros."

Rafe shot her a devil's grin, then slowly released her hand, letting his fingers stroke her palm as he pulled free.

She had to grit her teeth against the urge to keep her skin touching his, to absorb his warmth and strength. She refused to give him the advantage by showing him how he affected her. At least he'd never know that even when he'd threatened her back at the cabin she'd been aroused by his touch. Just thinking about her reaction made her cheeks heat. Luckily, Rafe took her blush as a positive reaction to his kiss on her hand.

With a wink, Rafe turned to her escort. "Be nice to her, McDermott. She's had a hard night."

Then he was gone.

"Right this way, doctor," the young man said. He led her through a secure door and down a long corridor toward the back of the house.

As she walked, she realized she'd made a mistake in trying to brush Rafe off. An alpha male bent on flirtation would only take it as a challenge.

Tough. She had no idea where she was, or even if Rafe and his men really were the good guys. She wasn't going to waste her energy flirting with him when he might have orders to kill her the next time they met.

McDermott stopped before a closed door of heavy, carved mahogany. He knocked, and at some signal she didn't catch, opened the door.

The man behind the desk rose and came around to greet her. He appeared to be in his early sixties with short, nutmeg brown hair silvered at the temple with a few gray strands. Standing around six feet tall, he had the trim, athletic build of a long-distance runner. His sharp gray eyes gave nothing away as he met her gaze.

"Dr. Montague, welcome to the Surgical Strike Unit. I'm Director Ryker." He shook her hand with pressure that was firm enough to be authoritative, but not so hard as to be aggressive or painful. "Please," he gestured to an old-fashioned wingback chair. "Sit down."

As she lowered herself onto the seat, he moved back around his desk. "I understand you have information on what our man Nate Ngoro has been put through." The steel underneath his friendly tone reminded her of Rafe.

Nate. Rafe's friend. Her memory was a bit foggy from exhaustion, but she thought the picture they'd showed her had been of a big black man. "I'm sorry, sir, but I never saw Nate at the compound. Kaufmann kept the work groups isolated, probably so we wouldn't understand the full scope and purpose of his program. So I can't say for certain what was done to him."

Gabby suspected that Kaufmann's research was far more complex than she understood. She'd hoped that the notes Laurel had stolen from the other sectors of the lab would present a fuller picture of the scope of Kaufmann's work. But with Laurel dead, those notes were lost to her.

Ryker nodded slowly. "Please, give me your best overview of what we're dealing with. We can get into specifics later. For now, I need to know which resources to assign to caring for Ngoro and the other men rescued."

Gabby nodded and launched into an explanation of what she knew. At the end, Ryker's expression was grim. "Since you have the best knowledge of Kaufmann's program, I'd like to offer you a job working with our doctors on reversing the damage done to Ngoro and the other men."

"You trust me enough to work with them?" she asked.

Ryker's eyes bored into her. "Yes, for now. We'll be monitoring you, of course, but you impressed Rafe with the way you cared for the men on the trip here. He's got good instincts and he says to trust you."

Gabby felt her cheeks heat with pleasure. Odd to think that Rafe's opinion mattered after the way he'd terrified her back at her cabin, but the way he'd interacted with his men and his willingness to reconsider his initial judgment of her had given her a degree of respect for him.

Ryker tapped the tips of his steepled fingers against his chin. "I also want you to work with Rafe on creating a map of the interior section of the lower lab, so we can return and remove the remaining subjects."

Gabby froze. Go back to the lab? Was he nuts?

Her face must have given away her emotion, because the corner of Ryker's mouth twitched. "My people excel at this type of rescue operation," he said.

"I'm sorry, sir. I didn't mean to insult them. It's just—"

"We understand the risks," he said with surprising gentleness. "That's why we need you to tell us every detail about the lab you remember, no matter how insignificant it seems. The more complete a picture we have of the facility, the safer our team will be."

Gabby nodded. She didn't want to think back on her time in the labs. But she'd do it in order to save the men left behind.

And if her heart beat faster at the thought of working with Rafe, she ignored it.

"Of course, sir. I'd be happy to help."

THE SCRABBLE of claws against the floor inside his cabin let Rafe know he had a visitor even before he opened the door. He barely had time to close the door and brace his back against the wall before his sister-in-law's golden retriever leapt at his chest, aiming an exuberant doggie kiss at his chin.

"Whoa, Monroe. Down boy."

"C'mon, goofball, leave my brother alone." Rafe's older brother, Niko, pulled Monroe down by the collar and dragged him into the living room, where Monroe was promptly distracted by his favorite chew toy.

"Welcome home, bro," Niko said in Greek. He bent down and snatched up a squat glass before Monroe's tail knocked it off the coffee table.

Rafe's throat tightened at the familiar language. Their father had been dead less than four months, and using the tongue of his birthplace still made Rafe choke up at his weaker moments.

To hide his reaction, he thumped his brother on the back,

then headed toward the open bottle of Ouzo that sat on his kitchen pass-through. It was too early in the morning for drinking, but what the hell. He needed something to dull the horror of watching Kaufmann's subjects die.

"Where's Jenna?" Rafe asked after the first fiery shot cleared his throat of any lingering emotion.

"With the hawks."

Rafe shot his brother a glance. "Kai okay?" Kai was Jenna's older brother. If he'd taken a turn for the worse, that could explain why Jenna needed time alone with the birds of prey. When the SSU had first moved into this compound, it restored the section that had originally been a wildlife rehabilitation center. Working with the various birds and animals had become part of the SSU's therapy program for agents recovering from both psychological and physical wounds.

"Yeah. They've got him stabilized, but he came damn close to dying. At least this time they've found some new drugs to help battle the malaria."

The mutant malaria parasite Kai had picked up in a warlord's prison in Indonesia had resisted even the latest experimental drugs, leaving their friend suffering from attacks every few weeks. And no one could predict how debilitating the attacks would be.

"Nearly losing Kai again has been rough on her," Niko admitted. "She just needs some time to herself."

Rafe heard the worry in his brother's voice. "You okay with that?" he asked.

Niko shrugged and tilted his head for another shot of Ouzo. "She's getting better. When she's upset, Jenna turns to me more often than before."

Over two years ago, Jenna had barely survived an attack that killed her parents and her fourteen-year-old twin brother and sister. She'd come out of that ordeal believing Kai was responsible. Determined to kill her brother in revenge, she'd trained with the SSU, trying to turn herself into an emotionless killing machine.

Jenna had discovered Kai was innocent only to almost lose him first to a vicious crime lord's torture, and now to his latest malaria attack.

Rafe and Kai had bonded during shared physical therapy sessions after a mission that finally took down Mexican crime lord Jaime Alverez. He hated seeing his friend suffer from the malaria, but at least Kai was among friends who cared about him.

For a moment Rafe thought about Gabby Montague and wondered how she was settling in. Was there anyone back at Kaufmann's compound who worried about her absence? Her background report had shown no living relatives. Since her obituary had run in her local newspaper, her friends surely believed her to be dead.

Monroe whined and butted his head against Rafe's knee. Rafe leaned down and rubbed the dog's head. Maybe he should check up on the pretty doctor. To reassure her that she was safe here. That he cared if she was frightened or lonely. The irony made his lips curl in a rueful smile. But it was true. He wanted her to start thinking of him as a friend. Hell, as more than a friend. He hadn't been attracted to a woman this strongly in years.

Shit. How had the woman burrowed under his skin so fast?

Rafe distracted himself from digging too deeply on that question by rubbing Monroe's ears and grinning down at the happy dog before straightening and reaching for his glass of Ouzo.

He probably needed to give the sexy doctor some space. After all, he'd nearly frightened her to death, then dragged her across the country to a place where she knew no one. So he doubted he'd be welcome at her door.

For some reason, though, that only made the urge to see her stronger. Cursing this inexplicable connection he felt to the doctor, he glanced over at Niko. "So, what brings you here, bro?"

"Heard you found Nate," Niko replied. "And brought back a sexy scientist." He tilted his glass toward Rafe. "Way to go."

Although Rafe had never hesitated to tell Niko about a woman before, he couldn't bring himself to discuss how he felt about Gabby. So he just shrugged it off and filled his brother in on the details of the mission.

"We're gonna have to go back," Rafe said. "Rescue the other men and shut the program down." He rubbed the back of his neck. He needed to get some sleep, then discuss this in more detail with Ryker.

He also needed to question Gabby. Find out exactly what was being done in those lower labs. Work on getting her to trust him so she'd give him the necessary information to plan a successful return raid.

And if his blood heated at the thought of spending more time with her, that was an unexpected bonus.

GABBY'S HANDS trembled as she blotted her hair with a towel. Showering had felt like a hard won luxury after believing Rafe and his men were going to kill her. That she'd been assigned this guest apartment instead of ending up in a cell for what she'd helped Kaufmann do seemed like a minor miracle.

But she felt most grateful for the privacy. She'd never been certain if Kaufmann had video or audio surveillance installed in the cabins. When she'd asked about whether the SSU monitored the guest quarters, Ryker had given her a sympathetic look and assured her that the SSU fully respected the privacy of its guests and the only cameras were in public areas, to alert the security team of any threats.

Maybe she was crazy, or so exhausted that she'd become gullible, but Gabby believed Ryker.

The knowledge that no one could see her now made her weak with relief.

Combing her damp hair back from her face, she slipped into the terry cloth robe hanging on the back of the bathroom door, then walked into the bedroom. She liked the surprisingly homey mix of mission and rustic style furniture that filled the apartment. The earth tone fabrics and black-and-white nature photos fit perfectly with the surrounding woods. Such a stark contrast to the sterile, institutional furniture of her cabin at Kaufmann's compound. The soothing environment added to her sense of safety.

Gabby turned on the bedside light. Maybe someday she'd stay in one place long enough to have a house of her own. A smile touched her lips. When she was thirteen, she'd seen a stone cottage tucked into the woods during a drive to the house of one of her aunt's interior decorating clients. For weeks after, she'd dreamed about growing up and living in the cottage. Imagined how she'd decorate it. Thought about what plants she'd have in the garden. And decided that she wanted two cats and three dogs.

But since leaving her aunt's house to go to college, Gabby had mostly lived in quarters provided by whatever medical facility she'd been working for. There had been no quaint cottage for her and no pets to welcome her home. Her last place had been a small low-rent apartment near the veterans' home. Ryker had said that during their pre-mission research on her and the other people in the satellite photographs, the SSU had sent a team to her old apartment. Her things were gone and the apartment had new tenants. What Kaufmann had done with her personal items and the few mementos she had of her parents and her childhood, no one knew.

Squashing a flare of melancholy, Gabby sorted through the clothing she'd bought at the SSU's general store. When he learned that Gabby had nothing but the one change of clothes in her overnight bag, McDermott had offered to take her shopping after her meeting with Ryker. Although she'd needed both clothes and toiletries, she'd told McDermott the shopping trip would have to wait until she found a way to pay for the items. She had only a few dollars in her wallet, left over from her vacation before Kaufmann had whisked her away. Kaufmann had deposited staff salaries into special bank accounts controlled by his finance department. Before her escape, Gabby had been unable to touch her money without arousing suspicion. And her purse with her credit cards had mysteriously disappeared between the moment Kaufmann approached her about the job and her arrival at his compound.

Yet McDermott had waved off Gabby's concerns about money. He'd been instructed by Ryker to set up an account for her at the store and explained that they'd work out the payment details later.

Though she hated being dependent on others for her basic needs, Gabby had given in and let McDermott lead her around the store. Used to the uniforms and generic toiletry items distributed by Kaufmann's supply team, she'd found the available choices overwhelming. Eventually, though, she'd settled on a few purchases, knowing that if she wanted to pay the SSU back she would have to either accept Ryker's job offer or quickly find a job in the outside world.

While she wanted to help Nate Ngoro and the others, part of her was afraid of ending up in another situation where her work was misused. Although her gut instinct said to trust Ryker, she had no way of knowing if his intentions would change once he had access to Kaufmann's data.

She sighed. Unfortunately, Rafe and his men had confiscated all her notes and test tubes. She didn't like having them out of her control, but even if another doctor got hold of them it would take months to replicate a program as heinous as Kaufmann's.

She tossed the damp towel on the bed and pulled on her new pajamas. If she accepted Ryker's job offer she'd have access to Nate Ngoro and the other escapees. She'd be able to take blood samples and check to see if they, too, had traces of Agent Styx in their blood.

If they did…

Her hands stilled on the knot of the drawstring waistband as hope fluttered deep inside her.

For years she'd listened to Vietnam veterans tell stories and pass along rumors of horrible acts committed under the influence of experimental chemicals, and of the terrible long term side effects. Finding one blood sample with the marker for Agent Styx in the blood of her patient back at Kaufmann's compound wasn't enough proof that Kaufmann had been using the supposedly destroyed chemical. But if Nate and the others all showed the Agent Styx markers in their blood, then maybe she could ask Ryker to help her investigate how Kaufmann got hold of the drug.

With any luck, such an investigation would lead back to the men who'd created the chemical in the first place. The men who'd given it to her father during the Vietnam War.

The same men her father had been trying to expose before his death. Even though she'd been a child, she'd understood that the mysterious phone calls that spooked her mother, and her father's insistence that Gabby stay inside as much as possible, had meant trouble.

Her suspicions had been confirmed when she turned twenty-one and the key to a special safe deposit box had been forwarded to her by a lawyer. What she'd discovered in the box had changed her life.

Medical reports from his time in the army that proved her father's rages had been the result of exposure to Agent Styx. A list of other symptoms. Vials of the chemical, along with a copy of the chemical's destruction order from the U.S. government. And several coded pages Gabby still wasn't able to read, no matter how hard she tried to crack the code.

The contents of that box had further fueled her desire to go into medicine so she could find other veterans like her father and help them before it was too late. She'd analyzed the samples of Agent Styx, then searched for those unique markers in the blood samples of her patients. When she did find veterans with traces of Agent Styx in their blood, she'd gone out of her way to pamper them. Done her best to ease their symptoms, even while she searched desperately for a way to lessen the rages and other symptoms.

With Nate Ngoro and the other men possibly the latest victims of the deadly chemical, could she really say no to Ryker's job offer? Gabby carried the damp towel into the bathroom and hung it up to dry. To be honest, she couldn't turn the opportunity down. She owed it to the victims of Agent Styx and of Kaufmann's program to help in any way possible.

Once she regained access to her notes, she expected to be able to continue isolating Agent Styx and working toward a counteragent. She'd also work on reversing the effects caused by Kaufmann's unique combination of drugs. With live samples from Nate and the others, maybe she'd even find a way to stop the physical deterioration before Rafe's friend also succumbed to death.

Then maybe you can get a real life. Gabby shook her head as the voice of her late aunt whispered in her head. It was an argument she'd had too often with the woman who'd raised her after her parents had died in a suspicious car crash when Gabby was twelve. Aunt Leticia felt the past was better left as dead as her sister and brother-in-law.

But Gabby couldn't forget the look on her father's face the night he'd died. The police had ruled the crash an accident. Claimed her father must have experienced one of his rages and lost control of the car.

Gabby never believed it. Her father hadn't had one of his fits for months before the accident. He'd been perfectly safe to drive. Otherwise, her mother never would have climbed into the car with him.

To this day, Gabby believed her parents had been murdered by the men he'd been investigating. Her parents had argued the night of the accident. Her father wanted both Gabby and her mother to stay at her aunt's house for a while. He'd insisted it was the only way to keep them both safe. Her mother agreed to send Gabby away, but refused to leave her husband. He'd been furious, but her mother had held firm.

From the way her dad had kissed her forehead before telling her to be a good girl and always listen to her aunt, Gabby had been scared she'd never see him again. She'd cried and begged him not to leave. She'd been mad at him for leaving her with Aunt Leticia instead of staying with her. She'd been equally mad at her mom for going with him when she suspected a threat.

When the police officer showed up early the next morning with news of the accident, Gabby had told the officer that her dad had known something bad was going to happen. But the police claimed there was nothing suspicious about the accident, and the matter had been dropped. In her heart, though, Gabby had always believed someone killed her parents.

With any luck, by working with the SSU she'd achieve both her goals. Restore the victims of Agent Styx and the men in Kaufmann's program to normalcy, and find the one responsible for her parents' deaths.

Kaufmann's Compound
Adirondack Mountains

"How many subjects did we lose?" Dr. Leonard Kaufmann glared at Rufus Cygan, his head of security.

"Five dead, sir. Eight missing. Three more with injuries that will take them out of the current round of testing." Cygan paused, then continued resolutely. "Half of sector seven suffered extensive damage from the explosion and will require significant repair before the staff can move back in. One doctor, two staff, and three guards are dead." He cleared his throat. "And Dr. Montague is missing."

Kaufmann stilled. "How is that possible?" Of all the staff, Dr. Montague had proved the most valuable, despite her reluctance to aid him.

"We believe Dr. Montague planned tonight's attack and that she had outside help. Our chase team fell under automatic weapon fire when they pursued the stolen transport truck."

"*Outside* help? Dr. Montague was supposed to have no contact with the world beyond this compound. Who assisted her in contacting an assault team? She worked with crazy, dying veterans. None of them could have participated in tonight's rescue."

"Unknown, sir. We're looking into it."

The pencil in Kaufmann's hands broke. If word got back to Wayne Jamieson about tonight's losses, the man would throw a fit. Kaufmann had enough trouble managing his egotistical funder without presenting the man with such a failure.

He couldn't afford to lose Jamieson's money right now. Or to lose the protection of Kerberos, Jamieson's ultra secret black ops group. Kaufmann's program was at a turning point. Even the slightest change could set their progress back weeks. "Did any of the papers or computers in section seven survive?" He needed Dr. Montague's research.

"No, sir. However, we will be able to retrieve electronic data from backup."

Kaufmann ground the broken end of the pencil into the scarred wood of the desk. "See that you do that as soon as possible. I won't let this attack slow down our progress." He'd have to assign another doctor to Montague's task and hope similar results could be obtained quickly. "Our location has been compromised. I want you to look into moving the facility. Keep the potential relocation a secret both from our staff and from the outside world. I don't want morale affected and I certainly don't want any more attacks."

"Understood, sir."

"You've sent a team out looking for Dr. Montague and the missing subjects?"

"Yes, sir. We should know where they went within a few hours."

"Good. When you find them, kill the subjects. But bring Dr. Montague back to me."

CHAPTER EIGHT

Early the next afternoon, Gabby headed across the SSU campus, looking for the communal dining room McDermott had mentioned. She'd slept long and deep, and while she didn't yet feel fully rested, she felt markedly better than she had during the past several weeks.

As she exited the apartment building, she once again had to appreciate the differences between the SSU's compound and Kaufmann's. No guards stood watch at the building's entrance and no one followed her as she walked. Strolling along the well-manicured paths through a cluster of cabins, she saw personal touches ranging from child-sized bicycles left on front lawns, to melodious wind chimes. A few runners nodded in greeting as they passed.

Kaufmann's housing complex had been as sterile as the labs, with interaction between staff strictly monitored. Runners and walkers were assigned times to use the special track set up behind the complex, but even there they'd been monitored. The staff had largely ignored one another as they focused grimly on their workouts. After a few tense runs, Gabby had instead chosen to perform a routine of ballet and Pilates moves in the privacy of her cabin.

Gabby hadn't realized how starved she'd become for normal human contact, free of fear and suspicion, until one of the runners smiled at her and Gabby felt her lips curl in answer. Basking in the peaceful atmosphere, she strolled slowly along the tree-lined path. Under the warmth of the sun, the terror-filled minutes when she'd thought Rafe and his team would kill her faded into memory. A burst of childish laughter coming from the yard to her right startled her into another smile. She couldn't remember the last time she'd heard a child's laugh. There'd been no kids at Kaufmann's compound.

Gabby took a moment and watched two girls and a boy, all under ten, race around the yard before she continued her stroll. Could this place possibly be real? It seemed impossible that yesterday she'd feared for her life working with Kaufmann, and now she was back in a world where happy children played.

A couple of houses later, the path forked. Remembering McDermott's instructions, she turned left. The trees grew closer together here, dimming the sunlight. She shivered, then paused as she heard the sound of male grunts and the unmistakable slap of boots on concrete. Frowning at the violent intrusion, Gabby hurried forward.

She emerged from the copse of pine trees and stopped in shock. On the other side of a low stone wall, a group of soldiers swarmed up a vertical net, climbed over, then dropped down the other side. The men's muscular bodies gleamed with sweat that plastered their tight t-shirts and shorts to their skin as they high-stepped through a tire course. One man in particular caught her eye.

Rafe reached the top of a giant net and easily swung himself over before dropping to the other side with feline grace. The man next to him landed badly and Rafe leaned over and helped his friend regained his balance. Then the two of them raced forward.

As Rafe reached the end of the tire course, a staccato burst of gunfire caused Gabby to gasp and jump back. But Rafe and his men just dropped to the ground and started belly-crawling through the mud under a series of low-hung nets.

Gabby inched closer to the wall separating her from the training field. Because of the way the land dipped, no matter how hard she strained or which way she moved, she couldn't see past the middle of the nets. Yet she needed to know that Rafe survived the obstacle course. Which made no sense. First, he was some kind of private soldier. He probably could run this course in his sleep. Second, she barely knew the man and what she did know confused her. He'd been ruthless last night, then flirtatious. She'd seen him controlled and deadly, then touched with grief. He intrigued her in a way she instinctively knew was dangerous. No matter how much Rafe appealed to her, she couldn't afford to get distracted from her work.

She stepped back into the trees, intending to find the correct path to the dining hall, but she'd already been noticed. A man in his forties with close-cropped brown hair and wearing a long-sleeved olive green t-shirt and matching pants approached her.

"May I help you?" His light blue eyes regarded her with curiosity.

Gabby shrugged self-consciously and stuck her hands in her jeans' pockets. "I think I took a wrong turn. I was looking for the dining hall." Unable to help herself, she glanced over the man's shoulder in hopes of seeing Rafe. "Um..." Oh, to heck with it. "Rafe and his men will come out of the exercise okay, won't they?"

The man grinned at her. "You must be Rafe's lady doctor, the one he rescued last night."

Gabby felt her cheeks heat. "Uh...I suppose. I'm Dr. Gabrielle Montague."

"Pleased to meet you, ma'am. I'm John Wilson." The man shook her hand. "Would you like to watch the rest of the exercise? We've got a viewing area in the middle of the field."

"I..." She didn't know what to say. This obsession to know everything about Rafe wasn't rational.

"C'mon." He held out his hand. "Rafe will work harder knowing he has a pretty woman watching him."

Giving in to her curiosity, Gabby let him help her climb over the stone wall. A few minutes later, she was seated in a low grandstand next to a couple of men in dress uniforms who Wilson said were observers from the Department of Defense. Apparently, even though the SSU was a private organization, it often performed contract work for the DOD.

She felt self-conscious and out-of-place at first, but soon lost her nervousness as she became absorbed in watching the training exercise. For as many years as she'd worked with veterans, Gabby had never seen soldiers in action before last night. Even if Rafe hadn't been among the men running this obstacle course she would have been fascinated with their sheer physicality. They easily handled tasks which would have driven her into the ground.

To her eyes, Rafe stood out as quicker and more graceful than the others. She bit her lip to hold back her smile, instinctively knowing Rafe wouldn't appreciate being called graceful. But his movements were performed so smoothly she couldn't think of a better word.

True to John Wilson's word, when Rafe spotted her he grinned, threw her a mock salute, then turned up his effort. At the end of the exercise, after the teams had huddled around the observers to get feedback, Rafe sauntered toward her.

Gabby's mouth dried up and her heart started beating erratically. She'd like to think she was experiencing a fear response based on the way Rafe and his men had terrorized her last night, but she couldn't lie to herself. This reaction was purely feminine.

Rafe's muddy clothes clung to his body, defining his lean muscles. It had been way too long since Gabby had been attracted to a man, and she'd never met anyone who shone with such wild vitality. Arousal curled in her belly. She shook her head, dismayed by her reaction.

"Hey, doc," Rafe greeted her with a self-satisfied smile. "Like what you see?"

She wanted to deny it, certain he received too much flattering female attention. A setdown would do him good. But she couldn't lie. So she said instead, "Just trying to understand what you do, since Ryker wants me to help you plan your return to the compound."

Just thinking about Rafe facing Kaufmann's trained killers and the insane rage of his subjects made Gabby's hands tremble. Yes, this exercise proved that Rafe and his men were extremely capable, but he didn't understand the unnatural power of Kaufmann's subjects. If they were let loose to attack Rafe and his men, only death would stop them.

"Hey." Rafe's finger stroked her cheek.

Gabby flinched in surprise, not realizing that he'd stepped closer.

"What's got that pretty face all somber?"

Gabby shook her head, afraid that if she gave voice to her fears she'd somehow jinx Rafe. Again, not rational. But it seemed that with this man she acted on instinct instead of intellect.

Rafe raised one eyebrow, but thankfully didn't push her. "So, what brings you out to the training field?"

"I got lost looking for the dining hall."

He glanced at his watch. "Give me ten minutes to shower and change and I'll walk you over."

She should tell him no. She had to tell Ryker she accepted his job offer, then start work before Nate and the others got worse. But the long-denied feminine core of her refused to pass up the chance to get to know Rafe better. After weeks of stress she needed something positive in her life. "Okay."

His rakish grin set butterflies dancing behind her breastbone and she wondered if she really understood what she'd just agreed to.

"My dad worked for the Drug Enforcement Agency," Rafe said during lunch. "One of the best field agents they had." He glanced down at the sandwich in his hand, but not before Gabby saw the flash of pain in his eyes. "When I was nine, he was shot in our driveway while washing the car with my older brother, Niko. Pop was paralyzed and spent the rest of his life in a wheelchair, but that didn't stop him from going back to work for the DEA."

"What about your brother?"

"Physically, he had just a few scratches. Psychologically?" Rafe shrugged. "It messed him up. He was only thirteen, but he blamed himself for not protecting Pop. No matter that Mexican crime lord Jaime Alvarez had ordered a hit on our father and no thirteen-year-old boy could've stopped it. Niko was already big on taking responsibility. He turned angry. Started getting in trouble."

"I'm sorry." She wondered how the change in his brother had affected Rafe, but didn't feel comfortable asking. Not when he'd given her such a deeply personal story. Given that she barely knew the man, she didn't know whether to be flattered or horrified that he felt comfortable sharing such a traumatic event.

"Yeah, well, Niko ended up putting his anger to good use. When he was eighteen, he accepted an offer from the DEA to unofficially go undercover in Alvarez's organization. Niko spent five years working his way up to being Alvarez's right hand man, until finally he had enough evidence to call in a raid that sent the bastard to prison."

"Did you know your brother was undercover?"

Rafe shook his head. "Alvarez sent us reports a couple of times a year, bragging about how he'd turned Niko into the type of man our father had spent his life working to put behind bars. Pop knew the truth, but not the rest of the family."

To her surprise, Gabby reached out and touched his hand. She wasn't the touchy-feely sort. Yet she left her hand where it was, wanting Rafe to have the comfort of touch. "That must have been hard."

Rafe turned her hand over and straightened out her fingers one by one. "I never believed Niko had gone bad. No matter what the evidence showed. Even when the DEA sent Niko to prison after the raid, as punishment for the things he'd done while undercover, I still knew he was one of the good guys."

Gabby's throat ached. She'd always wanted a brother or sister to love. Someone who would stand by her side no matter what. "Niko is lucky to have a brother who loves him so much."

Rafe grinned. "Damn straight. You stick around long enough, you can tell him yourself. He's also an SSU agent."

"Is Alvarez still in prison?"

"No." A feral expression swept across Rafe's face. "Long story short, Alvarez was released from prison after ten years, but then he tangled with Niko and ended up dead."

"I'd be interested in hearing the whole story some day," Gabby said, surprised to find how hungry she was for more information on Rafe and his family.

"I'll tell you, but only if you promise to stick around."

"That's something I need to discuss with Ryker first."

Rafe's eyes probed hers. "All right. So, what about you? Happy childhood? Your file says no brothers or sisters."

Gabby lowered her gaze to her plate. She didn't feel comfortable talking about her past, and never told anyone about her father's rages. Yet she owed Rafe some insight into her life, since he'd been so open with her. "Well, I was mostly raised by my aunt—"

"Dr. Montague?"

Gabby looked up to see McDermott heading toward her. "Yes?"

"Ryker would like to see you in his office now, if it's convenient."

"Of course." Gabby stifled her disappointment at having her time with Rafe cut short. What kind of spell had the man thrown at her to make her greedy for such intimate, two-way conversation?

Before she could stop him, Rafe stood up and disposed of their food trash. "I'll see you later," Rafe said, kissing the back of her hand. "McDermott," he acknowledged with a nod.

Then he was gone.

Gabby blinked at his abrupt departure. "Okay, McDermott, lead on. I don't know my way around yet."

Ryker met her and McDermott before they reached the administration building. "Hello, Dr. Montague." With a nod, Ryker dismissed McDermott, who flashed Gabby a grin before disappearing down a side path.

"Have you made a decision regarding my job offer?" Ryker removed the dark glasses hiding his eyes, making it easier for Gabby to answer.

"Yes, sir. I've decided to accept your offer...for now."

He nodded. "Good. Let's get you settled in right away. I know my medical team already has a list of questions for you." He started walking back the way she'd come, then took a right at the first intersection.

"If you don't mind, I'd like to see Kaufmann's men, sir," Gabby said.

"Let's hear what Dr. Smith has to say about that."

The medical building turned out to be the size of a small hospital. Inside, though, it looked like the same decorator who'd done her guest apartment had taken care to make the facility as warm as possible—painting the walls in warm earth tones and hanging plants and artwork where they best caught the natural light from skylights and windows.

"Of course," Dr. Smith said when Ryker passed on Gabby's request. "I'm afraid, though, that the men remain sedated."

"Dr. Montague, I'll leave you in Dr. Smith's capable hands," Ryker interjected. "Welcome on board. I'll check back with you later."

Five minutes later, Gabby stood on one side of a reinforced plate glass window looking into the room where the four surviving men slept on hospital beds. All of them were shackled at wrists and ankles. Even in deeply drugged sleep, they moved restlessly. She wondered what they dreamed of. Or did they remember what Kaufmann had done to them?

"I don't know if I can help them," Gabby admitted. "But I'll do everything I can."

"That's all we ask," Dr. Smith said. "Come, I've called a meeting in the conference room so you can meet the rest of the team."

There were five other members of the medical staff waiting in the small conference room. Two men and three women. Gabby made careful note of their names and wondered what they thought of her. How much information had Ryker given them?

Did they understand that she'd never intended her research to cause harm? That until the end she hadn't realized what types of experiments Dr. Kaufmann had been running? Or did they think she made that excuse to avoid responsibility?

If there were any doubters, they managed to keep their suspicions off their faces. Gabby decided to treat everyone like a respected colleague and hoped she'd win over any dissenters.

"I don't know much about what was done to Nate and the others," Gabby told the group. "There were two sections to Kaufmann's compound. The upper lab, where we believed we were working to resolve issues specific to veterans, and the lower lab, where Kaufmann worked to create his superhuman soldiers. I worked in the upper lab until last week." God, talking about this to a group of strangers was harder than she'd thought. She didn't see any judgment on their faces, but she couldn't help but feel guilty.

"My role was to find a chemical that would neutralize the rages Kaufmann's subjects suffer. The only time I saw any of the subjects on the lower level was when I first stumbled across the transport bay that led back to the labs." She took a deep breath and looked down at her clasped hands. "That's when I saw one of my former patients from the upper level tear out a man's throat with his teeth." She looked up and saw echoes of shock and horror on the faces surrounding her.

"As you've seen from the blood samples, the chemical mix used by Kaufmann contains a variety of known and unknown substances." Squaring her shoulders, she lifted her chin and delivered the bad news. "I know of no way to reverse all the damage done to these men. Right now, the best I can promise is some easing of their symptoms. Hopefully, the notes and samples I brought out will help us eventually develop a cure that will return Kaufmann's subjects to some degree of normalcy."

She paused, wishing she had better news. "Unfortunately, I don't think Nate and the others have that time."

Now for the tricky part. To give them what she could without exposing her knowledge of Agent Styx. "I've had some prior experience with one of the chemicals Kaufmann used, a chemical that is known to trigger rages even decades after exposure. I'll share the formula I developed to mitigate the rage. Kaufmann led me to believe the formula had some success, but he never let me see the men I was treating."

She glanced around the table. "I had no idea that Kaufmann's program included drugs that caused the acute organ failure and hemorrhaging displayed by the escapees on the truck. If any of you have suggestions on how to help stop the men from reaching that phase, I'd love to hear them. Otherwise," she shrugged unhappily, "we'll be starting from scratch."

To her surprise there was no grumbling over the lack of an

easy solution. The others just nodded grimly and started brainstorming a treatment plan. No one had any illusions. The men couldn't be saved. But they'd do their best to alleviate the men's symptoms and treat them like human beings for the last days of their lives.

SEVERAL HOURS LATER, Gabby finally left the conference room, more determined than ever to help Nate and the others.

"Dr. Montague!"

Gabby spun around as an unfamiliar young woman came hurrying down the corridor.

"I'm sorry," the woman panted. "I wanted to catch you before you left the building. I'm supposed to give you this." She handed Gabby a thick envelope.

At Gabby's raised eyebrow, she explained, "They found these notes hidden in the clothes of some of the men you brought with you."

Laurel. Tears stung Gabby's eyes. Her friend had managed to get the notes out of the lab after all, even though she herself hadn't made it. "Thank you," she murmured.

With a smile that said she was pleased to have fulfilled her duty, the young woman headed back toward the office at the end of the corridor. Clutching the envelope with chilled fingers, Gabby followed the written directions to the temporary lab she'd been assigned. There, waiting on the counter as promised by Dr. Smith, were several vials of blood and urine samples taken from Nate and the others.

The instant Gabby looked at one of Nate's blood samples under the microscope, she felt a thrill of recognition. He had the marker for Agent Styx. Unfortunately, Nate's blood also held traces of chemicals she didn't recognize, in addition to variations of both steroids and amphetamines. One thing stood out, however. Nate's body was deteriorating. Not so fast that she expected him to hemorrhage in the next twenty-four hours, but unless her team discovered a miracle solution, he wasn't going to survive.

Ignoring the weight of sorrow pressing on her shoulders, Gabby ran her first series of tests on each patient's samples. She jotted notes and made calculations, but in her gut she knew Nate and the others were too far damaged for her to save. The effects of Agent Styx were difficult enough to counteract. Once the chemical entered a person's system, it mutated, inserting itself into that particular body's weakest points.

That was one of the reasons it had made such an effective, although highly unstable, poison. Put it in the water supply and it was guaranteed to kill. Eventually.

Even the soldiers sent to disperse the agent couldn't escape it. Gloves had been issued to protect their hands after it was learned the chemical could burn through skin. But the government hadn't put protective measures in place to stop the men from inhaling the fumes when they poured Agent Styx into village wells in rural Vietnam. The long-term aggressiveness triggered by the fumes had worked to the U.S. government's benefit, giving them more ruthless, dangerous soldiers.

Soldiers like her father, who years after he'd been exposed still suffered from uncontrollable bouts of rage. But since the government insisted there had been no side effects to Agent Styx, none of the veterans had received specific treatment for it.

Until Gabby came along. Before she'd joined Kaufmann's group, she'd been close to finding a counteragent that worked to contain Agent Styx's effects in the body. Unfortunately, some of the chemicals used in Kaufmann's program enhanced the negative side effects of Agent Styx, making her wonder if the man had been briefed on the full spectrum of potentially dangerous side effects. And if not, then why had that information been withheld?

"What's got that pretty face scowling so fiercely?"

At the unexpected sound of Rafe's voice so near her ear

Gabby's hand jerked up in surprise and her pencil stabbed him in the cheek.

"Hey!" he protested, jerking back. His hand shot out and captured her wrist, moving her hand out of range of another attack.

She turned her head and glared at him. "Don't sneak up on me!"

Rafe's eyes laughed down at her. "I knocked, sweetheart. You were too focused to notice."

Knowing that she did have a habit of losing track of her surroundings when she was deep in thought, Gabby crossed her arms over her chest. "What are you doing here?"

"I brought you a welcome gift." Rafe pulled his hand from behind his back. There, cradled in his palm, sat a small teddy bear wearing a white lab coat and a stethoscope around its neck.

"Oh!" Her heart melted as she reached out to stroke the bear's silky fur. Tears unexpectedly filled her eyes. "No one's given me a gift in..." She let her voice trail off, aware of how pathetic she'd sound if she admitted it had been years. She hadn't had time to date and her friends had been casual, not the type to exchange presents.

Rafe placed the bear into Gabby's hands, then surrounded her hands with his much larger ones. "Shh, don't cry, *querida*. I wanted to make you smile, not frown."

She shrugged, but couldn't stop a tear from falling. "These are happy tears," she murmured.

Rafe nodded sagely. "Ah. Those mysterious tears that men never understand."

She gave him a watery smile. "Exactly." She glanced down at the bear in her palms. "He's perfect."

"I thought he could watch over you in the lab," Rafe admitted softly.

Oh man, he broke her heart. How did he know just the right words to say? "Thank you." With a gentle tug, she freed herself from Rafe's grip, then placed the bear on top of her computer. "How's that?"

"Just right."

Gabby grabbed a couple of tissues and blotted her tears. "Sorry, the stress is making me emotional."

"Nothing to apologize for. So, how are you settling in?"

She shrugged, then stared at the rack of test tubes. "I've started working with the samples Dr. Smith gave me and—"

Rafe's hands lightly gripped her shoulders and turned her to face him. "That's not what I meant, Gabby. How are you, the woman, not the doctor, settling in? Everyone treating you well?"

"Sure. They've all been very friendly."

His eyes searched her face and she wondered what he was looking for. Then the brown depths of his eyes heated. Tingles of electricity ran up her arm from where his fingers encircled her wrist.

Gabby suddenly couldn't breathe. She blamed the fire in his eyes, because surely it was eating all the oxygen in the room. Uh-huh. And that's why her skin flushed and her heart sped up. Lack of air, not an inexplicable flash of desire unlike anything she'd experienced. She couldn't want him so fiercely. She didn't do impulsive. Heck, she didn't really do relationships. Not for over a year, at least.

Maybe she was getting sick. Or maybe the stress was finally getting to her and making her weak, because she swayed toward Rafe and didn't turn away when he lowered his head. Then his lips touched hers. Her legs trembled and she feared she might crumble to the floor.

Oh, damn. She was in *such* big trouble.

His lips were warm and soft and fit against hers like they'd been custom molded. She kissed him back and his groan of male satisfaction made her shiver.

"*Madre de Dios*," he murmured, reaching for Gabby. "Come closer, baby."

She stepped into his arms and slid her hands to the nape of his neck. Part of her reeled in shock at her obedience to his command, but she couldn't resist the urge to touch him. His hair was shaved close at his nape and she stroked her palms over the short hairs, smoothing them down like she'd pet a cat, loving the sensuous feel against her skin. Loving the way Rafe bent his head to give her better access.

"Hell, yes, Gabby. Do that again."

Oh, God. The rough sound of his voice tightened parts of her body as if he'd physically stroked her. When was the last time she'd desired a man like this? Had she *ever* felt her heart race from just touching another man? From knowing that her caress had such a powerful effect?

No wonder women got drunk on their sexual power. She felt lightheaded and bold. Sliding her fingers deeper into his hair, she tugged until his chin lifted. Then she placed a kiss in the hollow at the base of his neck. She tasted him with the tip of her tongue and couldn't hold back her groan of approval.

Alarm bells blared somewhere in the back of her head, but she didn't care. This felt too good. After living so long with fear, she wanted heat. She wanted passion.

"Ah, Christ, you're burning me alive," Rafe said an instant before he took her mouth in another kiss.

This time she opened for him. The feel of his tongue inside her mouth, the spicy taste of him, had all her senses clanging. Shrilling in—

Rafe lifted his head. "Your phone," he gasped.

"Wha-?"

He nodded over her shoulder. "Your phone is ringing."

Trying to remember what a phone was and why she should care it was ringing, Gabby turned around and spotted the cordless phone sitting on the corner of her workspace.

Right. Lab. SSU. Patients!

She lunged and snatched up the receiver. "Hello?"

"Dr. Montague, Dr. Smith would like to see you as soon as possible. One of the patients is showing advanced symptoms."

Gabby bit back a curse. "Of course. I'll be right there." She glanced back over her shoulder. "Uh...which patient?"

"Gibson."

Gabby blew out a relieved breath. Not Rafe's friend, thank heavens. "I'm on my way."

She gently set the receiver back in its cradle. Talk about a harsh return to reality. Her body still sung from Rafe's kiss, and for the first time in her life the woman resented moving aside for the scientist.

"Bad news?" Rafe asked.

She nodded without turning around. "Gibson is doing worse," she said. "I need to go see Dr. Smith."

Rafe's hands settled on her shoulders and gave a comforting squeeze. He placed a gentle kiss on the top of her head. "I'll walk you down. These corridors can be confusing until you've been here a while."

"Thanks." She forced herself to step away from Rafe, when what she really wanted was to pivot and feel his arms enfold her against his warmth and strength. But she had to stay focused. Had to remember that her place here was still shaky, so she didn't have time for indulging her personal weaknesses.

Besides, she had patients to treat.

CHAPTER NINE

Rafe took a sip of Ryker's special blend of dark roast coffee and watched his boss spin the antique globe in the corner of his office while he spoke on the phone. Ryker nodded, even though the senator on the other end of the line couldn't see him. From listening to Ryker's side of the conversation, Rafe understood that the senator wanted the SSU to find his missing college-age daughter, even though she'd only been missing for twelve hours.

Ryker chose his words with extreme care, politely pointing out that the SSU was a counter-terrorist and national security organization. That, given the daughter's history of running away whenever she had a fight with her father, the senator would be better served by waiting a few days and then hiring a private investigator if she remained missing.

Ryker was freaking amazing, never losing his respectful, polite tone. Rafe would have told the man to get lost five minutes ago. Yet as the conversation drew to a close, Rafe couldn't see any tension in Ryker's expression or detect any sign of frustration or impatience in his voice.

"Why the hell did you pick *me* to train as your successor?" Rafe demanded when Ryker hung up the phone. "I hate crap like that." He'd been working with Ryker for seven months and still didn't think he'd be half as good in the position of director.

Ryker raised an eyebrow. "What makes you think I like it? Trust me, I have to work to stay calm and polite. I do it because we need support like his if we're going to stay in the game. You'll get the hang of it." Ryker poured himself a cup of coffee, added one cube of sugar, then perched on the edge of his desk.

"So, give me your impressions of Dr. Montague." Ryker's lips smiled around the rim of his coffee cup as he sipped. "Or should I say, of your little scientist?"

Rafe rolled his eyes. The SSU's gossip mill worked faster than the speed of light. Scary thing was, he did think of Gabby as his. But he'd die before he let his teammates know that.

"We scared her pretty bad," Rafe admitted. "Unless she's a world-class liar, I believe her when she says she had no clue Kaufmann was running a second program, and that she only switched sides in order to save her life. Still, we should keep an eye on her."

Ryker nodded. He took a long drink of coffee, then stared over Rafe's head. The hairs at the back of Rafe's neck stood up as he sensed Ryker struggling with some piece of information.

"I knew her father," Ryker finally said.

"What?" Rafe straightened. "I thought she was an orphan. Raised by her aunt."

Ryker shook his head. "After your team left on the mission, I finally realized why the satellite photos of her looked so familiar. She reminded me of a guy I knew in Vietnam. Dan Reagh. So I had the research department dig deeper into her background. Sure enough, she's his daughter, although someone went to great lengths to hide their connection. Her social security number is under Gabrielle Montague, which is her mother's maiden name. The small county where she was born only just joined the internet era and put all their old records online, which allowed our research team to locate her birth certificate and her parents' marriage certificate. They also found a death notice for her parents, killed in a car accident when Dr. Montague was twelve. That's when she went to live with her aunt."

Ryker tapped his index finger against the ceramic handle of his coffee cup. "Her father was part of a black ops group operating during the Vietnam War. I'd heard rumors of their group long before I met Reagh. Whispers about men who poisoned entire villages, but made it look like disease. Of opposition leaders dying from sudden heart attacks. And of the soldiers who could go for days without sleep and still remain sharp at the end, no matter how many miles they'd travelled to complete their secret missions."

Ryker stared into his coffee. "I met Reagh in the medical ward of one of our bases. We'd both been injured. But while I spent most of those first days in a drug-induced sleep, the nurses claimed Reagh never slept and never took his meds. His injuries were worse than mine, so I figured the nurses were exaggerating due to a misplaced case of hero worship. No man could endure the pain of such burns or such deep wounds." Ryker shook his head. "But it was true. I saw Reagh go into a berserker rage when they tried to force meds on him. They finally had to knock him out and restrain him in order to give him the antibiotics that saved his life."

A chill slid down Rafe's spine. No—

"They must have given him a tranquilizer, too, because when he woke up, he was mellow. We spent a lot of time talking. He never said too much, but reading between the lines, he was terrified of taking any medicine because of the side effects of the drugs given to his unit. Some of the drugs were pills, some were injections, and other side effects came from inhaling the fumes of the chemicals they handled on their missions. He said the drugs made them all crazy. He was afraid that if he didn't get out, he was going to end up dead. Because if the drugs didn't kill him, the government would—to stop him from talking about what they'd ordered him to do."

Ryker's eyes lifted, revealing some dark emotion that Rafe couldn't identify. "I helped make certain Reagh never healed well enough to go back into the field. We left the doctors with no alternative but to evacuate him to the States for more involved surgery. I returned to action, but never forgot how terrified he'd been.

"Now his daughter shows up at Kaufmann's compound. Working on a program that has similarities both to the one Reagh talked about in Vietnam, and to Nevsky's program. Further digging by our research team uncovered more than one domestic disturbance report that listed extensive property damage as a result of her father's uncontrollable rage."

"Christ. Did he hit Gabby?"

"Not according to the reports. And we didn't find any medical reports that would indicate abuse of either Dr. Montague or her mother."

"Thank God."

Ryker nodded. "Dr. Montague has focused on treating the side effects, including wild rages, caused by exposure to biological and chemical agents. Most of her patients have been Vietnam vets. Coincidence?"

Ryker set his coffee cup behind him on the desk and steepled his fingers underneath his chin.

"If her father told her his rages were triggered by drugs he was given in Vietnam, that would explain her life's work," Rafe mused. "Did you ask her about her father?"

Ryker shook his head. "She needs to trust me first. If I throw this out there, she might run. Some of the programs the government ran during the war were so secret, and so potentially damaging on a political and moral front, that even today the government will kill to keep them secret. I believe her father was part of such a program. Knowing anything about his work puts her in danger. If she's aware of that, she's not going to believe the coincidence that I happened to remember her father. She'll think I'm a threat. And we can't afford to lose her."

Rafe swirled the dregs of his coffee inside the cup. "You think Nevsky and Kaufmann were using some of the same components given to Reagh's team in Vietnam?"

Ryker shrugged. "We can't rule it out. To the best of my knowledge, all of those programs were terminated due to high failure rates. But that doesn't mean someone didn't keep a few samples." He stood up and walked over to the globe. Rafe waited while Ryker twirled the globe slowly.

Finally, Ryker shook his head. "We've confirmed the identities of the men you helped escape, plus the dead men Willits photographed on the way to the crematorium."

Rafe sat up at the sudden anger in Ryker's voice.

"Two of the men in our infirmary are FBI agents reported dead in action. The third is infantry, assumed dead after a roadside bomb in Iraq. All the other men you rescued were either current or former law enforcement or military reported as dead, but many of them hadn't yet been added to our list of missing personnel."

"What are you going to tell Jordaine?" Rafe asked. Matt Jordaine was their contact at the FBI. He'd turned the investigation into the missing personnel over to the SSU after four agents were killed while looking into the disappearances. Military intelligence had also lost agents during their investigation. So far, both the FBI and the DOD had failed to locate the people who'd leaked the details of their investigations.

Ryker walked his fingers over the globe. "I'm not going to update Jordaine yet. Nevsky was supported by both the Department of Defense and the CIA. Given the recent leaks, we have to assume Kaufmann has similarly well-connected backers."

"You think our mole reports to Kaufmann's sponsor?" Rafe asked. Ryker suspected the SSU had a mole, someone who was responsible for several mission failures over the years. They believed the mole had blown Kai Paterson's cover two years ago, resulting in the attack against his family that left everyone but his sister Jenna dead.

Because of the mole, Rafe's missions were a carefully guarded secret.

"I don't know," Ryker said. "I'm still trying to put together the big picture. Is our mole randomly creating trouble when he sees an opportunity to make money, regardless of who pays him? Or is his mission to slowly destroy our reputation?" Ryker gave a sharp spin to the globe, then turned abruptly to Rafe.

"Before your team heads back out, we're going to update the tracking program in your subdermal microchip. It will have stronger encryption to prevent anyone hacking into the signal and following you. We still can't track deep underground, but as long as the device is within ten feet of the surface, we'll know where you are."

The back of Rafe's neck tightened in warning. If any of his men got captured by Kaufmann's team, he prayed they died quickly. None of them wanted to end up like Nate.

MINDFUL of the way Gabby had reacted the previous afternoon when he'd walked into her lab, Rafe knocked loudly on her door. When she didn't answer, he gave the door a strong thump.

He was just about to give up and barge in when the door swung open.

"What?" Gabby snapped. She barely gave him a glance before she went back to reading the notes she held in her hands.

Rafe stood in the doorway, enjoying the unexpected opportunity to watch Gabby work. Her hair stuck up in sections behind a cloth headband, as if she'd pulled her hair while thinking through a problem. The right corner of her mouth was tucked in between her teeth and lines of concentration ran between her brows. He smiled when he spotted the little stuffed bear sitting on her computer, and thought about her next gift resting in his pocket.

Gabby muttered something to herself and turned back to her worktable. Grabbing a pencil, she began making rapid notations on the paper.

Rafe leaned one shoulder against the doorjamb, prepared to wait until she noticed him. But after several minutes, he realized she was so absorbed in her work she didn't remember he was there.

His male pride didn't like that. Especially on top of the way she'd refused to so much as look at him when he'd walked her to Dr. Smith's office after that mind-blowing kiss. Her presence drew his attention like a magnet. The least she could do was say "hi" to him.

He cleared his throat.

Gabby didn't notice.

When she reached for a test tube, he stepped forward. "Hold on a sec, doc." He grabbed her hand.

She started and blinked up at him in surprise. "What are you doing here?"

O-kay, this was scary. What if he'd been here to hurt her? "Gabby, you opened the door and let me in," he chided. He checked his watch. "Ten minutes ago."

"I did?" She frowned and then her eyes really focused on him. "Why are you here?"

"I came to bring you this." He pulled a tiny, posable ballerina doll out of his pocket and set it next to the bear on top of her computer.

"Oh, Rafe! Thank you. How did you—"

"You had ballet shoes in your go-bag."

She flashed him a quick smile, then adjusted the doll's position.

"I'm also here because it's seven o'clock and no one has seen you in the dining hall all day. I came to make sure you've eaten."

She shrugged. "Um…"

"Gabby, you're not going to do Nate and the others any good if you collapse. Let's get you something to eat." He tugged her to her feet.

"But—"

"Uh-uh. No buts." He ignored her attempt to free her hand and pulled her toward the door. "There's still an hour of full service in the cafeteria. You can take half an hour to eat."

"Rafe, wait! I've got to close these containers and turn the equipment off before I leave."

He raised an eyebrow, but at her no-nonsense look he let her go. While she puttered around the lab he crossed his arms over his chest and admired the curve of her ass when she bent down to retrieve a pencil from the floor. Then he frowned, noticing her skinny wrists as they peeked out from the cuffs of her lab coat.

"We need to put some weight on you," he blurted.

She stood up slowly, keeping her back to him. "Excuse me?"

Ouch. Rafe felt the chill even across the lab.

Gabby set the pencil back in its place, then turned to face him with her hands propped on her hips. *Now* she was totally focused on him.

Focused, and pissed.

Okay, so he knew better than to discuss a woman's weight. But still, someone needed to make certain she took care of herself.

"You've lost too much weight," he commented. Then his eyes narrowed. "You stumbled coming out of the lab the night we rescued you. Then you had trouble getting into the truck. You're so exhausted you're near the point of collapse, yet you're not doing anything about it."

She waved her hand toward her workspace. "Hel-lo. I'm working here. I think it's a bit more important for me to try and find a way to help Nate and the others than to break for meals."

"Nice words," Rafe said, snagging her arm and hauling her close. "But look at you. You're trembling. If you don't get something to eat and don't get a good night's sleep, you're going to end up in the infirmary. Then how will you help Nate?"

"Maybe I'm trembling because I don't like being manhandled and ordered around by a chauvinist jerk!" She leaned back, trying to break his hold.

He just wrapped his other arm around the small of her back and pulled her tighter against his body, starved for the softness of her breasts pressing against his chest. He bit back a satisfied grin as her pupils widened and she licked her lips. "Or maybe you're trembling because you're thinking about our kiss. Wanting another so much you can hardly breathe."

"In your drea—"

He shut her up by slamming his mouth over hers. Ah, hell. He wasn't supposed to do this again. Hadn't he given himself the lecture of all lectures yesterday afternoon? He was leaving on a mission in a week or two, tops. He had to stay focused on finding the best way to free the remaining subjects of Kaufmann's experiments.

He had no fucking business starting something with Gabby.

But damn if he could find the willpower to stop. The taste of her was like nothing he'd ever known. Even with her lips tightly closed she was more potent than the strongest shot of Ouzo. But when she whimpered and opened her mouth, her nimble little tongue reaching out to trace the seam of his lips, he was lost.

All he could think of was getting closer. Getting more. Slaking this thirst that only grew the more he tasted. Until he heard glass break. Years of training had him jerking his head back. He pushed her behind him as he scanned the room searching for the threat.

And felt like an idiot when he realized that during the kiss he'd turned and pressed her up against the counter. They'd knocked a glass beaker to the floor.

"Ah, shit," he said. "Sorry." He peered down at the fragments. "It looks like it was empty."

When Gabby didn't answer, he turned his head. Her face had lost the little color it had. Gabby swayed, then caught herself by bracing her hands on the counter.

Oh great, dickwad. You just finished yelling at her for pushing her limits and now your kiss has gone ahead and stolen the last of her reserves.

As much as he wanted to say something about that amazing kiss, he didn't trust himself to say the right thing. "C'mon," he said gently. "Let's get you some food, okay? I'll send someone over to clean up the mess."

He put his arm around her waist and led her toward the cafeteria. Even though he'd much rather be leading her to his bed.

CHAPTER TEN

"ARE you out of your freaking mind?" Gabby snarled at Rafe a week later, resisting the urge to destroy the mock-up of Kaufmann's lab that sprawled across the gleaming conference room table. Diagrams based on her memories of the lower lab's personnel schedules were tacked to the wall next to recent satellite photos. She gestured angrily at the glossy eight-by-tens. "Look at the photos! Kaufmann has an entire army guarding the compound now. Yet you're treating your return mission like some kind of party."

Sure enough, Rafe's mouth shifted into what she now considered his trademark teasing smile. She cursed as her mouth quivered, wanting to return a smile.

Dammit, sometimes she had trouble remembering that this was the man who'd pinned her to her bed that night at the compound. Who'd kept the flashlight directed at her eyes while he interrogated her.

The same man who'd nearly devoured her with those kisses she'd been trying so hard to forget. A week of giving him the cold shoulder hadn't stopped him from flirting with her, and it sure hadn't killed the low buzz of arousal she felt whenever he was near.

She rubbed her throat and took some petty satisfaction in watching Rafe's smile dim. His lips turned down and he shifted his weight as he stared at the faint pink scars that were the only remaining evidence of the night he and his men had terrorized her.

She let herself enjoy the small power of unsettling Rafe. Ever since he'd ordered her to grab whatever she needed from her cabin and then shoved her into the night, her life had been anything but comfortable. She'd been trying to shake up his world ever since, but nothing rattled him.

"Gabby, this is what we do," Rafe said. "We're good. My team can handle it, no problem."

Realizing she was close to throwing something at Rafe, Gabby closed her eyes and counted to ten. The infuriating man delighted in pushing her too far. He must have made it a personal goal to force her to unleash the temper she'd kept tightly chained since her childhood.

"Daddy, no!"

Gabby cowered behind the sofa as her father threw her favorite ballerina sculpture across the room. The delicate china shattered against the corner of the fireplace mantle and Gabby bit back a sob. She knew her daddy would be sorry about what he'd done when his nice side came back, but until then she clasped her arms around her middle and vowed she'd never get scary mad when she grew up.

Gabby jerked herself out of the past. True to her childhood vow, she never let her temper fly out of control. Even though she now understood that her father's rages had been a side effect of Agent Styx, the ghost of the child she'd been was still afraid she'd end up like her dad one day—so enraged that only destroying her surroundings would ease her. Then being unable to remember what she'd done the next day.

Just like her patients.

Not patients. Patient. Singular. Rafe's friend Nate Ngoro was the only escapee still alive.

But not for long. Today Nate's blood and tissue samples had confirmed her fears. His body had started self-destructing at a rate she had no way of countering.

Knowing she had to give Rafe the bad news only made her temper worse.

"Gabby, c'mon, give it a rest will ya?" This was from Muldovsky, Rafe's cherub-faced cohort. "Haven't you figured out by now we're the best?"

Gabby wanted to scream.

"Can you survive attacks by men as strong and mindless as Nate?" she threw back. Even in his weakened condition, Nate possessed extraordinary physical strength and unbelievably fast reflexes.

But if Rafe and his men felt any qualms about facing such a foe, they didn't show it.

"How's Nate doing?" Rafe asked.

Gabby winced as Rafe's expression moved from teasing to concern. She really didn't want to be the one to give him the news. He knew his friend's prognosis wasn't good, but Nate had been in such better overall mental condition than the others that she'd heard some of Rafe's men speculate their buddy might make it.

As Rafe watched her expectantly, Gabby sighed and forced herself not to look away. "He's dying, Rafe. His latest blood work shows his body has reached the same stage that killed the others."

She saw the quick flare of grief in Rafe's eyes and bit her lip. "I'm sorry. I wish there was something more I could do." Her throat tightened on a wave of tears. "But I can't help him because we're up against compounds we've never seen before!" What terrified her was that the notes Laurel had hidden in the clothes of the escapees contained comments indicating that even

Kaufmann didn't fully understand the drugs he'd been using. He'd stolen samples from someone he'd worked for before, a scientist called Dr. Nevsky, but Kaufmann didn't have the man's research notes and so had been unsuccessful in deciphering Nevsky's drugs.

Despite his maddened, almost animalistic behavior, Gabby felt both possessive and maternal toward Nate. Her team had managed to ease Nate's pain somewhat, but nothing could stop his body from self-destructing. She bit down on her molars, driving back the persistent feeling of helplessness. He was her patient now. She hated knowing she couldn't save him.

There was no consolation in knowing that tomorrow Rafe and his team were returning to Kaufmann's compound and might bring back the answers she needed. Nate didn't have that long. At the rate his body was deteriorating, he'd be lucky to still be alive in four days, let alone the six Rafe estimated his team would be gone.

She studied the tabletop mockup of the compound one more time. It looked just as she remembered. Which wasn't saying much. There were critical gaps in her knowledge of the lower lab. Empty spaces on the model indicated the places she'd been prohibited from entering. She'd only been able to give a rough estimate of the number of security personnel on duty inside.

The fact that the lives of Rafe and his team depended on her incomplete information terrified her. Yet Rafe seemed excited by the challenge. His dark mocha eyes snapped with the same excitement reflected in every one of his men.

She didn't understand the pitying glances the men threw her way, as if she wasn't really living because she didn't think risking her life was fun. What was wrong with a quiet, orderly life? A life without violence?

Nothing, that was what. But these maniacs would never see it her way, so it was time she left them to their final preparations.

"There's nothing more for me to add. Good luck tomorrow gentlemen."

She took one last look at each of Rafe's teammates, seeing their strength and their confidence. Wishing she could tamp down this choking fear for them.

Finally, she allowed herself to look at Rafe, and instantly regretted it. She felt singed by his heat and vitality. It wasn't fair. She finally met a man who brought her feminine side to life and he could end up dead before she'd even had a chance to explore the attraction.

An icy hand curled around her heart. No, she wouldn't picture Rafe dead.

Feeling tears threaten again, she spun on her heel and practically flew from the room.

"Gabby, wait!"

She heard Rafe's footsteps behind her in the hallway, but she didn't stop. The last thing she needed was to break down in front of him. She didn't want him pitying her or thinking she wasn't professional.

Dammit, she should have run the other way when he'd ordered her to pack her things and go with him that night. Her only excuse was that she'd still been off-balance from his interrogation and seeing the two dead bodies on the floor of her bedroom.

She wasn't used to violent death. Another difference between her and Rafe that should send her fleeing as fast as possible in the opposite direction.

She warned herself not to glance over her shoulder. Even though Rafe called to some feminine need she hadn't even known she possessed, she was damned if she'd give in to it. He was way too charming. Too dominant. Too accustomed to getting his own way.

And she'd been so lonely for so long that she soaked up Rafe's flirting like a dry sponge. The small collection of stuffed animals and figurines was a constant reminder of how well Rafe had come to know her. She didn't think she'd ever felt such an intimate connection to anyone, and it scared her to death.

Right. She was scared. Uh-huh. That was why her nipples were tightening just thinking about Rafe. Damn him to hell.

She gritted her teeth and focused on the door at the end of the hallway. Almost there.

"Gabby."

She slammed to a stop, frozen by the sound of Rafe's voice at her back. She hadn't realized that while she was thinking, she'd also been slowing down. Giving him time to catch up with her.

Rafe slipped around her, blocking her way.

"*Querida*, what's wrong?"

Hearing Rafe's chocolate smooth voice draw out the endearment sent a sensual chill racing across her skin.

No weakness. Do not let him get under your skin. First, he's leaving tomorrow. Second, Nate is dying. Keep your focus on your work.

Carefully keeping her eyes fixed on a chip in the corridor's paint, she mumbled, "Nothing. I'm just...tired and I still have a lot of work to do. Please let me past."

There. That sounded polite. She was pretty sure nothing in her tone gave her emotional state away. She sidled to her right, hoping he'd take the hint and move aside.

But no. Of course not. Instead, he reached out and tipped her chin up so she ended up staring into his concerned eyes.

Concern for her, when she was unable to save Nate. When she didn't know if the work she'd done for Kaufmann had helped or hurt his friend.

Why did he have to be so nice to her? Why did she have to find him so attractive? He was tearing her apart because she couldn't bear the thought that he was heading back to Kaufmann's compound. Rafe was the one bright spot in her life right now. How would she put her heart back together if something happened to him?

She felt the first tear slide like hot butter down her cheek. "Damn you! Just leave me alone." She jerked away and tried to run.

Rafe was faster. He wrapped her in his arms and set her head to rest against his chest. Within seconds his t-shirt was damp with her tears.

RAFE HELD Gabby against his chest and felt a lance of emotion pierce his heart. She was crying because of Nate. Because she cared so much about a man she'd only known as a rage-filled monster. Not the fierce, intelligent man Rafe had trusted with his life.

Rafe admired Gabby for not giving up despite the odds, but this crying totally undid him. Her tears didn't just touch Rafe the leader, they touched Rafe the man.

Rafe accepted the risks of his job. Each mission had the potential to end in death or disability. Just because he had no problem with the danger didn't mean he wanted those he cared about to worry. So he shielded them as best he could.

His heart ached because he couldn't protect Gabby from the pain of Nate's death.

She sniffled and started to pull away.

"It's okay," Rafe told her in a voice he hoped would soothe her into staying right where she was. "Just let yourself cry. Let it all out."

Christ. He sounded like some talk show shrink. But bottom line, he didn't want to let her go. It felt too right having her in his arms. Like she belonged here.

Unfortunately, someone forgot to tell Gabby that. After maybe another minute of crying into his shirt, she pushed away firmly enough that he had to let her go.

"I'm sorry," she mumbled as she pulled a tissue from her

pocket. She blew her nose, keeping her eyes down. "Things have just been a bit...much lately."

"Hey." He tipped her chin up and nearly staggered under the impact of her hazel eyes. More green today than brown, they glittered brilliantly through the magnification of her tears. He totally forgot what he was going to say. Poof. It was just gone. All he could think about was comforting her. Making her smile again.

Which is how he found himself leaning forward, kissing her wet cheeks and tasting her tears.

He felt her body go rigid, heard her sharp little inhale of surprise. He pulled back long enough to see her stunned expression. To confirm that she wasn't offended or scared. Then he leaned in again and finished drying her cheeks with his tongue.

Then, God help him, he moved lower and kissed her mouth.

RAFE'S CLOSENESS, his tenderness, threw Gabby completely off balance. The rasp of his tongue against her cheeks warmed her in places that should have been completely unaffected. Once again proving how dangerous he was to her equilibrium.

Then his lips settled over hers. He kept the kiss light. Tender. Yet her entire body jolted into awareness. When his tongue slipped between her lips she thought she made some husky sound of approval, but wasn't sure. All her senses were focused on the feel, the *taste* of his mouth against hers.

God, the power of his kiss. She felt it in her soul. Felt that if she didn't get more of his taste, she'd die. She pressed into him, sucking his tongue deeper into her mouth. Never wanting to let him go.

When Rafe raised his head, she whimpered and leaned forward, trying to recapture his mouth. He stared into her eyes, his expression clouded with desire. She was certain her own expression must be the same.

"Christ," Rafe whispered. He slid one hand to the back of her neck, the other to the small of her back and pulled her against his body as his mouth came down on hers.

Rafe nibbled softly at her lips and Gabby opened her mouth, eager to have him back inside. She gave a purr of approval when his tongue probed deeper and Rafe answered with a growl. The kiss flared, turning ravenous as they tried to devour each other.

Gabby lost her sense of self. The rest of her body simply ceased to exist. She became nothing more than a starved mouth, desperate not to let Rafe leave until this hunger for his taste, for the warm spice of him, was satisfied.

"Jesus, mate, get a bloody room will ya?" a sardonic Aussie voice drawled.

Gabby jerked away from Rafe, mortified. She didn't recognize the man standing in the corridor, leering at them. About Rafe's height, he had spiky, white blond hair, a surfer's tan and a grin that said he enjoyed her discomfort.

That was all she had time to notice before Rafe turned and put his body between her and the stranger. She put her hands between Rafe's shoulder blades and rested her forehead on the backs of her fingers.

"Playing voyeur again, Larson?" Rafe asked in a voice so chillingly polite, Gabby shivered. "Isn't it time you found your own lady?"

"Why? When it's so much fun stealing yours."

Gabby felt Rafe's muscles tighten underneath her fingers. "And yet I hear you're single again," Rafe responded.

Gabby heard Larson's sharp inhale. But before he could reply to Rafe, the beep of a cell phone interrupted.

"Ah," Larson murmured. "Duty calls. Dear lady, do keep me first in line when this oaf grows tired of you."

Gabby didn't bother to respond, and a moment later she heard his footsteps fading away.

Rafe's muscles relaxed. "Don't mind him. He likes to play the prick with other guys and steal their women, but he's a good operator."

Gabby stepped away from him. She wasn't sure how she felt about being classified as one of Rafe's women. Not that it mattered. She couldn't allow him to kiss her again. Hadn't she just warned herself about feeling anything for Rafe? Letting the nearly orgasmic power of his mouth distract her from her work would be the shortest route to heartbreak.

"I really need to get back to work," she said.

"Gabby—"

"No. Don't." She held up her hand in a warding gesture. "Just let it go. You're leaving tomorrow. I—" She shook her head. "Forget it. The kiss was amazing, but it's just a temporary thing."

"Like hell," he said with a sexy intensity that sent shivers of longing down her spine. From the look in his eyes, she was about sixty seconds from being pushed against the wall and racing toward orgasm.

He took a step toward her. Oh, God, if he touched her, she was lost.

So she took the coward's way out.

She fled.

RAFE WATCHED GABBY RUN. He wanted to go after her. To demand that she acknowledge the strength of the attraction between them.

But he had to stay focused on his upcoming mission. Letting Gabby worm her way into his emotions was the quickest way to distraction, and in the field distraction meant capture or death.

He was not going to lose another man to Kaufmann. Having Nate die was bad enough.

Rafe turned and headed back toward the conference room. He wanted another look at the mock-up. Wanted to run a couple more scenarios. Because shit happened and he was determined to be fully prepared no matter what Kaufmann's security team threw at them.

Yet as he walked down the corridor, he couldn't get Gabby's passion-clouded eyes out of his head. His poor little scientist. This past week had been one unforeseen, uncontrollable event after another for her. Outside her lab there was precious little order to this new world. The crazy, overwhelming lust between them had to be scaring her to death, because sure as shit there was no way to control the fire between them whenever they touched.

As that kiss proved.

His resolve weakened. But when he glanced back over his shoulder, she was gone.

CHAPTER ELEVEN

Rafe stared down at the man lying motionless in the hospital bed. "Damn, Nate," he murmured. "Guess I won't be pulling your ass out of any more midnight bar brawls."

He touched Nate's shoulder. Christ, but this was hard. Nate had lost weight, and his once robustly ebony skin was now tinged with gray. It reminded him too much of when his father had died.

The pneumonia had made his dad even thinner and more haggard than Nate. Sitting by his father's bed, Rafe had felt a burning mix of frustration and gut-wrenching grief. Even nearly four months later, he still couldn't stop his outrage at the injustice of his father dying from a bacteria. A fierce, proud man like his dad you expected to go down on the job. Not from pneumonia, for Christ's sake.

But at least he'd been able to say good-bye. Niko had been deep in Afghanistan, recovering from a bullet wound, when their dad went into the hospital. Rafe had said his good-bye to Pop, then hauled ass to find Niko and bring him home. But Pop had died before their plane landed in the States. Sometimes Rafe caught the bleak knowledge of the lost opportunity in Niko's eyes and he cursed fate all over again. If anyone should have been given the chance to say good-bye to Pop, it was Niko.

So yeah, Rafe appreciated being able to say good-bye to Nate. He understood what Gabby hadn't said. Nate probably wouldn't be alive when he returned.

He gave Nate's shoulder a squeeze. "You give 'em hell up there in heaven, Ngoro. Hear me?" He thought Nate's breathing hitched as if he understood, even deep within his coma. Picking up Nate's hand, Rafe murmured a brief prayer in French, the language of Nate's people back in Senegal. Nate always recited these words, basically a request for safety while ass-kicking, just before they dove into action.

Then Rafe set his friend's hand gently on the bed and walked away without looking back.

"There's enough trouble up ahead," Nate had once said when one of the men asked why he never took the rear-facing seat on any transportation. "Why look back at the trouble I left behind?"

"Amen, *mi amigo*," Rafe said as he let himself out of the room. "Amen."

Rafe headed down the corridor, wondering what to do next. He'd finished briefing his team. They'd run over their plans until they were confident they'd planned for every contingency. He'd said good-bye to Niko and Jenna. Sleep would be good, but there was a low hum in his body that meant sleep was still hours away.

Knowing this restless, almost melancholy mood wasn't good for his pre-mission preparation, Rafe decided to head down to the gym and work himself into his usual optimistic state of mind.

Instead, he found his feet leading him toward another hospital room.

"About fucking time," Kai Paterson snarled when Rafe pushed open the door. "Thought you were going to take off without saying good-bye, asshole."

Rafe laughed, relieved to find his friend awake. "Some of us have real missions to prepare for. None of this lazing about in hospital beds, flirting with the nurses."

He looked Kai over and frowned. While it was great to see Kai awake, his skin was almost cadaver pale and his amber eyes glittered with a touch of fever within his sunken sockets. His brother-in-law almost looked worse now than he had over two months ago when they'd pulled him broken and bloody out of Jaime Alvarez's dungeon.

"Christ, man, you still look like shit. I thought those new antimalarial drugs were working."

Kai narrowed his eyes and shot Rafe the finger. "I'm alive, right? That's good enough for me."

Rafe studied his friend. Kai looked like an academic, but he had a core of steel most people didn't catch when they first met him. Rafe knew what his brother-in-law had been through since the attack that killed his parents and the twins. In fact, thanks to a late night drunken confession, Rafe thought he was the only one who knew not just what Kai had done to the assassins, but what it had cost Kai in terms of self-respect.

Rafe supposed that compared to Kai's inner struggle to keep his rage and newfound thirst for violence under control, malaria would seem like a walk in the park. Even if the mutant variety Kai had picked up continued to threaten his life.

For Rafe, it was unsettling to realize how close he'd come to losing another friend. There had been too many losses in his life lately. First, Pop had died. Then the aunt he'd thought was dead had turned up alive, only to sacrifice herself in an attempt to kill Alvarez. Now Nate was on the brink of death.

It was almost enough to make a guy nervous.

AN HOUR LATER, Rafe knocked on the door of the cabin Gabby had moved into after accepting Ryker's job offer.

Gabby had spoken the truth when she said that taking their

relationship farther made no sense with him leaving tomorrow, but Rafe didn't care. He had to see her again. This attraction between them was special. Too powerful to ignore. He had every intention of jumping right back in when he returned from the mission. So she'd damn well better wait for him.

He'd just raised his fist to knock again, when the door opened. His jaw dropped. Gabby stood there in a short cotton robe. Her hair was messed up, as if he'd woken her from bed. His eyes flicked to the clock hanging above her kitchen sink. Almost two in the morning. He winced, knowing he probably *had* woken her.

But he wasn't sorry. She looked too good blinking up at him with her eyes slightly unfocused.

"Rafe?" God. Just the sleep-husky tone of her voice was enough to bring his body to full alert like a randy teenager.

"Is something wrong?" Her eyes sharpened and her brows drew together as that super-computer brain of hers started calculating probabilities. If he didn't say something fast, she'd worry herself into a panic over nothing.

But his tongue had frozen in place. Stunned by how much he wanted her, all he could do was stand there like an idiot, memorizing the way she looked so he could carry the image with him on his mission. Strands of golden hair clung to her cheeks and eyelashes, making him itch to reach out and smooth it into place. The sleepy look in her hazel eyes made him wish he was watching her from across a pillow after a long night of loving. Her lips were slightly parted, an invitation he didn't think she was aware of. Then her teeth worried her bottom lip and her gaze sharpened.

Knowing he had to say something before she concluded the world was at an end and raised the alarm, he stepped toward her. She instinctively moved back to let him into the cabin and he took full advantage, herding her inside. As soon as he'd cleared the doorway, he reached behind him and shoved the door shut.

Gabby's mouth formed a surprised "O" but before she could speak, his mouth covered hers.

Ah, God, yes. He hadn't intended to kiss her, but now he realized Gabby's sweetness was what he'd needed to calm his restlessness.

Just for tonight, he wanted to put all the ugliness of his mission aside and drown in Gabby's warm, fragrant female body. Her lips, soft as he remembered, moved underneath his hesitantly. He knew she thought this was a bad idea, so he finessed the kiss, molding his lips to hers without going deeper. He didn't want to scare her. To do anything that might make her pull back.

Despite the raging tension in his body, he thought he could spend the rest of the night chastely kissing Gabby with their mouths closed. Then she made an impatient sound deep in her throat, pulled him closer and opened her lips. That was all it took for the kiss to turn carnal.

She kissed him as if devouring him was her sole purpose in life. Making it very hard for Rafe to remember that he hadn't come here for sex. But as his tongue sparred with hers and she pressed her slender little body against his, all his good intentions crumbled.

Gabby pulled back, sucking in air as she stared up at him with heavy-lidded eyes.

Distance. Okay. This was good. Rafe forced himself not to reclaim her lips, no matter how enticingly shiny and swollen they were.

Say good-bye and get out of here, his conscience warned him.

Gabby's hands moved to the tie holding her robe closed. She undid the knot, fumbling a bit with the thick cotton ties before pushing the robe off her shoulders. It slid to the floor in slow motion.

Dear, merciful heaven, she was naked.

Rafe let himself just look at her, incapable of forming speech even if his life depended on it. Underweight or not, her body still had an innate feminine softness and grace that both made his knees weak with desire and made him feel as invincible as King Kong.

When her hands lifted to hide her pert little breasts with their pouting nipples, he finally found his tongue. "No." He sounded like he'd swallowed a box of razorblades, but that's how he felt, every breath, every word a painful combination of lust and awe. "Don't hide. You're so beautiful."

She made a sound of disbelief and his eyes flew to her face. The seductress who'd thrown off her robe was gone, replaced by a woman timid with uncertainty. "I know you think I'm too skinny. I'm—" Her teeth pulled on the corner of her lip and she searched his eyes as if looking for reassurance.

"Gabby." Her name was both prayer and thanks. "God, if you had any idea how many times I've imagined you naked. Reality is so much better. You're perfect. Your skin looks so soft, I can't wait to get my mouth on it."

She flushed and he felt a wave of tenderness. How long since she'd had a man in her life? Someone to make her feel special? In that instant he knew that what he felt for Gabby wasn't just lust or strong affection. He wasn't ready to put a name to it, but his focus shifted. Tonight would be about Gabby. About making her understand how sexy she was. How badly he wanted *her*. Just her. Gabby.

He tried to put all that into a long, heated gaze that traveled up her body. When he saw her nervousness fade, he reached for her.

She danced out of reach, stopping just short of the couch. Her eyes marked him from head to toe, destroying him with heat. "You have too many clothes on, Andros," she said. "I'm feeling at a disadvantage."

"Oh really?" He let his fingers hover over his belt buckle, waited until she focused on his hands, then darted forward and grabbed her around the waist.

"Hey!"

He ignored her shriek of protest and hauled her up against his body, taking her mouth in another kiss. Ah, shit. He was seriously drowning here. She tasted like nothing he'd ever known and everything he'd ever needed.

He slid his chest slowly side to side, loving the way her breath caught as the cotton of his t-shirt abraded her sensitive nipples. Then it was his turn to gasp as she shimmied against him. He tightened his hold on her and deepened the kiss, tangling his tongue with hers.

Her hands yanked his t-shirt out of his jeans, shoving the material out of her way so she could touch his bare skin. She stroked his back muscles, ran her nails up and down his spine, then, when he thought he was going to come if she didn't stop, she slid her hands down and tried to wedge them between the tight fabric of his jeans and his butt.

Ah, man. His little scientist was going to kill him.

"Hang on." He pulled back just far enough to pull off his shirt and undo his belt. Before he had the button on his pants undone, Gabby's hands were once again trying to slide down his butt.

He groaned, kissed her, and unzipped his jeans before the pressure against the denim cut off blood supply to a very critical portion of his anatomy.

Seconds later Gabby's questing hands reached their goal. She squeezed his butt cheeks and hummed in approval, the sound vibrating against his lips.

Jesus, if they didn't slow down, this was going to be over in about thirty seconds. Yet he didn't want to stop kissing her. To stop exploring her with his own hands, testing the softness of her. Finding that the good doctor had a surprising amount of sleek muscle for someone who sat in a lab all day. Loving the fact that his hounding her to eat three meals a day this past week had put a bit of much needed weight back on her bones.

Gabby hooked her fingers over the top of his waistband and shoved his jeans and boxer briefs down.

Rafe groaned. They weren't going to make it to the bed. Not when her eager fingers were kneading him, urging him closer to her hips.

To hell with it.

Without lifting his mouth from hers, Rafe hoisted her up his body. She immediately wrapped her arms and legs around him, aligning her core exactly where he needed it.

Gabby tightened her hold on him, all the while driving him crazy with hot little kisses along his jaw and throat. "Rafe, I need you inside me," she moaned.

Rafe managed to shuffle into a turn that put Gabby's back against the door and plastered him to her front.

"Yes." She arched into him. "Hurry." She reached down and took him in hand, her fingers cool against his heated flesh.

Then she squeezed and started to guide him into her. He felt her moisture against his tip and jerked back.

"Wait. Fuck, Gabby. Condom!" He turned slightly so she sat more on his hip while he reached down to his jeans, which were around his knees, fumbling with the pockets as he tried to remember which one held his wallet.

Gabby rubbed her clit against his bare hip and made a hungry, keening sound that sent barbed rivers of need slicing through his system.

Christ. Where the *hell* was his wallet?

His fingers finally touched worn leather, but in his haste he nearly dropped the thing on the floor. And that would have been a crying shame, because there was no fucking way he could reach the floor and keep Gabby on the edge of coming just from rubbing herself against him.

But, *mil gracias*, he finally got the damn wallet open and pulled out the condom.

"Give me." Gabby snatched the foil packet out of his fingers and with Olympic speed had the condom ready to go. Despite her hurry of a few moments ago, she gave him a wicked smile and took her own sweet time rolling the latex down his straining cock millimeter by millimeter until he couldn't take it any more.

He shoved her hands away, yanked the condom the rest of the way down, and slammed into her. *Dios.* She was hot and tight and fit him so perfectly, all he could think of was that he was home. He didn't want to move and risk losing this amazing mix of peace and razor-edged anticipation.

But then Gabby cried out and dug her heels into the backs of his legs. He moved, urged on by her choked gasps of pleasure. His thrusts rattled the door behind her, but Rafe didn't care. He braced himself, gave one last thrust, and exploded.

"Rafe!" Her scream of completion mixed with his satisfied roar as Rafe poured what felt like his heart and soul into this woman.

His woman.

GABBY AWOKE a few hours later cocooned in Rafe's arms, his chest against her back, his breath stirring the hair along her cheek. She was surprised he was still here. She'd expected him to sneak out while she was sleeping, to go get ready for his mission. The fact that he was relaxed enough, and trusted her enough, to fall asleep beside her, made her heart swell with so much emotion, she had to bite her lip to keep from whispering out loud how she felt.

Instead, she closed her eyes and let herself enjoy this feeling of safety and warmth. To imagine that she and Rafe had ordinary jobs and that there was nothing more pressing in their lives than to spend a leisurely day in bed, making love.

She pressed her cheek into the pillow and bit her lip. Oh, God, how had it happened? She'd fallen in love with Rafe. How could she do that? Hadn't she told herself not to care?

Yes, she most certainly had. Quite firmly, too.

But he'd wormed his way into her life too quickly for her to stop. She loved his flirtatious smiles. Appreciated the way he'd teased and bullied her into eating this past week. Liked how he'd sensed her nervousness when she'd acted out of character and dropped her robe tonight. He'd given her the precise words to boost her confidence, reassuring her that she'd done the right thing.

He always made her feel like the center of his attention when he was with her. She'd never felt so cherished.

A branch knocked against the window, causing her to jump. Reminding her sharply of the danger ahead. She tried hard not to imagine Rafe dead, bleeding from his eyes and nose, but the terrifying images flashed through her head anyway. What if—?

Stop it. Rafe and his team will be fine.

To distract herself, she thought back to when Rafe had carried her into the bedroom after their first frantic coupling against her door. He'd lowered himself onto her carefully and their gazes had locked. Then Rafe had flinched and murmured, "Christ, sorry." He'd started to lever himself off of her when she realized that like her, he was thinking of the last time he'd had her beneath him and how she'd thought he was going to kill her.

But she no longer feared him. So she'd locked her legs around him, trapping him in place, then raised her arms over her head, deliberately making herself vulnerable. She'd been rewarded by a brilliant smile and a torturously slow seduction. He'd reduced her to begging for an orgasm that arrived with such force, she'd nearly passed out.

She didn't want this night to ever end. But already a faint tinge of gray peeked around the edges of her drapes. It wouldn't be long before Rafe had to leave.

"Don't think about it," Rafe murmured sleepily. His fingers trailed across her breast, plucking at her nipple.

"Mind read much?" she gasped.

"Nah. Your body's so tense, a blind man could tell what you're thinking. Just let it go. We've got at least another hour. And I don't intend to waste it."

He rolled onto his back and turned her so she lay facedown on top of him. His eyes projected strength, confidence and passion. He tenderly stroked a strand of hair away from her cheek, then his lips touched hers in a kiss that started butterfly soft, but soon turned ferocious.

Gabby lost herself in his heat. But inside, her heart was crying.

RAFE HEARD A CHOKING little sound and glanced across the small table in Gabby's dining room. Ah, man, her eyes were so damn sad, she might as well have tightened a noose around his heart.

Lips trembling, Gabby's hand clutched the white teddy bear with the red heart on its chest proclaiming Be My Valentine that he'd given her when she woke up. Gabby quickly turned her head away, trying to hide the shine of wet cheeks, but it was too late.

"Gabby, I have to go."

"I know." Her voice was small and sad. Nothing like the passionate woman he'd made love to when he woke up this morning. He would have gone for another round in the shower, but she'd sidled out of his reach and promised she'd cook breakfast instead.

"I don't want you heading off on an empty stomach," she'd said, picking her robe off the floor. So he'd showered alone, then joined her in the kitchen for breakfast.

It was weird, but he felt peaceful with her. There wasn't any pressure to flirt, or make her laugh, or discuss their feelings. Just the quiet acceptance of two people enjoying a meal together.

He popped the last bite of toast and eggs into his mouth and drained his coffee cup. A quick check of his watch showed he had just enough time to run back to his cabin, grab his bag, and make it to the airstrip in time to meet his team.

Gabby stood, set the teddy bear on the center of the table, and stacked Rafe's plate on top of her own. "So...I guess you'd better get going."

She said it so casually, he knew she was hiding some deep emotion.

"No," he protested, despite the truth of her words. "I'm good." He reached for the dishes. "I can help."

She shook her head. "Rafe, it's better if you just leave." Her eyes met his for the briefest instant, too fast for him to tell what she was thinking. "Make it quick, before..." She bit her lip.

"Good-bye. Stay safe." Grabbing the stack of dishes, she pivoted on her heel and rushed into the tiny kitchen.

With any other woman he would have done what she'd asked. Avoided a scene and left. But not Gabby. Not the woman who'd cried over Nate. Who wasn't afraid to stand up to Rafe and who always looked surprised when he made her laugh.

The woman he was pretty sure he'd fallen in love with.

"Gabby," he pleaded, following her into the kitchen. "C'mon. Is that the best you can do?"

She set the dishes in the sink hard enough to make them rattle. When her hand reached to turn on the faucet, he stopped her.

"*Querida*, don't shut me out now. Let me have a proper good-bye." Gently, but firmly enough that she'd know he meant business, he guided her hands to the back of his neck and pulled her hips against his. "Just one more kiss for luck, yeah?"

Not waiting for her answer, he lowered his head. Oh, God, there it was again. Total combustion. Heat and homecoming and a promise he wanted desperately to keep.

"Don't you dare get yourself hurt," Gabby said fiercely when they finally came up for air. She poked him in the chest. "I want you back just the way you are."

"Yes, ma'am!" He saluted with two fingers, then kissed the tip of her nose. "We'll be careful. We always are."

He took her hand. "Come on. Walk with me back to my cabin to get my stuff."

Gabby looked pointedly at the robe she was wearing.

"Okay," he said with a grin. "You can throw some clothes on first."

To his surprise, she changed quickly, emerging in jeans and a t-shirt a couple of minutes later. The walk to his cabin was smothered with sorrow and longing until he thought he'd choke on it. But instead of making him want to run away, it made him want to pull Gabby close and never let go. He didn't even want to release her hand to get his bag.

What he really wanted right now was to take her back to bed. To watch the way her golden hair swung around her jaw line, bouncing slightly as she rode him. To make her lose her precious control.

Instead, he picked up his bag, locked his cabin, and headed back across the SSU compound, Gabby's hand held firmly in his own.

Five minutes later, they were at the edge of the airstrip.

Gabby placed a fast kiss on his mouth. "Go," she ordered. "Before I lose it."

Ah damn, she was starting to cry.

"Gabby—"

"Hey Rafe!" Muldovsky shouted.

Rafe waved over his shoulder to acknowledge that he'd heard his friend. "I'll see you when I get back," Rafe said.

"Yeah," Gabby said weakly, clearly unconvinced.

Man, she broke his heart. This smart, sexy woman destroyed every thought he'd had about what he needed. What his future would hold. Love and commitment had not been part of that.

He'd seen how worry had worn at his mother every time the DEA sent his dad on another mission, aging *Mamá* ahead of her time. He'd vowed never to do that to a woman. To keep his heart shielded and himself firmly in the bachelor camp.

But he wanted Gabby waiting for him when he returned, not just from this mission, but from every mission from here on. All he needed was her.

And damn if that wasn't a scary thought.

"I—" Rafe shook his head. There were words to describe how he was feeling, but this wasn't the time. "Bye, doctor. Don't forget to eat."

Turning his back on her was the hardest thing he'd ever done. He swung his bag over his shoulder and told himself not to look back. He was late enough as it was.

But when he got within feet of the short airstrip, he stopped.

To hell with it.

He spun around. Gabby stood with her left arm wrapped around one of the pine trees at the edge of the paths, her right hand shielding her eyes against the rising sun.

Their eyes met and he felt a jolt of awareness. No, it was more than awareness. It was more like the ah-ha moment when the last piece fit into a complicated jigsaw puzzle.

"I love you," Gabby mouthed. His throat tightened around a swell of emotion too sharp to bear. He mouthed, "I love you" back, then turned away. This time, he kept going.

Half an hour later, as Rafe watched the last of their gear getting loaded onto the plane, he felt an unexpected surge of superstitious dread crawl up his back. Something far stronger than his usual pre-mission nerves.

"What the fuck is wrong with me," Rafe muttered. Everything was going to be fine. The spot they'd picked out for a landing zone would be well out of range of known detection devices. They had Gabby's map of the compound, and while it wasn't perfect, it sure as hell was better than going in blind.

And he had more men this time.

There was no reason to be spooked.

No good reason except an uneasy gut to explain why he pulled his phone out of his pocket and dialed his brother while he waited for the team to finish loading their gear.

"Yo," Niko answered. "What's wrong, little bro? Thought you'd have left by now."

Rafe shook his head. God, this overwhelming relief at hearing Niko's voice was frightening. What was wrong with him? "I..." He shrugged, even though Niko couldn't see him. "I...um... We're just about wheels up, but I just wanted to say...I'm glad you're my brother. I love you, man," he blurted in Greek.

Jesus, it felt so much like good-bye, his eyes burned.

"Rafe?" All teasing disappeared from Niko's voice. "What the fuck is going on? You have a bad feeling about the mission? Call it off."

Trust Niko to understand what he wasn't saying. Sometimes his brother was too intuitive for his own good. "Nah, we're good. That was just something that needs saying now and then. To, you know, embarrass the shit out of you."

Across the tarmac, Depaoli signaled that the team was ready.

"Gotta go, Niko. Give Jenna a kiss and tell her I love her, okay? Bye."

As he snapped the phone closed and moved toward the plane, Rafe looked around the compound. Despite his assurance to Niko, he had the sinking sensation this was the last time he'd be back here. And damn if he didn't find his eyes blurring as he stepped onto the plane.

CHAPTER TWELVE

The Next Night
Adirondack Mountains

"I JUST LOST another of my guards to an attack by one of your freaks," Rufus Cygan snarled as he stormed into Dr. Kaufmann's office.

Kaufmann raised his head from the report he'd been studying, his eyes narrowing in annoyance at his head of security. "I've told you before not to bother me with such trivialities. Have the subject terminated and make sure a note gets put in his file about the attack." He lowered his eyes back to his report.

But instead of heeding the subtle dismissal, Cygan slapped his palms against Kaufmann's desk. "Your freaks are getting harder to control. It's taking up to five guards to hold one of your subjects when they get out of line. I want permission to bring in additional men. Double that when we move to the new facility."

Kaufmann slowly stood up until he looked Cygan in the eye. He wondered what combination of drugs would work to bring the man's lack of respect under control. "I have told you that the only additional men we can afford to give you are Level 1 subjects.

The project's funders are already skittish. If they get so much as a whiff of our problems, they'll shut us down."

Kaufmann leaned forward until Cygan had to back up. "If this project ends, I will personally see to it that you're thrown to the Level 5 subjects."

Cygan wet his lips and retreated as far as the visitor's chair. But then he seemed to find his backbone. "I'm telling you, my men won't work with any of your freaks, even the Level 1's. Because we all know even those don't last for long. What's the record now, three weeks?"

Actually, one of the subjects had recently made it four weeks without losing any of his cognitive or physical functions, the longest any of the Level 1 subjects had survived intact. "Then I suggest you find a way to handle the subjects with the men you've got."

"What about the extra security team? At least let me borrow a couple of those men. There've been no more intruders since the night of the explosions in the lab. Whoever helped Dr. Montague and the subjects escape is long gone. Odds are they got what they wanted. That team can spare four men."

Kaufmann shook his head. "Our funder claims his source is telling the truth and there's going to be a larger attack on the facility soon. I'm not reassigning the men from the external security team." He had several empty cells set aside for any attackers caught alive, and a new formula that was ready for testing.

"Deal with the issues in some other way, Mr. Cygan. Or you will be terminated."

Cygan's face paled.

Kaufmann let the faintest smile ghost across his mouth. There was something so delightful about watching a man realize how close he stood to death. "Do you understand?"

"Yes, sir."

Kaufmann waited until Cygan had closed the door behind him before returning his attention to his report. Damn Dr.

Montague. She'd been on to something. All the subjects she'd treated had made improvements in anger management. But as soon as her treatments stopped, the rages had come back threefold.

And she'd left no notes behind to assist him with duplicating her efforts. She'd even managed to erase her data from the backup. Such a setback was unacceptable. He had deadlines to meet and he needed Dr. Montague's data just as much as he needed the notes on Dr. Nevsky's microchip.

He'd just have to ask Jamieson to make certain Dr. Montague was returned to him.

Speaking of Jamieson...he checked the duty roster. All of the specially enhanced men Kaufmann had provided to Kerberos, Jamieson's private black ops group, should have two weeks left at Level 1. Add another two weeks at Level 2 and he had a four-week window before he'd have to replace the men.

Kaufmann tapped his finger impatiently on his desk. Of his current batch of subjects, he expected the group which had been given the old formula to enter Level 1, the phase with the highest performance, within two weeks. Unfortunately, the group which had received the new formula had not yet shown the anticipated results. More tests would be required.

He glanced at the calendar. There simply wasn't enough time. Damn Jamieson and his insistence on using the enhanced men to carry out the President's anniversary attack. Kaufmann required more time to perfect the formula, so that the subjects entered Level 1 earlier than four weeks and then remained at that level longer than the current month.

Also critical to ensuring the long-term viability of his program was halting the current rate of deterioration. Once the subjects reached Level 2, the decline in their physical and mental abilities occurred rapidly. Nothing his team had done to the formula so far had stopped the deterioration, which always ended in death.

Another reason he needed this new formula to work. He couldn't afford to lose any more subjects. It was becoming increasingly difficult to locate new subjects without arousing the suspicion of the authorities.

He pulled closer the report he'd been reading when Cygan interrupted him. At this stage of treatment all of the men were stronger physically than those under the previous formula. They also showed the insensitivity to pain and the ability to get by on one hour of sleep that was the requirement for Level 1 status.

Unfortunately, the mental results weren't as satisfactory. The formula had not sped up the mental breakdown required to achieve total mind control. It seemed that each man had an individual level of resistance to the various brainwashing techniques and nothing his team had tried changed that. In order to provide Kerberos and other organizations with reliable, enhanced soldiers, the time required for a subject to achieve Level 1's superior skills had to be shortened. And the cellular and mental deterioration had to be stopped.

He made a notation in the margin. Once Jamieson brought him Nevsky's microchip, he'd have the data necessary to get past these obstacles. Nevsky had achieved faster mind control in his subjects, but had refused to share his technique. The old bitterness rose, but Kaufmann pushed it back. Nevsky had been a paranoid control freak. He'd kept Kaufmann confined to monitoring the physical effects on both sets of subjects—the men who gained increased physical strength and endurance for long-range military operations, and the men who developed superior reflexes and speed that would assist them on espionage missions. But Nevsky had never explained the full scope of his program, leading to Kaufmann's current difficulties.

He'd almost run out of the samples he'd stolen from Nevsky's lab and his team had been unable to recreate over fifty percent of the substances in Nevsky's formula. The data on the microchip was the key they needed to start mass producing the necessary chemicals.

It was ironic, really. Jamieson worked for the CIA, but his goal was to put together an invincible private army for the President, so he was more interested in the strength side of the program. Men who could keep moving through any type of adversity, solely focused on achieving the goal their mind control handler had set for them.

Since Jamieson paid the bills, Kaufmann currently focused only on the aspects of the research that met Jamieson's goals for Kerberos. But Kaufmann's goal was far greater. Once he'd satisfied Jamieson's requirements and the man stopped breathing down his neck for new and improved soldiers, Kaufmann fully intended to restart the spy side of the program.

He'd then offer either type of subject for sale on the open market—mind-controlled brute, or super intelligent spy.

He flipped back through the report, checking one of the numbers. Before he could go public, he also had to find a way past what some of his researchers called the men's expiration date. The longest any of the men had survived after reaching Level 1 certification was eight weeks and two days. The program had made small advancements in extending the length of time the subjects lasted in the desirable Level 1 phase. But they inevitably started to deteriorate into Level 2 after three or four weeks. Once they reached Level 3, their bodies began to show outward signs of stress. An increase in clumsiness. Longer sleep cycles. Increased sensitivity to pain. Levels 4 and 5 followed quickly, with the end result being a man whose body broke down at the cellular level, and whose mind was so full of rage and insanity that even the simplest mind control command was ignored. If the men didn't commit suicide or die from their internal organs failing, then Kaufmann's rule was to give the Level 5 subjects over to more advanced Level 1 subjects for practice of assault techniques.

Unfortunately, he'd been unable to stop the deterioration. Nothing he'd tried had given the men longer life spans. He needed a new pool of subjects. Nevsky had initially used criminals, but had found that their lack of respect for authority interfered with the mind control program. Before he died, Nevsky had experimented on his first batch of soldiers stolen from the military and falsely reported killed in action. A recruitment method Kaufmann had continued.

Unfortunately, Jamieson had informed him that the FBI and the military were investigating disappearances of their personnel after some of their "dead" operators had been spotted during Kaufmann's trial missions.

Kaufmann planned on incorporating reconstructive surgery on his subjects once he'd finalized the formula and could provide his buyers with a guarantee of at least two years of remaining life per soldier. With a life span of mere months, Kaufmann couldn't afford to give his current subjects new faces, which meant it was time to find a new pool of subjects to pull from.

He needed young males in top physical condition. Maybe college athletes. His recruitment team could stage a few car crashes. Maybe even fake the crash of a team bus. That would net him a decent size subject pool.

Yes, he'd definitely look into that idea.

His intercom buzzed. Kaufmann scowled at it, but when it refused to be cowed and buzzed again, he pressed the talk button. "Yes?"

"Sir, Cygan asked that I inform you that an attack force is currently approaching the compound."

Kaufmann slapped his report shut. "Very good. Please tell Doctor Weis to have enough tranquilizer prepared and to make certain the cells are ready to receive our new guests."

"Yes, sir."

Kaufmann left his office and headed into the lower level of the security room. He wanted to watch the monitors and observe how the members of the assault team behaved during the attack. It would give him insight into how to break the survivors after their capture.

FACEDOWN ON A PATCH OF DIRT, Rafe struggled to lift his head. He needed to see how many of his men were still alive, but the drugs Kaufmann's security team had shot into his system prevented him from moving so much as an inch.

He did a mental recount. Muldovsky was dead. He'd fallen in the first attack by Kaufmann's security. Willits had been shot in the shoulder, but none of the others had taken hits that Rafe had seen.

Depaoli and his team... They'd been inserting from the other side of the compound. Rafe hoped they'd managed not to walk into another ambush, but he doubted it. The trap had been too perfect. Kaufmann's men had known exactly where Rafe's team would enter the grounds. Had waited until the last man was inside the fence before attacking.

Rafe's team had been on radio silence, so they hadn't realized until they tried to warn the others that their radio signal was jammed.

Someone at the SSU had betrayed them.

"Is this all of them?" The cold male voice rang with authority.

"Yes, sir."

The tip of a highly polished loafer poked Rafe in the side, rolling him to his back. "Only six survivors out of twenty-four." Rafe looked up into a face he recognized from the files. Dr. Leonard Kaufmann. The slightly scholarly aura about him contrasted with the utter soullessness of his blue eyes.

Rafe felt an infuriating mix of helplessness, grief and rage. Only five of his teammates were alive. He shoved deep all emotion except for his rage as he stared up at Kaufmann. Tried to open his mouth to speak, but the drugs had effectively paralyzed every muscle.

"Welcome to my program, Mr. Andros," Kaufmann said. "I will so enjoy breaking you and your men, and turning you into model subjects." Despite his words, his eyes showed no anticipation. No glint of satisfaction or pleasure.

Rafe had come face-to-face with crazed terrorists and vicious criminals, but Kaufmann's lack of emotion sent a shiver of fear down his spine. Rafe strained against the invisible bonds of the drugs and was rewarded with a slight twitch of his fingers.

Kaufmann shifted his gaze to someone behind Rafe and nodded.

A piece of metal jabbed into Rafe's shoulder. He heard a sizzle a second before hot pain exploded in his shoulder. His entire body jerked, then the world went dark.

Three Days Later
Late Evening, SSU Compound
Oregon

Gabby had just finished pouring hot water into her teacup when someone knocked on her cabin door. Strange, no one ever visited her. She hadn't made any friends yet, and no one from the lab ever bothered her at home.

Who could...? Rafe! Maybe he was back early.

She dropped the teakettle back onto the stove and dashed across the few feet of living room. Quickly smoothing her hair down, she yanked open the door.

Ryker stood on her front porch, the overhead light throwing his features into grim shadow.

"Gabby." The somber, almost pitying tone of his voice threw her into a panic.

Rafe. Something had happened to Rafe. Her heart lurched to a stop.

"No." She backed up a step and closed the door half way.

Ryker caught the edge of the door and pushed gently. "Please let me in. I need to talk to you about Rafe."

"No." Her eyes pleaded with him from behind the safety of the door. "Please, no."

"I thought you'd rather hear the news here, in the privacy of your cabin, than in the lab or my office," he said gently.

She froze. If she closed the door and denied him entrance, then she could live in her dream world. A world where Rafe came back to her and they started a relationship.

But Ryker was right. She didn't want people speculating about her grief, or seeing her reaction to what she knew was bad news. She released her grip on the door, then spun around and hurried into the living room, turning on every light as if somehow that would make the news more bearable. Finally coming to a stop behind the sofa, she rested her hands on the back.

Ryker stepped cautiously into the room, closing the door behind him without removing his gaze from her. He watched her with the wary attention of a hunter expecting a wild animal to attack.

"Perhaps you'd better sit down," he said.

She shook her head and gripped the back of the sofa so tightly her knuckles hurt. "Just tell me." Her voice was a hoarse, frightened thing that all but begged him to soothe her fears away.

He held her eyes for a moment, then nodded. "Three days ago, Rafe and his team missed their check-in. We haven't heard from them since. Our satellite has been out of commission since the day they left, but today we managed to get time on one of the European Union's satellites."

He paused, and Gabby wished she were sitting down after all. Her knees suddenly felt wobbly. "And?"

"The compound and the surrouding forest have burned to

the ground, Gabby. None of the tracking devices from Rafe's team are transmitting. We have to assume they're all dead."

Rafe was gone.

The room spun. Gabby's knees gave out. She distantly heard a wild keening rent the air before grief and pain sucked her under.

"GABBY, WAKE UP."

She came to her senses lying on the couch, a cold, damp washcloth on her forehead. Ryker had her hand between his and was lightly rubbing warmth into her icy fingers.

"What happened?" she asked.

Ryker's eyes met hers and the sympathy he gave her tore her heart in two.

"No." She shook her head. "He can't be gone. There's some sort of mistake. A malfunction in the tracking devices. He's alive. They're all alive. Just...somewhere out of range. Underground."

"Gabby, the U.S. Geological Survey recorded a minor seismic event at the compound's location two days ago. That's consistent with the size of explosion that would be necessary to destroy the underground facility. Once the site has cooled down from the fire, our investigators will go in. But there's little chance anyone survived."

Gabby pulled her hand away from Ryker and sat up. The washcloth fell onto her lap with a wet plop and she angrily tossed it onto the coffee table.

She refused to accept Rafe was dead. Not yet. As a scientist, she understood odds and probabilities. Even the strongest conclusion was often proven wrong when new evidence was uncovered.

"There's still hope," she insisted, standing up.

Ryker shook his head and moved back to give her space. "Gabby, if Rafe and his men did somehow survive the fire, it's likely they're under Kaufmann's control. Such a fire could be caused by a self-destruct mechanism similar to the one that destroyed Nevsky's lab." He walked around the coffee table and faced her across the short expanse of cheap wood.

"It would be better to be dead than subject to Kaufmann's experiments, wouldn't you say?"

Bile crept up the back of Gabby's throat as Ryker described her worst nightmare—Rafe turned into a maddened beast like Nate. She bit her lip and tasted salt. Surprised to find herself crying, she reached up and dabbed at her eyes.

"You're right. I wouldn't wish Kaufmann's program on anyone. I...it's better if he is dead. If they're all dead." The pain of that was too much, though. She wrapped her arms across her belly and rocked back and forth as the tears coursed down her cheeks.

"I'm sorry, Gabby. I know you cared for him. I..." Ryker cleared his throat. "He was like a son to me. He was going to be my successor when I retire. I'll miss him very much."

She couldn't deal with the grief she heard in his voice. Her own grief was more than she could bear. "Please. I need to be alone now. I...I know we'd only just met, but I love...loved him." She hiccuped out the last word, but wanted Ryker to understand why she was falling apart the way she was. Because Rafe was special. Because he mattered.

She sensed his hesitation before he spoke. "I'm sorry, Gabby. Come see me when you're ready to talk."

Gabby nodded. Then she curled up on her side on the sofa and cried.

CHAPTER THIRTEEN

One Week Later
Kaufmann's New Compound
Blue Ridge Mountains

"Mr. Teng, please step closer to me," Dr. Kaufmann ordered.

From his position chained to the wall, Rafe's heart sank as he watched his teammate shuffle toward Dr. Kaufmann. Teng kept his eyes on the ground, his head bowed in total obedience.

Fuck. Another one lost to Kaufmann. He hadn't seen Teng in two days and had hoped he was dead. Death was better than enslavement.

Now Teng was nothing more than Kaufmann's puppet.

"Tell me, Mr. Teng, what can I use to break Mr. Andros?" Kaufmann turned and ran his probing, assessing eyes over Rafe. "He's held out remarkably well against every tool we've used against him. Oh, we've managed to chip away at his resistance, but there's something that's keeping him strong."

Hell yeah, he stayed strong. Because he had the memory of Gabby to sustain him. Whenever the pain got too bad, she was there with him, soothing him. Telling him to hang on. Keeping him silent against the drug-induced compulsion to tell Kaufmann exactly what he wanted to know.

Gabby was the one person he loved that Kaufmann didn't know about, so hadn't been able to use against him. She was Rafe's secret strength.

Kaufmann faced Teng. "Tell me what's stopping Mr. Andros from becoming like you."

Teng cut his eyes toward Rafe, his expression tormented. Begging for forgiveness.

Rafe flinched. Teng had been part of the initial assault on Kaufmann's compound. He knew that Rafe had been attracted to Gabby from the start. Worse, he knew exactly how much Gabby meant to him.

Fear twisted through Rafe's gut, leaving ice behind. *No*, he mouthed.

Tears welled in Teng's eyes. Rafe tensed against his chains. He wanted to fight. To lunge across the room and stop Teng's mouth with his fist. But Rafe refused to let Kaufmann know how close he was to success.

"Gabby Montague," Teng mumbled to Kaufmann.

"What?" The surprise in the doctor's voice was almost comical.

"Rafe's in love with Dr. Gabrielle Montague."

"Excellent. You're dismissed."

Shoulders hunched with dejection, Teng left the room.

"Well, Mr. Andros. You surprise me. Dr. Montague doesn't seem like your type," Kaufmann purred evilly.

Rafe kept his face impassive. Deep inside his soul, he hastily built shields around his memories of Gabby. Praying it would be enough to keep her with him.

Kaufmann motioned for two of his assistants. "I believe we'll start with some physical torture," he told them. "One hour minimum. Then give him the next series of poisons. That ought to soften him up enough that he'll be ready for my next session."

Kaufmann's smile was pure triumph. "I will so enjoy using Dr. Montague to break you."

Rafe threw Kaufmann a cocky smile. "You can try. But I wouldn't bet on it."

An agonizing amount of time later, Rafe blinked at another photo through the blood and sweat dripping in his eyes. The poison was still in his system, although the double-vision and abdominal cramping were no longer as agonizing. This photo was different. Instead of showing Gabby having sex with Nate and other unknown subjects while lab-coated scientists looked on, this time Gabby was fully clothed, smiling as she passed a beaker full of blue liquid to Kaufmann.

The sex pictures Rafe had no trouble discounting. Gabby wasn't a whore. And he knew her ethics. She'd never have sex with a patient.

But the beaker...hell. He knew she'd worked for Kaufmann. This could be a perfectly innocent photo.

"Do you still think she was uninvolved in developing my program?" Kaufmann asked with a tinge of mockery. "Once she realized the power to be gained from controlling other human beings, she jumped right in."

Kaufmann reached for a beaker. "Recognize this? It's the same one from the photo. Only, you'll notice the level of the liquid is much lower." He held up a syringe.

"We've found the poison she helped us develop to be most persuasive. It's what finally broke Teng." With his other hand Kaufmann spread the rest of the photos on the table.

To Rafe's exhausted mind, they were damning. Gabby filling a syringe with what looked like the same liquid. Injecting it into a terrified man. Watching and taking notes as the man writhed on the examination table.

"Let's see if we can't once again duplicate Dr. Montague's excellent results." Dr. Kaufmann jabbed the needle into Rafe's arm.

Rafe's body arched against the restraints as the poison burned through his veins. His limbs convulsed. His vision darkened. His ears rang.

As if from a great distance, he heard Dr. Kaufmann laugh. "Oh yes, I'll have to thank Dr. Montague when she returns. I expect her back within the next hour."

Rafe shook his head, then moaned at the pain that caused. No. He wouldn't believe it. Gabby was safe at the SSU. She hadn't created this poison. She loved him.

The poison spread throughout his body and the world became nothing but blinding agony. Rafe writhed against his restraints, desperate to find some relief. Barely keeping his mind together.

But Gabby was there in his head. Smiling at him. Opening her arms and offering him shelter. And she pushed back the pain long enough to keep him from blacking out. To stop him from giving in.

"Hasn't he broken yet?" Gabby's voice demanded impatiently. "What's taking so long? Give him another dose."

"No!" Rafe bellowed. It couldn't be Gabby. Gabby wasn't here.

He struggled to open his eyes, but his eyelids were too heavy to lift. Unable to see, all he could feel were soft, feminine fingers holding him down while someone stuck a second needle in Rafe's arm.

"Rafe, give Dr. Kaufmann what he wants and the pain will go away," Gabby ordered. "Give Kaufmann control. Do it for me."

"Gabby," Rafe groaned. God, he'd missed her so much. Spent so much time dreaming about her soft words of encouragement. Her kindness. Her strength.

Sharp fingernails dug painfully into his wrists above the restraints. "Give in," Gabby ordered.

"Why are you helping him?" Rafe cried, head tossing against the table. Gabby wouldn't betray him this way. He had to open his eyes. Had to see what was really going on. Maybe Kaufmann was threatening her.

But no matter how hard he tried, he could not get his eyelids to lift. The poisons were stealing his strength and he needed all his energy to protect his mind.

"You're weak," Gabby whispered in his ear. "Kaufmann can make you strong. Just accept his control. So easy. Don't you want to make me happy? Do this for me."

No. Gabby was wrong. Giving in to Kaufmann would make him weak, not strong. Something wasn't right. But Gabby was his savior. If she said to do it...

"Pledge your obedience, Mr. Andros," Kaufmann said. "And I'll let you see Gabby again."

Feeling as if his soul were tearing in two, Rafe rode out another wave of pain as his back arched high off the examination table.

"Swear it," Gabby urged him. "Or I'll make you hurt even more."

Confused by her order, Rafe hesitated. Then a soft, warm, female form draped over his body, belly rubbing against his crotch, hands running over his chest. Fingers pinched his nipples. A tongue spiced with unknown bitterness thrust into his mouth, leaving the sensitive tissues burning.

"Stop," he heard himself moan as he yanked his head away. He choked on whatever she'd fed him with her tongue. The substance mixed with the poison already in his system to bring on an unbearable mixture of pleasure and pain. Mixing him up until there was nothing more he wanted to do than to please her.

"Give Kaufmann your pledge," Gabby whispered as she trailed kisses across his cheeks, leaving behind that powerful burning sensation.

He burned everywhere.

It didn't matter what he said. He wouldn't be alive much longer.

"Yes," he croaked.

"Say it, Mr. Andros," Kaufmann demanded. "Tell me you will obey me in all things."

"I will...obey you...in all things." As soon as he said the words, something broke inside Rafe. The defenses he'd held onto so fiercely crumbled.

"Excellent."

Gabby slid away from his body, but the arousal didn't go away. Headphones were slapped to his ears. Chimes and gentle ocean waves calmed him.

Then Dr. Kaufmann began to speak. And what was left of Rafe's soul crept into a deep hole and hid.

"Tell me who this is," Dr. Kaufmann ordered, pointing to the woman in the picture.

"Dr. Gab-ri-elle Mon-ta-gue," Rafe replied. Forming words was too difficult. It was easier to say nothing. Fighting was better.

"Is she your friend?"

"No." Rafe shook his head. "Bad woman."

"That's right. She's your enemy. What will you do if you meet her?"

"Kill."

"Excellent." Dr. Kaufmann waved his hand. Two assistants brought in a terrified, struggling woman who looked very much like the one in the photo. The assistants had their hands clamped tightly to her arms as they dragged her closer to Rafe.

Rafe glanced back and forth from the woman to the photo. "Not same woman," he said, struggling to put the words together. "Who this?"

Dr. Kaufmann smiled. "This is the woman who helped break you. She pretended to be Dr. Montague. She's just as bad."

The part of Rafe that was under Kaufmann's command

nodded. But the stubborn piece of him that refused to succumb gave an internal howl of fury, knowing he'd been tricked.

The assistants shoved the woman to her knees in front of Rafe.

"Show me what you'll do to Dr. Montague once you find her," Kaufmann ordered.

Rafe shook his head. He didn't want to obey Dr. Kaufmann. Hurting women was wrong. But the pressure in his head kept increasing until his body trembled.

"Kill her," Kaufmann ordered again.

Against his will, Rafe's hands rose. He fought, but the pain in his head grew so sharp, the edges of his vision started to turn black. Screaming inside, Rafe watched his fingers close around the woman's jaw. He twisted sharply, breaking the woman's neck, and felt the pain in his head vanish like fog.

"Excellent job," Dr. Kaufmann said with approval. He waved toward his assistants, indicating they should remove the body. "I'm very pleased with you."

Rafe's shoulders went back with pride. Why had he fought? It was his job to obey. To seek this man's approval.

"In fact, you've performed so well that I'm assigning you to a very special project. See this woman?" Kaufmann held up another photo. "Her name is Susana Dias. She has something very important that I need. I want you to retrieve it for me. This man might be in your way."

The man in the photo looked familiar, but it took Rafe a long moment to pull up a name. Kai.

"You will kill him and the woman if they get in the way. All I want is the microchip in the woman's abdomen." Kaufmann went on to outline Rafe's mission.

The sane part of Rafe didn't listen. It refused to accept the need to kill again.

Something had to be done. He could not be allowed to

succeed in this mission. Not this time. Kai was too important. His friend.

But the rest of Rafe didn't care. It just wanted to obey Dr. Kaufmann so the pain wouldn't return.

Six Weeks Later
Sunday, Morning

"Niko." Rafe clutched the phone to his ear like it was his only link to sanity. He could feel the madness pushing in on him again. The chaos that took over his mind gave the Voice in the white coat the power to control him. But this was important. He had to warn Niko. So he focused hard, making sweat pop out on his brow.

"Rafe. What's wrong? Where are you?" Niko's worried voice burrowed into Rafe, calming the jagged noise of pain and rage.

"God, we've been searching frantically for you."

Rafe gave a harsh laugh. "In trouble, bro. Ouch… Shit…" A headache sliced through his skull, the pain nearly dropping him to his knees. It meant the chaos was coming back. He didn't have much time.

"Rafe!"

"Ah…sorry…headaches…" He gasped at another bolt of pain.

"Stay with me, Rafe. What happened?"

Rafe took several shuddering breaths, forcing his way through the pain by using what meager self-control he still had. "Security…waiting for us… others dead… Gave me…drugs."

"Jesus Christ!"

"New…treatment…accelerated results…aagh!"

"Rafe, where are you?"

Rafe laughed. "New York City. Heading…to Brazil… They… ordered me…find Kai…kill him… Kill anyone…tries to…stop me…" The Voice insisted Kai had to die at Rafe's hand. Like

Willits. Like Depaoli. But this time it wasn't the same. Rafe wasn't in the killing room, with the Voice speaking in his ear as he circled one of his teammates in the fighting sand. Here he was free to listen to the part of him deep inside that said killing this man was wrong. Kai was tied to Jenna, Niko's wife. Hurting Kai would hurt Jenna and that would hurt Niko.

He wouldn't hurt his brother. "Ordered...get chip...get Susana Dias."

"Rafe, what has the drug done to you?"

"Body," Rafe panted. "Small changes...mind...shit, I'm losing it again...mind only sometimes my own...headaches when can think inde-pend-dent-ly...otherwise, only think of mission...shit...I'm losing control again...will try to...slow myself...down... Please, Niko, you gotta...stop me...do whatever you have to do...don't let me succeed... They tell me...hate you...hate everyone...can't do it...can't kill you all..."

"Rafe!"

Rafe tried to hold on to his brother's voice. There was something important he needed to tell Niko. But the madness swept in and took over his mind.

CHAPTER FOURTEEN

Nine Days Later
SSU Laboratories
Georgia

THEY BROUGHT Rafe back in a straightjacket.

Gabby had orders to stay inside so Rafe couldn't see her, but that didn't stop her from looking out the window of the sprawling plantation house that had been converted first into a CDC lab, and then the SSU's newest research facility. Only a few feet separated the back of the van and the rear door of the building, but even so, the two men in fatigues carrying Rafe could barely control him.

A couple stepped out of the sedan that had followed the van into the parking lot. The man lunged forward as if he wanted to help Rafe, but the woman put a restraining hand on his arm.

Rafe's brother, Niko, and his wife, Jenna. Gabby hadn't met them, but the man's resemblance to Rafe was too strong for him to be anyone else. Watching the way Jenna comforted Niko, a lick of jealousy flared to life. Gabby wanted that kind of closeness with Rafe. Yet the joy of knowing he was alive was tempered by the knowledge that he'd been subjected to Kaufmann's drugs. If she couldn't find a way to reverse the damage done to Rafe, she had only weeks left before she lost him to the same bloody death that had claimed Nate and the others.

She closed her eyes against a sharp wave of grief and fear. Her fingers snuck into her lab coat's pocket and stroked the worn fur of her valentine teddy bear. From the description Niko had given Ryker, Rafe sounded like he was just entering Level 3. Gabby crossed her arms tightly over her chest. Even when they'd thought Rafe and his team dead, Ryker had asked her to continue working on a way to counteract the effects of Kaufmann's program. He'd assumed that Kaufmann had relocated his lab and that there would be other men to rehabilitate once the SSU located the facility.

That's how Gabby had ended up here in Georgia, in this beautiful Victorian mansion with a team of scientists at her disposal. They'd made progress. She thought the drugs they'd come up with would halt the progression from Level 3 to Level 4, but since they'd lacked subjects to test the drugs on, she wasn't certain.

She believed that the only way to completely reverse the damage done was to directly counteract the drugs Dr. Nevsky had created. Those were the elements so unfamiliar that her team, like Kaufmann's, had had little success in replicating them, let alone creating counteragents.

Which left her terrified that even if Kai Paterson returned with the microchip containing Dr. Nevsky's notes, it might be too late for Rafe.

It would be better to be dead than subject to Kaufmann's experiments, wouldn't you say?

She gritted her teeth and pushed Ryker's comment to the back of her mind where it belonged. As long as Rafe was alive, she'd cling to the hope that she could find a way to return him to the man he'd once been.

She refused to accept anything else.

GABBY STOOD in the observation room watching Rafe through the one-way glass. The sob that had been sitting hot and heavy in her throat broke free, echoing through the empty room. She pushed the back of her hand against her mouth, trying to muffle it. Ryker had warned her what to expect, but still, it was so much harder to see Rafe like this than she'd expected.

Impossible to think only like a doctor instead of a woman. A lover.

She bit her lip. One night. That's all they'd had together, but it had been enough. Her heart belonged to Rafe.

The man in the cell below only vaguely resembled the man she'd fallen in love with. He had the same dark hair and eyes, but steroids had added layers of bulky muscle to his previously lean frame.

Gone were Rafe's amusement and love of life. Instead, this Rafe was constantly angry. In pain. His keen intelligence had dimmed until his eyes held only an animal's cunning. For Rafe, the world had narrowed to survival, with his mind the equivalent of an ape's.

Pain wrapped around her heart and squeezed. The world darkened momentarily and she staggered, feeling another piece of her soul shatter. She raised a hand palm out and caught herself against the window.

Rafe must have heard the impact, for he stopped his pacing and looked up. Even though she knew he couldn't see through the special glass, she shivered under the hatred in his glare. Her stomach rolled over and Gabby was profoundly grateful that she hadn't eaten anything that day. Vomiting all over the floor when she wasn't even supposed to be here would be a perfectly horrible way to end the day.

But she'd had to see for herself how far down the scale he'd progressed. She'd needed to reassure herself that he had not advanced past Level 3. The drugs her team had created didn't work on the later levels, only Level 3 and earlier.

She was just grateful Nate Ngoro had still been at Level 3 when he'd arrived at the SSU. Between him and the others, her team had samples from Levels 3, 4, and 5, giving them crucial data. Today they'd been notified that Kai Paterson had succeeded in retrieving Nevsky's microchip. With those notes added to her own data, she felt certain, given enough time, they could heal Rafe and return him to the man he once was.

The key element, of course, was time. She touched her forehead to the cool glass. *Please, let us succeed.*

As her stomach settled and she met Rafe's eyes again through the glass, she came to the realization that this wasn't enough. She couldn't simply stand up here watching Rafe as if she were just one more scientist studying him.

This was the man she'd made passionate love to. Who had touched a part of her soul that no other man had even recognized. She loved him. Had worried over him from the moment he left her bed.

She owed him so much more than just working to find a cure. He needed human contact.

Since he'd been brought in three days ago, Rafe had supposedly calmed down slightly. Enough that Niko had been allowed a face-to-face session with Rafe. They'd brought the brothers together in a small holding room yesterday afternoon, and Rafe had nearly broken his restraints in an attempt to kill Niko. Then, once Niko was gone, Rafe had beat his head against the wall, crying.

Several other visitors had been brought to see Rafe over the next few days, but none of them had been allowed in the same room with him. They'd all appeared on the other side of reinforced glass.

And Rafe had responded in exactly the same way.

Gabby didn't even want to imagine the type of pain Kaufmann had inflicted in order to turn Rafe against his brother and best friend. She rubbed her arms to ward off a sudden chill. Had Kaufmann known about Rafe's connection to her? Even if he'd tortured Rafe and his teammates, would Kaufmann have asked the right questions to learn about her relationship with Rafe? Possible, but unlikely.

A slow bud of hope unfurled inside her. What if she was the one person in his life Rafe hadn't been brainwashed against? The one person he wouldn't attack?

Still...the scientist in her warned that she had to be practical.

Was she willing to risk her life on a slim possibility? Yes. Would the rest of the team allow her to risk her safety? She shook her head, knowing all too well that Ryker would be the most opposed to putting her in danger. But the despair lurking behind Rafe's eyes broke her heart.

She *had* to find a way to get closer to him. She wanted Rafe to see her. To hear her. Even if it was through the barrier of a window, she needed to let him know he wasn't alone.

THE NEXT WEEK, Gabby asked the head of Rafe's psychotherapy team for permission to communicate with him through the two-way observation glass.

"I'm sorry," Dr. Winthrop said in his haughty voice. "But I cannot authorize that. It takes Andros hours to calm down after his rages and then more hours to earn back his trust again."

Knowing she wouldn't find any sympathy from the man, Gabby had pleaded with one of the other doctors on the psychiatric team. "Please, just show him my photo. All the other people he's been faced with from his past have been male. Maybe he won't react so aggressively toward a female." Even though Dr. Kaufmann had employed several women at his lab, Gabby had sensed a degree of chauvinism. It was likely

Kaufmann never considered brainwashing Rafe against the females in his life.

"Think of what it would mean if Rafe doesn't have a violent reaction to me," Gabby had added. "I could help him in a way no one else can."

The woman had given Gabby a look that bordered on pity, but nodded her head in agreement. "If he has an extended period of calm, we might consider showing him your photo."

Two days later, the psychotherapy team showed Rafe Gabby's picture, while Gabby watched through a one-way observation window with her fingers crossed. But when Rafe saw her picture, he growled and snapped at the photo. Shouted, "Bad woman. Kill."

Gabby hadn't been able to control her flinch, even though Rafe hadn't posed a physical danger to her. The therapist had tried to calm Rafe down, but left when it became clear he was ignoring her. Despite the disappointment swamping her, Gabby had continued to watch Rafe as her mind had tried to come to terms with the fact that he'd been programmed to kill her.

After a few minutes alone, Rafe's expression had turned from aggression to confusion. Then he'd grimaced in pain, put his hands to his head and squeezed his eyes shut. He'd started rocking back and forth, mouthing, "No. No."

Gabby's eyes had filled with tears and the weight of Rafe's pain had threatened to crush her heart until she couldn't breathe. It had taken fifteen minutes before Rafe had calmed down, but Gabby had hovered on the verge of tears for hours afterward.

The incident had only made Gabby more determined than ever to help Rafe. She examined his blood samples, looking for any nuances that would help her fine-tune the drug formula and stop his deterioration.

Because Kai had done work on the original formula while undercover at Dr. Nevsky's lab, he'd been made co-team leader with her. Now recovered from the poison he'd been exposed to at

Dr. Ivanov's lab, Kai had taken charge of reviewing the data the tech team had painstakingly retrieved from the encoded microchip so that Gabby could incorporate it into her research.

A week after Rafe had reacted so aggressively to her picture, Gabby's team administered the adjusted formula to him. Finally, they saw the results they'd been hoping for. They were ninety-nine percent certain they'd managed to at least temporarily halt his slide toward Level 4.

In fact, Gabby believed Rafe's intelligence had improved slightly. He appeared more alert when performing the tasks his cognitive therapists requested of him. The next day, Rafe had been shown Gabby's photo again. His only reaction had been a clenched jaw and hands that opened and closed into fists.

Yesterday, the curtain had been pulled back on the special observation window, allowing Rafe to see Gabby. He'd started, then stared at her with narrowed eyes. The medical team's sensors had reported accelerated breathing, but after a few minutes of intense scrutiny, Rafe had turned his back and walked away, leaving Gabby strangely bereft. Yet more determined than ever to be allowed into Rafe's room with him. To be the one friendly face among the strangers treating him.

Mindful of her safety, Gabby had waited with barely leashed impatience as she repeated the through-the-glass encounter several times a day for three days. Until finally the psychiatric team agreed that it appeared safe for Gabby to attempt a face-to-face meeting.

Gabby took a deep breath. Today it was time to show Rafe he wasn't alone.

"Are you sure about this, Gabby?" Kai asked. "Rafe may have regained enough cognition to be playing dumb in hopes of luring you inside."

"I'm sure." She patted the oversized pocket of her cardigan. "I've got the tranquilizer gun and the security team will be right outside in case something goes wrong. But the majority of his psychiatric team agrees that he's starved for contact with a human being who is not part of his medical team." Just thinking about how long it had been since Rafe had a normal, casual relationship with another person made Gabby's voice wobble on the verge of tears. Rafe had been such a gregarious man before his capture. She imagined the social isolation was as much a punishment as the physical torture he'd endured.

She firmed her voice, refusing to let her emotions make her appear weak to Kai. That was the surest way to have him ask Ryker to pull her off the project for lack of objectivity. And she needed to do this.

"He needs a friend. Hopefully, he's calmed down enough that he'll remember the positive time he spent with me, rather than the punishment Kaufmann inflicted on him. If I'm right, my scent should help break through any lingering conditioning." She'd overdosed herself with the cherry vanilla body lotion she'd been wearing the night they made love.

As they reached the door to Rafe's room, her heart fluttered in her throat. She'd insisted on seeing Rafe here, in the environment that was becoming his home, instead of in the more sterile holding room where he'd met Niko. And she'd chosen the middle of the night so his biorhythm would be slower.

God, she was scared. What if Rafe ignored her? That would almost be worse than if he attacked her.

"Ready? Keep your hand on the tranquilizer gun. There was a mild sedative in his dinner, so he should remain calm. There's also a restraint tying Rafe's leg to the bed, so keep at the distance we discussed and he won't be able to reach you. We'll be standing right outside. If we see or hear anything that indicates you're being threatened, we're pulling you out." Kai had four security guards with him, all armed with tranquilizer guns and restraints.

Gabby nodded. "I'm ready."

One of the security guards opened the door and let Gabby inside.

THE CHIME at the entrance to his room woke Rafe from a deep sleep.

Danger!

Rafe bolted from his bed and looked around wildly. His heart beat triple time as he tried to locate the threat he'd been expecting for days.

He checked the room once. Twice.

No one was there. The drapes were closed against the window. Everything appeared as he'd left it before sleep claimed him.

The lights overhead turned on, momentarily blinding him and sending him into a panic as he sensed someone enter the room. He held himself still, trembling on the edge of panic and aggression, while his eyes adjusted to the light.

A woman stood with her back pressed against the door, one hand in the pocket of her blue sweater. She stared at him with uncertainty. "Hi, Rafe."

He flinched. Her voice was soft, familiar. It filled him with a need to get closer. To hear her speak again. He stepped forward, his heart beating too fast.

"Do you remember me?" she asked.

His eyes flew to her face. Memory stirred. Her face... Yes. He remembered her face. Her smile.

Pain lanced through his head. *"If you ever meet this woman, kill her,"* the Voice ordered, showing Rafe a photograph. *"She is a traitor to this lab. If she catches you the pain will be unimaginable. To survive, you must kill her."*

Rafe trembled. The people holding him in this new location had told him the woman was not his enemy. She was a friend. The new white coats had also shown him her photograph, watching for his reaction.

Friend. Enemy. He hadn't known what to believe. So he'd forced himself to stay still, which seemed to please the white coats.

The next day the woman had appeared at his window. Again he'd heard the Voice in his head. *"Kill her."* But the new white coats were trying to help Rafe and they insisted the woman was a friend. He'd struggled to find the truth, but the pain in his head had been too much. The need to kill had started to grow. Yet the woman had been on the other side of the glass, out of his immediate reach. Instead of breaking the glass and attacking her, which might make these white coats abandon their gentler ways and hurt him, Rafe had turned his back and walked away.

But now she was here. And there were no white coats in the room. The voice inside his head telling him she was a friend became drowned out by the Voice. *"Kill her!"*

Rafe lunged toward the woman. The strap that had been fastened around his ankle broke with the force of his movement.

With her back already to the door, there was nowhere for the woman to hide. No chance she could escape him. He saw her hand start to pull something out of her pocket, but he slammed his body against hers, trapping her hand where it was.

Snarling, he wrapped his fingers around her neck and squeezed.

That's right, the Voice whispered.

The woman's squeak of alarm turned into a choked-off gasp. Her fingers clawed at his hands. Her hazel eyes widened in fear, but there was something else there, too. Something that made him hesitate and lessen the pressure.

"Rafe, please don't kill me," she gasped. "I'm Gabby. Remember? You helped me escape from Kaufmann. We m-made l-love the night before you left." Her eyes pleaded with him to remember. To have mercy.

Rafe shook his head. Those eyes. They...shouldn't...fear him. There was something wrong with her being afraid. It brought the memory of frightened eyes. Of him putting his arms around her to soothe away her tears.

"Rafe, I won't hurt you," she whispered. "I'm your friend. Your...lover."

Kill her, the Voice said inside his head. *She's lying. Just as she lied to you before. She told you to obey Kaufmann and the pain would go away. It got worse, instead. Punish her. She'll bring pain. Spill her blood onto your hands. Then you'll be safe.*

Rafe's fingers tightened again on her throat.

Tears leaked out of her eyes, wetting his hands. "I won't ever hurt you," the woman repeated. "I love you."

Love. He knew what that word meant. Agony. Electric shock. Cold so pervasive he couldn't think. Painful convulsions.

Yes, the men in white coats had taught him all about love.

The woman went slack in his hands. He continued to squeeze, waiting for the life to drain, when a scent barreled through his rage.

He paused. Sniffed. Moved his nose to the neck of the woman.

The scent was on her skin. He inhaled deeply and felt the red haze of rage recede, replaced by a curious calm that somehow silenced the voices. Instead, he heard soft laughter. Breathless moans of excitement. A sigh of bone-deep satisfaction.

The Voice tried to drown out the memories, making Rafe's head ache. But when he inhaled again, drawing the scent into his body, the voices went away.

Pain lanced through his head, followed by a strange sense of peace. This woman was important to him. Good. The Voice was wrong. Killing her would be wrong. He was supposed to protect her.

The new white coats were right. This woman was a friend.

He released her neck and lifted her limp body into his arms, tucking her face up near his shoulder and lowering his head slightly so he was closer to the special scent.

He carried her to his bed and set her gently on top of the covers.

The door at his back burst open. Pinpricks of pain blossomed along his back and upper thighs. He roared and turned around.

Soldiers rushed into the room. He knew what to do with soldiers.

Take them down.

He lunged toward them so fast, he saw surprise in their eyes. He grabbed the nearest man by his throat and flung him against the wall. Took down the next two. Felt more pinpricks of pain and looked down to see darts sticking out of his chest.

"We've got her."

"Get her out of here."

A man hurried to the door, the woman in his arms.

"No. Mine!" Rafe bellowed, trying to reach him. The woman was his to protect. But there were three men in his way. By the time he fought his way closer to the door, the man carrying the woman had disappeared.

Rafe lost it. He grabbed a chair and swung it into the men blocking him, then threw the chair against the large window. He overturned his bed and shoved it at the next wave of men, knocking them all down.

"Someone fucking restrain him, already!"

"What the hell do you expect us to do? The drugs aren't working. And Christ, he's strong as Superman even with the damn sedative in his supper. No wonder the restraint holding him to the bed failed."

He fought, but the drugs slowed him down.

Rafe kicked one of the men so he fell against the leader. They collapsed to the floor. Rafe raced toward the door. He needed to find the woman. To make sure she was okay. But three steps from the door he staggered, then fell to his knees as the drugs took effect.

"No!" he protested. He struggled back to his feet, but gravity slammed him face down on the floor.

He felt a boot on the small of his back and the nose of a rifle at the base of his skull. "Sorry, Rafe buddy," a vaguely familiar voice said. "This really is for your own good."

Cold plastic restraints snapped around his wrists, but all Rafe could manage was an enraged growl.

"This proves my point," a haughty male voice sneered. "He's an animal."

No, Rafe thought hazily as the drugs dragged him under. He *wasn't* an animal. He was still human. Just...different...

CHAPTER FIFTEEN

Later That Morning
Dr. Kaufmann's Lab
Blue Ridge Mountains

DR. KAUFMANN WATCHED his office door close behind the two Russian scientists who had worked at a lab run by Dr. Nevsky's Russian colleague, Dr. Ivanov. Arrogant bastards. They pretended not to speak very good English unless it suited them. Why they had a problem with him, he didn't understand. They should be grateful they weren't rotting in a Russian jail. But did they thank him for giving them the opportunity to continue their work?

No.

Instead, they stared down their aristocratic noses at him and informed him that Dr. Ivanov's program had been much more advanced than Kaufmann's program, so their talents were wasted here.

Worse, the machine that could read the microchip Jamieson's man Tonelli had brought out of Russia had finally arrived. The chip held notes about an experiment to test how

Ivanov's subjects fared in arctic temperatures. Not Nevsky's research.

Which meant that Kaufmann still didn't have the critical formula he needed to create more of Nevsky's drugs.

He shoved the report away from him and surged to his feet. He needed Nevsky's formula. His supply of the drugs that he'd stolen from Nevsky's lab was almost gone. Only with a regular series of injections of the drugs did the mind control retain its grip on the subjects. He'd tried rationing the drugs for one or two batches of subjects, but the weaker dosages had failed to achieve the desired results.

Rafe Andros had received the full dosage of the drug, yet Kaufmann didn't know if the mental block his team had created would succeed in preventing Andros from remembering details about the program. Kaufmann paced around his office, unable to sit still. According to Jamieson, not only had the SSU retrieved Andros, but Dr. Montague was working with the SSU to reverse the work done on Andros.

Kaufmann knew that Dr. Montague had stolen notes and samples before she left. There was no denying her brilliance, but even she didn't have a chance of fully reverse engineering the drugs without Nevsky's data. Unfortunately, since the microchip didn't contain Nevsky's notes, the chances of the SSU having access to the real microchip were high. If true, then Dr. Montague might succeed in creating a formula that would not only fix Andros, but all of Kaufmann's subjects.

That outcome was unacceptable. His credibility relied on the fact that once his teams of altered men were in place, no one could divert them from their mission.

He needed both Andros and Dr. Montague eliminated. But not before Dr. Montague was forced to return and fix the issue with the men's rages.

Because he very much doubted that Jamieson was ever going to be able to deliver Nevsky's microchip to him.

The Next Day
SSU Laboratories
Georgia

"Dr. Montague should be removed from the program," Dr. Winthrop insisted, scowling at the video screen showing Ryker in his Washington, D.C. office.

Gabby ignored him, while Kai sat back, crossed his arms over his chest and remained silent.

"Her reckless action ended in disaster. Patient Andros is now non-responsive. Truly little more than an animal." Dr. Winthrop shot Gabby a look that was clearly meant to make her quiver in her shoes and slink away.

"Sir, look at this section of video," she croaked. Her voice was hoarse and the words hurt coming out of her bruised throat. Rafe had nearly crushed her windpipe yesterday, but she was determined not to let Dr. Winthrop run her off.

She pressed the DVD player's remote control and an image of Rafe carrying her to his bed played across the screen. "See that?" she asked Ryker. "Look at his face. Notice how his expression changes. It goes from confusion, to something almost protective. Then here," she pointed to Rafe trying to fight through the security team. "He's trying to get to me. Listen to what he says. 'Mine.'"

She played the clip twice more before shutting the DVD off. "I got through to him, sir," Gabby insisted. "Just as I speculated, I believe my scent broke through his conditioning. The video clearly shows him pressing his nose to my neck, then calming."

Beside her, Dr. Winthrop snorted in derision. "Andros nearly killed you," he pointed out. "He was too enraged to notice any such thing. What Andros needs is to be left alone. He's like a wild animal. Dangerous to anyone who approaches him. We'll have to keep him tranquilized during all future sample extraction until he's calmed down. I consider him too dangerous to allow his cognitive team or the physical therapists in the same room with him. Until you have a formula to eradicate his rage, he's just too much of a threat."

Kai's eyes narrowed in speculation as he replayed the DVD.

Gabby turned her body toward Ryker. "Sir, I disagree. Rafe needs more human contact, not less. How else is he ever going to accept that his friends and family aren't the threats his conditioning claimed? What's more," she shot Dr. Winthrop a glare, "he needs to be treated with kindness and respect. Not called an animal, and particularly not when he can hear it!"

She paused and took a long sip of hot tea with honey to soothe her throat.

"I believe we can safely build up his tolerance to visitors. I'm not proposing that I go inside Rafe's room again just yet. What I want is five minutes a day with him. Five minutes on the other side of the window, while the cherry vanilla scent from my body lotion is piped into his room." God, how embarrassing. Everyone in the meeting knew the scent was a possible trigger because she'd been wearing it when she made love to Rafe.

Hoping none of the men noticed the way her cheeks heated, Gabby leaned forward and braced her hands on the surface of the conference room table.

"Let's give Rafe a chance to get desensitized to my presence," she suggested. "You've seen the follow-up video. He's been calm since he woke up from the tranquilizer." Calm only because he'd still been fighting off the heavy dose of sedative. Yet Gabby had seen on the video the sheer panic on Rafe's face when he'd realized he was fully restrained on his bed.

Not for the first time, she wished Dr. Lydia Tredmath wasn't out on maternity leave. Gabby had met the head of the SSU's PTSD unit right after her arrival at the compound in Oregon, and she'd found the woman both knowledgeable and compassionate.

Dr. Winthrop was on loan from the local Veterans Affairs hospital, but Gabby found his knowledge out-of-date and his compassion non-existent. She wanted him removed from the program altogether.

"Perhaps later, once he has his temper under control," Dr. Winthrop scoffed. "Right now, he needs to be isolated. He needs to know that acts of violence won't be tolerated."

Gabby gritted her teeth and took a deep, calming breath before answering. "Dr. Winthrop, Rafe's bursts of temper are not something he has control over. They are a direct result of the chemicals he's been given. Chemicals that are deeply integrated into his system. Until we find an effective counteragent, he will continue to go into rages." Even then, she didn't know if they could completely scrub Rafe's system. The new formula Kaufmann had used on Rafe had been absorbed into his system quicker, making the chemicals bond more deeply than with Nate. She'd tweaked her drugs since they'd given the first batch to Rafe, but each new formula meant using Rafe as a guinea pig. Testing her chemicals against Rafe's blood and tissue samples didn't necessarily translate into the reaction she wanted when injected into his system.

Which was why the sedative used in Rafe's food hadn't kept him calm. Blood samples taken after the attack had shown that one of the compounds from Kaufmann's drug had unexpectedly helped Rafe's body metabolize the sedative much more rapidly than expected.

She hated not knowing what side effects Rafe might experience, but given the fast deterioration of Kaufmann's subjects, they didn't have any choice but to give Rafe each new formula as soon as she created it and hope for the best.

"Kai, what's your opinion?" Ryker asked.

Kai's unusual amber eyes touched briefly on first Dr. Winthrop, then Gabby. As usual, she couldn't tell what he was thinking. No wonder Ryker had used him for undercover work.

But one thing she was certain of, Kai loved Rafe like a brother. He'd forgiven Rafe for nearly killing him a few weeks ago because he knew Rafe had acted under orders he couldn't disobey. Kai's story of how Rafe had attacked him in the Amazon jungle still gave Gabby chills, yet it didn't stop the man from working his butt off to save Rafe.

After Niko, Gabby knew that Kai was one of Rafe's closest friends. A part of her felt guilty because she'd been the first to go face-to-face with Rafe instead of Kai. Yet Rafe continued to react more aggressively toward men than women.

She just hoped Kai agreed that Dr. Winthrop was off base in his assessment of Rafe. She desperately wanted to open her mouth and make further points to her argument, but she sensed that would only make her appear desperate. So she waited for Kai to speak, forcing herself to breathe normally.

Kai switched the video to a shot of Rafe in his room earlier that morning. "What's Rafe holding?"

Gabby leaned forward. Rafe sat on his bed, clutching something to his chest as he rocked slowly back and forth. "I think..." She slanted her head to the side and squinted. "Um, I think that's the stuffed animal he gave me the morning he left. I...ah...had it in my pocket as a good luck token and it must have fallen out when he picked me up. I've been wondering where I dropped it." Watching Rafe cradle the teddy bear like it was precious to him had Gabby biting her lip to hold back tears.

"I think we should give Gabby's idea a shot," Kai finally said.

Yes!

"That's—" Winthrop began.

"I agree with Kai and Gabby," Ryker interrupted. "Rafe needs to get reacquainted with his friends. The ties to a lover are both physical and mental, so Gabby has a stronger chance of being accepted by him."

"Sir, I must protest! As head of the psychiatric team, I think you're making a grave mistake." Dr. Winthrop pushed past Gabby so he was closer to the video camera, as if the illusion of proximity would give him more clout with Ryker.

"Kai, work with Gabby to set up a viewing as soon as possible," Ryker said, looking past Dr. Winthrop. "Kai, you and Gabby are dismissed. Dr. Winthrop, please stay."

Gabby wanted to skip out of the room. Whether it was the victory over that pompous ass, Winthrop, or just the thought that she'd get to see Rafe again, she didn't know.

"Gabby, you know this might backfire," Kai warned as they walked down the hall.

"I know." Then she shook her head. "But I won't give up. He needs us, Kai. You, me, Niko and Jenna. He needs friends, not just scientists. If he reacts violently, then we'll back off for a few days and try again."

Kai shot her a speculative look. Then he smiled. "Rafe's damn lucky to have you on his side."

Gabby thought that may have been the nicest thing anyone had ever said to her.

GABBY FELT like she was six again, heading up the sidewalk to the school door on the first day of kindergarten. Butterflies danced in her stomach and her mouth was so dry she thought she could drink gallons of water and never feel hydrated.

But instead of the faded brick of her elementary school, Gabby stood in front of the observation window at Rafe's room. The drapes were closed, shielding Rafe from seeing her. But the security monitor to the left of the door showed his reaction to the scent of cherry vanilla that had been flooding his room for the past ten minutes.

He'd gone on alert when they'd started piping in the new smell. His head had swiveled, checking the entrance and potential hiding places for signs he wasn't alone. He'd paced around the room. At first he'd seemed agitated, then he'd seemed confused.

Finally, he'd sunk into an armchair and put his head in his

hands. She wished she knew if he had a headache, or if he was trying to block out her scent.

But this seemed as good a time as any to reveal her presence.

She nodded. Kai, who stood out of Rafe's line of sight in front of the security monitor, gave her a thumbs up and pushed the button to open the drapes.

Gabby had to force herself to appear relaxed despite her nerves. She'd dressed carefully for this, as if it was their first date. Because it was important that she trigger good memories in him tonight, she'd almost decided to wear her robe, since that's what she'd had on the night they'd made love. But in the end she'd gone with a simple t-shirt and jeans.

Rafe's head raised as the drapes swooshed open. When he noticed her, he surged to his feet. His eyes narrowed like a hunter spotting its prey and he took one aggressive step toward her. Then he stopped and his hands pressed against the sides of his head. She thought she heard him growl, although he was a bit too far away from the mic on his side of the window for her to be certain.

"Rafe, are you in pain?" This wasn't how she'd wanted to open this meeting, but from the way Rafe was shaking his head back and forth, and from the tension screaming from his taut body, something was wrong.

"Rafe, does your head hurt?" He understood language—the cognitive specialists had confirmed that. And they believed his brain was starting to process more complex commands even though his speech remained simplistic.

"Hurt. No hurt. G...G... Hurt. No hurt...G...Ga..." He lifted his head and met her gaze.

God, the torment in his eyes! It took all her control not to cry out or show Rafe how much his pain upset her.

She signaled for Kai to shut off the mic from her side and moved out of Rafe's view. "Hurt, no hurt? Kai, he could be experiencing some sort of intermittent pain. Should we abort?"

"No hurt, G-Gab—!" Rafe's anguished cry drew Gabby back to the window in time to see him charging toward her. She couldn't stop herself from backing up a step. But then she realized he was panicked, not violent, and she held her ground.

When he saw she was back, he stopped running. Instead, he walked almost tentatively toward the window. "No hurt...G-Gabby," he said.

Tears sprang to her eyes and her knees threatened to give out. He remembered her! She signaled for Kai to turn on her mic. "That's right, Rafe. My name is Gabby. I won't hurt you."

He shook his head and his mouth firmed into a stubborn line as he poked himself in the chest. "Me...no hurt..." He pointed to her. "No hurt Gab-by." He reached out and pressed his palm against the window with such a look of wary hopefulness it broke her heart.

Before he lost the ability to fully communicate, Rafe had told Niko that Kaufmann had tried to brainwash Rafe into thinking his family and friends were enemies. Yet only a month out from any contact with Kaufmann and his team, Rafe was already reaching for her without rage.

She mirrored his gesture, pressing her palm to the cold glass opposite his. Wanting so desperately to go into his room and feel his skin warm and alive against hers, yet knowing she didn't dare risk it. Not yet.

But soon, she promised herself. Very soon.

His eyes searched hers almost desperately and although she didn't see full recognition from him, there was an alertness that let her know some memory beside her name had punched through whatever noise filled his head.

"Rafe, do you remember who I am? Gabby Montague. I'm one of the doctors who was working on your teammate, Nate."

Rafe's eyes widened and he leapt back from the window in fear. "White...coat... No!" He slammed the sides of his fists against his temples, then dropped to his knees.

"Rafe!" Gabby shot a terrified look toward Kai. "What's going on?"

"No...hurts...white coat...hurts. Go 'way!" Rafe had his arms around his chest now, hunched over and rocking in pain.

Gabby signaled for Kai to close the drapes and shut off the mic. She joined him at the monitor, watching as Rafe collapsed into a fetal position. Oh, God, he was in such pain. Why had she thought this would be a good idea?

He's so alone.

Right.

"It was my mentioning that I'm a doctor that triggered his panic, wasn't it," she said quietly.

"Yeah, I think so." Kai put a comforting hand on her shoulder. "Don't beat yourself up. We're all new at this, Gabby. We're going to make mistakes. Look." He nodded toward the monitor. "He's calming down. Next time we'll be more careful."

She nodded, appreciating the way he said "we" when he could have heaped the blame on her. Then it struck her what else he'd said.

She swung her head around. "Next time? You mean—?"

"Yeah." His eyes warmed. "Rafe remembered your name. And he was the calmest he's been when faced with someone from his past. I'm definitely going to recommend to Ryker that we keep going."

"Thank you." She met his gaze and Kai nodded in understanding, letting her know that he wanted to help Rafe as much as she did. Would that apply to defying Ryker if he prohibited her from seeing Rafe? Yes, she suspected Kai would fight for her visits.

Now she only had to deal with Dr. Winthrop.

"Oh, by the way," Kai added. "Ryker sent Dr. Winthrop back to the VA hospital. It's just you and me in charge until he can find a replacement he trusts."

Gabby let her lips curl in just the hint of a satisfied smile. Anything more would be unprofessional.

But she really wanted to pump her fist in the air in victory.

"Come on," Kai said. "The cafeteria is still open. I'll buy you a cup of coffee."

Gabby took one last look at Rafe curled on the floor. "You know," she said slowly as they turned to leave. "It might be worth a shot to have an expert on autism work with him for a while. There's a woman I know. She's very knowledgeable and highly compassionate."

Kai nodded. "Makes sense to me. Let's ask Ryker for the go-ahead."

CHAPTER SIXTEEN

GABBY STARED at the data on her computer screen. Data that had been pulled from Dr. Nevsky's microchip. She didn't have to check her personal notes to confirm that this was the formula for Agent Styx. She had it memorized.

She sucked in a shocked breath and bit her lip. From what she'd been told about Dr. Nevsky's program, and what she'd heard about the components of the drugs Kaufmann had stolen from his deceased boss, she'd suspected Nevsky of either being directly involved with the development of Agent Styx or having access to the formula. But still, having the connection confirmed tilted her world sideways.

In addition to containing the formula for Agent Styx, this section of notes detailed the progression of the drug's development. Proving that Nevsky had been the primary researcher involved in creating Agent Styx.

He was responsible for her father's rages. And for her father's death.

She couldn't prove that her parents had been run off the road, but she knew in her heart that they'd been murdered. Killed to silence her father and stop his investigation into Agent Styx. The notes he'd left with the samples had described his search for other victims of Agent Styx and his attempt to locate the men who'd created the fatal chemical.

Too bad Nevsky was dead. She'd like to give him a dose of Kaufmann's formula. See how he liked being turned into a beast for the sake of science.

She chewed her lip. Nevsky might be dead, but someone had authorized his research. Gabby wanted that person held accountable. In case something happened to her, she needed to share the Agent Styx connection with someone.

Ryker? Right now, he was the only one she'd trust with the information. If anyone could find out who was responsible for letting Nevsky continue his work with Agent Styx, it was her boss. The SSU staff called Ryker a miracle worker, and had plenty of stories to back it up.

Besides, she'd heard that Ryker had served in Vietnam. He might know of the program.

She chewed her bottom lip. Her father had suspected a group of high-level military and intelligence officials in the initial cover-up of the dangers of Agent Styx. She had a list of suspects he'd put together, but she'd failed to crack the code. Not knowing who to trust in government, she'd decided that investigating the suspects was beyond her ability. So she'd devoted herself to mitigating the lingering side effects experienced by vets exposed to Agent Styx.

She shivered. Of course, at the time she'd also believed Agent Styx was no longer being used. If she'd found someone she trusted back then, someone in power who believed her and had been able to crack the code, would an investigation have been started? Was it possible the program could have been stopped before Nevsky further refined the drug?

Under that scenario, Kaufmann would never have gotten his hands on the samples he'd used to create his formula. Rafe would never have been turned into a beast.

And if she was going to dwell on what-ifs and might-have-beens, she might as well climb back into bed for all the use she'd be.

There was no way to know if she could have changed events. No crystal ball to counteract this pinch of fear inside her heart that said maybe she'd played a part in Rafe's suffering.

Gabby sucked in air, then let it out slowly. There were more important things to worry about than her potential guilt. She had to deal with facts. The reality of today.

Nevsky had continued to use Agent Styx. Even with all of his modifications over the years, he'd still been unable and unwilling to get rid of the primary side effect—murderous rage. He hadn't sought a cure for the rage because he'd believed that eventually he'd find a formula to allow him to control the rages in his subjects. Order them to unleash their anger only against chosen targets.

He'd come close. Too close.

And then Kaufmann had played with the formula. Gabby shook her head. Several of Kaufmann's alterations had wiped out years of Nevsky's progress, resulting in a quicker mental deterioration than with Nevsky's subjects.

She had to hope and pray that the counteragent she'd created from Nevsky's notes would bring Rafe's mind back before it was too late. She'd lost her father because of Agent Styx. She would *not* lose Rafe because Kaufmann had continued Nevsky's work.

CHAPTER SEVENTEEN

One Week Later
SSU Laboratories
Georgia

RAFE GLANCED at the chart on the wall, then the clock. Yes, the time matched the symbol next to the woman's picture. One of the nice doctors had created the chart for him. She had a soft voice and calming eyes. But not as soothing as his woman. Gabby.

A doctor.

That had scared him, at first. But not now. He'd learned that the doctors here didn't yell at him to kill. They didn't punish him with pain. They poked and prodded and took their samples, but then the discomfort was over.

And Gabby said each sample helped her. Rafe wanted to help Gabby. Partly because he wanted to get better. To get his mind back. But mostly because making Gabby happy made him feel warm inside.

He picked up the little stuffed bear with the bright red heart on it. He didn't remember much of Before. Mostly just bright fragments of color and sound, gone before they made sense. He'd seen flashes of the bear in those brief images. The bear, and Gabby. Always Gabby.

He bent his head and pressed his forehead to the bear's soft fur. The presence of Before was a constant pressure against the barrier in his mind. The barrier created by the bad doctors. Sometimes the pressure to remember Before built up until it became so strong, he thought he'd burst.

That was when he lost control and broke things until the pressure eased and he could breathe again.

Tonight, though, the pressure was small. Holding the bear helped. Knowing it belonged to Gabby soothed him and kept him from getting too angry when she had to leave him alone. But nothing made him feel safe like seeing her for himself.

He checked the clock again and paced restlessly around the room, impatient for the chime to signal that she was on the other side of the glass. Waited for the sweet smell that would announce her arrival, even though the glass prevented him from smelling her skin.

The room was silent except for the sound of his breathing and the scrape of his feet on the carpet. The people who watched him had brought him music and shown him how to work the player, but the sounds only increased the pressure in his head. Made him angrier because he couldn't remember what he had been or what had been important to him.

The white coats with their instruments of pain had destroyed him.

Rafe fought to keep the rage from growing. It would scare Gabby if he lost control and he wouldn't be able to stand it if he hurt her again.

The sweet scent he didn't know the name of tickled his nose. He inhaled and looked toward the drapes. The chime sounded and the heavy fabric opened, revealing Gabby on the other side.

Rafe's anger and frustration melted away. He couldn't name what he felt when he saw her. All he knew was that the promise of seeing Gabby eased him through his days.

"Hi Rafe." Her voice came through the speaker, filling him with warmth. "How are you tonight?"

"I. Am. O-kay, Gab-by." He'd worked hard to learn this response to her question. Speaking the words in his head was a struggle. They never came out of his mouth the way he wanted. Yet Gabby rewarded him with a smile.

He moved up to the glass and pressed his hand against it, as he always did. She matched her hand to his.

Rafe frowned. He usually liked this moment. Liked the way it made him feel connected to her. But tonight it wasn't enough. He felt some of the frustration sneak back.

For a long time he stared at their hands, then he lifted his eyes to search her face. She didn't look happy and it stirred some strong emotion he didn't recognize.

"Gab-by sad?"

Her smile wasn't as bright as usual. She hesitated and he sensed a lie coming, but then she shook her head. "I'm just tired, and frustrated that I haven't been able to make better progress at curing you."

Her words made her sadness sound simple, but there were tears in her eyes.

He wanted to wipe her tears away, but when he tried to reach out, the window stopped him. Frustrated, he banged against the glass.

She stepped back.

No. He didn't want her to go! He made a sound of protest. "No sad, Gab-by. Rafe help." His name sounded strange coming out of his mouth.

He looked toward his door, then back to the window. Door. Window. "Gab-by come." He stabbed his thumb against his chest.

"Rafe help Gab-by no sad." He pulled the bear from his pocket. "Bear help Gab-by no sad."

He waited. Not knowing if he'd said the words right. Only knowing that he wanted to touch her. To wipe her tears away and put his arms around her. The instinct to soothe was so powerful, he nearly shook with it.

If only he could touch her, all would be right. But first she had to trust him.

She glanced over to the door. "Rafe, if I come inside, will I be safe?"

He wanted to tell her he would never hurt her. Never.

But he *had* hurt her. Because the voices had been in his head. "No voices," he insisted, tapping his forehead. He didn't know how to explain that the voices ordering him to kill, the voices that caused pain inside his head, those voices now turned silent whenever she was near.

"Gab-by safe."

He met her eyes. He was desperate to touch her, to make her sadness go away, but he was afraid she was too frightened of him. "No scared, Gab-by. No hurt."

She searched his eyes, then gave a strange half smile. "In for a penny, in for a pound," she said. "Let's do it."

She walked over to the door.

Rafe's heart stuttered, then beat wildly. She trusted him!

Trusted. Him.

The door slid open. She stepped inside.

"Rafe." Her voice wobbled and her smile trembled. A tear tracked down her cheek. "I miss you so much," she murmured.

Rafe took a step forward. His vision swam. Another step and he was in front of her. Close enough to smell her sweet scent. To reach out with shaking fingers to brush her tears away.

And Gabby let him touch her. Without flinching. Accepting his comfort.

He handed her the bear and was rewarded with a watery smile. Memories flooded through him. Gabby stroking the bear's fur and looking as sad as she did right now. Gabby crying against his chest. Gabby yelling at him. Gabby with her mouth against his.

Rafe swayed as emotion followed the pictures in his head. Gabby reached out to steady him but his weight was too much for her and he ended up on his knees, his face pressed against the softness of her belly, his arms around her hips.

"Gab—" His vocal chords strained to form the word against a clot of emotion in his throat. "Gab-by. Re-mem-ber. You."

He cried like a little boy, his whole body shaking with his sobs. His arms tightened, pulling her close. Gabby. His lifeline.

But it wasn't long before happy memories of Gabby were replaced by painful visions of captivity. Of things the white coats had made him do despite his fighting them with every ounce of willpower he possessed. There, on his knees, Rafe nearly drowned in remembered shame, fear and pain.

"Shh. Rafe, it's okay." Gabby's hands stroked his hair, the soothing motion quieting some of the chaos brought by the memories. "You're safe. I'm not going to let anyone hurt you. We're going to help you. You're going to get better."

For the first time since he woke up in this room, Rafe felt soul-draining relief. Finally, he truly accepted that he was safe. Gabby was real. Her promises were real. This wasn't another trick to force him to bow to the will of the white coats. This was safety and comfort that wouldn't be yanked away.

Gradually his tears stopped. He continued to hold her, pressing his cheek tightly to her belly, even as his mind shut down, going into a sort of stupor.

"Hey, Rafe. Don't fall asleep on me. Let's get you to bed, okay?"

Gabby's hands nudged him up, so he stood. But he didn't want to let go of her. He kept hold of her hand, and with his other he smoothed her hair back from her face. He stared into hazel eyes damp with tears, but holding such love, he felt warmed to his core.

He traced his finger over her face. Her eyebrows. Nose. Mouth. Cheeks. Brushed away the tears that continued to fall.

Then gave in to an overwhelming instinct. He leaned forward and touched his lips to hers.

Her softness fascinated him. He pressed harder. She made a startled sound deep in her throat and he pulled back. Her eyes shone through new tears. He searched her face for some acknowledgement instinct insisted would be there.

She stepped back. When he reached for her, wanting more of her lips, or at least to hold her, she put up her hand.

"No, Rafe."

Rafe froze. What had he done wrong? "Rafe bad?"

Gabby shook her head. "It's not that." She hugged her arms across her chest. "Rafe, I'm a doctor and right now you're my patient first, my...friend...second. No kissing, okay? Not until you're all better. No hugging, either. We need to keep a professional distance. Do you understand?"

He was supposed to agree with her. It was how they'd trained him. Listen and obey.

But his soul protested. And this time he was free to express what he wanted. "No. Want kiss Gab-by. Want hold Gab-by. Want make Gab-by smile." He nodded his head for emphasis and drilled into her with his eyes. Tried to force her to agree to his demand, like the doctors used to do with him.

The corner of Gabby's mouth quirked up and he felt a spurt of satisfaction. But then she spoke and her words made him angry.

"Rafe, we can't break the rules. I need to have the respect of my team members when I make decisions regarding your treatment. They won't give me that respect if they think my heart is leading me."

Rafe didn't fully understand what she was saying. But he knew for certain she was trying to deny him. He took a step forward and touched his fingers to her lips. "Gab-by wrong. Rafe right."

When she didn't move away from him or yell at him to stop, Rafe got bolder. He reached out and pulled her into his arms, settling her head against his chest. "This right. Gab-by belong here. With Rafe."

Oh, God, she was in so much trouble. He was acting like the man he'd been before, the decisive team leader who wouldn't take no for an answer. Who expected the world to conform to his demands.

And he was correct. It did feel right to be in his arms again. Like coming home.

But professionally, this was a mistake. She should never have stepped through the door. Not that she thought Ryker would remove her from the team, but it set a bad example. Yes, everyone knew that she'd been Rafe's lover. And there was no getting around the fact that Rafe tolerated her presence when he still reacted aggressively toward his brother and Kai.

But there was a huge difference between standing on the other side of the glass, keeping a distance between them that allowed for some degree of objectivity, and standing with her cheek pressed over his heart, reveling in the steady beat that confirmed his body was alive and healthy.

Dammit, she didn't want to keep their relationship professional. Her heart ached for him, greedy for any little sign that the man she loved was returning to her. Soaking up each gesture of kindness like a barren desert drinking in rain. He'd touched her heart when he gave her back the bear that had become so precious to him, simply because he wanted to cheer her up.

Part of her jumped ahead, thinking of ways to convince Ryker and Kai that she should be allowed to continue having personal meetings with Rafe. After all, this was the first time he'd expressed a contrary opinion. It was a sign he was breaking through the brainwashing.

She sighed. Rationalizations wouldn't change the truth. Right now, theirs was a strictly professional relationship. Placing her hands on his waist, she lifted her head and stepped back.

Rafe grabbed her hands. "No!"

She tugged, but he wouldn't let go. It was so typically Rafe, she felt more tears welling up. "Rafe, I have to go. I need to sleep and then get back to work in my lab so I can find the drugs that will make you better. And you need to sleep, too."

Rafe tilted his head to the left, a hint of his characteristic devilment in his eyes. "Kiss Rafe," he insisted, squeezing her hands.

"No. If I kiss you, they might stop me from coming to visit you again." The instant the words left her mouth she knew they'd been the wrong thing to say. The devilment left his eyes, replaced by fear.

"No go!" He tugged her toward the bed.

Oh, no. Did he think to make love to her? Arousal stirred deep in her belly despite this being the wrong time. Everything that happened in this room was recorded. Bad enough that Ryker and Kai would see Rafe's first After kiss. She could not let this continue.

"Rafe, no. Wait." She tried to free her wrist from his grasp, but she couldn't budge him.

He reached the bed. But even as she shifted her weight back to resist moving any further, he used one hand to drag over the armchair until it sat next to the head of the bed. Then he tugged her picture off the evening spot on his daily activity board, and put it on the first line for the morning. Bringing in an autism specialist had been a major milestone. With Rafe's day scheduled out in a way he could easily understand and that allowed him plenty of time to mentally adapt to the next item on his agenda, the violent outbursts when he felt overwhelmed had all but stopped.

Looking entirely too pleased with himself, Rafe settled himself on top of the covers and used his hold on her wrist to make her sit in the armchair.

"Gab-by stay. No white coat stop."

Gabby fought back a laugh. "Ra-afe," she chided. "I can't stay here forever. I have work to do. Work to make you better."

Rafe pouted. Honest to God, the man stuck out his bottom lip just like a little boy. It was so endearing, she wanted to kiss him. Instead, she forced herself to think like a scientist, chalking this up as another sign of his personality returning. Secretly hoping this meant their treatment was working.

"Want Gab-by," Rafe insisted.

Gabby shook her head and sighed, but inside she felt lighter than she had in weeks. "Rafe, I'll stay until you fall asleep, okay? And I promise I'll come back tomorrow. Here, take your bear back."

Rafe accepted the bear, placing it on his chest. "Still want Gab-by stay."

"I can't do that. But wait—" She reached back, pulled the scrunchie from her hair, and slipped the elastic over his wrist. "You hold this for me until I see you again."

She checked the fit to make sure the elastic wouldn't cut off his circulation. Even worn and stretched out, the elastic barely fit around his thick wrist. "Okay?"

Rafe tightened his grip on her hand and put his other hand behind his head. "Rafe no sleep," he said confidently. "Gab-by no go."

Clever, but he'd lose this one. His body had started to reclaim the need for sleep that had been submerged by Kaufmann's drugs. Rafe now averaged about five hours a night up from the one hour he'd slept the first night here. To help the cause along, they fed him a carefully calibrated sedative with his dinner. She figured she had at most half an hour before the drug took him under. Until then, she'd enjoy the warmth of his calloused palm against hers, and treasure each sign that the old Rafe was returning.

CHAPTER EIGHTEEN

GABBY STARED at the blood smear through the microscope. With a sigh, she admitted that the sample on the slide wasn't going to change just because she wanted it to. Damn it, the new formula they'd tried wasn't helping Rafe. It wasn't hurting him, either, but right now she desperately needed a breakthrough. After five days on this regimen, Rafe had regained enough cognition to be able to understand his situation and feel hope.

She refused to be the one who told him he wasn't closer to being fully cured.

The image on the slide blurred and wavered, like a mirage. She blinked several times in succession, and when that didn't sharpen her vision, she swiped a hand across her eyes. To her surprise, her hand came away damp.

A tear trickled down her cheek and fell on top of the microscope.

Stop it! Don't you dare give up.

There had to be a formula that would break the block on Rafe's intelligence. Stopping Kaufmann's steroid-based drugs and applying one of her new formulas to counter Agent Styx had reduced Rafe's rages. Some of his cognitive skills had returned.

He spoke now in full sentences, although at an elementary school level. Made his own decisions, although with none of the complex strategizing he'd once been known for.

Gabby wasn't going to give up until he could once again hold a rapid conversation with her. Until he once again teased her and embarrassed her with double entendres. Until he could lead a team of SSU operators again.

She glanced at the flashing red light on her phone. Ryker had called again today, stressing how critical it was to get the location of Kaufmann's lab from Rafe. Apparently Kaufmann's subjects were soon going to launch a major attack. Ryker said he couldn't give Gabby details, but the key to stopping the attack was to shut down Kaufmann's program and get all of the subjects into treatment. Hundreds, if not thousands, of innocent people would die if the attack wasn't stopped.

While she understood the urgency of the situation, Gabby wouldn't rush Rafe. Each time someone questioned him about the coordinates of the lab, he flew into a rage and tried to kill the questioner. For hours after, Rafe would be in a near catatonic state. Gabby had finally insisted that no one mention the lab to Rafe. Trying to force the issue only set his progress back. Making Rafe feel safe and accepting him with his current limits, would, she believed, help his memory return in time. In the meantime, she needed to get his intelligence back up to normal.

Gabby rubbed at her temples and arched her back, easing muscles tight from hours standing at her workstation. The answer was here somewhere. She just had to try harder. She placed another slide on the microscope, comparing the results from a previous version of the drug.

Maybe if she—

"You're going to collapse if you don't get some sleep, Gabby."

Gabby spun around so fast, she almost fell over and proved Kai right. "Where'd you come from?" she demanded. Pain lanced through her chest as she remembered Rafe sneaking up on her, and how that had led to their first kiss.

Kai just smiled.

She was so used to seeing him in his lab coat that she forget he was an SSU agent as well as a scientist. He'd worked undercover for years. He was trained to move silently.

Kai's smile faded as he studied her. "Working yourself into the ground isn't going to bring him back any faster. When you're this exhausted, you're more likely to miss something. Let it go for the night. You'll do better once you're rested."

"I—" Gabby's voice broke and she looked away, embarrassed. She picked at a scorched spot on the counter. "Every time I leave the lab I feel like I'm abandoning him," she said quietly. "I can't..." She shook her head and a few tears broke loose, wetting her cheeks. She kept her head averted, hiding behind the fall of her hair and hoping Kai wouldn't notice she was crying.

"I can't imagine what it's like for him," she continued, "being trapped in a body that's so much faster and stronger than normal but unable to communicate any better than a seven-year-old." Kai made a sound of sympathy and somehow she found herself looking up and meeting his compassionate amber eyes.

"Kai, how does he stand it? Because he knows. I've seen the frustration and hopelessness on his face." She squeezed her eyes closed against the pain of failure. A flood of tears spilled over her lids and cascaded down her face.

"Hopelessness. From *Rafe*. He used to be so confident. So optimistic." She gave up pretending she wasn't crying and swiped her hands down her face.

"Yeah, that was Rafe," Kai said. "Never met a situation or a person he couldn't turn to his advantage with a smile or a joke."

His words conjured up memories of Rafe's smile. Of the sheer love of life he'd exuded. Of the mischievous glint in his eye before he'd made some outrageous statement.

Maybe it was exhaustion. Maybe it was her own helplessness,

but Gabby lost it. No more silent tears for her. She started sobbing noisily, her whole body shaking.

"Hey. Hey, there." Kai pulled her into his embrace. "We all love him, Gabby. We're not going to let Kaufmann win. No matter what it takes, we will get Rafe back. I promise."

She nodded against his chest, even though right now, that seemed as impossible as her sprouting wings and flying toward the moon.

CIA Headquarters
Langley, Virginia

MARK TONELLI KNOCKED on the unmarked door. He'd been working as part of the CIA's In-House Projects department for over a year now, and been a member of IHP Director Wayne Jamieson's private black ops group Kerberos for a couple of weeks, but this was the first time he'd been summoned to Jamieson's office. It was tucked away in an area with little traffic, giving Jamieson the privacy he craved.

Mark didn't even have his own office yet. Not that it had really mattered until recently. He'd been in Russia until just a few days ago, tidying up loose ends regarding the dismantling of a Russian lab run by Dr. Ivanov, and siphoning off as many of the research notes as he could for Kerberos.

As the door buzzed open, Mark walked inside.

The room was as opulent as he expected from a man with Jamieson's arrogance. Rich cherry bookcases and desk, a thick Persian carpet covering the floor, and dark leather chairs with brass studs. What did surprise Mark was the reproduction of the Mona Lisa hanging on the wall to Jamieson's left.

For a second Mark felt trapped by her eyes, as if she knew the secrets he carried and found them pathetically amusing. He shook off the odd sensation and turned to greet his boss.

Jamieson stood behind the desk. He held the phone to his ear while with his free hand he tapped the tip of a pen impatiently on the blotter. With a little jolt, Mark realized this was the first time he'd seen the man in person. All their previous interaction had been over the phone.

For a man in his early seventies, Jamieson still appeared to be in vigorous good health. He stood about five foot ten, with a slender frame that would have appeared fragile on a man exuding less energy. But Jamieson crackled with power. And anger. Even from several feet away Mark could feel the fury pouring off his boss. His ice blue eyes were narrowed and his thin lips flattened angrily with each syllable.

"No more excuses," Jamieson barked into the phone. Then he slammed the receiver down. The brooding look he shot Mark had the hairs on the back of his neck rising.

"The microchip you brought out of Ivanov's lab wasn't Nevsky's," Jamieson informed him. "And the Russian scientists aren't cooperating with Dr. Kaufmann."

Mark ignored the chill at the base of his spine. "I did say that I wasn't certain Ivanov had been honest with me about the microchip," he said with what he hoped was the right shade of disdain. "Even a dying man isn't guaranteed to tell the truth."

Of course, he'd known all along the chip was a fake. The SSU's Kal Paterson had swallowed the real microchip during the fight in Ivanov's lab. Before the SSU shut the place down and turned it over to the Russian authorities, Mark had grabbed a similar microchip he'd seen in a data reader, hoping it contained enough scientific data to fool Kaufmann. A risk worth taking in order to slide back into Jamieson's good graces.

Waiting with raised eyebrow to see where Jamieson was heading with his comments, Mark hoped the failure of the two Russian scientists to cooperate with Kaufmann wouldn't ruin his plans. Retrieving Nevsky's microchip had been his admission price into Kerberos. He wasn't going to let Jamieson kick him out of the organization now.

"Lucky for you the information you brought me on that other matter proved invaluable, or I'd be wondering why I didn't make certain you were killed in Brazil," Jamieson said.

Mark didn't let his surprise show on his face. He'd suspected that the assassination team he'd run afoul of on his assignment in Brazil had been sent by Jamieson, but he'd never expected his boss to admit it. So what game was Jamieson playing now? Softening Mark up by hinting that all was forgiven? Mark could work with that. Just as long as he remained part of Kerberos.

Mark had spent the past several weeks proving his usefulness to Jamieson. When his boss stated that retrieving Nevsky's chip was no longer enough to gain Mark entry into Kerberos, Mark had played along and asked what else he could do. Jamieson had hinted that he funded a scientific program similar to Nevsky's, and that it could use some new researchers.

So Mark had arranged for two of Ivanov's scientists to escape from jail in Moscow and sent them to Jamieson along with as many notes from the lab as he could gather. He wasn't a scientist. He didn't understand the notes, so he didn't know if what he'd provided to Jamieson had been valuable. He'd also taken half the notes he accessed and sent them to the SSU, along with copies of all the notes he'd passed on to Jamieson.

Luckily, Jamieson didn't realize Mark had a new agenda. His boss still thought he was the same ambitious man of a month ago. The man driven by two things: the need to avenge his father's death, and the need for such power that he'd never again feel as helpless as he had when his father died in his arms.

Before his visit to Ivanov's lab, Mark would have looked around this office and immediately started plotting the best way to take Jamieson's place. But the hours he'd spent at the Russian lab had changed him profoundly.

Ivanov had been proud that he'd succeeded in forcing men to commit acts that went against their personal moral code. Mark shivered. He'd thought himself immune to morality. He was the ultimate survivor, willing to commit any act to further his own agenda. Eight-year-old Mark had survived on the streets of Moscow because he'd been meaner and faster than the competition. And because he hadn't been squeamish about doing what was necessary to bring him the money to buy food for his ailing mother.

But watching the horrified anguish in a man's eyes as he killed his brother, unable to fight against the orders of the doctors who had him under mind control, had touched the conscience Mark thought long dead. What a shock to discover he still possessed a fragile moral code after all. Taking away a man's free will just to turn him into a killing machine was wrong. Mark felt a flash of sympathy for Rafe Andros. He'd learned that the SSU agent had been caught and put through Dr. Kaufmann's program.

A program Mark now realized that abused its subjects in the same way that Ivanov had. Which left Mark with the moral responsibility—he nearly gagged at the word, it was such a foreign concept—to shut down Kaufmann's lab. And to do that, he had to destroy both Kerberos and Jamieson.

Given Jamieson's power and the secrecy surrounding Kerberos, Mark's best shot was to undermine the organization from within. Then, once he'd secured the name of his father's murderer, he'd bring the SSU in to finish the job.

"You spent time at the SSU," Jamieson commented, indicating that Mark should sit down.

Mark nodded cautiously. A few months ago, he'd been part of an inter-agency exchange program between the SSU and the CIA and had worked with freaky Jenna Paterson on an assignment in Moscow. He moved toward the armchair closest to the desk. As he lowered himself onto the seat, a flash of bronze next to the phone caught his eye.

Only decades of deception saved him from giving away his

shock. It was ingrained in him to keep his gaze moving, never allowing an opponent to see what had caught his attention. Slowly, as if nothing was wrong, as if his world hadn't just shifted on its axis, Mark sat down.

"The SSU has become an increasing threat to Kerberos," Jamieson said. "I want your help in destroying them. In particular, we need to eliminate Rafe Andros and any other escapees from Kaufmann's program. I need you to tell me everything you remember about the SSU's security and the layout of their compound."

Mark nodded, glad that Jamieson appeared unaware that the only reason Mark had been allowed to leave Russia with the scientists was because he'd struck a bargain with the SSU.

But Mark's attention wasn't really on Jamieson's words. His peripheral vision confirmed what he'd thought he'd seen. A small, bronze, Etruscan horse with a dent on its left shoulder sat next to Jamieson's telephone.

Mark had last seen the figurine in his father's hand. It had been his father's good luck charm, handed down through the family for generations. But the little horse had been missing from his father's pocket the night his tortured, barely alive body had been dumped on their front lawn.

Mark had been desolate, desperately wanting the horse as a reminder of his father. Many years later, when he'd tracked down and killed the mobsters who'd kidnapped and tortured his father, Mark had demanded to know where the horse figurine was. They'd claimed ignorance with their last breath.

Now he understood why. All his martial instincts flared to life as he realized he was in the middle of a game with far deadlier implications than he'd anticipated. Jamieson had lied to him. Promised that in return for Nevsky's microchip, Jamieson would give Mark the name of the man who'd ordered the death of Mark's father.

His father had been a prominent judge in Massachusetts

who'd earned the enmity of the mob, so no one questioned the investigators' conclusion that his death had been a mob hit. Yet no one had ever been arrested. No one had been made to pay until Mark had joined the CIA and developed the skills necessary to ferret out and destroy the men he believed were responsible. Then Jamieson had hinted that the real mastermind still lived.

Mark had been played. All along the guilty party was Jamieson.

He wondered if today's summons was deliberate. Did his boss intend for Mark to see the horse? Was it supposed to be a warning that Mark was as disposable as his father had been?

Cold, hard determination settled in his stomach. No matter what he had to do, his goal had now changed. It wasn't enough just to shut down Kaufmann's lab and Kerberos.

Jamieson had to die.

JAMIESON WATCHED Tonelli leave the office. The man continued to surprise him. After Moscow, and Jamieson's decision to give the man another chance, Tonelli's attitude had remained as arrogant and ambitious as always. He appeared to be the same conscience-less man. Someone willing to do whatever necessary to get ahead. Yet the expression on Tonelli's face had flickered briefly into disgust when Jamieson had described Kaufmann's work.

Jamieson picked up the bronze horse and rubbed his thumb along the dent in its shoulder, trying to figure out the cause of Tonelli's disgust. The man hadn't visited Kaufmann's lab or seen any of the subjects at their worst, so there was no reason for the reluctance Jamieson sensed in him about becoming further involved in Kerberos.

Most likely, Tonelli had seen something at Ivanov's lab that he couldn't stomach, and he'd rightly concluded that Kaufmann's lab would be the same. Jamieson glanced over at the Mona Lisa.

She seemed to smile in agreement at his deduction. He returned her smile.

It was always satisfying to find a man's weakness. The more Tonelli showed a disinclination toward involvement with Kaufmann, the more Jamieson would push him in that direction.

Should the worst happen, and the President's anniversary demonstration fail, Tonelli needed to be in position to take the fall. The SSU was still sniffing around, trying to find out where Andros had been held. They already had reason to distrust Tonelli, with the way he'd turned Susana Dias over to Ivanov. So it would be a simple matter to throw evidence to the SSU supporting Tonelli's guilt. He didn't expect the SSU would look very hard at the evidence. If, after Tonelli's arrest, the SSU did figure out it was a setup, Jamieson would already be long gone.

SSU Laboratories
Georgia

NIKO WALKED UP to the covered observation window of Rafe's room. The last time he'd stood at this window, Rafe had flown into a killing rage and nearly shattered the window trying to get to him. But the doctors had finally decided that it was safe to let them meet again.

That moment continued to live in Niko's nightmares, along with the first time he'd seen his brother after his capture by Kaufmann. Under the scientist's orders, Rafe had tracked Kai into the Amazon jungle. Rafe had been pounding Kai's head against the jungle floor when Niko and Jenna showed up. Rafe had barely recognized his brother. Niko had fought Rafe, but in the end his brother had been too strong. The only way to stop him had been to tranquilize him.

Niko rubbed the scar tissue on his biceps. He still felt sick every time he remembered the sight of the darts sticking out of his brother's body.

Staying away these past weeks had been hell, but he wasn't a scientist and since Rafe had tried to kill him on sight, there'd been no reason for him to stick around. Still, Niko's protective instincts had insisted that it was his duty as big brother to help fix Rafe. Walking away from the lab had been the hardest thing Niko ever did, and that included his undercover work.

The second hardest thing had been explaining to his mother and younger sister that Rafe was ill, but that they couldn't see him. His mother had gotten that stubborn look he so feared and threatened Niko with her wooden spoon if he didn't take her to her youngest son. Niko had been forced to get Dr. Montague on the phone. Without giving away the truth of the situation, Dr. Montague had somehow managed to convince his *mamá* that Rafe would be fine, but that he couldn't be allowed visitors yet.

Niko hadn't wanted to leave the house he'd grown up in, wanting his *mamá* to have the security of one of her sons being present. But he'd also known that he'd go crazy staying home with nothing to do but worry.

Ryker had done his best to distract Niko by sending him out on physically grueling assignments. Jenna had been there to hold him in the middle of the night when he woke up from night-mares where Rafe killed everyone he loved. Dr. Montague had kept her promise to send him frequent updates on Rafe's progress. But nothing had filled the aching hole in his chest.

Now Niko took a deep breath, let his arms hang loosely by his sides, and nodded to Kai who stood off to the left. Slowly the drapes to Rafe's room opened.

Rafe stood facing his activity board, his finger touching what looked to be a photograph. Niko knew that Rafe's therapists had prepared his brother for this moment by adding Niko to Rafe's schedule. Niko had also given them the faded baseball cap that Rafe now wore backward.

As if sensing his brother's attention, Rafe turned toward the window. For a moment there was no expression on his face and Niko's hopes started to sizzle and die. Then Rafe's face broke into a wide grin. He whooped and grabbed the baseball cap off his head as he ran toward the window. "Niko!" He waved the cap at his brother. "Bro-ther!"

Niko tried to swallow past the stone lodged in his throat. "Hey, little brother," he said in Greek. "You feeling better?"

Rafe nodded. Then he glanced at the door. "In?"

Niko looked over to Kai for approval. His brother-in-law cleared his throat, blinked, then rubbed the tip of his nose. "Yeah, I think it's safe to let you in."

No sooner had Niko stepped into Rafe's room, than his brother swept him into a giant bear hug. "Missed you," Rafe declared.

Niko tightened his arms around his brother, so relieved at Rafe's attitude that his eyes grew damp. "Yeah, I missed you, too, Rafe."

Rafe pushed away and tugged Niko over to the easy chair. When Niko had settled himself, Rafe sat on the bed. "*Ma-má*? Ma-ri-a?"

"They're good Rafe. They've been worried about you."

Rafe's eyes widened in panic. "Know?"

Ah, hell. "No. Sorry. We told them you've been sick. Nothing more."

Rafe nodded. "Good. Thank you." He waved the hand holding the baseball cap toward the door. "What. News?"

Niko began to fill Rafe in on everything that had happened since his capture. Despite his simplified speech, Rafe nodded and seemed to understand what Niko told him. In his halting language Rafe explained how Dr. Montague and the other good doctors had been helping him. Rafe called Dr. Montague Gab-by and glanced fondly at a small stuffed teddy bear whenever he said her name.

Niko had never been so grateful that his brother had fallen in love before his disastrous mission. He wished he'd been the one to pull Rafe out of his painful memories, but the relief of being able to hold a conversation with Rafe again outweighed his regret.

Niko understood that Rafe might never regain his full cognitive abilities, but sitting here, seeing the same teasing, love of life spark in his brother's eyes, Niko didn't care. As long as his brother wasn't trying to kill him, all was good.

CHAPTER NINETEEN

SSU Laboratories
Georgia

"IT'S READY," Gabby announced, stepping into Ryker's office ten days later and shutting the door behind her. She'd finally hit on a formula she thought might break through Rafe's mental barriers.

Kai and Ryker exchanged glances of relief and guarded hope.

"There's still a danger it could drive him insane," Gabby warned. She gave each man a copy of her report, but she was too nervous to sit. Instead, she paced along the edge of the utilitarian office, waiting for them to finish the report.

Overall, the results were encouraging. Rafe was almost back to his original weight. He'd probably always carry ten or so extra pounds of muscle, but he'd shed the ungainly bulk from the enhanced steroid component. His reflexes and strength remained above average, but not so much as to make him a freak. Yet he still couldn't speak with adult complexity, and he still threw fits of rage when any reference was made to his imprisonment.

God, she missed the old Rafe so much. Being with him every day, yet with him unable to interact as before, was torture. After having failed in every other attempt, all Gabby could think to do was give Rafe a pure dose of Nevsky's original intelligence-enhancing drug. The one created for the side of his program meant to produce extraordinary spies.

Given alone, the drug had so improved the mental capabilities of Nevsky's subjects that their brains hadn't been able to handle the increased demand. Some of the men had literally burned out, dying when too many of their neural processing centers shut down due to overload. Others had gone insane.

Gabby's theory was that the drug's negative effects would be countered by what remained of Kaufmann's drugs in Rafe's system. Drugs that blocked mental pathways. Her tests confirmed that Nevsky's drugs should act on the sectors of the brain involved in keeping Rafe a prisoner within his own mind, but still, she was terrified. What if she was wrong? A note in Nevsky's files indicated that he'd once tried mixing his two drug formulas. The subject had experienced one day of both enhanced intelligence and superior strength. Then he'd fallen into a coma and died.

None of Gabby's tests had indicated such a severe reaction would occur in Rafe, but what if she'd missed some key piece of data? What if she'd incorrectly calibrated the dosage?

"Gabby, stop worrying," Kai chided. He'd learned to read her too well these past weeks. "The rest of your team has checked your data, reproduced your results, and agreed with your conclusion. This is Rafe's best chance. Even if it fails, it won't be your fault. Rafe gets the final go-ahead."

She knew that. She did. But a part of her didn't accept it. This was her formula. If Rafe didn't come out of this okay, it would be because she'd failed to account for some unforeseen variable.

Gabby bit her lip. "I know. It's just—"

"It's hard to give the go ahead to use Nevsky's formula on Rafe when we don't know what the results are going to be," Kai finished for her. "I know." He put a hand on her shoulder. "We'll monitor him closely. He's not going to die."

She nodded. To do nothing was irresponsible. Just because she was afraid didn't mean this was a bad decision. She owed it to Rafe to give him every chance.

She'd seen the pain in Rafe's eyes. Seen how frustrated he got when he failed to complete a basic test or was unable to communicate to her in anything but simple phrases.

If this formula would give him a chance at recovery, who was she to let her fear stand in the way?

She let out a long breath, forcing her fears to follow. "So, when are we going to ask him?" Gabby asked.

Ryker stood up. "How about now?"

Kai squeezed her shoulder. "It's the right thing to do, Gabby. You'll see."

She closed her eyes. *Please let him be right. Please let this bring Rafe back to us. He doesn't deserve to stay trapped the way he is.*

CIA Headquarters
Langley, Virginia

MARK TONELLI slowly ran the handheld scanner over the pages of the report Jamieson had given him. Finding out details about Kaufmann and his program was turning out to be much easier than Mark had expected. All he'd done was let a bit of his disgust show when Jamieson had given him a rundown on the program. His boss had seized on that and insisted on throwing tasks at him that drew him into further responsibility for the program. Mark suspected he was being set up to be the fall guy if the program became public, but he couldn't worry about that now.

He flipped a page of the report, then closed his eyes briefly and shook his head. He'd been naïve when he'd originally thought the drug program Jamieson supported was just about increasing body strength through enhanced steroids. He'd never guessed that men would go to such lengths to create superhuman soldiers.

But this report showed how much care Kaufmann's team took in picking their subjects. It was a catalog of male military personnel complete with photos. The report listed their vital statistics—age, height, weight—and rated key traits such as intelligence, obedience, and loyalty.

Jamieson had explained that as the program matured it became increasingly difficult to find men who responded well to the conditioning. So Kaufmann had put together a wish list of traits.

Mark had been tasked with sorting through this catalog, which was updated monthly, for men with Kaufmann's desired traits. Jamieson's contact at the Department of Defense would then help arrange for an "accident" where the man would be declared dead.

In reality, he'd be shipped to Kaufmann's lab.

While he read through the list, Mark kept an eye out for any mention of Faith's brother, Toby Andrews. Just thinking of the spunky former reporter brought a half-smile to Mark's lips. The woman had pulled a gun on him earlier in the week, in a desperate attempt to learn what had happened to her missing brother. Toby had been in military intelligence and the information he left his sister had led her to Jamieson. She'd seen Mark leaving a restaurant where she'd followed his boss and decided Mark was the easier target.

That move had saved her life. Jamieson would have had her killed on the spot. Mark, on the other hand, had found himself entranced by the woman. He'd agreed to help locate her brother in return for access to all the information her brother had gathered.

Unfortunately, he suspected Faith's brother had already been sent to Kaufmann. While Jamieson trusted Mark enough to give him access to the catalog in order to select potential new subjects, he'd yet to find any evidence of who was already in the program. He wouldn't tell Faith his suspicions until he had proof, because the odds of her brother surviving more than a few months with Kaufmann were slim.

In the meantime, Mark kept a duplicate list of potential candidates, which he'd send to Ryker tonight. He trusted the SSU director would make sure none of the targets actually ended up in Kaufmann's lab.

SSU Laboratories
Georgia

RAFE KNEW something was the matter the moment Gabby walked into his room, followed by Kai and Ryker. They never visited him all together.

Over the last few weeks the voices in his head telling him to kill had all but disappeared, taking with them the excruciating headaches. He'd been allowed to visit with Niko, and the love and acceptance he'd received from his brother had eased some of his soul-deep pain. After Niko, Rafe had slowly been reintroduced to in-person chats with Kai and Ryker. Niko had recently been called away on a mission, but Kai stopped by to chat every once in a while and Ryker had been by twice to talk about SSU business.

Ryker's visits had frustrated them both. His boss had clearly hoped that talking about the day-to-day operations of the SSU would trigger Rafe to remember more of his past. Ryker had explained that he'd been training Rafe to take over as director when he retired in five years or so. Rafe didn't remember and couldn't imagine ever wanting to sit behind a desk. All he wanted was to move. To release his constant restlessness. But he'd hated the hint of sadness and regret that had crept into Ryker's eyes.

He didn't like disappointing the man any more than he liked disappointing Gabby.

Rafe fought the urge to lower his head in shame. He still couldn't speak like an adult, but the memories of what had been done to him, and what he'd done, haunted him. Made him feel less than a man.

How could he look Ryker in the eye, knowing that Kaufmann and his scientists had ordered Rafe to kill, and he'd done so, even when it meant fighting Depaoli to the death. He'd watched the light go out in his friend's eyes after Rafe had stabbed Depaoli in the chest. Rafe could still feel the screams of denial pressing against his windpipe, demanding to get out. But the compulsion to obey the Voice had been too strong. The Voice had ordered him to kill, so he'd killed, while his tears splashed in a macabre polka dot pattern onto the dirt coating Depaoli's face.

For the rest of his life, Rafe would have nightmares about Depaoli's death. And yet every time Rafe tried to tell Ryker what he'd done, the splitting pain in his head returned. He couldn't even write it down. Kaufmann had fucked with his brain that much. Trapping him alone in here with his thoughts.

Fighting off insanity and feeling worthless.

Worse, he knew the information locked in his head was vital to finding Kaufmann and stopping whatever plans the scientist had for the upcoming anniversary attack. But dammit, he still couldn't remember anything about the lab's location.

Whenever he tried, blinding light speared through his mind, followed by shattering pain. The doctors had tried sedation, hypnosis, biorhythmic feedback. None of it worked.

Only Gabby kept him from going nuts. He anticipated her nightly visits with childlike excitement.

"Rafe," Ryker said. "We'd like to discuss something with you."

Rafe glanced from Ryker to Kai to Gabby. Kai had on his serious scientist face. Gabby held the clipboard with his chart stiffly in front of her. Her lowered eyes stared at the data on the chart as if it held the secrets to the universe. Yet even with the expression in her eyes hidden, the tight line of Gabby's mouth gave away her tension. She would suck at poker, because no matter how hard she tried, Rafe could always tell what mood she was in.

"What wrong?" Rafe demanded, directing his question at Kai. But, dammit, his words answered the question, didn't they? He still wasn't able to form grammatically correct sentences. His mind knew it, but there was still a block between his thoughts and his mouth.

Kai cut his eyes to Gabby. She sighed and finally raised her eyes.

The sorrow and fear there made him wish he was sitting down. "Rafe, your test results have flatlined. There's been no improvement on the cognition. Your mental skills. In fact, there's been a slight decline. If we don't do something quickly, we're afraid you're going to get worse."

She pulled her bottom lip between her teeth and worried it.

Rafe's hope deflated. He'd tried so hard on the test yesterday. He'd thought he'd done better, even though it still felt as if he was constantly watching himself through a thick layer of Jell-O. No matter how hard he focused on the right thing to do, his hands and mouth refused to obey.

"We want to try Nevsky's intelligence formula on you, Rafe," Kai said. "Gabby and her team have worked up a calibration that they believe will work well with your body. But the decision is up to you."

"Safe?" Rafe asked.

"We don't know," Gabby admitted. "We think so, but we can't be sure. We haven't anyone to test it on, except you. The test tube results indicate it's safe."

But Gabby was afraid, he could see it in her eyes. Kai held himself still, waiting for an answer. A part of Rafe's brain that remembered Kai from before interpreted this as tension, although Kai's expression was neutral. Ryker, as usual, had a face impossible to read.

"Die?" Rafe asked.

Gabby bit down hard on her lip and Rafe suddenly found himself unable to tear his gaze away as warmth filled him. He had the strangest urge to soothe her chewed lip with his tongue.

He jerked his eyes away, knowing this was the wrong time to be thinking such things.

"We don't know how dangerous this drug could be," Gabby said quietly. "It might kill you. It might make you insane. It might help you break through the barrier holding back your intelligence."

Rafe looked around his room. He was sick of this place. They now allowed him more time in other parts of the compound, but he was always escorted, and he always returned to this one room. He couldn't remember everything about his previous life, but he knew that living like this was a slow form of death.

And if he started to slide back to how he'd been in Kaufmann's hands?

No. He wouldn't regress. He trusted Gabby and Kai to have this formula right.

"Do—" Rafe shook his head. That wasn't the right response. "Yes." There. He'd said it.

"Are you sure?" Gabby took a step toward him and raised her hand as if she wanted to grab his arm and shake some sense into him. But at the last second, her hand fell away. "Rafe, Nevsky's subjects all died."

"Sure," Rafe answered. He tried to project through his eyes what his tongue couldn't express. He'd rather die than go back to what he'd been. "Never...monster...again."

Gabby's eyes filled with tears, but she nodded. "Okay." She glanced down at his chart.

"We'll start this afternoon," Kai said.

Rafe dipped his head in acknowledgement. He wanted to

hold Gabby. To tell her everything was going to be all right. But he remembered her words. This was work for her. He wasn't supposed to hug her in front of Kai or any of the others.

Even as his mind processed this information, he found his arms reaching for her. And when she rushed into his embrace and burrowed against him, Rafe forgot all the reasons this could be anything but right.

IT HURT.

The drugs feeding through the intravenous shunt burned Rafe's veins, making it nearly impossible to keep his face impassive. But that's what he needed to do. He couldn't let Gabby see his pain. She was already worried about using these drugs on him. He wouldn't give her any reason to pull back now.

But God, it hurt. He'd forgotten the sheer agony as the drugs scalded his veins. Kaufmann must have used a similar drug, because the pain reached the same excruciating level. It seeped into his every pore, leaving him no place to hide. He closed his eyes and breathed through his mouth in shallow pants, the way he'd done to survive Kaufmann's treatments.

"Rafe, are you okay?" Gabby's fingers were cool against the overheated skin on his forearm.

"Hurts. Burns."

Gabby gasped.

Horrified to realize he'd spoken out loud, Rafe opened his eyes. His attention snagged on her white lab coat. *White coats. Pain. Cold. Orders... No! Don't make me do it. Please—*

Terror shot through him. His body started to shake.

"Rafe!" Gabby's voice, sharp with concern.

"Go away!" Suddenly, he didn't want her here. Didn't want her seeing him like this. In pain. Afraid. Weak.

Didn't want Gabby and her white coat to become associated with this torture.

"Rafe, I'm sorry. I didn't realize this would hurt you. I'll—"

He reached out with the arm not being injected and grabbed her wrist. The pain clawed at his chest, threatening to cut off his breathing. He knew what would come next. Animal moans. Crying. Pleading.

He refused to let Gabby see him turn back into a beast. He glanced frantically around the room until he spotted Kai coming through the door. Good. Kai would understand.

"Kai finish. You. Go. Now!" Rafe squeezed Gabby's wrist trying to make her pay attention. But he used more force than he'd intended and she cried out. No, he didn't want to hurt Gabby. His soul shriveled back up and hid. He just wanted to be alone to ride out the pain.

"Leave!" he roared.

The pain in her eyes nearly stopped his heart. Then he felt another wave of burning liquid move through his veins, felt the increased saliva in his mouth, and knew he was seconds away from going into a fit.

"I've got it Gabby," Kai said, replacing her hand with his on the IV bag. He shoved her gently toward the door. "Hurry up and get out of here so he calms down."

"But—"

"You're making this worse for him, Gabby. He doesn't want you to see him in pain. Go!"

With an anguished look, Gabby left the room. The instant the door closed, Rafe's back bowed and he let out a groan of pain. Stars exploded behind his eyelids.

"Can you hang in there, buddy? I've got one more dose to go." Kai held up a second IV bag. "Or do you want me to stop?"

"D-don't...stop," Rafe gasped. The room started to spin as his body convulsed. "K-keep...G-gab-by...away."

Then he screamed.

CHAPTER TWENTY

One Week Later

RAFE LEANED BACK SO Kai's roundhouse kick missed connecting with his jaw. God, he'd missed sparring with Kai.

Anticipating his friend's next move, Rafe dipped into a lunge and swung his back leg out in a sweep. Kai jumped up and spun, avoiding being taken down. But Rafe had expected the counter-move and with a twist of his torso, brought his other leg up and around, landing a solid kick on Kai's thigh.

Flinching as one of Kai's fists slammed into his cheek, Rafe finally acknowledged how scared he'd been that he'd never regain his ability to anticipate his opponent and formulate a split second counterattack. Having superior strength didn't interest him if he couldn't use his brain the way he was used to.

Thanks to Gabby's drugs, his brain now worked fine. At least in his opinion. He'd taken another battery of intelligence tests this morning he hoped would show his improvement.

"She thinks you hate her, you know," Kai said, once again showing his uncanny ability to read Rafe's mind. "She thinks you blame her for your suffering." He flew at Rafe with a series of hand movements that forced Rafe to back up. "You broke her heart when you told her you don't want to see her."

"I don't hate her," Rafe replied several minutes later. Still wheezing from a chop to the throat, he reached for a bottle of water. "And I've never blamed her."

Kai crossed his arms over his chest and threw his don't-fuck-with-the-scientist look at Rafe. "Then maybe you should have come up with a better answer than 'Go away' every time she's tried to see you this past week." He paused. "You made her cry."

Rafe took a slug of water to hide his wince. "I never meant to hurt her," he finally said. "I just—" He glanced away, reluctant to confess how he felt. But he had to make Kai understand, so he could tell Gabby.

"Something snapped when she gave me the drugs," Rafe admitted, staring at the floor. "I had a flashback to Kaufmann's. Scientists in lab coats. Drugs. Pain. Having my will taken away." He shrugged. "I'm not avoiding Gabby because I'm afraid of her. I know she loves me and doesn't want to hurt me." He took another drink of water. "I...hell, I don't know how to say it. I just suddenly hated for Gabby to watch me fall apart, when I'd been struggling for so long to get back to the man she'd known before."

He crumpled the water bottle in his hand and tossed it toward the recycling bin. "Call it pride or shame or some combination of both. I just know that I can't face her until I'm back to myself. I..." His hands clenched. "We only knew each other a short time before I was captured. What happened between us was powerful, like nothing I've ever known. Yet..." Rafe paused, trying to put into words what he felt. "She's spent more time with me while I was closer to a beast than a man. I need her to see me as Rafe. Not as a victim to be pitied or helped, but someone she can love."

"She needs to hear this from you," Kai said.

Rafe shook his head. "I...can't. Not yet. Maybe this afternoon, if the tests come back normal. I feel almost whole, but I don't want there to be any doubt. I..." He bent down to pick up a discarded towel and snapped it against his leg. "I have to be her equal when we meet."

"Why?"

Rafe scowled. From the look in Kai's eyes, he knew. He just wanted to force Rafe to say it. Rafe added a glare to his scowl, but Kai just smirked.

"Fine. I'm not some helpless little boy. I'm her man and she's my woman. I love her and..."

Kai waited, one eyebrow raised.

"I'm afraid she won't be able to love me, now that she's seen me as Kaufmann's victim. I need her to see me as a strong man, one who's worthy of her love. Satisfied?"

"Yep." Kai shot him a grin and clapped him on the shoulder. "I've got a woman of my own now. I completely understand."

Rafe felt something tight inside him relax at Kai's easy acceptance. But, shit. If he was worried about his best friend thinking he wasn't good enough for Gabby, then maybe he needed to work on his confidence before he talked to her.

His watched beeped. Glancing down, he swore. "I've got an appointment with Dr. Steuart to go over my test results."

Kai nodded. "Good luck."

As Rafe headed back toward his quarters half an hour later, he saw Gabby talking with one of the male scientists at the other end of the hallway. She glanced at Rafe, then quickly looked away. Even with the distance between them Rafe noticed the way her shoulders hunched as she said something to the scientist before hurrying around the corner.

Rafe came to a stop, stricken. Gabby didn't want to see him. God. His heart ached so much he wanted to howl. Yeah, he'd known his refusal to talk to her had hurt Gabby, but...he shook his head.

You're an idiot.

He'd been so caught up in his own shit that he hadn't realized that his rejection would cut her to the bone. He'd just assumed that when he was ready to start up their relationship again Gabby would fall in with his plans.

But the way she'd just scurried away from him made him realize he'd wounded her far more deeply than he'd anticipated. Nodding absently at the scientist, Rafe hurried after her, hoping he wasn't too late.

To his relief, he caught sight of her around the next corner. "Gabby, wait!"

She ducked her head and kept going.

"Dammit," Rafe muttered. He broke into a run, not willing to let her vanish before he had time to state his case. He'd almost reached her when she sensed his pursuit. She darted forward and slammed her finger against the call button for the elevator.

Of course, the damn elevator doors opened immediately and Gabby leapt inside. Rafe barely got his hand in between the doors before they closed again. "Please, Gabby, don't run from me. I want to apologize."

She eyed him with such wariness, his heart nearly broke. "Apologize?" she asked hesitantly.

He let out the breath he'd been holding. "Yes. But not here." On a burst of inspiration, he blurted, "Have dinner with me tonight." While most of the staff had kitchens or kitchenettes in their apartments on the top floors of this old house, the SSU had also installed a small cafeteria that was open 24-7.

"Dinner?"

"Yeah." He nodded, clenching his fist so he wouldn't reach out and stroke a finger down her cheek. He didn't want to give her any excuse to say no. "C'mon, *querida*, we need to talk."

Gabby studied him for so long he feared she was going to say no. Finally, though, she gave a small nod and hope flared within him. "Okay. What time?"

He checked his watch. "How about six-thirty? I'll meet you at the cafeteria." He really wanted to pick her up at her door, but figured he'd pushed her enough.

"Okay," she said again. Then she looked pointedly at his hand, still holding back the elevator door.

He reluctantly let go, but what he really wanted was to crowd into the elevator with her just to be close enough to hear her breathing and smell her special scent. But he had to honor her wishes and let her go. For now.

Tonight, though. Tonight he'd make things right between them.

Gabby hurried through the corridors toward the cafeteria and checked her watch. Six thirty-five. Damn it, she'd promised herself she'd be on time tonight. Yet once again, she'd been so caught up in her work she'd lost track of time.

Nearly running now, she forced herself to slow down around the last turn before her anxiety made her sick. She tried some deep breathing exercises as she walked down the corridor, but the nervous butterflies in her stomach didn't settle until she saw Rafe pacing in front of the cafeteria door. Good. He was as anxious about their date as she was.

"Hi, Rafe. Sorry I'm late. I was working."

"Gabby!" The way his body relaxed and his face lit up made Gabby feel doubly guilty for making him wait.

He took her hands in his, then pressed a quick kiss to her cheek. "Hungry?"

Gabby nodded.

"Good."

Gabby followed him through the food line, marveling at how much Rafe piled on his plate. Once they were seated, Rafe pulled out a small gift bag and set it on the table. "For you."

"Oh, Rafe!" Her heart turned over. He'd remembered his tradition of bringing her presents.

He nodded at the bag. "Open it."

Inside the bag, nestled in forest green tissue paper, sat a little stuffed wolf cub. Gabby lifted him out and stroked the soft gray and white fur. "He's adorable."

"I wanted you to have something to keep you company in the lab, since I still have your valentine bear."

"I love him. Thank you."

Rafe's face relaxed into a smile. As he dug into his dinner and they made small talk, Gabby couldn't help herself from cataloging the changes in him. His hands and wrists bore a variety of new scars, visible reminders of the torture he'd endured. Worse, instead of facing life with the teasing, boyish charm he'd possessed before, Rafe now looked at the world through wary, watchful eyes with only the occasional glint of his old joie de vivre. It broke her heart that even here in the SSU's secure facility, part of Rafe remained braced for pain. Pain that had etched lines on his face, until there was no question that this man had been through hell and survived.

Gabby took a sip of water. No matter how her heart ached over the changes in Rafe, she had to stay positive. Every sign pointed to the latest round of drugs having returned his intelligence. So far tonight he'd only hesitated a couple of times over word choice, completely understandable given that his brain had been used to working at diminished capacity for so long.

Part of her was giddy with success, but the rest of her was afraid. Rafe had said he wanted to apologize. She didn't know what he thought he'd done wrong. She—

"I'm sorry I've been avoiding you since the last treatment," Rafe said.

Gabby blinked hard, startled by how he seemed to have read her mind. She lowered her eyes to the Formica tabletop. "It's okay," she said. "I understand. The drugs I gave you caused pain. It's to be expected that seeing me would remind you of Kaufmann and his scientists, and that you'd blame me for my role in their program."

"No!" Rafe grabbed her hand and squeezed so hard, her gaze flew up to collide with his. "Is that really what you've been thinking?"

"Of course."

Rafe relaxed his grip and turned her hand over. His thumb stroked over her palm. "Yes, the pain briefly threw me back to memories of Kaufmann. But I swear, I never for a minute mistook you for one of the bad guys." He took a deep breath, but didn't stop the slow, soothing movement of his thumb over her skin. "I didn't relive the moment when Kaufmann convinced me you'd betrayed me."

Gabby flinched. She didn't blame Rafe for giving up control to Kaufmann at the urging of the "fake" Gabby. He'd held on longer than most men would have. It still amazed her that Kaufmann had later confessed his deception to Rafe. And it humbled her, knowing that Rafe had been able to move past his anger, ignore Kaufmann's kill order, and remember that he loved her.

"I've been avoiding you because..." Rafe glanced away, the movement so uncharacteristically uncertain that she bit her lip to keep from offering comfort she knew he wouldn't want.

Finally, though, he looked back at her. "I'm tired of being your patient," he said. "Sick of being seen as weak and dependent. A victim." He shrugged and the ice that had formed around her heart at his rejection began to thaw. "Having you see me strapped to that chair while I writhed in pain was the final blow to my ego."

"I'm sorry. I never even considered that you might feel ashamed. You seemed to be handling our relationship so well up until then."

He gave a half smile. "Not so well for the week leading up to the last treatment. The more of my personality I gain back, the harder it becomes to be in a position of weakness around you. Your intelligence drugs have accelerated the return of my pride."

Rafe raised her hand and placed a kiss on her knuckles. "I never intended to hurt you," he continued. "I'm sorry you misunderstood. I always intended for us to start our relationship again. It's just...I wanted to be in a position of strength when I courted you again. I wanted to be normal again."

Joy poured through her. He didn't hate her! "You seem pretty normal to me."

"Yeah?" He grinned and leaned forward, his eyes dropping to her mouth.

She laughed and put a hand up between them, stopping his kiss. "Not so fast. We're in public, for one thing."

"Don't care." He shrugged, then slouched back in his chair.

Gabby bit back a smile, delighted to see the devilish glint in his eyes. This was her Rafe. "Don't you think we should take things slow this time? Get to know one another better?"

He jerked upright. "Hell, no! You've seen me at my worst. How much better do you need to know me, woman?"

True. "But...you still know very little about me," she countered.

"Yeah? I know you're smart, dedicated, and passionate. And you're more loyal than I possibly deserve." He reached forward and cupped her face in his hands. She didn't have the heart to push him away. "I'm always going to be thankful for you, Gabby," he breathed. "You never gave up on me. You saved my life."

He pressed a gentle kiss to her forehead and tears pricked her eyes. "Doesn't that fall into the imbalance of power category you're so afraid of?" she whispered. "How can you be sure what you feel for me is anything more than a side-effect of gratitude?"

This time he placed a light kiss on her lips and she felt him smile against her mouth. "Because I'm grateful to Kai for sticking by me as well, and I sure as hell don't want to strip his clothes off and tumble him into bed."

"Rafe!" she protested. But she shot him a brilliant grin, because that was something the old Rafe would have said.

"C'mon," he said, gathering their used dishes onto his cafeteria tray and rising to his feet. "Let's take a walk."

Rafe dumped their plates and utensils into the dirty dishes collection tub, then led Gabby out a side door into a little-used corridor. As soon as they were alone, Rafe took her hand.

"Where are we going?"

He shot her a sly look out of the corner of his eye. "Into the back garden so we can neck."

"Rafe!" Butterflies started dancing in her stomach. As much as she loved him, she found herself nervous about ramping up the sensuality between them. She had no idea whether the drugs had affected his libido. Even now she felt too shy to ask the question.

"Don't turn coward on me now, *querida*," Rafe said with a gleam of challenge in his eyes. Then he leaned down, and once again proved he could read her mind. "I guarantee, I'm feeling perfectly healthy in *every* way. I'm randy as a sixteen-year-old."

She blushed.

Rafe laughed and opened the door to the outside. The cool evening air felt good against her hot face as they walked down the steps and onto the brick path leading into the garden. Unlike the wide, unobstructed lawn at the front of the house, this back area had been turned into a walled garden. The garden contained a mix of practical and decorative plants, everything from fruit and nut trees to flowers and herbs.

Spotlights along the path provided adequate illumination. Rafe led her past the first of several benches, heading deeper into the garden where the trees and bushes provided more privacy from the windows of the house. Finally, he stopped underneath an arched trellis at the entrance to an open area where a fountain bubbled happily.

"Are you scared of me?" Rafe asked as he turned her into his arms.

She looked up at him, wishing the shadows weren't hiding his eyes. Afraid that she'd hurt him with the truth, but unwilling to give him anything less. "Yes."

He sucked in a breath, and she put a finger over his lips to stop his reply. "I know you care for me, Rafe, and that you don't want to hurt me. Your control over your temper has greatly improved. But..." She bit her lip. "Um...arousal can be a violent emotion. Particularly if it's had time to build up to a fever pitch. I..."

Rafe put his arms around her in a gentle hug. "You're afraid I'll lose control," he said against her temple.

She nodded against his chest, loving the feel of him warm and strong beneath her cheek. Soothed by the steady beat of his heart.

He stroked his hand over her hair. "I can't make any promises," he said after a long pause. "You know better than anyone how messed up I've been." He took her face in his hands and raised it so she was looking up at him. "But in my heart I know that no matter what happens, nothing could make me hurt you again." He lowered his head.

This time, the press of his lips was a declaration. A vow. She thought the earth held its breath and the evening insects and birds stopped their song to eavesdrop.

"If I do anything, no matter how small, that frightens you, speak out and I promise I'll stop." He smiled and the hint of sorrow, of acceptance that he might not behave, made her throat tighten up. "You can keep a tranquilizer gun close at hand if it will make you feel better."

"Are you crazy? I don't need to do that."

"Don't you?"

The fact that he'd even suggested it let her know how deeply his confidence had been shaken by his ordeal. "No. I trust you, Rafe. Even...even if you do end up losing control, I think you'll give me enough time to get away. You only ever hurt me that first time I entered your room, and then you started taking care of me again." She reached up and placed her hands on his face, pulling him down so she could initiate a tender kiss. "I just want us both to be sure before we get too involved again."

Because while her heart knew there'd be no other man except Rafe for her, she needed him to feel the same. Otherwise, if he later decided to leave her, he'd shatter her fragile heart.

"Knock, knock."

Gabby looked up at the sound of Rafe's voice. "Uh-oh. It's that late already?" She glanced at the clock over her lab workstation and found that yes, she was fifteen minutes late for her nightly dinner date with Rafe.

She made a face. "Sorry. I got—"

"—distracted. Yeah, I know, *querida*." Rafe laughed, the sound warming her heart. They'd been dating for nearly a week, yet she kept wanting to pinch herself every time Rafe acted like his old self.

"Let me just finish these notes," she said.

"Uh-huh." Rafe rolled his eyes. "Five minutes, or you're not getting tonight's gift."

Gabby smiled as she glanced at the rows of stuffed animals and figurines lining the shelf over her head. She had no idea how Rafe got hold of his nightly offerings. This SSU facility wasn't set up for families, or even long-term residence, so it didn't have a gift shop. Yet somehow Rafe always managed to show up with a whimsical present.

She wondered if he'd charmed one of the staff members into going shopping for him, knowing he wasn't allowed off the property yet. Or maybe, since direct deliveries to the facility weren't permitted, Rafe had shopped online and had someone pick up the items from the SSU's secure mail drop in town.

"Okay, five minutes." She bent her head to her computer, typing the last of her notes quickly. Acutely aware of Rafe's male presence at her doorway, she satisfied herself with a brief summary of today's findings. Enough to get her started in the right place tomorrow, but far less than the lengthy explanation she'd intended. Still, she'd committed to letting Rafe court her and she needed to show him that he mattered by honoring their time together.

"Ha!" she crowed. "Finished."

Rafe nodded slow approval. "Not bad. Four minutes fifty-nine seconds."

She stuck her tongue out at him.

"Come over here, *chica*, and I'll show you a better use for that pretty little tongue." Instead of following his statement with his usual sexy wink, Rafe held her eyes, one eyebrow lifted in challenge.

The heat in his gaze stormed through Gabby, stirring up a ferocious desire. Shocked by the sexual tension filling the room, she ducked her head and turned her back on him to straighten her papers and switch off the desk lamp.

"What's the matter, Gabby?" Rafe's hot breath on the back of her neck was the only warning she had before he wrapped his arms around her and pulled her against his body. "You suddenly afraid of me? Afraid of bedding the monster?"

"What?" She jerked free of his grasp and spun around. "How dare you?" She smacked him on the chest. "Don't you *ever* call yourself a monster. Do you hear me? You're still the smart, charming, caring man I fell in love with. Kaufmann didn't change you. You're still...you're still..." Her anger disintegrated into sobs. "You're still the Rafe I love. Just now you have all these dark edges that break my heart, because I don't know how to help you move past them."

"Ah, Gabby. Shh." Rafe pulled her into his arms and she settled her head against the familiar planes of his chest. "Don't cry, *querida*. Please don't cry. I'm sorry. I don't know where those words came from. I didn't mean to accuse you of looking down on me." He rocked slightly side to side, one hand cradling the back of her neck, the other pressing lightly against the small of her back.

"I guess, maybe..." Rafe blew out a breath. "What Kaufmann did to me, it damaged more than my body. More than my mind. It shredded everything that I thought I knew about myself. What I stood for. What lines I wouldn't cross. Sometimes, I remember the things I've done and I hate myself for breaking."

"No!" She tried to raise her head, but Rafe moved his hand and kept her pressed against his chest. "It wasn't your fault. Rafe, *no one* could have withstood Kaufmann's drugs for long. No one."

"Yeah, I keep telling myself that. But sometimes, like tonight, those feelings just bubble back up." He stroked his hand down her back and she felt his lips touch the tip of her ear. "I want so much to be worthy of your love, Gabby. But I don't always think I deserve you."

"Rafe! Don't ever think like that." This time she managed to push back hard enough that Rafe released her. She put her hands on his cheeks, reveling in the erotic press of his stubble against her palms. "I didn't turn my back on you just now because I was disgusted by the heat I saw in your stare. Never that. I want you. I just hadn't expected to go from studying blood smears to do-me-now arousal in one blink of the eyes."

His eyes laughed down at her. "Do me now? That sounds promising."

The hope in his eyes undid her. She hadn't realized how much he'd needed to be reassured that her opinion of him hadn't changed. She'd never been the aggressive one with her other lovers, but maybe now, more than even that last night together, she needed to show Rafe what she wanted.

So she grabbed his head, pulled him down and kissed him. His arms tightened around her, pressing her closer to his body as his mouth opened underneath her assault. For it wasn't a gentle kiss. She let every fear she'd had, every lonely night she'd cried out, reaching for Rafe in the dark, turn her kiss into a ravenous exploration. She needed him. Needed to know that he'd made it all the way back from Kaufmann's. That he was still hers in the most fundamental way.

She licked and nibbled and bit at his lips, let her tongue spar with his, and tried not to let Rafe take control too quickly. She wanted to devour him, then take a deep breath and dive back in to savor.

But Rafe had other ideas. His hands kneaded her butt through her lab coat as he rocked his pelvis against her. Her muscles clenched as she felt him hard and thick against her belly. She whimpered and tried to squirm closer.

A crisp three-tone chime startled her into jerking back. "Wha—" She blinked and looked around for the source of the noise, while Rafe placed a line of kisses up her jaw. Chime. Clock. Lab.

Right. The chime was her hourly reminder to get up out of her chair and move. "Uh, Rafe?" she gasped as his teeth closed lightly over her earlobe. "Maybe we can take this out of the lab? Away from poisonous chemicals?"

His teeth tightened just enough on her delicate flesh to let her know he didn't appreciate the interruption, then he straightened. Took a deep breath. Nodded. "Okay." Before she had time to guess his intent, he'd swept her up into his arms. "Your room is closer."

Ignoring her protests, he carried her out into the hallway, locked the door shut behind them, and strode toward the stairs to the staff quarters three floors up.

With one arm hooked around his neck, Gabby pressed her mouth to the hollow at the base of his throat and tasted him with her tongue. Rafe's sharp inhale emboldened her, and she nipped softly at his skin, then placed a kiss over the bite.

"Dangerous woman," Rafe muttered. "Give me your key."

Keeping her mouth on him, Gabby fumbled in her pocket until she found the key. A moment later Rafe shut her door behind them. His mouth lowered to hers in a kiss that promised sensual retribution, but when Gabby wriggled for him to set her down, he only tightened his hold and carried her into the bedroom.

Then, finally, he put her back on her feet.

"Need to see you," he murmured, his hands tugging at the hem of her long-sleeved jersey.

"Here." Gabby pushed Rafe's hands away. "Let me." Walking backward until she stood by the foot of the bed, Gabby pulled the shirt over her head and tossed it to the side. Her shoes, socks and slacks quickly followed, leaving her in the lacy, midnight blue bra and panties she'd bought with Rafe in mind.

"Amazing." Rafe's eyes traveled from her bare toes to her face and back down again, leaving heat behind. Her nipples tightened painfully against the soft lace and Gabby raised her hands to pinch and squeeze them, trying to find some relief.

"Lie down for me," Rafe whispered, taking a reverent step toward her. "So I can worship you."

Gabby shook her head. "No. I want you naked, too."

The awed desire on Rafe's face vanished under a flash of fear. "No." He backed up a step.

Gabby dropped her hands. "Rafe, I love you," she said gently, trying to squelch her sense of disappointment. "Please don't hide from me."

"I—" Rafe turned and walked away.

Great. She'd managed to completely ruin the mood. Fantastic. Gabby's throat tightened as she followed him. To her surprise, Rafe crossed his forearms, braced them against the wall, and lowered his head into the cradle he'd made.

"Don't want you to see the scars," he said so quietly she barely heard him. "Not sexy. Not strong."

"Rafe." She approached him like she would a frightened animal. "Give me some credit, please. I don't care if your skin is scarred or painted green with pink polkadots." Gently, she set her hand at the back of his neck. "You'll always be sexy to me. I'm so wet right now, just thinking about taking you inside me again." She stroked her fingers along his bare nape and down beneath the collar of his t-shirt.

Rafe gave a full body shudder and pressed back against her touch, so she moved in closer. "Let me undress you. Please. Let me show you that your body still turns me on. Okay?" This time she ran her fingernails lightly down the dip of his spine until she reached his waistband.

"What do you say?"

Rafe turned his head and looked at her. The uncertainty in his gaze undid her. She wanted to kill Kaufmann for destroying Rafe's confidence. After an agonizing moment, Rafe nodded.

"Excellent." Gabby pressed a quick kiss to his mouth. "Now, put your head back on your hands and let me work."

A flash of amusement lit his eyes. "Aye, aye, ma'am."

Once Rafe had turned away, Gabby wasted no time. She pulled his t-shirt from his pants and lifted it up his back, kissing each vicious scar she revealed until his shirt was bunched around his shoulders. She let Rafe finish removing the shirt, while her hands crept around to his front, undid his belt and zipper, and repeated the process with his pants. By the time Rafe was fully nude, tears filled Gabby's eyes again.

"You're so strong," she whispered against a particularly deep scar at the back of his left thigh. "Every single one of these marks is proof that you're a survivor."

"Can I lower my hands now?" he asked hoarsely.

"Not quite. Turn around, I want to see the front."

Rafe hesitated, then slowly pivoted. When he started to raise his hands overhead, she stopped him. "No, Rafe. I don't need you to take such a submissive a pose. Just keep your hands to your sides."

For a long moment, Rafe stared at her, his expression unreadable. Then he gave her a sensual smile and put his arms up. "I trust you, *querida*."

Those simple words sent a rush of arousal through her. Trying to ignore Rafe's erection, Gabby lavished kisses on every single scar on his chest, arms, and legs, taking side trips to worry his nipples between her teeth and run her tongue along the rim of his belly button.

"Gab-by," he finally groaned, looking at her with heated eyes. "No more. I'm gonna die if I don't touch you."

Letting her hand trail over his penis, Gabby took her time standing up. Then her hands went to the clasp of her bra as she started backing toward the bed. "Okay. Come and get me."

With a shout of triumph, Rafe sprang away from the wall. Gabby found herself on her back on the bed, her panties ripped off and Rafe's hands all over her. "Damn you," he muttered before he took her breast in his mouth. "I wanted to go slow. Savor you." His fingers dipped between her legs. "But you're so wet and I can't wait any longer."

She smiled up at him. "So don't wait." Wrapping her hand around him, she guided him to her center, then moaned as he filled her in one perfect stroke. "So good," she murmured. Her hands clutched at his back, urging him on, but Rafe seemed content to remain still, staring down at her in wonder.

"Home," he said, then buried his face in the crook of her neck.

"Yes." Feeling the dampness of tears against her skin, she pressed a kiss to his cheek. "Welcome home, Rafe."

She smoothed her hands down the muscles of his back. When after several minutes he still hadn't moved, she sank her fingernails into him. "Rafe Andros, if you're asleep I swear I'm going to kill you." Although she doubted he could sleep with his erection still pulsing hard inside her.

Rafe's muffled laugh vibrated against her throat. "Not asleep."

"Then move, damn you!"

"Bossy woman," Rafe grumbled. But when he lifted his head, his eyes danced with amusement.

"So glad you think this is funny," she snapped, wriggling her hips to ease some of the tension building inside her despite the fact that he still wasn't moving.

"*Dios*, how I love you." Rafe planted a hard kiss on her lips, then finally, the man withdrew. He held himself poised outside her entrance, looking down at her with his old devilment, then shifted forward until just the tip of him slipped inside her.

Gabby narrowed her eyes. "Oh, no," she snarled. "Don't you dare take this slow. I've waited too long for this."

Rafe raised his brows innocently and pressed inside another inch.

Growling in frustration, Gabby dug her nails into the nape of his neck, bringing his face down so she could take a sharp nip at his chin. "Damn you, Rafe Andros. Will you just fuck me already?"

The infuriating man actually chuckled, earning him a harder bite on his bottom lip. "All right. All right. I give up. Whatever the lady wants." Rafe pulled all the way out. Then, without any warning, he slammed into her.

"Yes!" Gabby's head went back and she arched into him as he started a furious rhythm. This is what she wanted. Rafe's strength pounding into her. Proving he needed her as much as she needed him.

Within minutes, a powerful orgasm tore through her. The edges of Gabby's vision wavered, then her body settled languidly back to earth. Only to find Rafe still hard inside her.

"Not done yet," he told her. He gathered her in his arms, then sat back on his heels without losing intimate contact. With Rafe's hands guiding her, his mouth at her breasts, and his dark chocolate eyes filled with love, Gabby soon found herself riding another orgasm. Only this time, Rafe was with her.

As they collapsed together on the bed, Rafe tucked her against him. And for the first time since he'd been captured, Gabby sank into a deep, restful sleep.

CHAPTER TWENTY-ONE

"Dr. Steuart informs me that your intelligence test came back normal, Rafe. Congratulations."

Rafe nodded at the image of Ryker on the videoconference screen in the underground conference room. His boss was currently back in D.C.

"Gabby and the others agree that except for your inability to remember where Kaufmann's lab is you're fit for duty again. Therefore, I'm having you transferred to the training compound in Oregon. Let's get you back to full fitness so when you do remember the location of the lab you'll be ready to go."

Satisfaction and pride filled Rafe. He couldn't wait to tell Gabby he was back in business. Yet he hated knowing that Kaufmann still had a hold on him. In the last couple of weeks he'd stopped experiencing the blinding headaches that had hit whenever he tried to remember the lab's location. But a thick fog still separated him and the memories, making it impossible to see clearly.

"Thank you, sir," Rafe said. "What about—"

The floor heaved, pitching the conference table sideways. Rafe heard the muffled boom of an explosion in the upper section of the house. Another explosion shook the videoconferencing screen off its anchor. Rafe dropped and rolled out of the way as it crashed to the floor and shattered.

Gabby! Rafe had left her upstairs in her apartment this morning after having convinced her to sleep in for once. If anything happened to her...

Staying close to the floor, Rafe scrambled for the door. Wait. Ryker would need an update and the director could tell him what contingency plans were in place. Rafe dashed over to the phone, but the line was dead.

Wishing he had a gun, Rafe cautiously opened the door into the hallway. According to an earlier conversation he'd had with Ryker, very few of the SSU staff in Oregon or D.C. knew this lab even existed. So who had leaked the lab's location?

He shook his head and assessed the situation. The corridor appeared structurally sound. A few ceiling tiles had cracks in them, and plaster dust covered some of the carpeting, but Rafe didn't get the sense the building was about to collapse on him. Still, being three levels underground with explosions above him and not knowing what type of reinforcements the SSU had added to the old building made him edgy.

Halfway to the stairs, another explosion nearly knocked Rafe to the floor. He braced himself against the wall until the shaking stopped. Praying that Gabby was okay, he raced toward the end of the hallway. Just as he reached the stairwell door, a security detail of four men stepped into view.

"Where did they hit?" he demanded, coming to a stop. "What are we up against?"

If the men were surprised to be faced with Rafe, they didn't show it. "Mortar strikes on both wings, sir," the closest man replied. Rafe felt the warm glow of pride at the man's respect. God, he'd missed this.

"There's a helicopter on the front lawn," the man continued. "Two platoons of men are fighting our exterior security team. The attackers are wearing black uniforms with colored stripes at the left shoulder under a gold insignia "

Everything inside Rafe went cold. Black uniforms. Gold insignia which he'd bet showed a three-headed dog. Colored stripes to indicate what level of stability the subject had reached. Christ. They were under attack by Kaufmann's men. "Tell—" He choked and had to clear his throat. "Tell whoever's in charge of security that the men you described are from Kaufmann's lab. Red stripes mean the men are at the peak of their physical strength and completely under Kaufmann's mind control. Orange stripes mean a bit less physical strength and speed and less reliable mind control." Yellow, green and blue subjects were too unstable to be sent on missions.

The man paled, but relayed Rafe's message via his radio. When he signed off, he explained, "We're to continue our original mission—checking this level for personnel and evacuating everyone down to the medical facility on Sub-basement 5."

Rafe nodded absently, trying to rein in his terror as he pictured himself being dragged back to Kaufmann's lab. Hell, no. He'd die before he let that monster touch him again.

"Dr. Steuart was in Testing Room 1 half an hour ago," he told them. "I don't know if she's still there, or if any of the other rooms are occupied."

Two of the men ran toward the testing room, while another started opening doors to check for injured staff.

One man hung back long enough to ask, "Do you need assistance, sir?"

Rafe shook his head. "Thanks, but I'm good." Leaving them to their work, he ran up the stairs. Gabby's room was on the second floor of the staff wing, but he had three flights to go just to reach ground level. He pulled on the railing, giving himself extra speed as he took the stairs two at a time.

Automatic weapon fire sounded from the floor above him. Cursing, Rafe pushed himself to move faster. Whoever was up there, whether SSU security or attackers, gunfire meant only one thing. More danger for Gabby.

Dios, please let him reach her in time.

At the top of the stairs he lowered himself to the floor and eased open the door so he wouldn't present a large target. The hallway was empty, but he heard booted footsteps heading his way from the front of the building. Staying low, he slipped out of the stairwell.

"There he is!"

The shout came from his right. Rafe rolled left, then sprang to his feet and bolted toward the nearby intersection of two hallways. As he made the turn, a dart embedded itself in the frame of a painting inches from his head. The familiar twang sent shivers down Rafe's spine. He was not a fucking animal to be tranq'd and tagged, as Kaufmann had done too often.

The uncontrollable fury that he'd worked so hard to bank rose up. His whole body shuddered with the effort to tamp down his rage. He stumbled. But his fear for Gabby beat against his skull, urging him forward. Telling him that fighting the men behind him wasn't worth his time. His priority was to save Gabby.

Even though he'd retained some of his enhanced strength and speed, the men chasing Rafe quickly gained ground. A quick glance behind him showed they had red stripes on their uniforms. Figured.

But he had one advantage they wouldn't expect. Thanks to the drugs Gabby had given him, he was able to anticipate where they'd shoot their darts next. He successfully zigged and zagged, narrowly avoiding being hit, until he reached the next staircase.

He grabbed the banister and vaulted over it. Two steps up and he was temporarily hidden by the wall. He used his advantage to fly up the stairs as fast as his legs could carry him, knowing he wouldn't have the advantage for long.

But all he needed was to get to the top of the stairs. He jumped up the last four stairs and landed in the common area.

On most days, at least one staff member could be found lounging in one of the comfortable, overstuffed chairs or cozy sofas flanked by a set of coffee tables. Today the space was empty.

Rafe grabbed the nearest chair and hurled it down the stairs, knocking his pursuers on their asses. It wouldn't slow them down for long, but he'd use every second to his advantage. He shoved a sofa across the opening to the stairs, then took a quick look around. Smoke drifted down the corridor to his left, from the direction of Gabby's room.

No!

Rafe burst into a run.

"Get your hands off me!" Gabby's enraged shout came from the end of the hallway where the smoke was thickest. Rafe increased his speed.

Through the smoke he saw two men drag Gabby out of her room. She had on a t-shirt and shorts and her hair was unbound. She dug in her heels and pulled back, trying to slow the men down. One of them lashed out with his fist and clipped her on the jaw. She collapsed into his arms.

Rafe bellowed in fury and charged. The man who'd hit Gabby threw her over his shoulder and ran towards the far stairs. The other man turned and charged toward Rafe with lowered head. His oversized muscles and the blank look in his eyes were clear markers that he was one of Kaufmann's men.

Rafe sized him up, saw his opening, and ducked to the side just as the man reached him. Rafe swung around, plucked the man's pistol off his hip, and in one smooth move slammed it into the back of the man's neck.

The man went to his knees, but he wasn't unconscious. Rafe didn't care. He pounded down the corridor where Gabby and her kidnapper had disappeared. The stairwell door banged shut when Rafe was halfway there. Even as he leapt down the stairs, he knew he was too late.

He reached the lawn in time to see Kaufmann's man toss

Gabby into a waiting helicopter. Rafe ran toward it, but he was too far away to even fire a single shot before the helicopter took off and banked sharply in the opposite direction.

"No-oo! Gabby!" Rafe dropped to his knees, howling his rage and grief to the sky.

Kerberos Headquarters
Outskirts of Washington, D.C.

"WHAT'S THIS?" Mark asked as he followed Jamieson into a military-style control room.

"The heart of Kerberos," Jamieson said with enough pride to cause Mark to do a double take.

Mark surveyed the room, hoping Jamieson would take his interest as being awe or at least respect for what he saw, instead of a way to burn the details into his memory to be reported to Ryker later. Men sat at workstations set into a long, u-shaped desk that reminded Mark of the bridge of the Starship Enterprise. Some of the men typed feverishly at keyboards. Others barked into headsets.

Screens lined three of the walls. One showed a global map illuminated by pinpoints of light in a variety of colors. Another showed a satellite photo of a village surrounded by lush jungle, viewed from above. That photo morphed into a night shot of a team of men climbing over rocks on a rugged hillside. One of the men toward the rear of the group paused. He slammed his forehead once, then twice, into the rock in front of him. The man behind him reached into a pocket, withdrew a syringe and jabbed it into the man's neck. Before Mark could figure out what was going on, the image changed to an open, empty sea under a storm. The final screen was split between security shots of the interior and exterior of this building.

"Jonas," Jamieson said. "Bring up the training exercise please."

The image on the middle screen changed to show a group of men in fatigues working through what appeared at first glance to be an ordinary obstacle course. Then Mark noticed that the walls were extremely high. The distances the men had to jump or swing seemed excessive. The speed at which the men completed each obstacle made them appear to be moving at double time.

These must be Kaufmann's men.

"Kerberos has recruited men from every branch of the military, law enforcement and intelligence community to form the most elite assassination squad in the world." Jamieson glanced at Mark, no doubt wanting to see how he reacted to the news that the assassins that had almost caught him in Brazil had come from Kaufmann.

Mark wasn't an amateur, though, and his face remained devoid of emotion.

"But that isn't enough," Jamieson continued. "Why settle for ordinary men? There are jobs the President needs done that a normal man just can't handle."

Jamieson waved at the monitor. "This is the latest batch of recruits from Dr. Kaufmann's program. Men with physical abilities that put them worlds above the elite of any special operations group in the world. Men who obey our every command without fail, no matter the physical toll. Men who are already presumed dead, so if they die on a mission, there's no one to mourn them and raise questions."

Mark checked the image for signs of Faith's brother Toby, but the camera angle wasn't close enough to allow facial identification. All the men had similarly bulked-up bodies that spoke of heavy steroids use, so he couldn't even use body type to guess at Toby's presence. "How far into the program are these men?" Mark asked. He made sure his tone was stiff with distaste, but with an underlying curiosity, as if he was fascinated despite himself.

"Excellent question. I see that despite your personal objections, you've been paying attention to the reports I sent you. These men are in the last week of Level 1. They are part of a recently modified program, and have been with Kaufmann for about eight weeks."

That was the right time frame for Toby. Mark tried harder to determine any distinguishing characteristics of the men, but they were running a complicated pattern across a field, so Mark gave up trying to make an identification. He'd just have to go about this another way.

"Why are you showing me this?" Mark asked.

"Because these men are training for a very critical upcoming mission dear to the President's heart. I need you to understand what's at stake, so that you can run interference with the SSU."

Mark hoped the chill that came over his body at those words didn't show in his body language. He hadn't wanted to believe that the President would go behind the backs of all the legitimate organizations tasked with protecting the nation to create his own squad of soldiers. But it fit with what Mark had learned.

According to Ryker, the SSU had been asked to investigate disappearances of military and law enforcement personnel. Every time the agencies involved had started an investigation, they'd hit stone walls. No one had wanted to believe the interference originated at the White House, but Ryker had expressed doubts that anyone else could have so effectively stalled the investigations.

Mark acknowledged the irony that he now trusted Ryker more than Jamieson, when once he'd considered the SSU to be beneath his contempt. Strange what a reawakened conscience could do to a man.

At a softly spoken command from Jamieson, the middle screen returned to the satellite shot of the village in the jungle. "This is an island in the South Pacific," Jamieson said. "A place hated by our President."

"Why?" Mark asked with feigned confusion, even as it felt like a giant fist had a vise grip on his heart. He'd heard rumors, but the shreds of his idealism that had survived the death of his father had refused to believe them.

"This village," Jamieson said, gesturing to the screen, "Is the birthplace of three of the men who carried out the attack in Jakarta that killed then Ambassador MacAdam's son. It's been five years since the boy died. President MacAdam has decided it's finally time to exact retribution. His weapon will be Kerberos's soldiers."

The rumors had been right. For a moment Mark was five again, watching the man he admired most, his father, die in his arms. He'd felt the same bone deep cold then as now. Only this time the cause was betrayal. He hadn't wanted to believe the President capable of targeting innocent civilians as part of a scheme for personal payback. Mark managed to keep his breathing even and his face expressionless as he studied the image of the village, trying to commit to memory details that would help the SSU figure out which of the thousands of islands was the target. He'd never heard a specific name tied to the terrorists' home.

The image showed a typical, sleepy village. Brightly colored laundry hung around what seemed to be a communal well. Pens held farmyard animals. Children played in dusty streets. "I don't understand," Mark said.

As Jamieson went on to outline the basic plan, Mark realized that before he'd disappeared, Toby had been way ahead of him in discovering Jamieson's purpose. But who'd been feeding Toby information? And was that person still around for Mark to use? He needed the name of that island. Even without the name, he had to get this information to Ryker and hope the SSU could stop the plot that would leave an island of innocent people dead.

Kaufmann's Lab
Blue Ridge Mountains

"WE HAVE THE WOMAN, sir. She is in transit to the facility."

Kaufmann smiled and shifted the cell phone to his other ear. "Excellent. Update me when you are half an hour away and I will have a team escort you in."

He disconnected the call and replaced the phone in its belt clip. This was how Jamieson must feel when his teams successfully completed a mission. Elation. A feeling of such power, he felt capable of taking on the most challenging opponents and winning.

No wonder men became addicted to power. Because of him, Dr. Montague's life was at risk. He could just as easily tell his men to kill her as to transport her.

That wouldn't serve his purpose, of course, but his blood hummed at the possibility of causing her death. This was the first time he'd deliberately set out to harm another human being for no other reason than she stood in his way. All of his subjects' deaths and tortures contributed to science. This, though, was personal. He knew Dr. Montague had sicced the SSU on him. He wanted her to suffer.

But his revenge had to wait. First he needed her help boosting his formula.

Kaufmann scowled. He didn't like being beholden to the woman he hated. But all his attempts to stabilize his subjects at Level 1 had failed. Montague had worked with Rafe Andros. If anyone could come up with the breakthrough he needed, she could.

After...well, then retribution would be served.

Three Hours Later
SSU Laboratories, Georgia

"Rafe, what's going on?" Ryker demanded.

Rafe spared a second to check over his shoulder, long enough to notice that Ryker had brought Kai and two security guards with him, then returned his attention to the lab assistant.

"Get it now," Rafe ordered.

The young man shot a frightened look in Ryker's direction.

"What's the problem, son?" Ryker asked.

"He...uh...he wants..." the young man stammered.

"I want more of the drugs Gabby gave me before she was kidnapped," Rafe bit out. *Dios*, it hurt just knowing she was gone. He couldn't even think about what she might be going through or he'd turn back into a raging beast.

Rafe looked quickly around the lab, trying to find what he needed on his own, but there were too many bottles to choose from and he didn't understand the scientific labeling. He turned to Kai. "He's afraid to give me the drugs. So you do it. Give me the highest dose you can."

Kai looked at him as if he'd lost his mind. "Are you crazy? You know the danger."

Rafe got up in Kai's face. "I don't fucking care about the danger," he snarled. "Kaufmann. Has. *Gabby*." The anger and fear inside him was a thick, swirling cloud that threatened to choke him. "I can't rescue her if I don't remember the location of the lab, and I can't do that until this damn mental block is gone. The drugs she gave me last time helped. I can almost remember. So give me more."

"Rafe, that's too dangerous," Kai protested. "Nevsky's subjects went insane on high doses of these drugs. Gabby has made some alterations, but even she doesn't know the potential side effects."

Rafe swallowed back words that would turn this into a fight, wasting time he couldn't afford, and clenched his fists. "If I do nothing, Gabby is lost. She's not a fucking SSU agent, so she hasn't been chipped. How the hell are we supposed to find her unless I remember? No one else has a goddamned clue where Kaufmann is."

Gabby was alone. Scared. Probably hurt. Rafe wanted to tear Kaufmann apart with his bare hands, but first he had to rescue Gabby.

"Do you have any fucking idea what Kaufmann will do to her?" Rafe shouted. "Do you know what it feels like to have his needles slide into you? When the drugs are injected into your blood they burn like acid. The pain goes on and on, until you're lucky you don't lose your mind trying to escape it." Even thinking about it had his heart racing in fear. "When the pain finally stops you discover that you *did* lose your mind, because you're now under Kaufmann's control."

How much worse would it be for Gabby? Rafe knew she wouldn't willingly work with Kaufmann again, which meant the scientist would have to use drugs to force her cooperation. Yet all of Kaufmann's subjects were male. Would the scientist calibrate the drugs for a woman's body? Even if he did, how could Gabby survive such treatment?

"Every second we stand here arguing is a second more that Kaufmann has to hurt Gabby. It took Kaufmann less than two weeks to break me, but I had training. Strong as Gabby is, her mind won't survive long." He sucked in a deep breath. "I have to do everything in my power to help her. If I go insane, fine. At least there's a chance I'll reveal the lab's location before I flip out."

Uh-oh. The room had fallen so quiet, he could hear the faint ticking of the clock. Ryker and Kai stared at him with identical looks of horror.

"What?" Rafe demanded.

"That's the first time you've talked to us about what happened," Kai said gruffly. His expression was nearly impassive thanks to years of undercover work, but Rafe sensed his friend's shock.

On second thought, maybe it wasn't a hint of pity Rafe saw in

Kai's eyes. Kai had been tortured recently. He knew about pain and helplessness. Maybe his eyes held understanding.

"Can we find an acceptable dose to give Rafe?" Ryker asked.

Kai looked over Rafe's shoulder to the assistant. What he saw there must have reassured him. "Yes," he said.

"But Rafe, there's no guarantee this is going to lower your mental barrier," Kai warned. "We don't know all the steps Kaufmann took to block the memories."

Rafe crossed his arms over his chest. "Hypnosis didn't work. Regression didn't work. Psychotherapy didn't work. The barrier feels thinner since Gabby gave me the drugs. It will work."

"If it doesn't," Ryker said, "that doesn't mean Gabby is lost. We're actively searching the region where the helicopter disappeared from radar. We *will* find her."

Rafe gritted his teeth. Finding her wasn't good enough. He needed her unharmed. Unfortunately, every second in Kaufmann's presence equalled agony.

CHAPTER TWENTY-TWO

Later That Night
Kaufmann's Lab
Blue Ridge Mountains

"Why isn't she awake yet? I need to question her."

Floating between consciousness and unconsciousness, Gabby froze at the sound of Kaufmann's arrogant voice.

No!

What had happened? Where was she? Her memory was a warm, fuzzy blur, punctuated by bursts of pain from the side of her jaw. That's right. Someone had hit her. Yes. Kaufmann's men had dragged her from bed. When she'd fought back, one of them knocked her out.

Her kidnapping had been so well orchestrated, the SSU must have a spy in its midst. A flare of anger helped burn away some of her lethargy.

"The men gave her too large a dose of the sedative." The unknown voice was more nasal and less emotional than Kaufmann's. "They misjudged her weight. We don't know how long it will take to wear off."

"So give her something to wake her up," Kaufmann said.

Oh, God. Gabby wanted desperately to drop back into darkness, but she was too terrified of what Kaufmann might have planned for her. So she kept her eyes closed and let herself continue to drift in semi-consciousness.

"If that's what you want," the other voice replied. "However, I have to remind you that she's been given so much of the drug that forcefully bringing her back to consciousness will expose her to the side effects. Even with wake-up drugs she won't be sharp enough to interrogate for several hours."

Kaufmann cursed. "Fine. Let her come out of it naturally. But I want to be alerted the second she's conscious."

Gabby heard the door close as Kaufmann left, but the other man continued to move around the room. Gabby kept her breathing shallow, terrified that at any moment the man would discover she was awake and call Kaufmann back.

The scientist muttered under his breath. Gabby heard papers shift, then the click of a retractable pen. Great. Wasn't he ever going to leave her alone? She didn't know how much longer she could play possum. The need to move and stretch was becoming increasingly urgent.

She tried to relax. Tried to drift back into the hazy state between awake and asleep. But her body decided it was ready for action. As if trying to force her to move, the center of her right foot started to itch.

The sensation started out mild, so she had no problem ignoring it. But the need to scratch quickly grew. Gabby's muscles tensed and it became a struggle to keep her breathing deep and even. If the scientist looked at her, he'd surely notice she wasn't nearly as relaxed as she'd been a few minutes ago.

Finally, the scientist muttered a curse and slapped what sounded like a soft cover notebook against a hard surface. She heard his footsteps cross the room, then the door banged open and slammed shut.

Gabby was too wary to let out the breath she was holding. This could be a trap. If she handled this wrong and bolted awake, she might find herself facing a silent a guard.

Still, she couldn't do nothing. So she mentally crossed her fingers and cracked her eyelids open.

She was lying on a narrow bed along the right wall of an exam room. Cabinets and counters ringed the other three sides, with a gap only for the door. A microscope sat at the edge of the counter directly to Gabby's left. To the right of the microscope a spiral notebook lay at a haphazard angle, as if slammed down in anger. Test tubes sat empty in a drying rack. Other tubes filled with unknown substances sat in well organized holders.

Gabby desperately wanted to get up and look through the notebook while she had the chance. She hoped it would show information on what drugs they'd given her. And maybe she'd be able to find a drug to take to counteract the lethargy that still had a grip on her mind.

Yet she hesitated, remembering Kaufmann's paranoia. Normally he didn't place security cameras in the labs because he was afraid someone might leak the tape to people on the outside. This was hardly a normal situation, though. He'd made clear that he was impatient to talk with her. She had no doubt he wanted to question her about Rafe's progress.

Oh, God. Rafe. Did Kaufmann have him prisoner as well? It would kill Rafe to be back under Kaufmann's control. No. Kaufmann hadn't mentioned his name, so she had to believe Rafe was free.

So what should she do? Continue to pretend to be unconscious on the assumption that the room was being monitored? Or take a chance and gather as much information as she could about what was going on?

She gave a mental sigh. Everything she knew about Kaufmann pointed to him having cameras in the room. And if she was caught trying to escape, it might cause Kaufmann to let his subjects go to work on her.

So, without lifting her head, she lifted her eyelids just enough to let her scope out the room. The door was the only exit. The air vents were too small for her body to squeeze through. The pen on the counter could be used as a weapon, if she could snatch it without being stopped.

Likewise the beakers and test tubes. She could break them and hope she ended up with a shard long enough and sharp enough to serve as a makeshift knife.

She wished she could count on the SSU to come to her rescue, but unless Rafe's memory had miraculously given up the lab's coordinates since this morning, or the security team had managed to track the men who brought her here, no one would be able to find her. Gabby needed to stall Kaufmann's plans long enough to escape. Because once he got his hands on her, she had no illusions. She'd give him exactly what he wanted.

Mark Tonelli called Ryker with the intention of turning over some new information, but the first words out of the man's mouth were, "Do you know where Kaufmann moved his lab?"

"Not yet." Jamieson kept the location secret and Mark hadn't been able to discover the data on his own.

He lined up the pencils on the desk in front of him so all the erasers were side-by-side. "I have more important information, though." Here it was, his big bargaining chip. But he needed Ryker's promise first.

"Before I continue, I want your promise that if the SSU gets involved, they'll leave one of the subjects alone. He's the brother of a friend of mine and I don't want him hurt, just contained."

He had the sudden urge to roll his eyes. Just months ago he would have been horrified to think of being reduced to bargaining with the SSU. Willing to beg to make sure Faith's brother wasn't killed if the SSU used force to stop Kaufmann's men. Before Moscow, Mark had worked with Jamieson to arrange for the SSU's destruction.

Now he only trusted the SSU.

"I also want the doctor who defected from Kaufmann's lab to talk to me and my friend," Mark continued. "We need to understand what's been done to her brother, what behavior to expect and what the doctor can do to help him."

If Ryker thought it odd that Mark was making a request on behalf of a friend, he didn't give any indication. "Done. Unless your man tries to kill one of ours, we won't use lethal force. My men will defend themselves."

Mark thought that situation was all too likely. While he understood Ryker's point, Faith would have a hard time accepting the death of her brother under any circumstances. So he just wouldn't tell her about Ryker's condition, and hope that it all turned out all right in the end. "Agreed."

"We have a problem, though," Ryker added. "Dr. Montague was kidnapped by Kaufmann's men."

Mark cursed. "I'll do what I can to find the location of the lab for you."

He took a deep breath, knowing he was about to cross a line that would forever change his future. "I've learned that a team of Kaufmann's subjects is scheduled to carry out an attack on an island in the South Pacific in a few days. By order of the President."

"The anniversary demonstration," Ryker said. "Damn, the rumors were right."

Mark felt a great weight lift off his shoulders. He didn't have to explain the situation or the consequences to Ryker. In truth, the man probably understood far better than Mark. Which made the next part of his mission even easier.

"I've been ordered to distract the SSU," he said.

"Find me the lab and our assault team will appear suitably

distracted. No one expects us to be large enough to stage two nearly simultaneous attacks," Ryker said. "Can you give me any details that will help us locate the island?"

"My boss claimed that the island is where several of the terrorists grew up, but I've been unable to find any information linking the suspected terrorists to any of the regional islands." As best he could, Mark described the scenery shown in satellite photo. "They're going to put something in the water that will kill everyone."

Ryker cursed. "Something they already have access to? Or is a new product from Kaufmann?"

Mark thought back. "I don't know. My boss said they were very proud of the chemical and that the test runs had been perfect. I think..." He closed his eyes, picturing Jamieson in his mind. "I think he said that after years of trials they'd finally achieved the results they wanted."

"I need everything you can get me on this chemical so we can create a counteragent," Ryker said.

"I'll do my best." Despite the rapidly approaching anniversary date, Mark had to proceed very carefully or risk being caught.

SSU Laboratories
Georgia

RYKER STARED at the e-mail from Gabby sitting in his inbox. The subject line read "In case of my death or disappearance."

Mouth set in a grim line, he opened the e-mail. Thank God, Rafe wasn't here with him. The last thing Rafe needed was proof that Gabby had not only anticipated an attack, but hadn't expected to survive. And it said something about the persistent danger in her life that Gabby hadn't trusted the SSU to keep her safe.

Five minutes later he pushed out of his office chair and

stalked across the room to the window. His office hadn't suffered anything more than a few cracks in the ceiling during the attack. Several holes had been blown in the exterior walls, and two of the administrative offices had collapsed ceilings, but overall the physical damage had been limited. The assault team had known exactly where to place their explosives for maximum impact. They'd moved in, split up and headed without hesitation toward two locations: The lower level where Rafe had been in one of the treatment rooms, and Gabby's apartment on the second floor of the staff wing. Whoever had provided the information to Kaufmann not only had detailed knowledge of the inside of the buildings, but knew the schedules for both Gabby and Rafe.

SSU cleanup crews had already patched the walls, and Ryker had put enhanced security measures in place in case another incident occurred. He considered that unlikely. Kaufmann had Gabby and right now, she was more valuable to him than Rafe.

Luckily, Rafe hadn't been captured. Despite Dr. Steuart's assurances that Rafe's mental condition was stable, Ryker didn't think the man would survive being under Kaufmann's control again.

Ryker glanced out the window, watching with approval as a pair of security guards walked the perimeter. He didn't want to believe that another traitor existed within the SSU. He'd hoped that after discovering how Gonzales had betrayed Rafe's team to Kaufmann, then later worked with Tonelli to turn Susana Dias over to Dr. Ivanov, the SSU was finally clean of moles. Another series of background checks was underway, but so far nothing suspicious had been discovered.

However, thanks to Gabby's e-mail, he realized that the people behind Kaufmann's lab were much more powerful than he'd expected. Throwing into question the results of this latest background search. With the right connections, a past could be created that even the SSU's prime hackers wouldn't find a hole in.

Rubbing his hand over his jaw, he paced back and forth in

front of his desk. Knowing the ramifications of Gabby's discovery had the potential to destroy lives.

Gabby had found traces of Agent Styx in Kaufmann's subjects.

Christ. No wonder Rafe's temper had reminded him of the soldiers he'd seen in Vietnam. According to Gabby, the data on the microchip included evidence that Nevsky had been part of the team that created Agent Styx. Something Ryker had never even suspected.

Gabby's email included a transcription of notes from her father detailing his investigation into Agent Styx. He'd been close to uncovering Nevsky's involvement. Had already determined that two other scientists had been involved in the original program but neither had survived the war. Based on that information, Ryker had to agree with Gabby's assessment that the car accident that killed her parents had been staged to stop her father's investigation.

His hand automatically reached out to give a calming spin to his antique globe before he remembered that he wasn't in his D.C. office. He closed his fingers into a fist and stared out at the front lawn.

Gabby's email had also included a coded list of people her father suspected had covered up the misuse of Agent Styx during the war. Gabby hadn't been able to break the code, but Ryker recognized it. The key wasn't something he could pull accurately from his memory today. Too many years had passed since the special ops units had used this unique code during the war.

But he had the key in a box of wartime paraphernalia he kept in a secure vault in his basement. Part sentimental mementos, part reminders of how wrong things had gone, for once he was glad he'd held onto the items. Because if he was right, then the man or men who funded Kaufmann might very well be on her father's list.

He sighed. Under the current circumstances, bringing down

the powers behind Kaufmann no longer held top priority. Based on Tonelli's information, Ryker was certain that Kaufmann planned on arming his soldiers with Agent Styx for the upcoming anniversary attack.

He needed Gabby back. Her email explained that she'd worked with samples of the chemical over the years, trying to mitigate its side effects. With the anniversary of the death of the President's son fast approaching, Gabby was the SSU's only hope of creating a counteragent in time.

Unfortunately, the key to finding Gabby was locked in Rafe's memories.

CHAPTER TWENTY-THREE

The Next Day
SSU Laboratories
Georgia

As Rafe marched down the corridor toward the psychiatrist's office, he felt the knowledge of the lab's location lurking just out of reach behind that damned veil in his mind. Since the second injection, he'd remembered more of his days at the lab. The torture. The conditioning. The sounds of men going insane. The look and smell of the cell he'd been chained in.

But no matter how hard he concentrated, no matter how many times he ordered himself to break through and *remember*, the location of Kaufmann's lab remained hidden. He tried every mental trick he knew. Hell, he'd even let the doctors hypnotize and regress him again.

Nothing.

Meanwhile, his fear for Gabby had grown claws and tore at his soul because instinct told him she was nearly out of time.

And yeah, he knew that made him a bastard. His primary concern should be to help locate the lab so the SSU could stop

Kaufmann's soldiers from killing scores of innocent civilians. The life of one woman shouldn't matter.

To Rafe, though, Gabby's life was everything.

"Tell me again why you think this will work," Kai muttered beside him. "You really think Kaufmann let you keep the knowledge of the lab's coordinates?"

"Yes," Rafe snapped. "I told you. Last night I dreamed about Kaufmann sending us out on test missions with instructions to call him when our mission was complete. At that time he'd give us the command that would allow us to remember the coordinates and return to the compound."

"You really think that hearing a recording of Kaufmann is going to open up your memories?" Kai asked.

Gabby's friend Laurel, the one who'd helped plan the initial escape, had smuggled several of Kaufmann's dictation tapes out of the lab, hiding them in the clothing of the escapees. The tapes had been given to the SSU's top techs and they'd put together a new tape following the script Rafe had written.

"What if his voice sends you into attack mode instead?"

Rafe shot Kai a sideways glare. "You vetoed my other suggestion," he reminded his friend. "So this is our best shot."

"More drugs are not the answer," Kai retorted. "You're already on a dose that's barely safe. So yeah, in comparison, making a tape of Kaufmann's voice seems sane."

Rafe would've cut the knowledge out of his brain and handed it to Ryker if he could. Anything to save Gabby.

He yanked open the door to the psychiatrist's office. Dr. Steuart and Ryker were already in the room.

"Are you sure you're ready for this?" Dr. Steuart asked as Rafe moved toward the cell phone resting on her desk. The phone had been set up to connect directly to a computer that would play the fake message from Kaufmann. "There's still a chance that hearing Dr. Kaufmann's voice might send you into a rage. Or worse."

Rafe gave an impatient shrug of his shoulders. "Objections noted," he growled. "Can we pleases get the fuck on with this?"

He picked up the cell phone and dialed a number from memory. The cell phone was programmed to connect to the computer message no matter what number Rafe dialed. After the "call" the SSU's techs would take a look at the numbers Rafe had actually dialed and see if they could get any information on the lab's location from tracing the phone number.

As the last number went through there was a second's pause, then the phone rang three times, just like in his dream.

"Who is this?" Dr. Kaufmann's voice answered.

Rafe froze, swamped by fear and rage. His hands started to shake as he fought back the instinctive need to grovel and obey.

Waiting for orders. Waiting for punishment.

Then Kai elbowed him, bringing him back to the moment.

"This is subject 82431, sir," Rafe said crisply. "I've completed my mission."

"Good. Listen for my order."

"Yes, sir!"

"You will now remember how to return to your cell. If you are not in your cell within forty-eight hours, your memory will lock again and you will be terminated. Do you understand?"

"Yes, sir!" he replied.

The other end of the line clicked as the call ended.

Rafe staggered as the dam inside his head burst open. He caught himself with a hand on the desk, fighting against dizziness. Then his eyes cleared and in his mind he saw a clear image of the compound.

He gestured for Kai to give him paper and pencil. Grabbing the pad his friend set before him, Rafe sank into the doctor's office chair and started scribbling.

Ten minutes later, he not only had the coordinates of the compound, but had drawn a rough map of all the paths through the forest toward the facility, how they were guarded, the best way to enter the building, and the fastest route to his cell.

"Amazing," Kai breathed when Rafe stopped writing. He pulled the paper toward him, then held it out to Ryker. "Take a look at that. He actually remembered."

Rafe scowled, not liking the surprise in Kai's voice.

"Good job, Rafe," Ryker said.

"I'm not a second-grader you need to praise because my drawing finally resembles a real person," Rafe grumbled.

Ryker raised his eyebrows at his outburst, making him feel even more like a child called before the principal for rude behavior.

"Is there anything more you want to tell me before I take this to our research department?" Ryker asked.

Rafe glanced at the drawing. "It was humid and hot outside, but the interior was naturally cool. I think, like in the Adirondack compound, part of the structure must have been built into the rock itself." He struggled to make sense of all the images that now crowded his head. There were almost too many for him to assimilate.

"I remember lots of trees. Like...maybe it was in or bordering a state forest. Someplace far away from people, so that our outside activities wouldn't be noticed. That's all for now."

Ryker nodded, then clapped Rafe on the shoulder. "Thank you." He turned toward Dr. Steuart. "Are you done here?"

She shook her head. "I'd like to have a brief session alone with him, please."

Rafe struggled to keep his annoyance off his face. He was damned tired of her poking around in his brain. When would he earn the right to keep his thoughts to himself? But knowing he needed to continue earning Ryker's trust, he nodded agreement.

With a final smile of approval in Rafe's direction, Ryker walked out the door, followed by Kai. Leaving Rafe with a disturbing sense of abandonment.

That Afternoon
Kaufmann's Compound
Blue Ridge Mountains

GABBY OPENED her eyes the next time Kaufmann entered the room. She'd been unable to come up with an escape plan and had decided to stop postponing the inevitable.

"Ah, I see you're awake." Kaufmann's voice lacked even the minimal warmth he'd once used when addressing her and the other scientists. This voice rang with pure, cold cruelty that made Gabby shiver and her stomach cramp.

But she would not let him see her fear. If he'd wanted to kill her, he would have done so. Which meant he needed her.

"I won't bother with social niceties, Dr. Montague," Kaufmann continued. "I've brought you here for one purpose only. To share the knowledge you've gained from working with Rafe Andros and Dr. Nevsky's notes."

Gabby shook her head.

"You won't help me?"

"No." Her voice was hoarse and the refusal barely audible, but Kaufmann's lips thinned.

"Have you suddenly developed a conscience? You had no problem helping me before."

She would not discuss her morals with him. The only thing she had to say to Kaufmann was no. Since she'd already stated her position, she simply returned his stare.

"I take your silence to mean you truly believe you can refuse to help me and I'll permit it?"

Gabby didn't answer, although her stomach turned over uneasily. She didn't like the malicious glint in his eyes, but she'd spent the time since she'd awakened coming to terms with the idea that he'd use pain to control her.

From the moment she left the first compound with Rafe and his men she'd considered the possibility that Kaufmann would come after her. Maybe even kill her. All she could do now was endure his torture long enough to escape. Because once he realized she'd never cooperate, he'd have no reason to keep her alive.

"Speak to me, Dr. Montague. I want to make certain that I understand you. Will you help me strengthen my program with the knowledge you've obtained?"

"No."

"Even if I tell you that I can make you obey me? I would enjoy putting you through our mind control regimen, but there's not enough time. So I will have to use other methods."

The slow, thin smile that stretched his lips was pure evil. "I have quite an extensive arsenal of poisons at my disposal. They're bundled with an antidote which kicks in with enough time to stop the subject from dying. But the results are…excruciating."

Gabby swallowed tightly but kept her chin up. Rafe had survived Kaufmann for weeks. She was determined to survive as long as possible. "My answer is still no."

Kaufmann's eyes lit with anticipation and Gabby trembled all the way to her bones.

"Excellent," he said. He flicked his eyes over her body as if measuring her. Everywhere his eyes touched her skin felt singed. "I will have to calibrate the poisons for your smaller body. In the meantime, have something to eat." He gestured to the door and a lab technician brought a tray of food into the room.

"It might be the last untainted food you eat for a while." With that parting remark, Kaufmann left the room. The tech placed the tray on a low table near Gabby, then followed his boss out of the room.

Gabby's stomach grumbled. But as tempting as the mashed potatoes, vegetables and meat with thick gravy might be, she didn't trust that it was safe. It would be just like Kaufmann to poison it. And even if it was safe, it was better to keep her stomach empty.

She was certain that whatever Kaufmann had in store for her, she'd soon be losing any food she managed to choke down. Better not to have anything ready to vomit up.

Closing her eyes against a surge of fear, she concentrated on her breathing and tried to put herself into a light trance. Anything to distract her from the torture she knew was coming.

BURNING, electric pain jolted Gabby awake. The last thing she remembered before unconsciousness had claimed her was being on the bed and smelling a sickly sweet odor.

The pain that had brought her awake receded slowly, as if reluctant to let go of its hold on her. She opened heavy eyelids. Her vision was blurry, but she made out the shape of two figures standing nearby. She blinked furiously again and again until her eyes finally brought into focus Kaufmann and the face of an unfamiliar female in a white lab coat.

The woman held an electric probe in her left hand.

Gabby shivered, and as her skin prickled with goose pimples she realized she wasn't wearing her clothes. Instead, she was covered in the same easy-to-clean gray coverall she'd seen Kaufmann's subjects wearing. She tried to sit up, but her hands and feet were strapped down.

"This is your last chance," Kaufmann said, "Will you agree to help me?" The anticipatory light in his eyes made it clear he wanted her to refuse. He was looking forward to hurting her.

Gabby wet her lips. "No."

"Very well, then." Kaufmann turned his back and spoke quietly to the woman.

Gabby took a good look at her surroundings and realized she'd been moved to a different room. The only furnishings here were the examination table she was on, a tall cabinet, and a long counter with a built-in sink. Sitting in the middle of the counter were a single vial and a syringe.

Gabby's stomach tightened in dread, but she couldn't look

away from the vial. She barely registered Kaufmann giving the woman instructions. The woman hung the electric probe up in the cabinet and moved to Gabby's side. Gabby was so focused on trying to keep her breathing calm and even, mentally preparing herself not to beg or cry, that she flinched when the woman grabbed hold of her arm and pushed up her sleeve.

With calm, deliberate movements, Kaufmann picked up the vial and inserted the tip of the syringe. Everything inside Gabby urged her to shout, to scream, to plead with him not to do this. She didn't like pain. She didn't deal well with pain at *all*.

But she wasn't going to break down. She had to be strong. *Sometimes, the only way to fight is just to endure. And that's the hardest thing of all.* She remembered the bleak look in Rafe's eyes when he'd told her that. She'd been awed by his strength, knowing that most men wouldn't have been able to survive what he had. Not and also keep their sanity.

She only hoped she could draw on some of Rafe's strength.

The needle stabbed into her arm. Heartbeats later the poison hit her system. Gabby's head went back on an involuntary gasp. Her hands clenched as waves of agony crashed over her.

As the first scream broke free from her soul, she prayed she'd pass out quickly.

CHAPTER TWENTY-FOUR

The Next Morning
SSU Compound
Oregon

"SIR," Rafe began as he followed Ryker down the hallway of the SSU operations headquarters in Oregon. They'd arrived just hours ago in preparation of meeting up with the team Ryker had requested for Gabby's rescue. "Send me ahead with Niko and Kai. Put someone else in charge of the men."

Ryker glanced over his shoulder without breaking stride. "No."

Hell. Was Ryker crazy? He wasn't ready. The drugs had brought his intellect and memory back, but now Rafe was dealing with a new set of issues. He processed information almost too fast to handle, causing dizzy spells and small migraines. And he was still prone to fly into an uncontrollable rage if he was pushed too far.

He'd done his best to hide the extent of his symptoms from the doctors, but they were aware he wasn't fully back to normal.

So he was the dead last man who should be leading Gabby's

rescue team. Besides, what soldier would want to follow a man who got his last team captured, then personally killed several of his teammates while in captivity?

No one, that's who. Which was why he'd been avoiding his friends since he'd returned to Oregon. Losing his self-respect to Kaufmann ate at him like a damn cancer, but seeing pity or disgust on the faces of his friends and colleagues would hurt worse than all the physical torture he'd endured.

Ryker pushed the release bar on the exterior door that led onto the assembly grounds. "For the record, I didn't order anyone to join this team. I made it voluntary."

Which probably meant only Niko and Kai were going to be waiting for—

"Holy shit," Rafe breathed in awe. Then he muttered a Greek prayer of thanks.

The assembly area was packed with men and women in fighting gear. Rafe did a quick head count and gave up after reaching fifty. It looked like the whole freakin' roster of available SSU agents had shown up.

Rafe could only stare at them, dumbstruck.

Paul Chin, a well-respected SSU team leader and a former SEAL, stepped forward and saluted Rafe. "All the volunteers are assembled and ready for your selection, sir!" He grinned. When Rafe just stared back, unable to speak past the lump in his throat, Chin winked at him.

"Of course," Chin said, "maybe picking a team to go after those mad scientists is too tough an assignment for a mere Ranger."

Rafe gave Chin a mock offended glare, then let his gaze roam over the assembled mass. Niko stood front and center next to Kai. Niko and Kai usually worked undercover, so wouldn't normally volunteer for an assault mission. Yet because it was such a small agency, the SSU cross-trained all its agents. Rafe had no hesitation in nodding at each of them, indicating he accepted their presence on his team.

Seeing the pride on Niko's face, it hit home again just how deep his brother's love ran. And for the first time, Rafe really got what Niko meant when he'd said he wouldn't have survived prison without Rafe's unconditional love and acceptance. When you'd fallen so far you figured not even your family could still love you, life became a special type of hell. But Niko and Kai hadn't given up on him any more than Gabby had. Knowing that had helped Rafe through his recovery.

Jesus, his throat felt tight and his eyes itched. He'd never imagined...had never even dared to hope he could slide back into command of this elite group. He'd been born to fight. Born to lead. Here, in the company of strong, honorable men and women was where he belonged.

He'd thought Kaufmann had stolen this from him.

Chin cleared his throat and Rafe nodded. What the hell was he supposed to say? Rafe swallowed and turned to face the crowd. "Thank you."

His voice echoed off the walls, then the crowd erupted in a raucous cheer. "This community represents all that is good and honest about this country. I've been proud to call myself an SSU agent all these years. I thought—" He shook his head, unable to believe what he was about to confess. "I thought after what Kaufmann did to me, that I'd never be fit to lead again. I'm still not convinced I belong up here. As many of you know, I've experienced both physical and mental changes because of Kaufmann's program."

He forced air into his lungs, firming his voice. "But I promise you this. I will not rest until Dr. Montague and the other victims of Kaufmann's program have been rescued. I will not stop until Kaufmann and his team are eliminated."

The crowd responded with supportive hoots and hollers.

Chin stepped forward and grabbed Rafe in a one-arm bear hug. "Welcome back, Rafe."

Shit. His eyes were tearing up. Way to earn everyone's respect. Rafe blinked them away before Chin released him, hoping his friend hadn't noticed.

But damn if Chin's eyes weren't bright with moisture. And when Rafe looked out over the crowd, he saw several other wet eyes.

All right then. Maybe this once he would just go with it. Let 'em see him cry.

Just a little.

Two Days Later
Kaufmann's Compound
Blue Ridge Mountains

RAFE LOWERED his binoculars from his lookout point over Kaufmann's new compound. God, it seemed like a million years ago that he'd stared down at the first compound, wondering how deeply Gabby was involved in Nate's disappearance. Now here he was, struggling to pull out mission-critical details from his memories of this place, while suppressing echoes of pain, degradation and forced obedience.

He stifled a sense of déjà-vu and slipped farther into the trees. In the end, he'd had to turn away SSU agents who'd volunteered to join this mission. The result was three assault teams, headed by Rafe, Chin and Niko. A fourth team lead by Kai would collect Kaufmann's data and securely store all chemical and biological samples.

As Rafe moved over to a new observation spot, he tried not to think about the responsibility of leading so many people into a danger he wouldn't wish on his worst enemy. But yeah, part of him was totally freaked. Kaufmann had trained him to follow orders instead of giving them. Before his capture, leading men had been second nature to Rafe. Then Kaufmann's conditioning convinced him his job was to submit, not to think.

He continued to fight against the urge to give in and let someone else take control. Having two dozen men and women looking at him with trust and respect went a long way toward restoring his confidence, even though he didn't fully deserve their respect yet. His men might not have had time to recognize all Rafe's differences, but he was acutely aware that he still wasn't free of side effects.

His job, in addition to keeping his team safe, was to see that the man he'd become earned their respect. Which meant he had zero room for error.

He took a deep breath. Good thing he'd always loved a challenge.

Checking the compound from this new angle, Rafe raised his brows. Kaufmann must have been damn confident that Rafe's mental blocks would hold, because security hadn't changed all that much. Two electrified fences topped with barbed wire enclosed the facility. According to the data leaked by Tonelli, Kaufmann hadn't installed any advanced security measures such as infrared or radar.

Kaufmann had never been able to use guard dogs as part of his defenses. The animals sensed something different in the altered men, something that made aggressive dogs attack and timid dogs slink away. Kaufmann hadn't wanted to waste time overcoming the guard dogs' reactions, so he'd banished them from the premises.

All the better for Rafe and his team.

Rafe studied the patterns of the teams of normal men patrolling the perimeter. The only time Kaufmann's subjects ever left the compound was their weekly shift as part of the security team. Whenever Rafe had joined a patrol, the regular guards had treated him with the same caution they'd use around a feral dog.

Rafe had barely acknowledged the guards' existence. All that mattered was the mission Kaufmann had given him. Which sometimes included killing a guard who wasn't living up to expectations.

After watching for half an hour, Rafe motioned for Andersen and headed back to base.

GABBY PANTED and fought to remain conscious through the haze of pain. Kaufmann and his prize torturer had dumped her on the floor after this latest session, and the chilled concrete felt good against her overheated, oversensitive cheek. Her body still tightened with residual spasms from the electric shocks they'd given her. Her mouth tasted like sour eggs and although she still couldn't get her eyes to open, she smelled vomit close by.

During this round of torture, Kaufmann had questioned her about Rafe and the SSU. Did Rafe remember his time at the compound? Could he find his way back here?

"No," Gabby had screamed, giving him the truth while she fought back hopelessness. Because if Rafe didn't remember this location, then how could he possibly rescue her?

She didn't know how much longer she could stand Kaufmann's abuse. Each day her body grew weaker, eroding her resistance. Yet perversely, the casual way Kaufmann and his scientists hurt her gave her the strength to continue to say no to the most important question—would she cooperate? These weren't the type of people she wanted to be in the same room with, let alone provide them with critical research to allow them to make their subjects even more monstrous.

What terrified Gabby all the way to her soul was the fear that in Kaufmann's attempt to force her cooperation before his deadline, the worst was still to come.

RAFE KNEW it was going to be bad when Niko cornered him the moment he returned to camp.

With a nod, Rafe dismissed his team, then let his brother herd him farther into the forest. When Niko finally stopped and turned around, his grave expression caused Rafe's world to freeze. He knew in his gut Niko had bad news. And only one topic would make Niko bring Rafe so far from camp no one would hear them.

"No." The denial was out of his mouth before Rafe could take it back. "Gabby's alive." She had to be.

"Yes, but—" Niko shot him a look of pained sympathy. "I'm sorry, Rafe. One of Chin's scouts overheard two guards talking as the shift changed. They were joking about a female prisoner. Someone Kaufmann has been torturing. The guards placed bets on whether Kaufmann would give the woman to the normal guards or the freaks when she breaks."

"No!" Rafe shoved Niko away from him. He knew. Ah, *Dios*, he knew what it felt like to be in Gabby's shoes. The pain...

He shuddered. The pain had almost been too much to bear, and he'd been trained to resist torture. The thought of Gabby's delicate, feminine body suffering a fraction of that agony, or even the bone-numbing chill of the water chamber, made him want to throw his head back and howl.

Rafe stood in a tiny, tile-lined cubicle just tall enough for him to stand upright and so narrow that he couldn't sit or lie down. He'd lost all track of time.

"Tell me what I want to hear, Mr. Andros," the Voice crooned through the overhead speakers. "Then you can go back to your room."

This was the dangerous voice. The voice that wanted his agreement to do something bad. This voice he had to ignore, even though he knew what the consequence would be.

"Still no answer? Very well, then."

The pipes groaned and Rafe braced himself as a deluge of icy water spurted out of the hole directly over his head. He clamped his teeth together and closed his eyes. The water sluiced over his body, pooling at the bottom of the chamber until it reached his knees. Then the water stopped and a new voice came out of the walls.

"Do you feel tired Mr. Andros? Do your muscles hurt? Do you feel cold?"

"Cold."

"Nothing else?"

"No."

"Thank you."

It bothered Rafe that he wasn't physically tired. Somewhere in the back of his brain he knew he'd been standing here for too long. At least a day, maybe longer. His muscles should hurt. He should feel sleep deprived.

Instead, all he felt was cold. But that ice was layered over an inferno of molten rage.

Rafe pulled himself back to the present with difficulty and let fury wipe out his fear. Anger would give him additional strength to take down Kaufmann. But right now he had to think. "I want to hear the report directly."

Niko nodded, his expression wary. "You...okay?"

"What the fuck do you think? No, I'm not okay." He was as far from okay as he'd ever been. Out of his head with terror and the nearly overwhelming need to hurt the ones holding Gabby. But losing control wouldn't help him save her. "After I talk to Chin's scout, we need to prepare the teams. We're going in tonight."

Niko opened his mouth as if to speak, then shrugged. "It's your call. You know I've got your back."

"Thanks."

Niko clapped Rafe on the shoulder, then led the way back to camp.

As he followed, Rafe felt his brain working overtime, weighing and discarding options with abnormal speed. The backs of his eyes ached and a spot at the base of his neck tingled. The sensations still freaked him out and made him want to check in a mirror to see if he had smoke coming out of his ears like a cartoon character. Worse, a hot, painful pressure built in his skull until he thought his brain might explode. Relief only came when his brain finished processing the data and slowed down again.

At moments like these, Rafe could understand why so many of Nevsky's subjects had committed suicide. But he had to hang on. His increased intelligence was his strongest advantage. Kaufmann believed his mind control to be ironclad, and would never consider that Rafe could break it, let alone retain enough intelligence to communicate the location of the compound to anyone.

He looked forward to seeing Kaufmann's face when he realized he was wrong.

CHAPTER TWENTY-FIVE

Washington, D.C.

"I AGREED to your request to kidnap Dr. Montague," Jamieson said into the phone. "Because you promised it would result in the complete stability of your men. So where is my new team?" He drew the heavy gold silk drapes tighter against the picture window in his home office. He suspected someone had been following him and no longer trusted the security of his office phone at Langley.

Here, at least, he was guaranteed not to have some underling walk in on him. Plus, he had the best security system, including top-of-the-line anti-eavesdropping equipment.

Nevertheless, he resented the need to skulk around like a common thief. He was working at the behest of the President. He should be immune to scrutiny. Yet he couldn't shake the feeling that there were forces closing in on him. Forces determined to see him fail.

"Dr. Montague is proving to be more of a challenge to crack than we anticipated," Kaufmann explained in his arrogant voice. "Don't worry, you'll have your team."

Jamieson stared down at the executive order in his hands. Kaufmann had less than a week to get his formula tweaked so that the next batch of men would remain stable during the anniversary demonstration.

"If I order you to break Dr. Montague's resistance by the end of tomorrow," Jamieson asked, "what's the quickest you could have the new team ready?"

The men on his current team were already showing signs of deterioration. In a week they would start losing coordination and balance.

"I can't give you a definite time," Kaufmann explained with a hint of impatience. "I don't know what techniques Dr. Montague used to reverse the side effects in Rafe Andros. Gene therapy, drug formulation...each option poses different challenges. Assuming nothing goes wrong, we're talking ten days at the minimum to incorporate the changes into our program, strengthen the desired effects, and run tests. Two to three weeks is more likely."

Jamieson squeezed the phone so hard the plastic groaned in protest. "Unacceptable. The President needs the new team ready to deploy in five days."

"Impossible!"

"Make it possible," Jamieson said. "Or I'm going to destroy you. And then I'll throw you to your subjects."

He slammed down the phone and stood at his desk, hands fisted to stop their trembling. Years of careful planning, of lying and manipulating to achieve his dreams, and it all stood on the verge of collapse because of Kaufmann's incompetence.

Kaufmann should have killed Dr. Montague months ago. If she didn't provide the necessary information immediately, Jamieson would make certain to rectify Kaufmann's oversight.

Kaufmann's Compound
Blue Ridge Mountains

DR. KAUFMANN STARED at the unconscious body of Dr. Montague through the one-way glass in her cell. She'd proven to be remarkably resistant to both the pain of poison and of physical torture. Oh, she'd given up data about Andros and the SSU, but she still refused to reveal how she'd broken Kaufmann's mind control and cured Andros of his rages.

Kaufmann tapped his foot. He had to get her cooperation by tomorrow, or he'd never be able to implement the changes to his formula before Jamieson's deadline.

Unfortunately, should Dr. Montague fail to cooperate, he didn't have any fresher subjects to send to Kerberos. He had a few men who, like the current subjects serving with Kerberos, had already been at Level 1 for almost four weeks. Even under this new, accelerated regimen that was the longest a subject had remained at Level 1, where the mind control was strongest. For such a sensitive mission, the President required the fully controlled men of Level 1.

Kaufmann had managed to slow most of the physical deterioration, delaying full body breakdown until the eighth week. But the subjects' mental deterioration was more rapid than before. They experienced increasingly violent rages as the mind control eased, lashing out at anyone within reach. Including their controllers.

No, worse than that. The subjects *targeted* their controllers.

Kaufmann pressed his palm over the stabbing pain in his lower abdomen. When the mind control was in effect, disobedience was met by excruciating headaches that disabled a man. But just last week, one of the subjects had beat his controller to death, his extraordinary strength making it impossible to contain him. When even tranquilizers hadn't slowed him down, the guards had been forced to kill him.

If Jamieson sent the current team to the anniversary demonstration there was a strong possibility one or more of the men would break free of their handlers and go on a rampage. Then Kaufmann could kiss his career good-bye. He'd worked too many years to fail now.

Which meant he needed to force Dr. Montague today to reveal how she'd countered the mind control and rage in Rafe Andros. Kaufmann had just enough time to rework the formula, inject it into his current subjects, and send them to Jamieson in hopes the changes would make the men more stable.

Unfortunately, the scientists in charge of her torture believed Dr. Montague had reached her physical limit. If they hurt her any more, they couldn't guarantee her mind wouldn't snap.

So Kaufmann had to try another way.

He pressed the intercom button to the left of the cell door. "Has Cygan returned?" he demanded of his assistant.

"He's just entered the compound, sir."

"Good. Have him meet me in the Sector 3 interrogation room."

The sound of a metal door sliding open roused Gabby from her stupor. When she'd woken up after the last torture session, she'd found herself shackled to the cold rock wall in this cell with her arms over her head and her legs slightly spread.

Footsteps echoed down the corridor, silencing the moans and cries from the other prisoners. When she heard the rattle of a key in her cell door, Gabby raised her head and squinted against the faint light coming in through the bars. Even that small motion made her senses spin. She didn't remember when she'd last eaten. Couldn't imagine ever wanting food, or even water, again after the poisons had turned her insides into a writhing, biting mass of agony. But she knew Kaufmann needed her clear-headed. So she suspected they'd been giving her intravenous sustenance while she was passed out.

How had Rafe found the strength to survive? How had any part of his sanity remained? She was lucky. Kaufmann didn't want to break her mind. And he couldn't give her the mind control drugs because interfering with her independent thinking would defeat the purpose of having her able to manipulate the formula to achieve the results he wanted. She couldn't imagine how much worse it had been for Rafe to have his will taken away and be forced to kill his teammates. Yet he'd not only survived, he hadn't lost his ability to laugh. To love.

Gabby clung to the memory of that last night with Rafe as she braced herself for more pain. So far her torturers had been careful not to damage her eyes or hurt her so badly she couldn't work. Still, Gabby didn't know how much more pain she could take before her mind broke. She swallowed thickly, hearing the echoes of her screams in her mind. Feeling the throbbing on her back, belly and thighs from where strips of skin had been torn or burned off. The thin hospital gown she wore did nothing to protect her from the chill that seeped out of the rock behind her, but at least the cold numbed the pain, making it almost bearable.

The door opened and Kaufmann stepped into the cell. He regarded her with the intensity of a man determined to crack a particularly difficult puzzle. "You have proven to be much more resistant to pain than I expected, Dr. Montague. My deadline looms near and we are no closer to a resolution."

Gabby held her breath, knowing he would make her pay for interfering with his plans.

"So I have decided to try another method of persuasion." He crooked a finger over his shoulder, and one of the security guards entered, dragging a kicking, twisting, gagged young boy no more than ten or eleven years old.

Oh, no.

The weight of defeat threatened to smother Gabby as the boy

was brought further into the cell. The poor child was little more than skin and bones, and in desperate need of a wash. His clothes were stiff with dried mud and other unidentifiable substances. His hair was a brown rat's nest. His eyes, wide with fright and pain, pleaded with her for help. Gabby saw the unmistakable bulge of a collarbone out of place and wanted to strangle the guard with her bare hands.

Where had Kaufmann found the boy? He didn't allow children at the compound.

A female scientist stepped into the cell holding a syringe in her left hand. At her nod, the guard raised the boy's arm and pushed back his sleeve.

"No!" Gabby had barely survived the poisons. They'd kill a child. She swallowed against a lump of bitterness, aware that everyone in the cell watched her with anticipation. They knew what her response would be. What any decent human being's response would be.

"Don't hurt him," she said, forcing the words through vocal chords shredded from screaming.

"This boy is a trespasser," Kaufmann told her. "We found him living like an animal in the woods. Why shouldn't we test our poisons on him? Think of all the knowledge we can gain."

"Leave him alone and I'll help you." Defeat left a sour taste in her mouth. The boy's eyes flared briefly with hope, then settled into a watchful wariness.

Kaufmann gave a tight, satisfied smile. "You agree to share your knowledge of Dr. Nevsky's formula, and the work you did with Rafe Andros, to help me strengthen the mind control of my subjects?"

Gabby nodded. "Yes."

"If you fail, if any changes you make do not deliver results, the boy will be given the exact same dosages of poison that you received."

Gabby's stomach turned over, knowing she was truly trapped.

There was no way she could allow that boy to suffer. "I understand."

"Good." Kaufmann waved at the guard. "Take the boy away."

"No," Gabby protested. "I want him with me, where I can watch over him. Because if you go back on your word and hurt him, then I won't give you what you need."

Kaufmann's mouth flattened into a cruel line.

Gabby notched her chin up and met his eyes with all the determination she could muster.

"Very well," Kaufmann said with quiet menace. "Cygan, call some of your men to escort Dr. Montague to Lab 1. You will accompany them with the boy."

Kaufmann stepped closer to Gabby. "You will begin work now," he said. "I want results by the end of tomorrow or first the boy, then you, will suffer far beyond what you've already experienced."

He turned and stalked from the cell, followed by the female scientist.

Gabby let out the breath she'd been holding, but otherwise kept her relief from showing. One day. If she could stall that long, maybe a miracle would happen and she'd find some way to escape.

The guards freed Gabby from the chains, then handcuffed her and shoved her after Kaufmann. Unable to stop herself, she peered into the other cells as she stumbled down the corridor. The weak illumination from the walkway lights allowed her to see the men chained to the rough stone walls. They were naked. Many had oozing burns and bleeding cuts crisscrossing their bodies.

Some of the men appeared to be unconscious, or asleep. Others writhed in pain. As Gabby and her guards walked past one cell, the man lunged forward against his chains. Face contorted in rage, he snarled and snapped at the passing group.

Even though there was no way he could reach her, Gabby

sidestepped. The guard to her right laughed and shoved her closer to the cell. The other guard grunted something uncomplimentary, grabbed Gabby's arm, and pulled her toward the end of the corridor.

Keeping her eyes straight ahead, Gabby didn't take a deep breath again until the door to the cellblock closed behind her. God. Her heart ached. No wonder Rafe had been such a vicious beast when they'd brought him in.

And she understood so much better why Rafe had insisted she see him as the strong man he'd been before his captivity, not the battered, maddened prisoner.

"If you fail me," Kaufmann said conversationally from up ahead, "after we've tortured the boy, we'll bring him into our program."

Gabby glanced over her shoulder. The boy's terrified gaze was fixed on Kaufmann. Gabby slowed her pace until he caught up with her. "Don't worry," she whispered. "I won't let him hurt you."

The boy was so scared, she wasn't certain he believed her. "I'm Gabby," she offered, hoping to show him she wasn't a threat. "What's your name?"

"W-William," he stammered.

"Remember, Dr. Montague," Kaufmann called back to her. "If you fail me, I will turn you over to my subjects. Who knows what they'll do to you before you die."

Gabby suppressed a shudder, not wanting her terror to make William more afraid.

No matter what happened, she had to keep the boy safe. If that meant going along with Kaufmann, she'd give him what he wanted.

For now.

CHAPTER TWENTY-SIX

"I don't have a photographic memory!" Gabby snapped at Kaufmann three hours later. The stimulant from the energy drink they'd forced her to down had long since faded, leaving her dizzy with pain and fatigue.

Kaufmann only added to her anxiety by checking in with her every hour. "I'm doing the best I can. It took me weeks to figure out how to counteract what you'd done to Rafe, and that was with Nevsky's data to work with," she told him. "I didn't memorize his notes, and even if I had, you've changed your formula since you used it on Rafe."

Kaufmann's eyes narrowed. Gabby knew she was pushing her luck by talking that way, but dammit, his expectations were unreasonable. Even if she'd been on board with his goal she would need more time than he'd given her and access to her research back at the SSU.

Why he thought it possible to coerce her into producing the results he needed was beyond her. She was beginning to think the man was slightly crazy. The changes she'd noticed in this version of his formula didn't make sense. It contained fewer components that opened the mind to exterior control, yet he claimed that better mind control was his primary goal.

She glanced to the other side of the room where William was chained like a wild animal. The boy had confessed that he'd run away over a week ago during a family camping trip in the nearby state forest. He'd quickly gotten lost and had been trying to find his way home when Kaufmann's men caught him. A little while ago the poor thing had dozed off, but he'd jerked awake when Kaufmann entered and now huddled fearfully in the corner.

"If you can't remember the formulas you need," Kaufmann said, "then I'll bring in the hypno—"

An alarm blared and the two-way radio carried by the guard at the door squawked. The man engaged the speaker and listened to what was being said, his expression growing grimmer by the second. When he was done, he turned to Kaufmann. "Sir, there's been a breach of security."

Gabby's heart soared. Rafe!

"Details," Kaufmann demanded.

"One of the exterior guards was found dead, and the security system has been disabled." The guard drew his gun and aimed it at Gabby.

Kaufmann dragged a spare lab coat off the rack by the door, laid it on the floor, then swept Gabby's notes into the center. "Tie it up in a bundle," he ordered.

She opened her mouth to refuse, but then Kaufmann shifted, letting her see the gun he had aimed at William. Meeting the boy's terrified brown eyes with a nod of encouragement, Gabby slipped the capped syringe in her hand into her coat pocket, then knelt down. She took her time tying the coat into a manageable pack.

Kaufmann probably had an escape route, but if Gabby had anything to say about it, she and William would make their own escape. And she was going to take these notes with her.

"Time to go," Kaufmann said.

"Corridor is clear," the guard announced.

"Good." Kaufmann motioned Gabby to her feet.

She shook her head and reached out toward William. "Unchain him."

Kaufmann grabbed her arm and shoved her toward the door. "We don't need him. Move."

"No!" She wasn't leaving this defenseless child to huddle terrified and alone until rescuers arrived. She planted her feet and Kaufmann ran into her.

"Fool," he hissed. "Do you think I'll delay our escape because you want the boy with us?" Kaufmann's gun hand moved too quickly for Gabby to stop him. He fired toward the corner.

William's body went stiff as the shot entered his chest. The guard put a second bullet in the boy's head and William slumped forward. Gabby screamed and turned on Kaufmann, hand raised to strike.

Kaufmann shoved the hot barrel of his gun under her chin and Gabby froze. The pain of her skin burning had the odd effect of calming her down. William was dead. She couldn't help him. Her job was to get out of here alive.

Her arm fell to her side. Kaufmann stared into her eyes. What she saw there terrified her. Mad resolve. Cold calculation. No remorse for having taken a child's life.

"Cuff her," Kaufmann ordered.

The security guard tightened a pair of zip-ties around her wrists.

Then Kaufmann grabbed her throat and squeezed until her vision dissolved and her consciousness shattered.

RAFE STEPPED over another inert body, making his way farther into Kaufmann's compound. Once they'd breached the outer security, they'd tossed canisters of fast-acting, quick-dissipating knockout gas into the building. Gas that had been specially formulated to knock out Kaufmann's subjects.

The gas had worked like a charm. While Chin's team secured the unconscious men and guarded against further attacks from the rear, the other teams headed deeper into the compound, searching for Gabby and Kaufmann.

For Rafe, it meant walking back into the scene of his worst nightmares. As he moved through familiar corridors, he heard echoes of the past. Exerting all his newfound self-control, he kept his face impassive while inside he trembled in fear. Just around this corner was the cell where he'd been held. His pace slowed. His breathing turned ragged and his heart tried to beat a retreat through his spine.

Fuck. He could do this. He had to do this. What if Kaufmann had Gabby down here?

"Rafe? You okay, bro?" Niko asked over the microphone. His team was on the other side of the building. Rafe didn't know if there was another cellblock over there, but he hoped not. He didn't want his brother seeing the conditions Rafe had endured.

"Yeah. I'm good," Rafe said. His team didn't need to know he was terrified of facing his old cell. He'd push through the fear. Get the job done. All that mattered was rescuing Gabby as quickly as possible.

"Let's go," he said. Taking a deep breath, he stepped around the corner and into hell.

GABBY CAME AWAKE to the disorienting sensation of falling. Her head banged against something hard and her eyes flew open. She was upside down, arms dangling overhead as she hung over the shoulder of one of Kaufmann's guards. The man's powerful arm pinned her thighs to his chest and his shoulder dug painfully into her belly. With each running step he took she bounced against his back, which rattled her teeth and jostled her head. Her vision whirled and for a moment she thought she was either going to pass out or throw up.

She coughed, trying to draw air into her starved lungs, and found her throat tight and painful from where Kaufmann had squeezed. Hoping to see where they were, she lifted her head. But the corridor was dark, illuminated only by a thin strip of emergency lights at baseboard level.

Gabby caught snatches of conversation between the guard carrying her and Kaufmann. Enough to understand that Kaufmann and his key scientists were heading toward an escape tunnel where a helicopter waited to take them all to safety.

Gabby knew her chances of being rescued were next to none if she let Kaufmann take her into the tunnel. But all the wriggling in the world didn't break the guard's hold on her legs. She tried pinching him, then balling her bound hands into fists and punching him in the kidneys, but it was like hitting a wall. He didn't so much as flinch and all she got were sore hands.

She tried screaming, but her damaged throat barely managed a croak.

Okay, so if she couldn't force him into dropping her, then maybe she could grab a weapon. She raised her bound arms and skimmed her hands over his sides, not close enough to touch, but close enough to feel any weapon. She thought she remembered a holster at his belt. If she could just find it...

Well, hell. Her fingers met an empty leather holster. A quick search didn't locate any other available weapon. She closed her eyes to think, then realized that the hard object jabbing into her stomach wasn't part of her captor's shoulder holster, but the syringe she'd put in her coat pocket.

Her eyes flew open. Ah-ha!

She tightened her back muscles and lifted her torso off his

back mere inches, just enough to allow her to slowly work her fingers through the folds of her coat. She had to rest several times, letting her body sag against his while her aching back muscles protested the strain.

Lifting herself one more time, she inched her fingers forward until she met plastic. She slid the syringe out of the pocket and held tightly to it while she let her torso go limp and her hands dangle again. When she'd recovered some strength, she flicked the cap off.

She had no idea what effect the contents of the syringe would have on a man, since the drug was one of Kaufmann's creations and had always been mixed with two other drugs before being administered. Since it was the only weapon she had, she had to hope it would disable the guard long enough to let her break free and run.

While she waited for the right moment for her to strike, she grabbed hold of the guard's belt with her other hand, steadied herself so that her head and torso didn't bounce so much, and settled in for the ride.

FUCK.

All Rafe's resolve to stay strong crumbled when he stepped through the door into the main cellblock. The chill, the damp, the scent of desperation and fear hit him with the strength of a knockout punch, nearly sending him to his knees.

He grabbed the doorframe for balance. He...his...

He shook his head. Christ, he didn't want to think about it. Didn't want to walk down to the fifth cell on the right and see if his former cell now contained another prisoner.

"Sir, are you all right?" Jerome MacTavish asked quietly.

Rafe nodded and pushed away from the doorframe. "Yeah, I...uh—"

"That's okay. I understand. You were held prisoner here, weren't you? Got to be hard to come back."

"Yeah," Rafe muttered. "You've no idea." He wasn't that man any more. He'd survived. He was free. But the men inside the cells weren't.

He forced himself to move forward. To peer into every cell, searching for Gabby. Some of the men noticed him and snarled, straining against their chains. Others hung limply with heads down. A few men stared straight ahead but without registering the presence of Rafe's team, too locked within their own hell.

Memories swamped Rafe. The shame of being chained to the wall. The fear of knowing he was completely helpless, with no chance of rescue.

In the beginning, the cold and damp ate away at a man's resistance. Then the drugs kicked in, numbing the system so that nothing caused discomfort and only near-crippling injuries caused even the faintest pain.

Rafe's hands trembled. Each step felt like he was slogging through tar. But he knew that if he stopped, he'd be lost. There was only a thin barrier holding back his rage. He had to stay focused on the job or he'd end up tearing this place apart with his bare hands.

As it was, each cell he passed, each prisoner he left behind, weighed him down. But he couldn't act. Not yet.

These men could not be released from their cells while conscious. No matter how disconnected some of the men appeared, they'd all been programmed to attack strangers. Several agonizing minutes later, Rafe's team finished canvassing all four corridors. With a nod, Rafe sent Andersen and MacTavish back to the main entrance into the cellblock to detonate more tranquilizer canisters. That would keep the prisoners unconscious for several hours, denying their aid to Kaufmann's team. And allowing Chin's team to come through and secure the men for transport back to the SSU.

But there was still no sign of Gabby, and Rafe was getting worried.

"Niko, any sign of her?" Rafe asked.

"Negative. We've just got one more lab to clear. Ah, shit. Hold on."

Andersen and MacTavish returned, signaling that the canisters had detonated. Rafe waved his teammates forward and followed at a slow jog.

"Rafe?" Niko's voice came back over the comm link.

"What happened?"

"We found the body of a young boy chained in the corner of the lab. He can't be more than ten. Looks like he'd been living in the woods or something. He's filthy and undernourished. Christ. Someone fucking shot him in the chest." Even over the link Rafe could hear the anger in his brother's voice.

Rafe swore in Greek.

"You got that right," Niko said. "Listen, Kai's team is here. I've got to move on to the next wing. Later."

The comm clicked, then Rafe heard Kai's broken curse.

"Kai. You okay?"

"Yeah." Kai's voice cracked. "Ah, sorry. Wasn't expecting a child."

"I hear you." Rafe rubbed the back of his neck. Kai had his own disturbing memories of captivity, having spent time chained first in an Indonesian warlord's prison, then in the dungeon of Mexican crime lord Jaime Alvarez. But like Rafe, Kai had been an adult during his imprisonment. The idea that Kaufmann would treat a child that way turned Rafe's stomach.

"Any sign of Gabby?" Rafe asked, steering the topic back on less painful ground.

Kai cleared his throat. "The lab shows recent signs of use, although there aren't any notes, but...hmm..."

"Kai?"

"Sorry. Had to check the microscope. Looks like Gabby was here. There's a slide that has a piece of tape in her handwriting."

Relief crashed through Rafe. He kicked up his pace. If Gabby had been able to write, she couldn't have been hurt too badly. Now all he had to do was find her.

GABBY DIDN'T KNOW how long the guard ran with her over his shoulder, but eventually she felt him slowing down. Good. Maybe he was tiring. She wriggled and kicked her legs, but he hadn't weakened enough to let her slip free.

Not much later, the guard stopped.

"Do you have your pass card?" Kaufmann demanded.

"Yeah...I mean, yes, sir!" The guard shifted his hold on Gabby and started to lower her down in front of him. "Just let me put the girl..."

Gabby formed a two-handed fist around the base of the syringe, arched her back and swung her fist over her left shoulder. When she felt the needle sink into flesh she jammed her thumb on the plunger.

"Aagh!" The guard instinctively brought his hands up to yank at the syringe, letting go of Gabby. A second later, he jerked and pitched forward. Gabby twisted and pushed back against his shoulder as he fell, ending up sprawled along his back and legs. The man didn't move, even when her knee dug into his hamstring as she scrambled away.

Oh, God, was he dead?

Don't think about it. You have to get free, not worry about whether you just killed a man.

Kaufmann's fingers closed around her ankle, but Gabby kicked back with her other foot and he let go. She lurched to her feet, stumbled once as her body adjusted to being upright again, then dashed forward.

A bullet ricocheted off the wall beside her.

Damn. She'd forgotten that Kaufmann had a gun.

"Get up you fool! Get her back," Kaufmann shouted.

Gabby ignored the pain in her body and ran faster. She raced around a bend in the corridor.

And ran smack into an oncoming team of Kaufmann's security men.

CHAPTER TWENTY-SEVEN

GABBY SLAMMED into the lead guard's chest before she realized he was there. Unfortunately, he had great reflexes. He grabbed her by the shoulders, spun her around before she'd taken more than a half step, and shoved a gun between her shoulder blades.

"Walk," he ordered.

Tears of frustration stung her eyes as she walked around the corner and back along the corridor, which seemed like a much shorter trip than when she'd run from Kaufmann.

Kaufmann met them almost immediately. "Good, you've retrieved her. Follow me." He turned and headed toward the faint outline of a door set in the wall.

So, she still had value to him. How far did that extend? If she put her life in danger, could she force him to release her?

While she ran possible scenarios in her mind, Kaufmann swiped a key card through a reader set beside the door, then pressed his thumb to the biometric plate. The light changed from red to green and the door slid open.

The guard nudged Gabby forward. But her attention was riveted on the unmoving man on the ground with the syringe still sticking out from the base of his skull.

"Lucky kill, bitch," the man behind her snarled. "We won't be so easy. Search her."

Another guard yanked her coat off, then ran his hands quickly, but thoroughly, over her body. "She's clean."

"Good. Let's go." The man behind her shoved her shoulder with the palm of his hand, sending her staggering forward.

Gabby barely noticed. She'd *killed* a man.

She shuddered and ran her tongue across suddenly dry lips. As a doctor, she'd devoted her life to helping others. She swallowed back the taste of bile. She hadn't meant to kill the guard. Only to disable him. Yet that didn't relieve her guilt.

The roar of a giant engine coming to life snapped her out of her thoughts. Gabby glanced around her and discovered that they'd entered a giant cavern. Most of the space was bare. To her left, a guard manned a command console, working a series of switches and keeping an eye on several monitors.

In the center of the cavern a transport helicopter squatted menacingly. Its rotors shoved currents of air toward Gabby that nearly sent her off her feet. About half a dozen people in lab coats walked toward the helicopter from other entrances into the cavern.

Kaufmann was evacuating his people. If he got away, he'd be able to go underground again. Start his program anew. Subject another batch of men to his hideous program.

Somehow, she had to stop him.

But how? She wasn't a fighter. This was Rafe's area of expertise. Searching the area for inspiration, she noticed several metal barrels she thought might contain fuel for the helicopter. So, was there a way she could get close enough to the barrels to set off an explosion without killing herself?

As Kaufmann's group reached the boarding area near the helicopter, one of the guards near the nose dropped to his knees, then toppled over. Another guard fell. Bullets pinged against the metal skin of the helicopter and ricocheted off the concrete floor.

More guards collapsed.

The scientists who were farthest from the helicopter broke into a run. Someone screamed. One of the scientists already in the boarding area pounded on the side of the helicopter, shouting for the pilot to open the door and let them in.

Kaufmann reached back and grabbed Gabby, using her to shield his body as he turned to face this new threat. He pressed the tip of his gun against her right temple while his left arm pinned her in front of his chest.

Gabby looked across the cavern and blinked in surprise. Men in assault gear had taken up positions behind a low wall, weapons aimed toward the helicopter.

Only... Gabby glanced around. There wasn't any return fire. All the guards, including the one closest to her, were on the ground, either wounded or dead. No longer a threat.

A man walked out from behind a pillar.

Rafe! Gabby nearly whooped in relief. Tears burned her eyes. With his black assault gear and the faceplate of his helmet raised, Rafe looked every inch the fierce warrior she'd first met. Her heart swelled with love and pride. She wanted to run across the cavern and hurl herself into the safety of his arms, but Kaufmann tightened his grip and shoved the gun harder against her head.

"Let Dr. Montague go, Kaufmann," Rafe called. His voice echoed hollowly in the cavern. "You can't escape."

"I think not," Kaufmann replied. "You still belong to me, don't you Mr. Andros? No matter what Dr. Montague has done, there is no possibility she completely reversed my control." His voice changed, becoming deeper. More authoritative. "I am your master, Mr. Andros. Listen to me. I have a task for you."

Gabby bit back a cry as Rafe stiffened. *Oh, no. Rafe, please. Don't give in. Don't let Kaufmann win. Don't listen to him.*

"You will turn around, Mr. Andros. You will order your men to lay down their weapons. Then you will fire upon your teammates. When every one of them is dead, you will drop your weapon and surrender to me. On my count. Three...two...one...!"

FOR THE BRIEFEST SECOND, Kaufmann's voice raised a need to obey in Rafe. He remembered pain, humiliation and the compulsion to carry out whatever task the Voice commanded.

Agony speared through his head. He inhaled sharply.

The pain brought reality back. He wasn't a slave to Kaufmann any more. He was free. His own man. Yet in his arrogance, Kaufmann refused to acknowledge the possibility that Gabby had succeeded in reconditioning him.

"I'm going to play along with him, boys and girls," Rafe breathed into his lip mic. "D'Argent, do you have a clear sight to Kaufmann?" D'Argent was the team's sniper. Rafe had sent him and half of his team to take positions along the perimeter of the cavern where there were enough natural outcroppings of rock to provide plenty of hiding places.

"Affirmative, sir."

Rafe didn't allow himself to look at Gabby again. His killing rage was too close to the surface. For now, he had to pretend she was a stranger. It was the only way to keep his head cool and get the job done so she'd be safe. Slowly, he brought his hands up to his head, as if the pain of fighting Kaufmann's order was too much to bear.

"Remember," Rafe said into his mic. "If possible, we need Kaufmann alive." They needed to question Kaufmann about the anniversary attack, and about who'd been funding the lab. Then they had to find out if there were any ancillary facilities and if backup of the data existed.

Kaufmann's program had to end.

Rafe had no doubt that Kaufmann would spend the rest of his life in prison. Yeah, deep down he wished for five minutes alone in a room with Kaufmann to get a little personal retribution, but

Rafe wouldn't let himself take the law into his own hands like that. He wanted to be a better man. For Gabby.

"Roger that, sir. Shoot to disable."

"Rafe," Carpenello said from his position on the far side of the helicopter. "You have another set of security guards sneaking toward you from this side."

"The pilot is armed and moving into firing position," Dobson reported. "Looks like he's got an automatic rifle aimed your way, boss."

"Acknowledged," Rafe breathed. "Gentlemen, on my mark."

As if obeying Kaufmann's command, Rafe turned around and raised his arm.

"Rafe, no!" Gabby screamed.

Part of Rafe flinched at her lack of trust in him. But he couldn't allow himself to dwell on that. He dropped to his knees. "Go!" he ordered.

As the men in front of him raised their weapons to take out the new contingent of guards just rounding the front of the helicopter, Rafe pivoted toward Kaufmann and brought his weapon up.

Gabby raised her arm toward Kaufmann's face, ready to scratch his eyes out despite the gun jammed into her temple. Yet before she made contact Kaufmann grunted in pain, his head jerked back, and he dropped to his knees.

The hand holding the gun to her head relaxed slightly, but his arm was still crooked around her neck. As he fell, he dragged her with him. Gabby barely got her hands out in front of her just in time to stop her nose from colliding with the stone floor.

The sound of gunfire echoed around the cavern. The window of the helicopter's cockpit shattered, spraying pieces of glass onto the tarmac.

The scientists who'd been lined up to get into the helicopter were screaming. Some in pain, some in anger or fear. The smarter ones dropped and hid underneath the helicopter. The panicked ones continued to beat on the side of the helicopter, demanding entrance.

Normal security guards in plain black uniforms returned fire, while Kaufmann's subjects, marked by the colored stripes on their uniforms, responded with varying degrees of violence. Those wearing a red stripe remained calm and used their weapons in a rational, orderly manner. Many of those with yellow stripes dropped their weapons and surrendered, despite orders from their commanders to keep fighting. The men with orange, green and blue stripes charged recklessly into the fight, lashing out at whoever was closest, whether friend or foe.

"Open the helicopter door!" Kaufmann screamed. He started a one-armed crawl toward the helicopter, dragging Gabby with him.

No! She pulled back against his hold and twisted. She felt his gun scrape along her cheek as she moved, but she didn't care. She just wanted to get free.

But despite the shoulder wound Gabby could see oozing blood through his shirt, Kaufmann still had enough strength to tighten his grip on her neck. His eyes burned with a crazed light and his lips curled off his teeth. In that moment he resembled one of his subjects instead of the impeccably groomed man she was used to seeing.

Gabby struggled to get free, but Kaufmann's grip was ironclad.

Then a booted foot kicked Kaufmann's good shoulder, forcing him onto his back.

Kaufmann's arm relaxed and Gabby scrambled away from him.

"You turned him into a monster!" The anguished cry came from a man wearing the all-black uniform of a normal guard. He dropped to his knee and slammed his fisted hands into the sides of Kaufmann's neck.

"Hands up!" one of Rafe's men ordered. "Do it now!"

The guard stepped away from Kaufmann. Two empty syringes fell to the ground as he raised his hands above his head. His face crumpled in grief.

"You turned my brother into a monster," the man sobbed, glaring at Kaufmann through his tears. "Then you killed him. Now it's your turn. You're going to die slowly and painfully."

Rafe's men moved in, secured the man, and escorted him away.

Kaufmann pawed at his neck, then screamed. The muscles along his throat spasmed.

Gabby flinched. She knew all too well the searing pain of the drugs. She'd wanted to claw her own skin off to stop the pain. Yet as much as she hated Kaufmann, watching him suffer went against everything she believed in as a doctor.

She glanced away and found herself staring at a familiar, scarred male hand extending toward her.

"Here, *querida*," Rafe said, the gentleness of his voice a contrast to the fury in his eyes.

He pulled her to her feet, quickly cut her zip-ties using his utility knife, then yanked her into a bone-crushing hug. She squeaked as his hold caused her wounds to flare with pain, but her hands didn't release their death grip on him. Then Rafe placed frantic kisses on her cheeks, her forehead, her eyebrows, even her nose before he finally took her mouth.

Only to immediately pull back. "Shit, I'm sorry, sweetheart," he murmured. "I didn't mean to hurt you." His finger gently traced her swollen, cut lips.

"That's okay. I'm just so glad to see you. I—" Tears of relief filled her eyes. She'd really thought she wouldn't make it out of here alive.

A man cleared his throat. "Excuse me, sir, but Andersen wants to know what to do with Kaufmann."

Rafe looked at her as if he never wanted to let her go. So she leaned up and pressed a brief kiss to his mouth. "Your men need you," she said. "Go. I'll be fine."

"I love you," he said fiercely.

"I love you, too," she told him. "Go finish being a hero. I'll see you back at headquarters."

He gave a reluctant nod. "Lynch," he barked at one of his men. "Make sure Dr. Montague stays safe."

"Yes, sir!"

With a final kiss, Rafe handed her off to his friend. Then he walked over to where two of his men knelt on Kaufmann, pinning his arms to the ground.

"Doctor?" Lynch prompted.

She started, so absorbed by watching Rafe move that she hadn't heard a word Lynch said. "I'm sorry?"

"Why don't you come over here and sit down until we have everything mopped up?"

Straightening her shoulders, Gabby started to follow him. Then she heard Rafe speak, and she stopped in shock.

"No, we're not going to help you," Rafe said in the cold, hard voice Gabby hadn't heard since the night he'd infiltrated her cabin. "Not unless you give us the details on the anniversary demonstration."

She couldn't hear Kaufmann's response, but Rafe's reply carried clearly.

"We've got Dr. Montague. She cured me. She and her team can help you. But if you don't tell me what I need, you can writhe in agony forever for all I care."

Yes. That's what Kaufmann damned deserved. The man should suffer for what he'd put Rafe and the other men through.

Gabby glanced over her shoulder.

Rafe's hand shot out and connected with Kaufmann's body, making the man yelp in pain.

To her surprise, she heard Rafe give a low, cruel laugh in response to something Kaufmann said. "Hell, no. We're not going to shoot you and let you out of your misery. If you refuse to cooperate, we're going to let these drugs take full effect. Maybe, if you're lucky, you'll survive. Hey, maybe you'll respond to mind control...by me. That's my kind of justice."

"Doctor, come on," Lynch entreated, pulling on her arm. "You don't need to witness this."

He was right, Gabby realized with a jolt. She was a doctor, for pity's sake. She was supposed to relieve pain and suffering, not feel a spurt of satisfaction that Kaufmann was experiencing a degree of the torture he'd inflicted on his subjects.

Yet as she let Lynch lead her away, she understood that in Rafe's world, different rules applied. Survival of the fittest took on an entirely different meaning, one wrapped in violence and questionable choices.

Gabby couldn't fault Rafe for taking advantage of Kaufmann's pain. Not when the lives of innocents were at risk if they didn't stop the anniversary attack. But it didn't mean she had to give in to her own need for retribution and watch.

CHAPTER TWENTY-EIGHT

Rafe knelt beside Kaufmann, waiting while the other man rode out another painful contraction. He didn't allow himself to think about Gabby, or hold her image in his mind. If he did, Kaufmann would be dead within seconds.

The only thing that had kept Rafe sane once he'd learned Gabby was being tortured was the hope Kaufmann would go easy on her. That maybe he'd only use some of his milder drugs to confuse her mind so she'd agree with him.

He'd prayed that Gabby hadn't been beaten.

But she had. Her face was bloody and bruised. There were finger marks on her throat that pointed to near strangulation. And *Dios mio*, her arms.

Swollen, red needle tracks. Deep bruising. A thick, rectangular burn on the inside of her right wrist. And there were five bloody strips where skin had been cut away. Bile crawled up the back of Rafe's throat just thinking about Kaufmann taking one of his specially crafted knives to Gabby's tender skin.

Rafe's muscles tightened and his heart began a vengeful beat. He was so close to reaching out and wringing Kaufmann's neck that he had to look away. To distract himself, he instructed his team to start herding the captured scientists toward the door.

When he had himself under control and felt confident he could talk to Kaufmann without attacking, Rafe met the man's eyes.

The pain must have eased, because Kaufmann had regained his typical expression of cold condescension. "You will have Dr. Montague provide me with counteragents to whatever drugs that guard gave me. Once I am assured I am in no more danger, I will give you the information you want."

Rafe shook his head. "You can suffer for days for all I care. I'm not lifting a finger to help you until I have the information I need. Where is the anniversary demonstration taking place and how do we stop it?"

"I told you, I don't know what you're talking about."

"Right. Try again. We know you're providing men to Kerberos and Wayne Jamieson for the President's attack against the terrorists who killed his son. Give me the details, and maybe you'll live."

Kaufmann shook his head. "You're too late," he said with a smirk. "The men are already on their way."

"Don't lie to me. You were waiting for Dr. Montague's help in stabilizing the men." Unable to resist, he glanced back over his shoulder to where Gabby sat on a wheeled stool, staring into space while Lynch hovered protectively by her side. Had she broken in time to give Kaufmann the final details he needed?

He wouldn't blame her if she had. SSU agents underwent extensive training on how to withstand pain, but Gabby wasn't an agent.

Rafe turned his head in time to see Kaufmann's expression shift from surprise to calculation and he knew Kaufmann was going to lie again. Then the pain hit Kaufmann, leaving him panting. "She didn't give me the information I needed," he spat. "Stubborn bitch refused to break. As a backup, Jamieson already has a team of less stable men in place. You know how it is. Once they've been armed and deployed, they won't stop until they succeed."

He smirked. "You'll never find them in time."

Rafe thought back to the attack on Susana Dias's archaeological dig. The mission had been simple. Grab Susana Dias. Having been on the flight down to Brazil, Rafe knew the scientists on board had possessed enough chemicals to keep the men under tight mind control. Yet the men had somehow broken free. After dropping Rafe at his observation post near the dig, the men had killed their handlers, then returned to the dig the next night and used napalm to obliterate the site. They'd almost killed Kai and Susana.

No one knew why the men had attacked the site or what caused them to break free of the mind control. Rafe shuddered. He didn't want to think about how much more damage a larger group of Kaufmann's subjects could do if they raged out of control.

"Where is the attack taking place?" Rafe demanded.

Kaufmann shook his head. "I don't know. I wasn't given their exact destination."

"Bullshit." Even Level 1 subjects were never sent off on a mission unsupervised. Kaufmann would have given the destination to the team's handler.

Kaufmann gasped at another wave of pain. His eyes watered. "Please. Help me."

As Rafe listened to those words a very strange thing happened. Kaufmann had been a trigger for fear and hatred since the moment Rafe had been captured. An all-powerful master. But now, as he watched Kaufmann suffer, Rafe saw him as just a man. A man with insane ideas and a total lack of compassion. A man who could be hurt. Who could be...no *was*...defeated.

"You're not done talking yet," Rafe informed Kaufmann. He

motioned over two of his men. "Take him out of here. I want him in an isolated medical unit back at headquarters. And make sure Douglas is on hand to interrogate him." Douglas possessed an uncanny ability to get information from prisoners without resorting to torture.

"Yes, sir."

When they led Kaufmann away, Rafe felt a weight lift from his chest. For the first time since his capture he felt in control. As if he truly had his life back.

Across the cavern, Niko stepped out of the cellblock corridor carrying the front end of a stretcher that held one of Kaufmann's subjects. The tight, angry expression on Niko's face promised murder if he got within striking distance of Kaufmann. Luckily, the path Niko took with the stretcher led in the opposite direction from where Rafe's men were escorting Kaufmann away.

After he'd placed the stretcher next to the line of other victims, Niko remained kneeling on the ground, head bowed. Then his fist slammed onto the tarmac.

Christ. Rafe started toward his brother. He hadn't wanted Niko to see the cells where he'd been held. He'd wanted to spare his brother that pain. As he drew near, Niko climbed wearily to his feet and turned around.

The agony in Niko's eyes threatened to undo Rafe's veneer of calm. He cleared his throat. "So..." Rafe glanced toward the door to the cellblock. Felt shame tighten his throat.

"God damn, I don't know how the hell you survived," Niko said in Greek. His arms engulfed Rafe in a tight bear hug. "I knew it had been bad," he added. "But, Jesus..."

Rafe heard the tremor in his brother's voice and understood exactly how Niko felt. Rafe had experienced the same shock when he'd seen Alvarez's dungeons, knowing that Niko had been tortured there whenever he'd disobeyed the crime lord's orders.

Rafe tightened his arms about his brother. "Yeah, well, you and me, we're tough sons of bitches."

"Damn straight." Niko laughed, thumped Rafe once on the back, then let go. "Just don't let *Mamá* hear you say that."

"Hey, I might be tough, but I'm not crazy," Rafe countered.

Niko's eyes flicked toward the cellblock door, then back again. "I'm proud of you, bro." Then Niko stepped back, shot Rafe a salute, and returned to work.

Rafe took a good long look around the cavern and the SSU agents rounding up Kaufmann's men. Yeah. There was a lot here to be proud of.

Walking toward Gabby, Rafe activated his comm unit. "Kai, how's the data retrieval going?"

Kai's response was a grunt, followed by the sound of something heavy hitting the ground. "Good thing we brought those hand trucks," Kai finally replied, sounding out of breath. "This place is a data goldmine. Got some interesting notes from the main labs, but Grainger is still trying to break the security on Kaufmann's private office. He says no one outside of the highest levels of the intelligence community is supposed to have access to this technology yet."

"Make sure you tell that to Ryker. It will help him narrow his search for Kaufmann's boss."

While Rafe filled Kai in on the situation with Kaufmann and explained about the team that had already deployed for the anniversary demonstration, Rafe motioned for Lynch to move Gabby out. "I'm going to send the guard that attacked Kaufmann to you. Maybe he'll know of a way to breach Kaufmann's security. We have to discover the location of the men."

"Good. We need a break."

"Assuming he can get you into the office, what's your estimate on when we can blow this joint?"

"Give us another hour," Kai said. "We've been planting the explosives as we go, and we've only got one more room in addition to Kaufmann's to check."

"The subjects all out?"

"Yeah. Fuck." There was a wealth of emotion in that word. Sympathy. Anger. Horror.

Great. First Gabby, then Niko, now Kai had seen where he'd been held.

But his friends didn't pity him. They admired him for surviving. Understood his torment a little better.

As for Rafe, with Kaufmann in custody, maybe now his sleep would be nightmare-free.

KAI NODDED to the man on his left, then slowly pushed open the inner door to Kaufmann's private lab. Kai's team had donned biohazard suits when they saw the symbols on the exterior door. The danger was confirmed when he spotted equipment necessary for handling volatile and deadly biochemical agents. Ten minutes later, after reading the labels on the bottles and jars, then skimming through the research notes, Kai's stomach dropped, even though Ryker had warned him to be on the lookout for something like this.

This hidden lab wasn't part of the regular program. It was far worse.

Notes described what amount of finished product had been introduced into various water samples, then each sample's toxicity was given a rating from Mild Gastric Pain to Severe Organ Failure. Time from exposure to death was charted alongside major and minor symptoms. Skin samples treated with the agent sat in various states of degradation upon microscope slides. Photos of people with burns and bloody boils on their skin crowded a cork board.

One whole chart listed the optimal amounts of product per gallon of water in order to kill populations starting at twenty and rising to two hundred thousand people.

Christ. They could wipe out entire cities with just a liter bottle of this stuff. While the notes indicated that gallons had been produced, all that remained here were a few partially filled vials of the components of the deadly agent, plus ten test tubes of Agent Styx that hadn't finished maturing before the staff evacuated.

Kai motioned to his companion and they started the slow, meticulous process of safely packing everything up for shipment to the SSU.

Each carton got a similar label: Agent Styx. Highly toxic. Hazmat suit required.

CHAPTER TWENTY-NINE

RAFE STARED out the helicopter's open door, watching an inferno devour Kaufmann's compound. His team's expert placement of the explosive had ensured that nothing would remain.

Dios, he needed to hold Gabby so desperately. Wanted to see for himself every mark Kaufmann had made on her skin and heal it with his kiss. Needed just to hold her and inhale her scent and know from the warmth of her body pressed against his that she was alive.

One brief hug and a few kisses didn't come close to satisfying him. And he hated knowing that after days of captivity she'd been herded away by other members of his team, all strangers to her. She should have been given weeks off and treated to every sort of pampering her heart desired instead of being put back to work before she'd even had time to heal.

He should be the one pampering her.

When he'd realized that Gabby would be returning to Georgia without him, he'd nearly thrown a fit. He'd thought Gabby would accompany him back to Oregon.

Instead, Ryker had explained that Gabby had knowledge of the chemical agent Kaufmann's men would use in the anniversary demonstration. Only the Georgia facility had the necessary protections to allow Gabby to safely handle the chemical while she tried to develop an antidote.

As the helicopter zoomed forward, Rafe felt the connection to Gabby growing dimmer with distance. And the rage he'd worked so hard to tame started to rise. He hated being separated from her. Balling his hands into fists, he clamped his teeth together and wrestled his anger into submission.

Because he would not lose control in front of his team.

But he swore that when this was all over, he'd spirit Gabby away to some tropical island and spoil her for at least a month.

Kerberos Headquarters
Washington, D.C.

JAMIESON LOOKED at the useless bank of computer monitors, his fists clenched in rage. The one monitor that mattered at this moment, the one showing Kaufmann's compound, was blank. Four hours ago Kaufmann had sent a garbled message. He'd stated that his compound was under attack and that he'd ordered an evacuation.

Not a word since.

"Sir, we have a backup satellite coming online in four... three...two...one..."

The screen lit up. Jamieson took one look at the collapsed building that had been Kaufmann's compound and wished the damn satellite had stayed out of operation. At least the President wasn't here to witness the failure, *again*, of Kaufmann to keep his program safe. By the looks of it, not a single building remained intact.

Jamieson didn't have to see the attackers to know they'd been sent by the SSU. Kaufmann should never have insisted on taking back Dr. Montague. He should have recognized that the SSU would attempt a rescue.

The cold hand of fury threatened to squeeze all the air out of his lungs. The fool. The utterly naïve, incompetent fool! He hoped Kaufmann was dead, because the thought of the scientist being interrogated by the SSU gave Jamieson chills. He didn't delude himself about the chances of Kerberos and the demonstration remaining a secret for long under that scenario. Kaufmann was weak. He'd spill everything he knew, then try to manipulate the situation so Jamieson took all the blame.

All his plans, ruined! Because Kaufmann couldn't manage to keep his mind on security instead of his damned research.

Thank God the backup team for the demonstration was already in place. There was still a chance Jamieson could prevent this disaster from reaching the President's ears. It would be the biggest bluff of his lifetime, acting as if Kaufmann's program was fully intact, when in fact everything had been destroyed except the backup files Jamieson had insisted be stored off site in case such an event occurred.

He needed to find a replacement for Kaufmann. But he couldn't worry yet about how he was going to find a scientist capable of filling Kaufmann's place. First he had to make certain that no other security threats loomed. Had someone on this end betrayed the compound?

Jamieson pivoted on his heel. "Major," he said to his head of security. "I want a report on what went wrong at the compound, delivered personally by you no later than seven o'clock tonight. I also want to know if the SSU has taken prisoners, and if so, if Kaufmann is among them. Have an assassination squad on stand-by."

Jamieson didn't wait for agreement. He stalked out of the room without another word. The major would obey or risk death. In fact, in addition to killing Kaufmann and any of his surviving staff, it might be necessary to eliminate every man who'd witnessed the destruction of the lab, just to make certain the President didn't learn of the disaster. Kerberos could not be tied to such a failure.

Jamieson strode down the corridor toward his office. When he read the report from his communications expert that was sitting on his desk, Jamieson shook his head. It looked like Tonelli was going to have to die earlier than he'd planned.

Mark Tonelli awoke to the feeling of cold linoleum beneath his cheek and a pounding in his head.

"Ah, I see you're finally awake."

Every cell in Mark's body froze at Jamieson's deceptively mild tone.

Damn, damn, damn. The word resonated inside his skull with the rhythm of his headache.

What had he done to give himself away? More important, how was he going to get out of here alive and get back to Faith? The questions gave him something to focus on besides the pain in his head, and the pressure at his wrist and ankles from zip ties.

He had no illusions about Jamieson's plans for him. His hands and feet were bound. Duct tape covered his mouth. Four men stood guard around him in what looked to be a small kitchen, although it was a place Mark had never seen before.

Even though most of his intelligence work was done in restaurants or meeting rooms, Mark had maintained his survival instincts, the ones that had kept him alive on the streets of Moscow as a boy. A good thing, since the hunt for Nevsky's microchip had put him in more physically dangerous situations these past few months than he'd experienced in years.

Adrenaline pumped through his system, sharpening his mind and heightening his senses. He took note of the distance between him and his guards. Jamieson and one of the guards were the closest to the only door. What he needed to know, but couldn't tell from his position on the floor, was whether or not the guards were normal, or Kaufmann's monsters.

It would be better if—

Jamieson knelt down in front of Mark, extending his palm to reveal Mark's father's little bronze horse. For once, Mark didn't look at the miniature with longing or a burning anger. Instead, he just felt sad.

"You're as much trouble as your father was," Jamieson said conversationally. "I was able to stop your father before he revealed my name to the investigating committee. Don Marrone was more than pleased to order the hit in return for my arranging for certain pending charges to be dropped." He shook his head. "I had hoped your time on the streets of Moscow would wear away all that moral superiority your father instilled in you. Yet here you've betrayed me just as surely as your father."

Mark made an angry sound behind the duct tape. After all these years, he'd finally found the man responsible for his father's death and he was helpless to seek his revenge.

"Unfortunately, you managed to do what your father couldn't. You interfered in my plans." Jamieson rubbed his thumb over the dent in the horse's shoulder. "We discovered your transmissions to the SSU. Tell me, have you been working for the SSU since the beginning? Nod yes or no, please or Victor will break your leg."

Mark shook his head no.

"Strange. I believe you." Jamieson tilted his head to the side. "What turned you? Was it Ivanov?"

Mark nodded.

Jamieson's lips pressed together. "Idiot." His hand closed around the horse, then he straightened out of his crouch.

"You've ruined my plans for you, Mr. Tonelli. You were supposed to be my scapegoat, but only after the anniversary demonstration. Now, with Kaufmann's lab destroyed and the SSU in possession of Kaufmann, I'll be forced to have you killed. Records will show that you'd been embezzling funds in order to support Kaufmann's lab. The investigation will center on you. Meanwhile, the anniversary demonstration will go off as planned. Afterward, Kerberos will remain in high favor. We'll free those scientists currently in custody and then we'll start the lab again using our backup notes."

Jamieson sighed. "It's a pity, Mr. Tonelli. For a while there, I had high hopes for you." He turned to go.

Mark was about to watch his father's murderer walk away and there was nothing he could do about it. Yet oddly enough, he didn't feel bitter. Instead, he felt relieved to know the truth. Revenge didn't matter right now. Getting free and getting to Faith before Jamieson discovered her brother's connection to Kerberos was all that mattered.

Jamieson spoke briefly to the guard by the door, then one of the men accompanied him out of the room.

Leaving Mark and three men.

He tensed. He had a plan, but the only way it was going to work was if he could get someone to take off this damn duct tape. He needed to speak.

But before he could figure out a way to convince one of his guards to cut the tape and let him talk, a boot slammed into his temple and the world went black.

CHAPTER THIRTY

SSU Laboratories
Georgia

GABBY REMOVED the slide from the microscope, replaced it in its empty slot in the organizing box, then propped her elbows on the countertop and rested her head on her hands. She was exhausted. Along with Kai and the rest of their research team, she'd been working around-the-clock since her rescue trying to create an antidote to Agent Styx.

Unfortunately, the version of Agent Styx removed from Kaufmann's compound contained alterations from Nevsky's original formula that almost made it impossible to counteract. Thanks to Kai's knowledge of biochemical weapons, the various dispersal methods, and what biochemicals were the best neutralizers, they'd eventually come upon what they thought was an antidote.

Based on this latest test data, they'd succeeded.

Unfortunately, the antidote was still highly unstable, which would interfere with Ryker's attempt to stop the anniversary demonstration.

She shook her head. Ryker had explained about the team of Kaufmann's enhanced men and their role in the upcoming anniversary attack. It sickened her to think that innocent lives could so easily be put at risk.

Not to mention the lives of the men under Kaufmann's command. She had no illusions that the men would survive the mission. They were nothing more than disposable weapons. Just like Rafe had been.

Rafe.

Gabby bit her lip. God, she missed him so much. She hadn't seen him since he'd given her a quick kiss good-bye back in the cavern before he headed off to Oregon to prep for the mission.

She'd worked twice as hard to find an antidote to Agent Styx because she knew Rafe and his men faced potential exposure when they moved in to stop the attack. The threat of them falling prey to the chemical in its current, ultra-lethal formula had been filling her sleep with nightmares. Yet, even given the danger of the scenario she was about to present to Kai and Ryker, it was their only viable option.

Thank heavens she wouldn't be the one to tell Rafe her plan. She knew he was going to go ballistic.

Gabby finished typing up the last of her notes and shut down her computer. After locking up, she strode down the hallway to Kai's lab. She knocked once, then pushed open the door.

"We're good to go," she announced as she stepped into the room. "The final test was a success."

Kai held up his hand to indicate he'd be with her in a second. He put another droplet of green liquid into the vial in front of him, then quickly capped it. "That's great," he said.

He checked the clock on the wall. "Give me fifteen minutes and meet me in the conference room so we can call Ryker together. I need to finish this up."

Twenty minutes later, a grim faced Ryker stared at Gabby across the video link. "Are you sure?"

She nodded with as much confidence as she could muster. "Yes, sir. The only way to keep the formula stable enough to be effective is if it's created on the ground and handed to Rafe and his men as they head out."

"Kai?"

Considering she'd hit Kai completely out of the blue with her insistence that their team needed to head to the island, he remained remarkably calm. For which she wanted to hug him. "I agree, sir. We need a mobile lab on the ground with the team."

Ryker raised a brow. "Gabby, I hope you appreciate what hell Rafe's going to put me through when I tell him."

She winced. "I do, sir. Sorry." She took a deep breath. "I don't want to go. Honestly. I've had enough danger to last me a life-time. I know the chances of something going wrong and our team getting exposed to Agent Styx are high. But there's no other choice."

"Very well. Go get some sleep. I'll call when I've made arrangements, and when we've figured out which island is the target."

THE NEXT TIME Mark woke up, he was hit by the nauseating stench of diesel fuel and the bone-jarring vibration of tires underneath a corrugated metal floor. Before opening his eyes he flexed his muscles, confirming that his hands and feet were still bound. His mouth, however, was no longer taped.

He cracked open his eyes then immediately shut them again as the faint gray interior of the van he was in spun around him, igniting another headache. He didn't understand why he wasn't dead yet, but he didn't plan on letting this opportunity escape him.

"Don't move," a man's voice said behind him.

Mark flinched. How had he missed that he wasn't alone?

Something sawed through the bindings at his wrists and the

thin plastic restraints quickly broke. Mark didn't dare move his arms in case this was some kind of sick game.

"It's okay to move," the man said. "No one in the driver's compartment can see back here." A moment later the restraints at Mark's ankles were cut away.

Mark rolled gingerly to a more comfortable position, then ignored the screaming pain in his head and pushed himself to his knees. "What's going on?" he demanded in a voice gone hoarse.

In the faint light from the rear window Mark recognized one of the men from Jamieson's assassination squads. Not one of the men who'd been in the kitchen.

"Call it an attack of conscience," the man said. "I don't approve of what Jamieson has done with Kerberos, muddying the purity of our mission with those freaky monster men. You were right to help the SSU shut down Kaufmann's down. Now I want you to stop the demonstration."

Mark shook his head, sure he must have misheard. "Excuse me?"

The man nodded toward Mark's hip. "I put a flash drive in your pocket. It has the personnel roster and battle plan for the anniversary attack. Give it to the SSU. Stop Jamieson from killing everyone on that island."

Mark opened his mouth to speak, but the man held up his hand. "I don't have the contacts to get this information acted on immediately. The SSU trusts you. Me and my men will disappear in a few days. We'll tell Jamieson we dumped you in the ocean if he demands proof of your death. By the time he becomes suspicious, your friends at the SSU should have taken care of him for us."

Mark didn't know what to say. He wasn't used to people helping him without asking for something in return. But the man's voice rang with the truth of conviction. So Mark settled for a simple, "Thank you."

"Don't thank me too much," the man said. His teeth flashed

white as he smiled. "I still have to make this look good." With that the man opened the back door of the still moving van. Before Mark had any idea what he intended, he found himself picked up and flung toward the side of the road.

Mark had a second to think, "Oh shit, this is going to hurt." Then the ground rose up and smacked him.

Before he passed out yet again, he thought he heard the sound of the man's laughter.

Two Days Later
National Arboretum
Washington, D.C.

"I HAVE proof that the President is planning an attack to mark the fifth anniversary of his son's death," Ryker announced to the four men sitting around the secluded picnic table. The sun slipped behind a bank of clouds. "Half of the assault team will be Kaufmann's enhanced soldiers." He paused, still stunned by the information on the flash drive Tonelli had brought him. "They're going to drop an updated version of Agent Styx into the water supply."

Ryker listened to the collective round of cursing. The five men —Ryker; Matt Jordaine of the FBI; Roger Brown of the CIA; Four Star General Aldrick Wehrig, and Brit Remington of the House Judiciary Committee—had met in Vietnam and become the sort of inseparable blood brothers war often produced. None of them would forget the bloody massacre they'd stumbled upon during a routine security sweep of a Vietnamese village, or the shock of seeing maniacally enraged American soldiers attacking each other when there were no more villagers left to kill.

They'd later learned that those soldiers had been affected by exposure to Agent Styx.

"How the hell is that possible?" Jordaine demanded. "All

samples and all data on Agent Styx were destroyed in seventy-one."

Ryker kept an eye on Brown and Wehrig as he answered. "Dr. Nevsky. The data on his microchip indicated that he was one of the creators of Agent Styx. I suspect that when the CIA and the DOD hired him to create their super spy and super soldier programs they didn't ask for proof that he'd destroyed his data on Agent Styx."

Jordaine swore. Wehrig looked disappointed. And Brown shook his head in resignation.

Ryker rubbed the bridge of his nose. "Plus, someone in one of those organizations must have been a co-creator with Nevsky. Because our teams found the lab being used to create the new version of the drug. I know we didn't leak the formula, so Kaufmann must have received outside help."

Remington sat forward. "Give me details of the attack."

Ryker placed manila file folders in front of his friends. "This is what we know. Nevsky incorporated Agent Styx in his program to create superhumans for the CIA and DOD. After his death, his second-in-command Dr. Kaufmann started a similar program using drugs he'd removed from Nevsky's lab before the fire. These samples included compounds that had been mixed with Agent Styx. Based on Kaufmann's formula, our expert believes that Kaufmann didn't fully understand the full range of side effects of Agent Styx. Which is why she believes someone else must have provided the data to recreate Agent Styx for the demonstration."

"Your expert?" Brown demanded. "How can you have an expert on Agent Styx?"

"More connections to Vietnam," Ryker replied. "Dr. Montague, the woman who reversed the damage done to Rafe Andros, is Dan Reagh's daughter. Montague is her mother's maiden name. Reagh apparently saved a few vials of Agent Styx and left them to her after his death. Since her father experienced the periods of rage that are the primary side effect of Agent Styx, she's focused her career on finding a way to help veterans who'd been exposed to the drug. According to her, the version of Agent Styx Kaufmann teams will disperse is even more lethal than what we saw in Vietnam."

Four grim faces stared back at Ryker. "Reagh," Wehrig finally commented. "No shit. Small world." They'd all heard the rumors during the war about Reagh and his extraordinary black ops unit. Including the tales that the men had become overly aggressive due to exposure to Agent Styx.

"Can we tie Kaufmann's men directly to the President?" Remington asked. He'd play a key role if impeachment became necessary.

"Yes. My source provided data that shows the President has commissioned a group called Kerberos to carry out an act of retribution on behalf of the United States."

"What's Kerberos?" Jordaine asked.

Brown nodded slowly. "The name rings a bell, but I can't say where I've heard it."

"How about Wayne Jamieson and CIA's In-House Projects? My source says Kerberos is Jamieson's private army and that Jamieson provided funding to Kaufmann for enhanced soldiers."

"Jamieson." Brown shook his head. "Should have figured he'd be behind this. Arrogant prick. Thinks rules are for everyone else. I never approved of In-House Projects to begin with."

"Someone care to clue the rest of us in?" Jordaine asked.

"In-House Projects was created to clean up the messes left when a sanctioned CIA mission goes sour or there's risk of a breach of secrecy." Brown braced his forearms on the table. "Ryker, you're saying Jamieson has formed his own paramilitary group?"

"Of course. The freak trainees," Wehrig muttered.

"What?" Brown shot a puzzled glance at Wehrig.

"There have been stories for months about crazy men with

incredible strength who showed up for army maneuvers, accompanied by orders that the men were to be trained like everyone else. Rumors of regular units going out on training missions and finding the targets already destroyed." Wehrig shrugged. "Never saw proof, though."

Ryker nodded. "We've all been aware of assassinations the news media never reported. Hard assets of hostile governments or competing businesses being damaged by so-called terrorists that were supposedly built like the Incredible Hulk. That might have been Kerberos at work."

Including the mindless decimation of Susan Dias's archaeological dig.

"So let me summarize," Remington said. "This Jamieson fellow has been tasked by the President with carrying out the anniversary demonstration. Jamieson has an unsanctioned paramilitary group called Kerberos which is made up at least partially of Kaufmann's enhanced soldiers. These men are going to unleash Agent Styx on an unnamed target."

"Not unnamed," Ryker said. He laid out a map. "We've narrowed the possible targets to twelve. By the end of the day we expect to have confirmation of the primary target."

"How can we help?" Jordaine asked.

"This is what I need…"

The Next Day
SSU Compound
Oregon

RAFE WALKED down the hall toward the briefing room. The heavy oak paneling and high ceiling with its intricate molding were more appropriate for a university than a special operations group. But Rafe had always liked the warmth of the building and now, after so many months away, he felt the contentment of a successful homecoming.

He was back in business. Yeah, he still had some side effects to deal with, like a brain that functioned like a Cray computer, lingering enhanced strength, and the occasional killer headache. But only the headaches were a problem. He actually didn't mind being smarter or stronger, just as long as he didn't stand out as a freak.

So far, no one had commented, so he figured his differences weren't that noticeable to anyone but him. Probably he just felt smarter because he'd spent so much time unable to process even basic information.

Even his rage wasn't as big a problem as before. Yeah, his temper was sharper, more vicious and quicker to ignite than before, but it had eased from the once constant pressure. And he'd learned how to control it, so he rarely had incidents where he lashed out uncontrollably.

Since his team had landed, he'd barely had time to breathe. He'd forced the pain of being separated from Gabby out of his mind and focused on working on a plan to stop Kaufmann's men. His team was now ready to go.

Rafe pushed open the door to the briefing room. Ryker stood at the opposite end of the long table, speaking into a Bluetooth earpiece while paging through a report. He glanced up and lifted the corner of his mouth in greeting to Rafe.

Behind Ryker, heavy drapes hid the leaded glass of the large bay window and its view of the side lawn. Open maps and piles of documents covered the top of the twelve-seater dining room table. The wall to his left contained a giant screen displaying a digital map of the world. Rafe closed the door behind him and studied the latest pinpricks of red light that showed possible locations for Kaufmann's men.

He frowned as he counted the dots. Twelve. Twice as many dots as before, but while two days ago the dots had been spread throughout the world at known terrorist hot spots, now they were all focused out within the multi-island nation of Salaqut to the east of Indonesia.

"You've narrowed the target area?" Rafe asked. As Indonesia had cracked down on terrorists, Salaqut's main island Jumawat had become the latest terrorist training ground. But these dots covered more than just Jumawat.

"According to the data on the flash drive Tonelli—"

"Tonelli? You've got to be kidding me." The last time they'd met, Mark Tonelli had left Rafe to bleed out on the tarmac in Cozumel. Tonelli hadn't shot Rafe but he hadn't done a thing to help him, either. Just pumped him for information and left him to die.

If that wasn't enough reason to be wary of the guy, Tonelli been responsible for Jenna nearly getting raped during their assignment in Moscow. Rafe would never forgive him for that.

Ryker raised his brows at the disgust in Rafe's voice. "So far, the information he's given me has panned out. He has his own reasons for wanting the attack to fail."

Rafe rolled his eyes. He'd wouldn't trust Tonelli if the man suddenly sprouted angel wings and a shiny new halo. When trouble hit, the only agenda that mattered to Tonelli was his own. Everyone else had better get out of his way.

"As I was saying," Ryker continued, "Tonelli's data shows that the President has given Kerberos orders to attack more than just the terrorist camps. He wants their homes and villages destroyed."

"That's what he wants Agent Styx for," Rafe concluded. Ryker had already briefed Rafe and his team on the deadly chemical found at Kaufmann's compound.

"Exactly. These aren't tiny villages. We're talking thousands of people dead."

"*Madre de Dios*. He's the fucking President. He can't just go off on a vendetta. When this comes out, it will throw the country into war."

"Tonelli doesn't know how the President plans on spinning the attack. Whether he'll pretend ignorance, since only a few members of Kerberos will know the truth, or whether he'll wave it as a warning to all terrorists that the game has changed and the United States can no longer be counted on to play nice."

Working outside the rules, hitting hard and playing dirty without sullying the reputation of the United States government was one reason private operations groups like the SSU existed. To hurt the terrorists and other wrongdoers in ways that the government couldn't. But the SSU didn't breach ethical boundaries. They didn't kill innocents.

Rafe met Ryker's eyes and saw the same bleak knowledge. If this attack succeeded, the whole international power balance would be overthrown, with the United States cast in the role of villain. Destroying everything the SSU stood for.

"What's the plan?" Rafe asked.

"According to this data, there's an attack team assigned to each village. At least two men on each team are Kaufmann's enhanced soldiers. Some of those men are reaching Level 3, which means they're barely sane enough to be controllable. From what we can tell, the plan is to keep Kaufmann's men contained until the day of the attack, then set them loose on the villages with the command to first attack the family homes of the terrorists, then kill everyone else they meet. The regular soldiers will act as backup during the attack, protect Kaufmann's handlers, and kill any villagers that escape. Afterward, they'll put Agent Styx into the water supply in case there are any survivors."

"How fast does Agent Styx work?"

Ryker's mouth flattened into a thin, tense line. "Gabby says this version has been significantly enhanced from what was used in Vietnam. It's three times as virulent. Fatal even if the fumes are inhaled. At the dosage we're talking about, ingesting half a cup of tainted water will kill a healthy adult male within twenty-four hours as the biochemical agent eats the body from the inside out. If the water is used only for bathing, it takes Agent Styx forty-eight to seventy-two hours to eat through the skin and start destroying the underlying nerves and muscle to the point the body can't survive."

Holy shit. Rafe stared at the map, imagining the horror of watching the ones you loved turn into bloody, indistinguishable mass of flesh like something out of a monster movie.

And he felt a chill snake down his spine. The drugs Kaufmann had given him contained at least one element of Agent Styx. That's why, if his subjects lived long enough, their bodies started to break down. Once again he realized how much he owed Gabby. She said she'd finally managed to neutralize that aspect of the formula. So he was safe.

For now.

"We can't field a force big enough to stop those men once they're deployed to the villages," Rafe said. "There are too many ways they could slip by us."

"Agreed. Ideally, we do a mass evacuation, but the situation is politically sensitive. The people on our side who have contacts high up in the Salaqutian government are all under oath to our President. We don't have time to identify someone open to believing the President capable of such an act. Someone who the Salaqut government also trusts and will listen to."

"So our best bet is to find out their staging location and hope we're not too late. Tonelli have any info on that?"

"No, but there are several possibilities listed. I'm guessing the data we received was downloaded before the plan was finalized. I have other contacts culling satellite images. Fortunately, with all the terrorist cells based on the islands, the area has come under increased satellite surveillance recently." Ryker crossed his arms over his chest and grimaced at the map. "Tonelli also said he'd be heading for the island and would call with any updates."

Yeah, if the guy wasn't just yanking their chains.

"In the meantime," Ryker continued, "we've got another complication. Gabby has found a counteragent, but it's extremely unstable."

Atta girl, Rafe thought. There wasn't a problem his woman couldn't solve. But...

"Unstable. How does that affect us?" Rafe asked.

Ryker slanted Rafe a wary glance.

Rafe tensed. "What?"

"The formula starts to break down at two hours, despite Gabby's attempts to keep it in the form she needs. The good news is that her antidote can be added to the water supply to neutralize Agent Styx and also be given as an injection to affected people. But both treatments have to be given within that two-hour window."

Even their fastest plane couldn't get a shipment of the antidote to Salaqut in under two hours. Some of the islands would take at least another hour to reach from the capital. Which meant...

"No. *Hell* no. She's not coming to Salaqut with us."

Ryker raised his eyebrow and stared Rafe down.

Fuck. Ryker didn't have to speak. Rafe knew that from a mission perspective he was being unreasonable. But the thought of Gabby anywhere near that hellhole under normal circumstances was terrifying. Add in the potential threat from physical attack by Kaufmann's men, the real possibility that the SSU team could be exposed to Agent Styx, and his blood ran cold.

He couldn't lose Gabby.

Yet he couldn't leave those villagers to the mercy of Kaufmann's men either. He spun away from the map and slammed his fist down on the heavy oak table. "Dammit! We're going to weaken our force by protecting her."

"We don't have a choice," Ryker said. "In order to have a workable antidote, Gabby's team has to produce the antidote in the field. The CDC is loaning us two of their portable hazmat labs. On the flight over we'll have them tricked out to look like the local delivery trucks. Gabby's already gathering the chemicals she needs. She and her team will be on a plane within two hours. You'll meet them at the airport then all of you, along with the portable labs, will fly to Salaqut. Hopefully, I'll have the staging location of Kaufmann's men by then. Gabby and Kai will equip the labs in the air so when you hit the ground you can move out immediately."

Rafe put his hand to the back of his neck and squeezed. Gabby had already suffered enough at Kaufmann's hands. The thought of losing her to Agent Styx opened up a yawning, spinning void deep inside Rafe's chest that made him want to throw back his head and howl.

"Great," he said, letting frustration push back his fear. "Just fucking great. Did she mention if this antidote can be used as a vaccine to protect against contamination?"

"It can't."

Not the words he wanted to hear.

"We'll keep her safe, Rafe," Ryker said, clapping him on the shoulder. "She'll be stationed as far from the staging area as possible. She won't be in any danger. Trust me."

Rafe looked at Ryker. People at the SSU called his boss the miracle worker. If anyone could manipulate events to keep Gabby safe, Ryker could.

But, a little voice warned, *she'd been under Ryker's protection in Georgia and Kaufmann's men still took her.*

Fuck that. If Rafe had to personally stand guard at her side to protect her, he would.

CHAPTER THIRTY-ONE

The Next Day
Washraiti Island, Salaqut

INSIDE THE AIR conditioned climate of the mobile lab, Gabby waited for the final hermetically sealed case of antidote to finish the decontamination process. They'd been lucky. The data from Ryker's contact Mark Tonelli had pinpointed this island as being the target for the attack. Gabby had charge of this mobile lab for supplying Rafe's assault team with the antidote, while Kai worked a second mobile lab a few miles away to supply Niko's team.

A few seconds later the green light went on over the decontamination chamber. Gabby grabbed the first case and walked outside to where Rafe and his team were waiting. In just those few steps, the nearly one hundred percent humidity plastered the high-tech, moisture-wicking fabric of her loose olive-green tank top and cargo pants to her body.

"Remember," she told Rafe as she handed him the case, "the timer on the front of each case will show you how much of your two-hour window is left."

Early morning sunlight filtered through the dense jungle vegetation, painting Rafe in primitive shadows. Making him look so darkly sexy that she wanted to pull him down for a hot kiss.

Get your mind back on the job, girl.

Gabby sighed. Despite being on the same plane, they'd both been kept so busy that they'd only managed one brief kiss hello. Her arms ached with the need to hold Rafe close. To protect him.

To protect herself from the pain of losing him.

Disgusted with her selfishness when they had lives to save, Gabby went inside and picked up the next case. This time when she handed it over to Rafe she focused over his shoulder, afraid that if she kept looking at his beloved face and worrying that he wouldn't make it back, she'd break down and kiss him. With his teammates waiting at the edge of the jungle, she didn't want to jeopardize their respect for Rafe by making a public display of affection.

The trees were actually quite fascinating to someone who'd never lived in the tropics. Thick, lush, and covered in flowering vines. Rafe had chosen this section of dense jungle and volcanic hills for his base because of the existence of rocky overhangs like the one sheltering their mobile hazmat lab. Between the overhang and the surrounding vegetation, the unit was nearly invisible until you were right on top of it. Something of a miracle, given that the truck housing her lab was painted with a bright seascape with frolicking fish on one side and a vibrant jungle with playful monkeys on the other. Not what she considered camouflage, but once they'd hit the highway she'd understood. Every vehicle here was painted in outrageous, exuberant colors. Driving a plain truck through the countryside would have been a mistake.

Rafe signaled one of his men. The man took the two cases and headed toward the team's motorbikes. One of the guards assigned to protect the lab passed by, moving away a little bit when he neared them so as to give them privacy.

Gabby picked up the final case, then just stared at it. So much was riding on luck. What would she do if Rafe didn't come back?

The team from Kerberos—a mix of Kaufmann's enhanced soldiers and normal men—had been on the island for several days. They'd already started wreaking havoc, if news reports of strange attacks on the outlying villages were to be believed.

But now Kerberos's men were gathering at a place deeper in these hills. Ryker's source, a man called Mark Tonelli, said this was when the men would get their vials of Agent Styx and head to their targets.

Rafe and Niko's teams would attack before the men separated, then contain the area. Each SSU agent would carry either the antidote to Agent Styx or the tranquilizer needed to subdue Kaufmann's men. The tranquilizer would be delivered via dart gun. The antidote could be given via injection to someone who'd already been exposed to the chemical. Dumping the antidote into contaminated water would neutralize it. Those vials had a special quick-release cap that could be opened with one gloved hand.

"Remember," she warned, "you have to use the antidote within two hours, otherwise it's useless. And you have to use the special masks and gloves."

He nodded.

As she passed the case to Rafe, his fingers closed over hers. Startled, she looked up and saw heat flare in Rafe's eyes.

"You're so damn beautiful," he murmured. "Inside and out. I've missed you so much."

Then he shocked her by planting a brief, hard kiss on her lips. "Stay safe for me," he growled. "Keep alert and do exactly what the guards tell you. I'll be back soon."

He gave her one more kiss, turned, and disappeared into the jungle.

Leaving Gabby staring after him, her heart soaring and a prayer on her lips.

Thirty Minutes Later
The White House
Washington, D.C.

IT WASN'T every day the country needed to be saved from the whims of a crazed President.

Ryker followed the President's aide through the lower corridors of the White House toward the entertainment room. He ground his teeth together. President MacAdam had ordered the deaths of thousands of innocent people and he was going to watch the live video feed from his lavish entertainment room as if it was a Hollywood movie.

The Chief Justice of the Supreme Court walked slightly ahead of Ryker, just behind the aide and next to the Vice President. The White House legal counsel walked beside the Secretary of State. Jordaine, Brown, Wehring and Remington were acting as representatives of their various agencies—FBI, CIA, DOD and the House Judiciary Committee.

No one stopped the grim group as it walked through the halls. True to his word, the aide had made certain all the Secret Service agents on duty tonight were aware of the situation and would not interfere.

The radio on Ryker's belt vibrated. "The room is secure, sir," the Marine on the other end announced.

"Good," Ryker said. "We're just coming around the corner."

As the group turned into the hallway, the guards opened the double doors into the entertainment room.

"Close the door!" the President snapped. "I told you, I'm not to be disturbed."

The group filed silently into the room and the guards shut the doors behind them.

The President shot an annoyed glance at his aide. "It's the fifth anniversary of my son's death and I'm finally going to get revenge. Leave me alone."

The full-size movie screen was broken into twelve squares around the perimeter, each showing a village on Salaqut. In the center was a view of an encampment in the middle of the jungle. Men stood in line in front of a truck waiting to receive small packages.

Agent Styx.

The White House legal counsel cleared his throat. "Your revenge is why we're here, Mr. President. We can't allow you to do this."

The president laughed with crazed jubilation. "Too late." He nodded toward the men on the screen who had started dispersing. "They're on their way."

Ryker watched the countdown clock in the lower right hand corner. At precisely the correct time, the screen went black.

Rafe was right on schedule.

Salaqut

RAFE CHECKED HIS WATCH. Twenty minutes until Ryker confronted the President. He confirmed that his men were in place, then signaled them to move toward the clearing in the middle of this dense section of jungle. In the distance he heard the welcome sound of an aircraft. Tourist planes weren't common on this part of the island, but scientists occasionally used old crop dusters in their atmospheric studies, so the plane wouldn't raise suspicion until it was too late.

As his team approached Kerberos's meeting place, Rafe confirmed that Niko's team was similarly slipping into position.

"Bro, looks like Tonelli told the truth," Niko said in Greek over their comm line. "I count two dozen of Kerberos's men, with more arriving."

"Son of a bitch." Rafe pulled up to the clearing. Straight ahead, men formed a line in front of a truck very similar to

Gabby's mobile lab. The men wearing Kaufmann's signature black uniform with colored stripes outnumbered the normal Kerberos agents. If any of Kaufmann's men broke through their mind control and let loose the rage Rafe knew they were feeling, the normal agents didn't stand a chance of reining them in.

A man stepped out of the lab section of the truck holding a Styrofoam cooler. Overhead, the noise from the plane's engine increased. Rafe pushed a button on his phone, signaling the team back in the States to start jamming the President's satellite link.

On Rafe's mark, his team donned their gas masks and protective gloves, then dropped to their bellies as the crop duster unleashed its special cargo directly onto the clearing.

The nerve agent acted immediately, knocking every unprotected man in the area unconscious. Rafe and his team quickly stood up and began searching for anyone left awake. The airplane circled around and dropped a load of dissipator, and within ten minutes the sensor on Rafe's gas mask beeped to let him know the air was safe to breathe again.

Rafe finished securing the hands of the man at his feet, then removed his gas mask and gloves. Across the clearing, Niko gave him the thumbs up to indicate all the hostiles on his side were out of action as well.

Rafe crossed over to the truck and did a thorough search. Once he'd determined that none of the vials of Agent Styx had been compromised and that the lab was empty, he locked it down.

Taking his satellite phone out of its holster, he dialed Ryker. "Mission successful, sir," Rafe announced. "The area is sec—"

"Rafe!" Andersen hurried over, waving frantically.

Everything inside of Rafe tensed at the man's stricken expression. "The team at the mobile lab reports an attack by two of Kaufmann's men. They think the men got lost and mistook our site for their meeting place. They're trying to break into the lab."

"Sir, we have a situation at one of our mobile labs," Rafe curtly informed Ryker. "I have to go."

Rafe shoved his phone back in the holster. "Which lab?"

"Dr. Montague's, sir."

No!

Rafe motioned for six of his men to join him, then quickly relayed the news to Niko.

"Go," Niko said. "We've got this covered."

Dammit, Rafe thought as he turned away, they were half an hour away from the lab. Too long for him to be of any help to Gabby.

"What else?" Rafe barked to Andersen as they broke into a run toward the motorcycles.

"The men have taken down four of our guards and are pounding on the mobile lab, trying to break down the door," Andersen said. "Lewellyn is inside the lab's security room and he doesn't know how to stop them. The attackers are wearing hooded uniforms that repel the darts and bullets can't fully penetrate the material, either."

Rafe spared a glance at one of Kaufmann's unconscious men. Sure enough, this close he could see the bulk of a rolled-up hood at the collar. He stopped and knelt down so he could feel the material.

Fuck. It was some sort of super flexible armor.

He surged back to his feet and sprinted toward his motorbike. "Where's Gabby?"

"Dr. Montague is trapped in the lab's interior. She was working on another batch of antidote when the attack began."

Rafe leapt onto his bike and kicked it into life. He didn't know what terrified him more. The idea that Kaufmann's men might break into the lab and hurt Gabby, or that by pounding on the lab they might cause Gabby to spill some of the deadly chemicals on her and somehow she'd be killed despite her hazmat suit.

Rafe sent a prayer up in every language he knew and turned his bike toward the lab.

Gabby concentrated on holding her hand steady as she poured one of the less toxic ingredients of the antidote into the measuring container. After this step, she'd have to head into the hazardous material room and don a full protective suit to finish mixing the antidote. But for now—

A man yelled and something large slammed into the observation window. Gabby's hand jerked and the chemical spilled onto the counter. She instinctively jumped back so none of it would get on her, even though the safety equipment she wore—goggles, mask, apron and elbow-length gloves—would protect her.

Gabby gasped as the entire lab shook and braced herself against the counter. A second later, Lewellyn's body hit the splintered glass of the observation window. The reinforcing wire inside the glass bent, cutting into the guard's back as some incredible force shoved him forward. Then, with a loud crack, the wire broke and Lewellyn fell through onto the floor of the lab.

Alarms sounded and warning lights flashed.

Gabby tore off her mask and goggles and raced to his side. Oh, God. Blood seeped from under his back.

"Don't move," she ordered, coming to her knees beside him, thankful for the thick apron shielding her knees from the broken shards of glass. "Let me see how badly you're hurt."

"No," he gasped. "Run!"

"What? Why?"

"White coat," a voice bellowed from the other side of the shattered window.

"Kill," shouted another voice.

She didn't recognize the voices, but she recognized Rafe's term for Kaufmann's doctors and heard the familiar rage and madness behind the words. A glance at the ruined window showed two men wearing Kaufmann's black uniform with red stripes. But these men weren't acting like highly controlled, rational subjects of Level 1. Instead, their eyes were wild with fury. Spotting Gabby, one of the men bellowed, then leapt into the room through the window, easily clearing the high pane.

Gabby screamed and tried to scramble back, but the heavy apron weighed her down. She yanked off her gloves and fumbled for the safety catches at her neck and waist. *Come on. Come on!*

There! The catches released. She shoved the apron toward the man heading for her and stumbled to her feet, searching for escape. Oh, God, she was trapped. There was only the one entrance to the left of the observation window, and the second man now stood between her and the door.

Knowing she had to do something, Gabby turned and ran toward the hazardous material room.

She wasn't fast enough. The first man grabbed her by the neck, lifted her off the ground, and with an incoherent yell, threw her across the room.

Gabby crashed onto the counter, knocking over beakers and test tubes as she slid along its surface until her head hit the wall. Dazed, she put her hands down to prop herself up and felt the sharp edge of broken glass cut into her wet palm.

She had only a moment to panic about which of the hazardous chemicals she'd touched when the man grabbed her feet, swung her around, and slammed her head first into the corner of the supply cabinet.

The world went dark.

CHAPTER THIRTY-TWO

Mark Tonelli had ambushed Faith's brother Toby ten minutes ago and tried to break through the man's mind control by playing a voice recording of his sister. Instead, a woman's scream had sent Toby racing through the jungle, with Mark struggling to keep up with the man's enhanced speed.

Mark followed Toby into a clearing and pulled up short at what he saw. Shit. The bodies of four guards lay scattered around a truck that must be one of the SSU's mobile labs. Two of the men had broken necks. One had multiple stab wounds and a slit throat. The other man looked as if he'd been beaten repeatedly with a blunt object about the head and chest. Despite the damage he'd suffered, he was trying to pull himself toward the truck.

Mark threw a quick glance to where Toby had disappeared through the twisted door to the lab, then hurried over to the man. "What happened?"

"Kaufmann's men...two...caught us by...surprise...wear...ing... protective suits...tranq darts...bullets...bounce off..." His eyes turned toward Mark, pleading. "Help...Dr...Mon...tague..." He coughed violently, then collapsed.

Mark bolted toward the lab. If the men killed Dr. Montague,

then who would return Toby to normal? How would he explain to Faith that he'd failed her?

Mark jumped over the mangled ruin of the door and into an antechamber that must have been the security command center. Broken monitors littered the floor. A chair stuck out of the far wall. All that remained of the observation window were jagged pieces of glass and fragments of wire.

Beyond that, a growing pool of blood seeped out from under the body of another guard. Dr. Montague lay in a boneless heap at the foot of a supply cabinet. One of Kaufmann's men kicked Dr. Montague repeatedly in the face and torso while a second man smashed beakers and shoved everything from the counter-tops onto the floor.

The man attacking Dr. Montague threw back his head, yelled in primal fury, and pulled a knife from his belt.

With an answering bellow, Toby charged the man. The pair went down in a tangle of flying fists.

The other attacker was too busy trying to pry a cabinet off the wall to notice the fight. But Mark knew it would only be a matter of time.

The man's hood had slipped off his head, leaving the back of his neck exposed. Mark raised his pistol and fired just as the cabinet broke free of the wall. Kaufmann's man staggered back under its weight. Mark fired repeatedly until the man landed on his back under the weight of the cabinet.

Satisfied that the man was dead, Mark turned in time to see Kaufmann's man kick Toby in the stomach. Toby landed on his back with a grunt.

Kaufmann's man ignored Toby and rushed over to Dr. Montague. Dropping to his knees, he raised his knife and plunged it into her chest.

"No!" Toby struggled to sit up, reaching out as if he would choke the man. Tears streamed down his cheeks as his mouth twisted in horror. "No hurt Faith!"

Shit. Dr. Montague was roughly the same size as Faith, and with her straight blonde hair hidden under a protective cap, Toby wouldn't realize this wasn't his curly-haired sister. He must have thought Faith was close by because of the voice recording Mark had played for him.

The man yanked the knife out of Dr. Montague.

A second later, Rafe Andros dove through the window and tackled the man.

Mark sensed another man heading toward Toby and he threw himself at Faith's brother, pushing Toby to the floor and shielding him with his own body. "Jurassic Park," Mark said, giving the code word to indicate he was friendly. "Don't hurt this one. This is Toby. I—" A wave of pain bit off the rest of his sentence.

Kaufmann's man yanked his knife free of Mark's lower back as he and Andros rolled away.

Mark's vision tunneled. "Don't...hurt...Toby..." he gasped. Then he lost consciousness.

RAFE LOST his grip on Kaufmann's soldier for one freaking second and the bastard managed to stab Tonelli. Snaking his arm around the soldier's middle, Rafe yanked him away from the wounded man.

The knife arched toward Rafe's face. He blocked it with his forearm, trying to hit hard enough to shatter the man's bones, but the man changed his angle and Rafe didn't get the impact he needed. All he managed to do was halt the knife inches from his face.

Rafe let his fury give him strength. This man had stabbed Gabby. Bad enough that he'd hurt her. But if he'd killed her...

Rafe felt the beast he'd been under Kaufmann raise its head and roar. He drove his knuckles hard into the man's kidney.

The man didn't so much as grunt in annoyance. The knife

pressed closer to Rafe and his forearm started shaking. Shit. He couldn't hold the man back any longer.

He dropped his forearm and rolled away with millimeters to spare as the knife plunged toward the spot where his head had been. Rafe barely managed to avoid a quick series of follow-up jabs.

Screw this. He was never going to equal this man's strength or speed. And he didn't have time to waste. He had to get to Gabby.

Rafe pulled his tranquilizer gun out of its holster, then dodged a kick that nearly turned him into a soprano. He quickly ejected one of the tranquilizer darts into his hand. In the few seconds it took to accomplish that, Rafe lost his focus on his opponent.

The burn of a knife slicing shallowly along his biceps jerked Rafe's attention back to the fight. He didn't waste time on the pain. He brought his fist up and around, jabbing the tranquilizer dart into the man's exposed carotid artery. He pushed, making certain all the drug was expelled. The soldier bellowed in rage and swatted at the dart.

Rafe spun out of the way as the man's eyes rolled up and he collapsed.

Rafe scrambled over the man's body, raced across the lab, and slid to a stop on his knees next to Gabby.

Blood trickled from her mouth and soaked the front of her lab coat where the knife had stabbed her. "Gabby?" he whispered. He couldn't tell if she was breathing. She was so battered, he was terrified to touch her. Afraid he'd only add to her pain. And there were so many shattered beakers around her, Rafe didn't know what lethal chemicals she'd been exposed to.

Panic beat frantically inside him. He didn't...he couldn't...

If he lost Gabby, he wouldn't be able to go on. But staring down at her damaged body, he couldn't remember what he was supposed to do. All his training in emergency field medicine was trapped in some inaccessible place within his head, held prisoner by his fear. His shaking hands hovered over her body. "Gabby!"

"Hey, man, let me see." Owens, his team's medic, gently shoved Rafe out of the way.

Rafe grabbed the man's wrist. "Don't hurt her," he snarled.

Owens looked back, his eyes softening. "I won't," he promised. "But I need to touch her to see how badly she's hurt. What we need to do to save her."

Save her. The words penetrated the fog of anger and fear. Rafe felt himself nod, and saw his fingers release Owen's wrist. He cleared his throat. "Yes. Save her." He swallowed hard. Gabby's face seemed paler than a minute ago and her lips were turning blue.

He barely registered the curt commands Owens gave to other members of the team. All Rafe could think about was Gabby's smile. How she'd never given up on him. How the memory of her laughter and her sometimes sharp tongue had anchored him during his captivity.

"Breathe, dammit," Owens cursed. "C'mon Dr. Montague, don't leave the boss like this. Be a good girl and breathe."

Rafe swore he felt his own breath freeze in his lung. "Don't die," he ordered Gabby. A tear slid off his chin and fell onto the bruised back of her limp hand. He wiped the teardrop gently away with the tip of his finger. "Don't you dare die, Gabby. I love you. How will I live without you?"

"What's the ETA on that chopper?" Owens shouted. "We need her out of here!"

"Two minutes," a familiar voice said. Niko. "Come on, bro," Niko added in Greek. "Let's get you out of their way so they can prepare Gabby for evacuation."

Rafe shook his head. "I need—"

Niko reached down and pulled Rafe to his feet. "No. You need to let Owens do his job."

Rafe looked helplessly from where Owens was working frantically to save Gabby, back to Niko. The pained sympathy he saw in his brother's eyes was too much like a confirmation of Rafe's worst fears.

He squeezed his eyes shut and shook his head. "No." His soul was breaking apart at the thought of losing her. With every curse from Owens's lips Rafe's control threatened to snap. All the progress he'd made since his captivity started to erode. His carefully rebuilt sense of self wouldn't survive without Gabby.

Niko put his arm around Rafe and led him to the far corner of the destroyed lab. "Don't watch, Rafe. It won't help."

"Then what the fuck am I supposed to do?" To his horror, Rafe's voice cracked and he felt another tear slide down his face.

"Just pray, bro," Niko said softly. "There's nothing you can do but hope and pray."

"I still don't have a pulse," Owens snarled. He raised his head and Rafe flinched at what he saw in the man's eyes. Grief. Anger. Resignation.

"No," Rafe protested. He took a step toward Gabby. "No!"

Owens glance down at Gabby and shook his head. Then he squared his shoulders. "Bouchet, get your ass over here and help. We need a fucking miracle."

Niko blocked Rafe's path with his arm. "Let Owens work," he said. "If anyone can bring her back, he can."

Rafe stared at Owens and Bouchet working feverishly to save Gabby. "I never even told her she's my world," he whispered on a ragged breath.

"She knows, Rafe. Trust me, she knows."

Rafe barely breathed for the next several minutes. But then Owens's head lowered in defeat. His hands fell to his sides. Bouchet reached out and closed Gabby's eyes, then laid his jacket over her face.

"NO!" Rafe yelled. "Gabby!" His knees buckled. He would have gone down except for Niko's support. "I've got you," Niko said. "Hang on to me."

Niko's voice was thick with grief and the sound of it, the acknowledgement that Gabby was gone, felt like a vise screwing tightly into Rafe's heart. Unbearable, unending pain flowed through him, hurting worse than all of Kaufmann's torture.

He couldn't move. Couldn't breathe. Gabby was gone. His fault. He should have insisted she stayed home. Or insisted on guarding her himself. Tripled her protection.

He should have shown her in a million ways how much she meant to him.

Now it was too late. His soul had been ripped out, leaving him with such emptiness, he didn't know how he'd keep on living.

For the first time since he was a boy waking from a nightmare, Rafe turned his head into the comfort of his brother's shoulder, and cried.

CHAPTER THIRTY-THREE

A COMMOTION at the door to the mobile unit announced the arrival of the medevac team. Rafe lifted his head and watched the men carry the stretcher in, feeling as distanced as if he watched a football game from the nosebleed seats.

Kai followed just behind the team. As Gabby was transferred onto the stretcher, he picked up her left hand and eyeballed her palm. Then he leaned down and took a cautious sniff.

He pulled back quickly, shaking his head and wrinkling his nose as if he'd smelled something nasty. The team carried Gabby away, but Kai didn't follow. Instead, he focused on the wreck of glass and chemicals on the floor. He picked his way carefully through the debris, then leaned down and gave another sniff.

Nodding to himself, he pulled a pair of latex gloves out of his pocket, slipped them on, and continued searching until he'd uncovered a small vial that hadn't been broken. Checking the label, he gave a satisfied smile and tucked the vial into his pocket.

Then he took off at a run after the stretcher.

Rafe shook his head, thoroughly confused. But at least for a few minutes he'd been distracted from his pain. The thought of leaving this room and following the stretcher terrified him. If he left, he'd have to acknowledge Gabby was dead. Have to see her treated as a corpse instead of a person.

He couldn't stand that.

"C'mon, Rafe," Niko prompted gently, nudging him toward the door. "Let's get out of here. Make sure we get to say a proper good-bye to your lady."

The White House
Washington, D.C.

"I AM THE COMMANDER IN CHIEF," President MacAdam stated with an arrogant sense of entitlement. "I have every right to sanction action against the enemies of this country."

"You are not above the laws of this nation, Mr. President," the Chief Justice countered smoothly. "And what you proposed to do today wasn't about keeping our country safe. It was about revenge for your personal loss. While we're all sorry about your son's death, you have a greater duty now. A duty to the entire population of the United States. A population that is not made safer by you ordering the murder of thousands of innocent civilians."

The President glared back. "You have no right to tell me how to conduct our national security. Get out."

The Chief Justice only shook his head. "It's over, Byrne. Come peacefully and let the Vice President take over."

The President surged to his feet. "It's my right!" he snarled. "My right to see that justice is carried out."

"That wasn't justice you had planned," Brown from the CIA corrected. "It was murder."

Several agents surrounded the President. "Byrne MacAdam, you are under arrest for the attempted genocide of the entire population of northern Salaqut."

Ryker watched the confrontation with an ever growing weariness. And a sense that it might finally be time for him to retire.

Listening to the President's angry justification had destroyed the last shred of his idealism. He rubbed the back of his neck, feeling old, tired and disillusioned.

But there was someone else watching the proceedings with interest. Someone edging closer to the back exit.

Ryker moved to cut the man off. "Wayne Jamieson, I presume?"

The man pulled a gun. Instincts honed from martial arts had Ryker shifting to the side as Jamieson fired. Before the man could fire again, Ryker moved forward and slammed his fist against Jamieson's throat.

The man froze and his eyes widened with horror when he realized there was a syringe stuck in his neck. "What have you done?" Ryker knew he feared the syringe contained one of Kaufmann's drugs.

Ryker smiled coldly and stepped back. The syringe held a standard tranquilizer, but Jamieson didn't need to know that.

"It was his idea," Jamieson accused. His words slurred slightly as the sedative took effect. "MacAdam came to me with the idea of using Kerberos for his demonstration. It was his plan all along. I'll tell you all the details. Just please, give me the antidote."

Ryker motioned two Marines over. They caught Jamieson just as he collapsed. "Cuff him and escort him out of here," Ryker said.

In the center of the room, the President shoved the Chief Justice into the man behind him, then tried to ram himself through the group and escape. Within seconds he, too, had been tranq'd and was out cold.

"Do you think he'll deal?" Ryker asked Jordaine as the agents carried the President's unconscious body away while the Chief Justice gave the presidential oath to the Vice President.

Ryker's friend rubbed his chin. "I don't know. He's not the rational man I thought I knew. This man seems crazy enough to put us through a trial just so his opinion can be heard."

Ryker shook his head. "The country doesn't need that. He should take the offer." If the President resigned, agreed to stay out of the public eye and agreed to be monitored for five years, then no charges would be brought against him. Otherwise, he'd be charged with attempted genocide.

Ryker's cell phone vibrated. Looking down, he read the text message from Niko.

Plot stopped. Gabby and six others, dead. Tonelli stabbed and critical.

Ryker closed his eyes on a sharp wave of grief. Giving the President the option to get off scot-free no longer seemed the best choice.

Salaqut

KAI WAS ARGUING with Owens and Bouchet when Rafe followed Niko onto the helicopter. Rafe's gaze darted away from the body underneath the sheet in the middle of the floor. That couldn't be Gabby. There had to be some mistake. Maybe this was a nightmare and he'd wake up soon.

With a swirl of dust, the other helicopter lifted into the sky, carrying Tonelli and the living wounded to the hospital. Several unhurried minutes later, Rafe's helicopter followed with its cargo of dead.

Telling himself to stop being a coward, Rafe dropped to his knees beside Gabby and pulled the sheet back from her face. Even beneath the blood and bruises she was the most beautiful, most precious sight in the world.

He reached out and smoothed her hair back from her face. "Thank you, *querida*," he whispered. "You saved me. I only wish..." His throat closed up and he fought to get the next words out. "I'm sorry I wasn't able to save you."

"For God's sake, let me give her the injection," Kai shouted at Owens. "What harm can it do? You think she's already dead!"

"And you're crazy if you think you can bring her back to life, man," Owens scoffed.

Rafe's head whipped around. "What?" Hope burst inside him. He surged to his feet.

Kai moved around Owens to stand directly in front of Rafe. "I've been trying to tell Owens that I think Gabby cut her hand on a broken vial of Agent Medusa. It's a powerful nerve agent that in small doses can put the body into a sort of hibernation that resembles death." Kai turned back to Owens.

"You've covered the knife wound and drained the chest cavity of blood?"

Owens nodded.

"Put the drainage tube back in and let me give her the antidote. If her heart starts, you keep the fluid away."

"Please," Rafe heard himself beg. He tugged Kai toward Gabby. "Do it."

"Rafe, man, it's been too long," Owens protested. "Even if she comes back there's a good chance she won't be the same."

Rafe knew he meant brain damage. But he didn't care.

"She'll be fine," Kai snapped as he knelt beside Gabby. "Agent Medusa prolongs the time the brain and other organs can survive on minimal oxygen without permanent damage." He filled a syringe from the vial he'd taken out of the debris in the lab, then injected it right over her heart. He stared at his watch for two minutes, then nodded to Owens.

Owens placed his stethoscope over Gabby's chest. "Christ," he breathed. "We have a heartbeat. Bouchet, get over here. We've got our miracle, man."

Rafe found himself sandwiched between Niko and Kai. Both men were laughing and slapping Rafe on the back. But Rafe shoved them out of the way. A great big bubble of joy tried to push its way through his system, but he refused to set it free. Not until he was certain this was real.

He sat by Gabby's head, stroking her hair as the medics worked.

All the while his lips formed a silent prayer. *Please, let Gabby live. Please, let Gabby live.*

CHAPTER THIRTY-FOUR

Three Days Later
SSU Medical Facility
Oregon

THE JAGGED PAIN of the knife wound had given way to peace and an enveloping veil of warming light. Gabby floated blissfully in the light, then something plunged her back into darkness. Pain returned, along with awareness. She caught snippets of conversation, enough to know that she'd been declared dead and that no one knew if she'd survive emergency surgery.

Gabby wanted to return to the light, but every time she managed to reach that peaceful place, something kept pulling her back.

No. Some*one* kept pulling her back.

Rafe.

His voice was an almost constant companion. Words of love, of grief, of apology. Pleading for her to return to him. And as she regained more of her senses, she felt his touch. Smoothing back her hair. Stroking her cheek. Squeezing her hand.

Anchoring her to the world until finally she let go of her search for the light and opened her eyes.

Rafe slept in a chair pulled up close to the side of her hospital bed. His arms were stretched out to keep hold of her right hand, while his head rested against the high back of the chair. The position looked uncomfortable, yet Rafe's mouth was open slightly as he slept deeply.

Gabby kept very still, not wanting to wake him. He looked exhausted. Dark circles shadowed his eyes and his cheeks were sunken underneath several days' growth of beard. From the bloodstained, dirty appearance of his clothes, he hadn't changed or showered recently.

And still, he took her breath away.

She drank in his appearance with all the gusto of a desert flower sucking in the first rain after a long drought. His hair had grown long enough that a stray curl tickled his forehead, making her fingers itch to brush it away. Yet even as she thought it and raised her hand, her strength waned and she fell back into darkness.

The next time Gabby opened her eyes, she found Rafe's dark chocolate gaze upon her.

His face lit up with joy, bringing him from the grim man sleeping by her bedside closer to the laughing man he'd once been.

He leaned forward and pressed a quick kiss to her lips. "Welcome back, *querida*," he whispered. "You scared me near to death." Then Rafe buried his face against the bed and cried.

With great effort, Gabby lifted her right hand and placed it on his head, loving his warmth under her palm. "It's okay, Rafe. I'm here. I'm alive. You brought me back."

He raised his head. "No, Kai brought you back." He squeezed her hand almost painfully. "Owens, the team medic, gave you up for dead, but Kai said you'd been exposed to some special chemical and you weren't really dead. He gave you some injection and your heart started. So you owe Kai your life. Well, you flatlined a couple of times in surgery, but you never would have made it to the hospital if not for Kai."

"And I wouldn't have made it back from where I went when I flatlined if not for you, Rafe." She wanted to kiss him, but didn't have the strength. The best she could manage was a weary smile. "I love you, Rafe."

"Ah, *querida*, I love you so damn much. Don't you ever leave me again."

"I won't. I promise."

One Month Later
SSU Offices
Washington, D.C.

Rafe helped Gabby into a chair at the end of the conference room table. Jenna, Niko, Susana and Kai were already seated. Ryker stood at the far end of the table, watching the group with a small, proud smile. Yet something seemed off. There was tension in Ryker's body that set Rafe's instincts on edge.

Reaching out to close the door, Rafe was shocked when Mark Tonelli walked through, his arm around a woman with wild, curly blonde hair.

For a second, Rafe could only glare at Tonelli. "I still haven't forgiven you for Cozumel," he snarled.

Tonelli tipped his head in acknowledgment.

"But thank you for helping us stop Kerberos." Rafe stepped aside and let the man into the room. He still didn't fully trust the guy, but from the sappy way the woman by his side looked up at Tonelli, there must be a few redeeming qualities to the man.

"Faith Andrews, meet Rafe Andros," Tonelli said. "Faith's

brother Toby is one of Dr. Montague's patients. He was the man who tried to stop Kaufmann's other men from attacking Dr. Montague on Salaqut."

"I'm sorry for what your brother is going through," Rafe said. "But if anyone can help him, Gabby can."

"I know. She's been wonderful." Faith gave Rafe a sweet smile and he wondered how the hell she'd ended up with a bastard like Tonelli.

"Thank you all for coming here today," Ryker began after the newcomers and Rafe had taken their seats. "The current President has asked me to personally extend his heartfelt appreciation for your help in stopping the anniversary demonstration and for bringing down Kerberos."

"Hear, hear," Susana called out. She started clapping and was quickly joined by Jenna.

Rafe grinned. He liked Susana and the way she lightened Kai's often too serious life. And because she was Dr. Nevsky's daughter, and had received some injections from her father before she'd even been born, Rafe felt an odd kinship with her. Best of all, he got to tease Kai for the rest of their lives about marrying a former supermodel.

"My heroes," Jenna crowed.

Niko rolled his eyes and planted a fast kiss on his wife's mouth.

"As some of you may have heard," Ryker continued, "former president Byrne MacAdam's attorney was pushing for him to be declared insane, but MacAdam took offense and fired him. He continued to insist it was his right as Commander In Chief to attack the terrorists who'd killed his son in the manner he saw fit."

Rafe saw the shadow of some dark emotion pass over Ryker's face. Gabby must have seen it too, because she glanced over at Rafe in question. Not knowing what had the Director on edge, Rafe shook his head and gave her hand a squeeze. He still found it hard to care about much of anything besides Gabby's health, but it was unusual for Ryker to show any wayward emotion. That worried Rafe.

"What you don't know is that all the key players in the anniversary demonstration plot, including MacAdam, Jamieson, and Kaufmann have died during the last forty-eight hours."

Rafe sucked in a breath. Yeah, that would explain Ryker's dark mood.

Gabby's fingers tightened on Rafe's as she stared at Ryker in shock. Niko cursed, while Kai crossed his arms over his chest and regarded Ryker with narrowed eyes.

"House cleaning," Tonelli muttered in disgust.

Rafe had to agree, but the thought didn't make him happy.

"Other victims include the man in the DOD who asked Jamieson to stage the accident that killed Dr. Montague's parents. Also, Dr. Winthrop from the VA. He gave Kaufmann the location of our Georgia facility along with our security details, allowing Kaufmann's men to stage a successful kidnapping."

Rafe felt Gabby tense beside him. He knew she'd been told that her parents had indeed been murdered to stop her father's investigation into Agent Styx, but she wouldn't have wanted the man responsible to die without facing trial.

"This information is not yet for public distribution, so I have to ask you to promise to remain silent." Ryker looked pointedly at Tonelli's companion, so Rafe figured she must have some ties to the media. "The reason I'm telling you this is to warn you to watch your backs. The SSU currently knows more than any other group about the scope of Nevsky and Kaufmann's programs. We possess the only samples of the drugs and have the only copies of the research notes. The data provided by Tonelli linked key officials within the DOD to Jamieson and Kerberos, but I'm not certain that we have caught everyone involved."

"You're expecting an attack?" Rafe asked. If so, he was getting Gabby the hell out of here.

"I don't know. With both Gonzales and Winthrop dead, I believe the SSU is now free of traitors. However, I no longer trust our former government allies. So while I have no data that suggests an attack has been planned, I'm not ruling it out. All facilities will be on high alert until further notice."

Rafe glanced over at Tonelli, wondering why he was being allowed to hear this. Ryker caught the direction of his gaze. "Tonelli will be serving as a part-time liaison between the SSU and the CIA while we finish dismantling Jamieson's network. And Faith will be providing Dr. Montague with any personal details about her brother that might help move him toward full recovery."

Ryker looked around the room. "Any questions? No? Right, then. Let's talk assignments..."

AN HOUR LATER, Ryker's hand crushed the velvet drape as he held it away from his office window. He was high enough up that he could see the Mall and the Lincoln Memorial. If he squinted hard enough he could make out the Capitol's dome at the other end, and with some careful orienteering he could locate the roof of the White House.

He used to enjoy this view. It used to give him peace to look at the enduring symbols of honor and truth. But now everything he looked upon seemed tainted by corruption, greed and arrogance. Nothing new to the political heart of the country, but before recent events he'd always trusted that there were enough honorable men to counteract the vices.

That belief had been shattered by the encrypted e-mail he'd received informing him of the deaths of MacAdam, Jamieson, Kaufmann and several other men involved in the anniversary demonstration. The e-mail had gone into details, each line making Ryker more and more ill. Which was why he hadn't shared that information with his team

Ryker stared bleakly toward the Lincoln Memorial. He'd been assured that all men would stand trial, even the President. Ryker would never have believed the men would be assassinated.

Ryker didn't kill because of expediency or to avoid a messy situation. He'd thought his friends from Vietnam had been like-minded. But the details of these deaths made him realize that getting to all the victims would have been impossible without collaboration across several different agencies.

Implicating his friends. Putting Ryker forever on the outside. Because no matter what their crimes, Jamieson and the others had deserved better than to be killed without having a chance to atone for their actions.

Ryker stared through the rain blurred glass at the sea of umbrellas on the sidewalk below. The people down there trusted their government to protect them, and to uphold the laws that made the United States unique.

Not to kill simply because it was easier than dealing with the potential fallout.

Ryker briefly closed his eyes. He'd just drawn his personal line in the sand. His friends, whether directly involved or merely complicit, had taken one too many steps toward becoming the type of men he'd always fought against. Ryker could not follow them and still retain what was left of his soul.

He rubbed the back of his neck, feeling unutterably weary. Old and jaded. Abandoned. Uncertain if he had the strength to keep fighting alone. Wondering if this was a fight he could ever win.

But...he couldn't just walk away. Not yet. He had to make certain the SSU continued fighting as an honorable organization. He had to ensure that his successor was well-trained to handle the moral complexities of this job. To handle disillusionment.

To be prepared to find himself nearing retirement and realize he had nothing to show for years of sacrifice except the somewhat bitter knowledge that the world would have been in even worse shape if not for him.

Shaking his head at his melancholy, Ryker let the drape fall back into place and returned to his desk. Until he found his new successor, he had work to do.

CHAPTER THIRTY-FIVE

Three Months Later
Paros, Greece

THE SUN WAS EDGING toward the horizon when Gabby made her way down the dusty lane toward her rented bungalow. Swallows danced in the air above the little cove, while on the dock not far from her front porch half a dozen octopuses hung off a clothesline stretched above the dock while a fisherman tenderized his latest catch.

Gabby's mouth quirked up in amusement. The odd custom was just part of the magic of this island. Magic that over the past two weeks had allowed her to finally relax all the way down to her bones after working herself into exhaustion.

As soon as she'd been declared fit, Gabby had jumped right back to work. Her team had tweaked the regimen they'd created to help Rafe and managed to return Toby Andrews and several other victims of Kaufmann's program to near normalcy. With no additional victims located, Ryker had decided to shut down the Georgia facility and move the personnel into new positions at the Oregon compound.

Once the final patient had been released from treatment, all of her team's research had been bundled up and locked away in secure storage, along with samples of the drugs they'd used. Accessible only in case someone restarted Kaufmann's program and counteragents were needed.

Ryker swore that access to the data would be extremely limited so it wouldn't fall into the wrong hands again.

Gabby was still surprised that Ryker hadn't closed the Georgia lab after mentioning he thought there might be another attack. But the facility would have been too hard to replicate on short notice, and Kaufmann's victims had too short a window in which their deterioration could be stopped, so Ryker had instead tripled the security.

Luckily, the feared attack had never materialized.

Ryker had offered her a permanent position with the SSU's medical team in Oregon and she'd accepted. The work would be straight medicine, with an occasional case of someone who'd run afoul of a new biochemical weapon. Kai would be getting a new, specialized lab at the far edge of the campus to work on counteragents to biochemical weapons. After that facility was built, Gabby would have the option of joining his team, but she wasn't sure she wanted to continue working with dangerous chemicals. Straight medicine would be a welcome change.

Muscles aching pleasantly from her long hike, Gabby strolled toward the beach. The only thing she needed to make this vacation perfect was Rafe. He'd planned on coming with her, but at the last minute Ryker had activated him for a special assignment.

Gabby scowled and kicked at a stone in the path. Was it too much to ask for a little concentrated alone time with her guy? She felt as if she'd barely seen him since the afternoon Ryker had dropped the news about the deaths of Kaufmann and the others. He hadn't even been able to phone her these last few weeks.

But Gabby's sour mood evaporated on a flash of joy when she turned down her lane and spotted the man lounging on the beach's low rock wall. Rafe's thick black hair had grown out from its mission ready buzz cut. A day's worth of beard darkened his cheeks, making him look like a rakish pirate.

He wore a steel gray t-shirt untucked over rough khaki pants. The pants were rolled up to mid-calf and his bare feet dangled in the water. A battered pair of leather hiking boots sat on the sand by the base of the rocks.

He looked healthy and tough and so edible she wanted to bury her face in the crook of his neck and nibble. She'd missed him so damn much.

He sat in profile to her while he chatted with the fisherman. Rafe hadn't spotted her yet, but someone else had. A dark shadow leapt from Rafe's lap and trotted toward her, purring loudly in welcome.

"Hey, Pirate," Gabby greeted the cat, a laugh in her voice. She squatted down and rubbed the back of his head, then ran her finger between his ears and down the line of black fur separating the tawny right side of his face from the chocolate colored left side. Pirate butted his head into her palm, demanding a deeper caress. She picked him up in her arms and gave him a serious head rub.

"Lucky cat," Rafe said.

Startled by how close his voice sounded, Gabby looked up and found that Rafe had left his rock and stood right in front of her. Her breath caught and her heart tripped over itself at the way his eyes devoured her.

She found herself grinning idiotically back at him, because his reaction was so typically Rafe. No beating around the bush for him. Just straightforward lust.

Pirate meowed and kneaded her with his claws, chastising her for neglecting her petting. Gabby gave him one more vigorous rub on the top of his head, then set him on the ground. Pirate rubbed himself against her legs and looked up at her. When he didn't get the attention he needed, he moved to Rafe. But Rafe was fully focused on Gabby. With an unhappy swish of his tail, Pirate stalked away.

Leaving Gabby staring at Rafe, not certain what to say. *I missed you. I love you, will you give me the rest of your life*, seemed far too direct. She didn't want to scare him off.

Dios, she looked fantastic. It was all Rafe could do not to haul her into his arms and kiss her senseless. But he'd made himself a promise. This time he'd court her properly. Give her all the romantic trappings she deserved. Show her every day how much he loved her.

Rafe cleared his throat to break the uncomfortable tension between them. "Hey, Gabby," he said. "You're, uh, looking good." Ugh. Good? She looked fantastic. So sexy, heat pooled in his groin.

Her hair was different. Kind of full and stacked in the back. The ends of her hair now formed longer points in the front, highlighting her cheekbones and making her eyes look enormous.

Eyes that watched him with a mix of wariness, hope and heat.

He focused on the heat. As long as she still wanted him, then everything was going to be okay.

Even if she didn't seem willing, or able, to speak.

"So, um..." he began. "Sorry it took so long to join you. Mission turned out more complicated than expected." *Stop acting like a bumbling idiot*, he told himself. *Just say it.*

"Okay, here's the deal," he said on a rush. He took a deep breath to steady his voice before continuing. "We haven't had what anyone would call a normal relationship, so I think we should start over and do this right."

He held out his hand. "Hi. I'm Rafe Andros. I'd really like to get to know you better. Will you accept me as your tour guide? My father's family comes from Mykonos, an island not far from here. I'd love to show you around."

Gabby placed her hand in his and beamed up at him with such radiance, Rafe felt as powerful as Zeus himself.

"Pleased to meet you, Rafe. I'm Gabby Montague." She moved toward him. "I'd very much like a tour guide. But I'd like something else even more."

She was close enough that he could smell suntan lotion, sweat, and underneath it all, Gabby's cherry vanilla scent. He would have closed his eyes and let himself get lost in the scent, except he was captured by the way her eyes darkened and her tongue slipped out to wet her lips.

He almost groaned.

"Anything you want, you get," he said hoarsely. "It's all about you."

Her lips curled in a sensual smile that damn near sent him to his knees. That was all the warning he got before she leaned in and took his mouth in a hot, ravenous kiss.

"I need you," she murmured.

His arms clamped around her and he dragged her closer until their bodies were aligned chest to thigh. Gabby hummed deep in her throat, a low sound of pleasure that made Rafe forget all his good intentions.

Almost. "You sure?" he said raggedly, pulling away slightly so he could see her expression. "I had a slow, romantic wooing all planned out."

"Yeah," Gabby said with a shaky laugh. "I've missed you so damn much. Romance can wait." She nipped at his bottom lip. Rafe groaned and took her mouth again, giving himself completely over to her.

A heavy slap on his back and the laughter-tinged voice of the fisherman congratulating Rafe on his good luck broke the sensual spell.

Rafe pulled back from the kiss. Gabby blinked up at him, her face dazed with arousal. He reached down and laced his fingers in hers. "How about dinner in town?" he suggested. "We can finish this later."

She nodded and let him lead her back toward her bungalow, her head leaning on his shoulder. "You won't leave me?"

He shook his head and smiled down at her. "Just because I want to take it slow doesn't mean anything has changed. You're mine. I love you. I just want you to get to know the new me."

Gabby rubbed her cheek against his shoulder. "Silly man. I loved you even when you were more beast than man. Nothing's going to change that. Still, romance sounds nice."

He laughed. "All right then. How about we start by watching the sunset?" He pulled Gabby down to sit beside him on the low wall surrounding her patio and put his arm around her.

As the sun slowly sank out of sight and the night took over, Rafe knew that his life was just beginning. A life of love with this amazing woman by his side.

DEAR READER

Thank you for spending time with Rafe and Gabby. I hope you enjoyed reading *Retribution* as much as I enjoyed writing it!

Retribution is the one book that still makes me cry when I reread it. Poor Rafe! When he first walked on stage in *Vengeance* I had no idea what a rough ride he was in for, but I knew that he'd need a very special heroine. He couldn't have ended up with a better lady than Gabby.

Here's a piece of trivia that early subscribers to my newsletter may remember. The cat hanging around Gabby at the end of the book is based on a cat I met while on the Greek island of Paros. Like Gabby, I didn't know who he belonged to or what his name was, so I called him Pirate.

Finally, if you enjoyed reading *Retribution*, please consider recommending it to family, friends, and anyone else you think might be interested in Rafe and Gabby's adventures. Leaving a review on the retail store where you purchased it or on Goodreads will also help other readers discover *Retribution*.

Thank you for your support!

If you'd like to learn more about Faith Andrews, the woman Mark Tonelli fell in love with, pick up *Payback*, the fourth book in the SSU series.

Happy reading!

Vanessa

ACKNOWLEDGMENTS

Once again I'd like to thank my critique partner Virna DePaul, my editor Valerie Susan Hayward and my proofreader Angela Pike. Thanks also to Frauke Spanuth of Croco Designs for creating another awesome cover.

Most of all, a huge thank-you to all the readers who have made this series a success!

ABOUT THE AUTHOR

Photo by Gigi Pandian

I confess. I spend way too much time thinking up ways to torture my characters. As a worst-case scenario thinker, I channel my persistently dark what-if questions into writing romantic thrillers that combine intense emotion with action-packed plots.

I'm best known for The Surgical Strike Unit series about a privately run special operations group. My new series, WAR, is set in West Africa, where I lived for a time.

When I'm not writing, listening to music, or playing puzzle games on my mobile device, I help writers learn Scrivener and take long hikes in the nearby hills.

JOIN THE KIERDEVILS

Receive snippets-of-life stories, writing updates, sneak peeks, and other exclusive content such as *The SSU/WAR Bonus Pack* when you join the KierDevils newsletter.

www.vanessakier.com/kierdevils